THE FRACTURED MAN

by

Juliet Conlin

*

The Fractured Man
Juliet Conlin
First Published 2013
Published by Cargo Publishing
SC376700
© Juliet Conlin 2013

ISBN 978-1908885234

Printed & Bound in England by Martins Ltd.
Cover design by Chris Hannah
www.cargopublishing.com

Also available as:
Kindle ebook
Epub ebook

To my family

PROLOGUE

London, Pimlico, December 1919

Elliot enters his father's office unannounced. It is something he has never dared to do in the past, and yet it does not occur to him to question why he is doing it now. Perhaps something has stirred his subconscious, something that will lead him to witness a scene that will change him forever. As he enters the room, his brain registers the sight immediately. The silhouette of his father's bulky form against the window; head bent oddly to the left, revealing a segment of pallid skin above his collar; right arm propped up on the desk, the hand clutching an item of brutal, elegant black. Elliot recognises the gun although he has never actually seen it. A military revolver, promised to whichever of his two sons was the first to "become a man". Naturally, that had been Ed.

Ed, yes, this has to do with Ed. Of course.

These thoughts scramble around the neural structure of Elliot's brain, tunnelling, colliding, seeking out through electrically charged pathways the target for their associations, before finally sliding into place. And so, although Elliot's brain registers the sight immediately, it takes a while before the image takes on meaning. Because he sees what he does not want to see. Because he is in terror of what he sees. Because the sight of his father placing a cold, hard revolver against his warm, soft temple seals Elliot's guilt forever.

'Don't.' His lips form the word, but his terror has disrupted the interplay between thought and speech. He swallows, forcing his tongue to come unstuck from his dry palate, and tries again.

'Don't. Please.' His voice is hesitant, gelatinous.

His father opens his eyes and looks at Elliot. His eyelids are pink and swollen; Elliot thinks he might have been crying, but he cannot be sure. He has never been able to read his father's eyes. All he knows is that he has never before seen this level of desperation in his father. Grief, denial, rage, the emotions have come and gone over the past year since Ed's death, their residue sticking to the atmosphere like fingerprints on barely cured lacquer. But desperation, this is new. And terrifying beyond belief. Elliot looks straight back into his father's eyes, trying to find traces of hesitancy, indecisiveness, but finds nothing. His father still holds the gun to his head.

'Why?' Elliot asks, taking a step forward. His father does not react. It is a good sign. A flutter of hope rises up and out of Elliot, hovering in the air between them, its wings beating as fast as Elliot's heart. It dares to suggest that what is coming – what is *surely* coming – is not inevitable. Then his father speaks.

'I do not wish to discuss the matter. Leave. Now.'

'I can't do that,' Elliot says.

'You left him there to die.' It isn't an accusation, merely a statement of fact.

'No, I – '

'You left him there and now he is dead.'

'But I didn't want him to die. I didn't want him to die. You can't punish me for his death,' Elliot says, suddenly angry. He pauses, nervously awaiting a reaction to his defiance. He cannot remember when he last invited confrontation with his father. The improbable sound of carol-singing blows in from outside. *God rest ye merry gentlemen.* The accomplished harmonies appear displaced, almost exotic, in this setting.

Elliot's father straightens his posture. The gun barrel is perpendicular to his temple. His hand is trembling slightly.

'Elliot.' He speaks as though it pains him to say his son's name.

'Yes?'

'Elliot. It should have been you.' And he pulls the trigger, sending 18 grams through his skull. It is a neat, precise shot. The noise is sharp and swift, a whip cracking, a car backfiring; loud, but not loud enough to interrupt the carol-singers. *Oh tidings of comfort and joy, comfort and joy.*

ONE

London, Bloomsbury, 1920

There was a knock at the door; a sharp, precise knock, hard enough to rattle the stethoscope that hung on the brass door handle. Elliot looked up from his papers, noticing only now how dark the room was beyond the pool of viridescent light that shone from the green glass banker's lamp onto the centre of the desk. He checked his watch. Twenty to eight. It was probably Nurse Robinson, wanting to wish him season's greetings before she left for the Christmas break. Elliot reached over and grabbed an envelope, which was propped up against the desk lamp, and hastily slipped it under the pile of papers. It was a letter Nurse Robinson had asked him to look at, and recalling her evident embarrassment at her request coupled with an underlying urgency, he felt slightly guilty that he had forgotten all about it until now.

'Come in,' he called, but the door stayed shut. He sighed and got to his feet, catching sight of the silver-framed calendar that sat on his desk, reminding him that it was the anniversary of his father's death, and that he hadn't yet found the time to visit the cemetery.

He went to the door and opened it. It was a man Elliot didn't recognise. He had an oddly angular frame; his coat hung from his shoulders in a straight line, and he was tall, about six feet, the same height as Elliot. He looked at Elliot expectantly but did not speak.

'Can I help you?' Elliot asked, trying to sound impatient. The man was presumably some other doctor's patient and had knocked on the wrong door.

'Yes, Dr. Taverley. I believe you can help me.'

The first thing Elliot noticed was the man's accent. It sounded Eastern European, but he couldn't place it exactly.

'Did Stanislav send you?' he asked. It was unlikely that his friend had sent someone to the clinic, especially without informing him beforehand, but it was the best explanation he could come up with. As so often, he felt drained at the end of his day's work. The man continued to look at him; his shoulders, already stooped, seemed to drop forward even more. Elliot found his vulnerability difficult to withstand. He sighed.

'Look, I don't know what Stanislav told you, but I don't think I can be of any help to you. If you just wait here, I'll get an address for you. It's a charitable organisation in Bethnal Green; just go there and explain your situation.' He paused, awaiting some kind of response. When none came, he added, 'I'm sorry. I can't help.'

The gloom had become oppressive, but it seemed oddly inappropriate to switch the light on before the man had left. The room was saturated with a dark stillness, Elliot wondering what else he had to say to make the man leave.

'I do not know a Stanislav,' the man said finally. 'I came to see you, Dr. Taverley, because I believe you can help me. I have not been well. Please, you must not send me away. My mind, it plays tricks on me. I do not know how. They tell me I become another person, when –'

'I understand,' Elliot interrupted gently. This was

not one of Stanislav's charges, but presumably one of those unfortunates in need of psychiatric care who was unable to afford private fees. The night porter must be sleeping on the job, Elliot thought wearily. He longed to close the door, but the man's helplessness had triggered a concern in him, a deep-seated inclination to heal, to mend things, reaching way back into his childhood, when he had made futile attempts to reattach the spiders' legs that his brother had pulled out.

'Look here, Mr ...'

'Najevski. Raphael Najevski. But please, call me Raphael.'

'Look here, Raphael. I think you have come to the right place. Sadly, the clinic is closed now for two weeks. If you come back in the New Year, I can arrange for you to be seen. By myself, if you wish.'

He felt intensely relieved that the matter had been resolved so easily. Perhaps he would sleep here tonight, save himself the effort of the journey home. He kept a spare blanket in his office for just such occasions. He smiled at Raphael, nodding gently in expectation of assent.

But Raphael didn't leave. Instead, he said, 'I cannot wait that long. Please.'

It was the melancholy with which he made this statement that disarmed Elliot completely. He reached past Raphael to the light switch on the wall, blinking rapidly as his pupils contracted suddenly in the sharp light.

'Please, come in, sit down,' he said.

Raphael stepped into the office and took a seat in one of the two large armchairs. 'Thank you,' he said quietly.

Elliot perched on his desk to face Raphael. He had no intention of keeping the man here longer than necessary. A preliminary diagnosis should suffice for now; for many patients, the experience of being listened to, taken seriously, was enough to instil a sense of comfort and temporary psychological stability.

'You say you have not been well. In what way, Raphael?'

'Itisdifficulttoexplain.Ihavesuchbadheadacheswhen it happens. Then it is as if I am floating, and then – vagueness, confusion.'

'When what happens?'

'Well, I am not really sure. I have ... episodes. They tell me I become another person, but when it is over, I have lost the memory. Almost. It is like when you wake up and remember your ... stories in your sleep?' He paused, then smiled apologetically. 'I need to find the words in my head; this is not my language. I struggle with it sometimes. I mean *dreams*.'

'Your language is fine,' Elliot said, picking up a pencil and notepad and writing down the words *short-term amnesia?* He put down the notepad and interlocked his fingers on his lap. 'Please don't worry about the words you use, Raphael. I will tell you if anything is unclear. To begin with, I'd like you to describe one of these "episodes" if you can. Is there anything in particular that precedes them?'

Raphael rubbed his face with both hands. Elliot wasn't sure whether he had heard the question.

'When was the last time this happened?' he asked.

'Last week. I was at the house of an acquaintance

when I felt a headache beginning. I was making a copy of a letter to the Immigration, for a working visa for this acquaintance. I do that sometimes, help other foreigners with their paperwork. There are many who cannot read or write. They need someone to help with important documents, you know? Well, I was copying a letter for someone – the house was full of other people, children, it was very noisy, making it difficult to concentrate. Soon after I had begun, very suddenly, I could not stop writing. I felt a – what is the word? – ah, compulsion, to continue; I could not stop, and the pain was getting stronger, seeping into my whole body now, and I went on writing, writing, until I felt like I was floating ... and then suddenly, nothing.'

He stopped. 'May I have a cigarette, please?'

'Of course.' Elliot pulled his cigarette case from his pocket and offered him one. When he had given Raphael a light, he lit up his own. He gestured for him to go on.

'When I became aware again of what was happening,' Raphael continued, in a softer voice than before, 'there were people all around me, laughing. My legs were shaking, and I couldn't stand. Someone offered me vodka, but I felt sick. I looked down and saw ...'

'Yes?' Elliot probed gently.

Raphael's voice was barely audible. 'I saw that I had urinated on myself – you see, I had no idea what had happened. I was just afraid that I had made a terrible fool of myself. It was humiliating. Later, I was told that I had impersonated somebody's elderly aunt, mimicking her hoarse voice and irksome manner in every detail. Apparently, I had been hilarious.'

He stopped talking and bowed his head, as though it were too heavy for his neck to carry. He was clearly distressed now; his hands were trembling and his loosely held cigarette was in danger of burning right down to the skin. Elliot watched as the ash fell to the floor.

He leaned forward and touched Raphael's hand. 'But you cannot recall doing this?' he asked. 'Any of it?'

'No, Dr. Taverley. I have no memory of it at all.'

He lifted his head; he was blinking back tears.

'I need to make sure I understand you properly,' Elliot said softly. 'You say you have headaches, and that you feel compelled to continue with whatever it is you are doing at the time.'

'No. It is only when I write. In words that are not my own.'

'What do you mean, not your own?'

'When I copy a handwritten document. A letter or something. It frightens me, because I can only imagine afterwards what happens to me.'

Elliot was puzzled. Raphael's accent was tiring to listen to, and he wasn't sure he had understood fully what the man was trying to tell him.

'So you make a copy of someone else's letter, and then you get a headache?' he asked.

Raphael nodded. 'And I lose my mind, my memories.' He sounded desolate.

'How often has this occurred?'

'Three, maybe four times. But it is terrible, and gets worse every time. Please, doctor, will you help me?'

Elliot got up and walked around his desk. 'I'll be

honest with you, Raphael. It is my policy not to give my patients any guarantees. If you want to become my patient, and I decide to treat you, any success is largely dependent on how willing you are to get better.' He placed his hand on Raphael's shoulder. Raphael continued to look straight ahead. 'I can't merely give you some medicine to make your symptoms go away. Treatment can take a long time. It can be months, sometimes even years, until you are cured. It is important you understand that. Now, I suggest you go home and come back in the New Year. We can arrange an appointment now, if you like.'

Raphael looked up at Elliot and let out a soft moan. 'No, Dr. Taverley. I cannot wait that long. Please. I fear ... I am so afraid I might lose my mind. I might lose it and never get it back. Please,' he whispered. 'Please help me.'

Elliot thought hard. The clinic – which took its nickname "the Chapel" from its location in Chapelford Lane – was closed to patients for the holidays. But this man was desperate, that much was obvious, and the alternative – a closed psychiatric unit – didn't bear thinking about. The clinic's director, Charles Beaumont, was planning to spend Christmas in the country with his daughters; he had probably already left London. Elliot poured himself a glass of water and took a sip. He could arrange to see Raphael over the next two weeks, just to get him over the worst, and register him formally at the clinic in the New Year. It wouldn't be unethical, just a little unorthodox, and in any case, he had no grand plans for Christmas. His fiancee Helena would be visiting her parents in Brighton, and he had planned a quiet few days working on some patient notes.

'Very well, Raphael,' he said, his determination growing as he spoke. 'Come back here for a proper consultation tomorrow evening. Let us say seven pm. Any sooner than that is out of the question. Try and put things out of your mind in the meantime.'

Raphael rose from his chair. 'Thank you, doctor. I am sure you will be able to help me.'

Elliot stayed behind for another hour to clear up his desk. As always, he feared that unless he was exhausted and ready for sleep by the time he got home, he would spend half the night ruminating on the day's events and the work that lay ahead of him. He accidentally caught his sleeve on a tower of papers that rested dangerously close to the edge of his desk. Before he could stop it, the tower toppled over and the sheets slid, one by one, off the side of the desk, settling on the floor in a random arrangement. He groaned. That was his morning's work wasted. Dozens of handwriting samples, brief snippets of half-finished letters to Elliot, ranging from the unimaginative:

Dear Dr. Taverley,

My name is Robert Kollin and this is a specimen of my handwriting ...

and the slightly more educated

I apologise for the untidiness of my scribbles – though I admit I am intrigued to learn what they might reveal ...

to the self-consciously uneducated

I hope you can reed my ~~riti writting~~ writin ...

But it wasn't the content of these short written passages that interested Elliot. It was the writing itself; those graphical revelations of mental qualities, personal characteristics, intrinsic psychology. That morning, in hours of patient drudgery, Elliot had managed to work his way through five specimens, drawing up detailed charts of each patient's graphological profile in relation to their particular neurosis. There was the round, bouncy handwriting of Mrs Derby, the manic-depressive, who had lost her husband and two sons at the Somme: the regular pressure and pronounced garlands in the writing suggesting a convivial, optimistic woman, but the mass of internal contradictions, the disparately angular connections and downward slopes, indicated diametrically opposed impulses. Jenny Wilson, one of Elliot's younger patients, revealed her insecurity and self-hatred in the over-corrected letter formations and constant retouching. Her childish signature appeared tiny, almost to the point of illegibility, at the bottom of the page.

When Elliot had finally finished piling up the papers on his desk, his stomach growled. He checked the time. It was almost half past nine. A low droning from beneath the window reminded him that the heater was still switched on, but it was producing more noise than warmth. Elliot shivered. It had been a miserable day. The odd visitor aside, he had promised himself that morning that he would make time to visit his parents' graves, and he hadn't yet been. The cemetery would undoubtedly be closed now. Should he walk past, just to make sure? He went over to the window and wiped the condensation off with his hand. The darkness outside was grey, not black; the sort of damp, cold grey that renders everything it touches colourless. His stomach complained again. He registered the foul taste of hunger in his mouth, and decided that it was time to go home. He placed his notebook uppermost on the pile of papers and read *short-term amnesia?* on the top page. He shrugged, then suddenly remembered Nurse Robinson's letter.

Earlier that day, following a therapy session with Mrs Derby, Nurse Robinson had brought in some patient files that Elliot wanted to take home during the Christmas break. She had made a great deal of squaring the files in line with the corner of his desk, cleared her throat several times, and checked to make sure that her hair was properly pinned beneath her cap – an unnecessary exercise, since her appearance was always impeccable.

'Is there anything I can help you with, nurse?' Elliot asked, half-guessing she wanted to get off early on the last day, a request he would have gladly granted her.

Nurse Robinson looked up brightly as though she were feigning surprise. She appeared unusually fidgety, almost nervous.

'Oh, no, nothing.' She wiped her hands on her apron, and then sighed. 'Well, actually, Dr. Taverley – no, it's nothing.'

Elliot smiled. 'Please. What is it?'

'Well.' Nurse Robinson took an envelope from the pocket of her apron and stared down at it. 'It's this. A letter from my sister. I mean, not from my sister, not to me. It's a letter someone – a gentleman – has written to my sister, and – ' She paused and gave Elliot a strained smile. Elliot waited for her to continue.

'It's a little *delicate*. She isn't sure, you see, whether he is being truthful in what he writes, and I thought, well, with your expertise, you could perhaps – ' she suddenly shook her head and thrust the letter back into her pocket. 'No. I'm so sorry I troubled you. It was very silly of me. Please – '

'No, not silly of you at all,' Elliot interrupted. He felt surprised and flattered, yet at the same time shared her obvious discomfort. This was a very unusual – and awkward – conversation.

'Do let me see the letter,' he said softly. 'I'm sure you wouldn't be asking me if it weren't important.' He held his hand out, hoping his words would put her at ease.

Nurse Robinson hesitated, then slid the letter from her apron and handed it to him in one swift motion, as if to prevent her from changing her mind.

'In your own good time,' she said. 'I realise how busy you are.' Her eyes swept his cluttered desk. 'And I've taken the liberty of, um, deleting some of the more personal details.' She cleared her throat. 'I don't think my sister would want anyone reading those.' These words came out in a whisper.

Elliot took the letter and propped it against his desk lamp.

'Fine,' he said, trying to sound casual. He didn't intend on prolonging the situation any longer than necessary. 'I'll do my best and let you have my thoughts as soon as possible. In writing, perhaps. Then your sister will have a proper graphological assessment at her disposal.'

Nurse Robinson let out a little sigh. 'Thank you, Dr.

Taverley. I'll, well, I shall return to my office, then.'

She turned and left, closing the door behind her with the gentlest of clicks.

On his way out, with Nurse Robinson's letter in his pocket, Elliot stopped by the night porter's desk. Tanner was fully engrossed in a crossword puzzle.

'Good evening, Mr Tanner,' Elliot said.

Tanner looked up. 'Oh, Dr. Taverley,' he said. 'You're the last to leave tonight.' He smiled and added, 'well, 'xcept for me. But someone's got to keep an eye on the place, eh?'

'Quite,' said Elliot. He liked Tanner, and generally took time to stop and talk before he left – that is, Tanner did most of the talking; typically about the latest escapades of his eight children.

But tonight, rather than enquire about Tanner's children, Elliot frowned and said, 'By the way, I had an unannounced visitor this evening. I don't mean to get on to you about this, but security is no trivial matter here. You need to be more vigilant.'

Tanner blushed. 'There was no one came past me, I swear. I don't let no one in who's got no business here.'

'It's all right.' Elliot felt suddenly sorry for putting the man on the defensive. 'We all make mistakes. Well, enjoy your evening.'

'Same to you, doctor. And Merry Christmas!'

Two

Viewed from the street, the Chapel was nothing remarkable to look at. Its grey brick facade was embellished by stucco, white in colour only when the brightest of sunshine fell on the face of the building. To most passers-by it was fairly inconspicuous, its purpose announced almost surreptitiously on a small brass plaque on the brick to the left of the large oak doors: *Chapelford Lane Clinic for Psycho-Therapy and Psycho-Analysis, Director: Dr. Charles Beaumont, MB, MRCP, FRS, FMPA.* It was set back from the road, sandwiched between Evans's Restaurant on the right, an establishment that boasted upstairs dining rooms, popular prices and quick, friendly service, and on the left, the headquarters of the self-proclaimed "Protestant Truth Society". One of Beaumont's favourite anecdotes, which Elliot had heard told on at least three occasions, was that in the very early days of the Chapel, its proximity to the Truth Society had been a cause for great annoyance to the Society's evangelical proprietor, Mr J.P. Randall: many patients had unwittingly taken Mr Randall's promises of "spiritual healing", which were advertised in the window, at face value, and had wandered into the building in the belief that this was where they would receive psychological salvation.

The day following his encounter with Raphael, Elliot stood at the front of the Chapel, waiting. The clinic had officially closed its doors for Christmas and Elliot would need to let Raphael in himself. It was dark already; no chance for dusk at this time of year, night had fallen quickly and vehemently. Elliot lit a cigarette. On the side of the neighbouring restaurant, a banner had been hoisted in preparation for the New Year's celebrations. 'Welcome 1921!' it proclaimed in large silver and black letters. The banner flapped in the breeze, making a smacking sound when it hit the side of the building. Elliot had read in the paper recently that a group of Hindus in India considered 1921 to be the beginning of the new millennium, having discovered a calculation error in the Gregorian calendar. It was seductive, the promise of Great New Beginnings.

Not a man for New Year resolutions, Elliot nonetheless found himself considering the year ahead. He and Helena were due to get married in June; the date long planned and set, and he felt a quiet thrill of excitement at the thought of a single event that would so shape his future. He disliked, and as a rule avoided, matters that necessitated finality; things that were impossible to retract in the event of a mistake. More than once he had fallen into a slipstream of procrastination, delaying the inevitable for fear that he would make the wrong decision. But it was different with Helena. She was not quite twenty-three, seven years his junior, not even old enough to vote, and yet she was sure that she wanted to commit the rest of her life to him. Her assurance confirmed his conviction that he had never been as certain about anything as this.

The air was thick; dozens of neighbouring chimneys were zealously excreting charred clouds of sulphurous smoke. After a minute or so, Elliot's lungs tightened uncomfortably, so he flicked his cigarette to the ground and pulled his collar up, then shoved his hands into his pockets.

It was another cold evening. He hoped Raphael would be on time. He looked down the street to his right, past one or two customers entering the restaurant, and then to his left. The street was empty. He let his mind wander back to the days when he had dealt exclusively with a patient's physical disorders. He had enjoyed the practical, hands-on aspects of medicine; it had been so much more straightforward than psychology, the human body so much more treatable than the human psyche. But it was the connection, or rather the disconnectedness between body and mind, that really fascinated him. Soldiers, for example, who had lost their limbs but retained an intact mind. Or the shell-shocked nurses who hadn't sustained a single physical injury. A body could be touched, examined, surgically dissected if necessary, to uncover what lay beneath: a fractured bone, a cancerous tumour, a withering organ. The mind, psyche, spirit, soul – the fact that there was no unifying label for it offered a clue to its intangibility, its ephemerality. Defining the mind was like trying to gather up quicksilver with your hands.

Elliot paced up and down to stamp out the cold that was beginning to creep up his legs. Another minute, and he would head back inside. He heard a "Good evening" behind him, and turned to see Mr Randall locking up his shop. He returned the greeting, and then spotted Raphael walking towards the Chapel through the intermittent, circular pools of light given off by the street lamps. Elliot felt strangely relieved. He smiled, pleased that his earlier concerns over whether Raphael would come had been unwarranted.

Once inside the office, Elliot helped Raphael out of his bulky overcoat. He could see that Raphael was nervous.

The man's apprehension seeped out of him, and Elliot had a sudden, urgent wish to comfort him, assure him that he was quite safe, and that no harm would come to him. He looked tired, as if he hadn't had a good night's sleep for quite some time; he was unwashed and unshaven, and his clothes were in need of cleaning.

'How have you been feeling?' he asked him.

Raphael's breathing was shallow; his dark eyebrows were pulled together in a frown.

'Very well, thank you, doctor. Just a little tired.' He forced a smile. 'A lot of work, you know?'

'I know,' Elliot replied, smiling back.

They sat down facing each other, the lower halves of their faces illuminated by the small green lamp that sat on the desk between them. The rest of the room lay in shadow. Elliot looked down at Raphael's hands; his fingers were tightly interlocked, as if he were praying.

'You may remember that I told you that the clinic is closed, at least officially, until January,' Elliot began.

Raphael nodded.

'There is a certain protocol with regard to new patients. I will register you formally when the clinic's administrators are back, but in the meantime, I would like you to write down your details for me.' He picked up a sheet of blank paper and handed it to Raphael.

'Name, address, nationality, date of birth. And any physical complaints you may have.'

'I have no physical complaints, doctor, just the headaches.'

'Very well. Now, have you ever received any kind of

psycho-therapy before?'

'No.'

Elliot handed him a pen and watched him write his details down. It was only a half-truth, really, the request for the man's details. Elliot could well have waited until January; he would have to use an official registration form, anyway. But he couldn't resist what he regarded as data collection, acquiring a specimen of the man's handwriting, in black and white. It was always a shame to let such opportunities go to waste.

Raphael handed him the sheet back. Elliot quickly scanned the page, noting the tight, scratchy upper zones with softening, almost rounded middle-zone letters and larger than average spaces between the words. Nothing obviously pathological, Elliot thought, but he would have to subject the script to a full graphological examination later to be sure.

'You are Russian?' he asked, as he put the sheet of paper aside. 'How long have you been in London?'

'Two years.'

'And are you in employment?'

'Yes, I work at the docks, painting ships. When there is work to be had.'

'Do you enjoy it?'

'It is work. I can feed myself.'

He let Raphael speak about work for the next few minutes, taking notes and occasionally interjecting with questions.

'And these ... episodes you described to me last time you were here, where did they take place?' he asked.

'In different places; the first time in a public house, then twice at the house of some acquaintance or other. I do not like to remember the occasions, they are ... painful, frightening.' His voice was very quiet.

'It's all right,' Elliot said gently. 'Now, normally when I have a new patient,' he leant forward and rested his forearms on the desk, 'I ask him or her about themselves, we talk about how they feel, their memories, their dreams, things that make them feel sad, or angry.' It was part of Elliot's approach to therapy to explain to the patient as much as he could about the treatment that lay ahead. That way, he hoped to establish the patient's trust in him and relieve him of any undue fear of the psycho-analytic process. Fear of the unknown was the worst kind of fear. He turned his arms on the desk so that his palms showed upwards. Nothing to hide.

'In your case, however, I feel it is necessary to begin somewhere else. What I need, in order to understand the nature of these episodes more clearly, is for you to copy someone else's handwriting for me. That way, I can determine more specifically what form of treatment is best suited to you.'

Raphael shifted on his chair; Elliot could tell he was not quite relaxed, but enough at ease to proceed. To proceed with what, only moments before, had occurred to Elliot might be the trigger for a dissociative episode. He steadied his breath as his thoughts began to rearrange themselves into coherence. There was a slight, *very slight*, possibility that the episodes Raphael had described to him were in fact symptoms of a multiple personality disorder. He leaned back in his chair until his face was in shadow. He had come shamefully unprepared for this meeting, he knew; but then, he had acted more out of charity than anything when he had agreed to meet the patient while the clinic was closed. If he had listened more carefully to what Raphael had told him yesterday evening, *They tell me I become another person*, he would have recognised the symptoms immediately. He had never treated a multiple personality himself, but had, of course, read many articles on the subject. For many such patients, it took only a smell, a sound, to trigger the "splitting" from one personality into another. Perhaps, with Raphael, it was the action of writing.

He leant forward again to face his patient. 'I will ask you to copy down a letter, Raphael. I'd like you to try and duplicate the handwriting as best you can. Do you understand?'

Raphael nodded. His hands remained tightly clenched.

'Whatever happens, I'll make sure you're all right. No need to worry. Is there anything you'd like to ask me?'

'You just want me to copy the letter, is that it? You will watch me?' he asked.

'Yes, and I promise ...' Elliot leant forward even further so that he could see Raphael's face clearly, 'I promise, you will come to no harm.'

He would need an appropriate sample, Elliot thought, from someone whose script was easy enough to read. Before he was sure exactly what the man's problem was, he didn't want to confuse the issue with problems like illegibility. He had many handwriting specimens from patients here on his desk, but he discounted them immediately; they were clinically confidential. It seemed an odd exercise, something in his years of utilising a wide range of therapeutic techniques he had never dreamed of doing. He wondered briefly if he was too eager for Raphael's condition to be something out of the ordinary. It was more than likely that the man was merely an epileptic.

He unlocked the slim drawer that nestled just underneath the desktop. Here he kept his private correspondence and a journal. He had once returned home early to find his housekeeper Mrs Blake searching through some of his papers; she had denied it, claiming that she was merely cleaning up properly, but her reaction had been suspiciously defensive. Since then, Elliot had kept his private papers under lock and key. No one else used his study, and the cleaner here was reassuringly careless in her duties.

He leafed through several piles of letters that lay in the drawer. Uppermost lay a bundle, tied together carefully with a white ribbon, of Helena's love letters to him. He smiled but laid them aside immediately. Far too close, too personal. Next, he picked up a pile of black-framed condolence letters from distant relatives and friends of his parents, professing their utmost sadness at receiving news of his mother's death. Elliot flicked through them, scanning the pages for the most legible handwriting, when he spotted a pile of yellowing sheets of paper at the bottom of the drawer. They were from Ed. Elliot slid them out cautiously. He didn't bother reading them – he knew their content intimately. As he appraised the texture of the paper with his fingertips, slivers of guilt merged with a swell of excitement. His brother's handwriting would be perfect for the task. Bold and clear, showy almost, letters formed speedily but remarkably easy to read. Ed's character had been so strong, so clearly formed, and yet ... Elliot couldn't quite suppress the feeling that it was distasteful to exploit his brother's memory in this way. Hurriedly, in an attempt to stop the feeling from mounting, he plucked one of the letters at random from the pile and tidied away the rest of the papers, taking care to lock the desk. *Surely if it helps the man*, he thought.

He looked up at his patient. Raphael's breathing appeared slightly more rapid than normal, but the tension in his hands had diminished; Elliot could see the white knuckles turning pink again, until finally, he unclasped his hands. When he felt sure that Raphael had understood what was being requested of him, he placed a blank sheet of paper, a pen, and his brother's letter in front of him.

Raphael lifted the pen from the table and held it loosely in his hand. For a while, he focused his gaze on the handwriting sample before him. The writing on the page was large and flamboyant in appearance; the black ink soared and plunged across the sheet, like the recordings of an angry seismograph. Elliot's brother Ed was the sort of man one could not easily forget; the kind of man for whom the word "charisma" had been invented. His handwriting was a clear reflection of his character. He always made extravagant use of the page, signifying a confident and unbridled approach to life. His t-strokes aimed high in cheerful optimism, and it was only in the rhythmic altercation in pressure, and the slightest of tremors in the proud upper loops, that any indication was given that this was written by a man surrounded by the confusion and wretchedness of war.

Although he had been five years Elliot's senior, everyone had considered Ed the youthful, vigorous one, while Elliot had looked on from the sensible, sober sidelines. Elliot had admired his older brother for as long as he could remember. Growing up, he had always felt the need to be close to his brother's side, despite their obvious differences in temperament. As children they had had the unspoken understanding that Ed would let young Elliot join in with his games and adventures, while in return, Elliot was sworn to secrecy over anything – or anyone – forbidden they might encounter. These encounters were frequent when they were young – travelling to areas of the city that were out-of-bounds; Ed's clandestine meetings with the housekeeper's plump niece – and Elliot, the straight-laced boy that he was, frequently felt filled to bursting point with the strain of it all. The keeping of secrets, especially from their mother, the dread of being found out, was one of his most intense childhood memories; that, and the feeling of admiration for the effortlessness with which his brother kept his secrets.

When Elliot began to receive letters from the trenches, he realised how the Army had suited Ed's temperament. In one of his letters, Ed had written of how the war wasn't breaking him; instead, *it was breaking him in.* Elliot had lost count of how many times he had analysed these final letters, and wished he never had.

The extract he had given Raphael to copy was a typically humorous one from the early days of the war; an anecdote about a trench cat that walked across No Man's

Land at leisure. This was a strictly neutral feline, aptly nick-named "Woodrow" by the soldiers, and who was shrewdly aware of the mealtimes on both sides. In his letter, Ed joked about what it must mean to have nine lives in the midst of shelling and sniping. His letters were always cheerful; he very rarely spoke of the horror and desolation of life in the trenches. Even when he did, it was always couched in terms of the most remorseless optimism: *I'm living in conditions that would have driven me insane six months ago, and yet I've never felt better in my life!*

Elliot looked up from the letter, and glanced at Raphael. He was consumed by concentration. His eyes seemed to stare at the pen in his hand, almost questioningly, and with great effort he worked his fingers around it. Elliot watched with fascination. Raphael appeared to struggle to find a natural position for his fingers; it looked as though he had never held a pen before. When he was finally comfortable, he leant forward, seemingly at ease now, almost stroking the paper with the pen. Elliot had read the letter countless times and knew almost every word by heart.

Dear Elliot,

Just a brief note to let you know how things are. Have written you a couple of letters, but have not heard from you or anyone else. Some dimwit must be in charge of distributing the mail here. As I write this, Jerry's having another good go at us. He never seems to tire of it. I shall be as deaf as a bat by the time I return!

Last night, we lost three men in No Man's Land, stupid buggers; they came out of the dugout without waiting to be re-lieved, they don't understand the importance of maintaining <u>control</u> over that strip of mud. If it weren't us in there, it would be

Jerry. I shan't pretend that we are all having a jolly time here – the food is rotten and the rats so big they would give a dog a run for its money. But, mustn't gripe, it's great to feel so ALIVE!

Speaking of pets, we have a trench cat here...

As Raphael began to write, Elliot watched him intently, not knowing what to expect. He caught himself hoping for something extraordinary to happen, and the suspense was almost unbearable. His eyes darted from Raphael's hand to his face, and back again. The room was completely still; all he could hear was the hot, tremulous pulse in his ears, and the sound of the pen moving across the rough paper, scratching, scribbling. The desk lamp illuminated the back of Raphael's writing hand, as the words crept one by one out of the shadow of his hand. The words... it was unbelievable... they were *exact* reproductions of the originals – every t-stroke as sharp, every lower loop as rounded, even the i-dots appeared as carefully placed as those in the original script. It was flowing, effortless, as though he were writing in his own hand.

And then it began: the first thing Elliot noticed was the change in posture. Raphael began to sit up straight – more than that, his shoulders were pulled back and down, as his chest thrust forward and his back straightened. No longer a reserved, self-effacing emigre; here sat a proud, self-confident man of the world. His eyelids, which had seemed, moments ago, to wear the heaviness of an onerous life, opened wider to reveal sharp, lucid eyes. The purplish shadows under his eyes disappeared; or was that just a trick of the light? Then, it seemed, the transformation was complete. Abruptly, Raphael stopped writing. He looked up and gazed straight through Elliot, not a flicker of recognition in his eyes.

'I don't think,' he began, 'that I could ever really find the words to describe the smell.'

Elliot almost called out in disbelief. It was – it couldn't be – but it was unmistakably Ed. The influence of their Scottish mother was evident in the smooth inflections in his voice, the soft low vowels, the rolled 'r' faint, but not imperceptible – no trace of a Russian accent, or was he just imagining it?

'It's the noise most men complain about, the rifle fire, the incessant shelling. It drives some of them mad. But you can learn to block that out. It's the smells that catch you unawares, the pleasant and the putrid; and, worst of all, they stay with you for such a long time, as though they bury themselves deep in your memory, to torment you for years to come.' Ed/Raphael leaned back in his chair and looked up at the ceiling, folding his hands across his stomach.

'I decided one night that we could all do with a hot drink, and took the risk of brewing some cocoa in our dugout. For no apparent reason my fool of a signaller stood up, spun 'round, and then fell, shot through the head and helmet by a sniper. His brains splattered onto my sleeve, and I could smell it, the fresh, sharp stench of human cerebellum, intermingled with the sweet aromatic smell of cocoa. Now I can't smell chocolate without smelling the signaller's brains.' He sat upright again, to look at – or through – Elliot. He pulled back his lips into a generous smile.

'And that's why I like the cold. It numbs your sense of smell. Anaesthetises your nose, if you like.'

Elliot was trembling all over. How was this possible? Had his brother really appeared in all but body, in unimaginably accurate detail? Or had he just been hearing what he wanted to hear? He tried to steady his thoughts. It must be a trick of the light, some neurally-based illusion. He was a psycho-analyst, for Christ's sake! This must be some form of unconscious projection. But as he dug his fingernails ever deeper into his thighs in the weak hope that the pain would shatter the illusion, shock his consciousness back into reality, he knew that he must discount these rationalisations, for that is all they were. This, he knew with alarming clarity, was real.

He missed his brother so much! All shades of grief and sorrow – long since buried, but not forgotten – wove themselves into an angry tapestry around his heart. Cruel and painful, they squeezed and squeezed, ever tighter, until he felt his lungs contract and he gasped for air. Putting his hand to his face, he noticed that he had been crying. He opened his mouth to speak, but no words came out. He struggled to think of something – anything – to say, to keep Ed alive, here, in this room. When he finally spoke, his voice was strangled with emotion.

'Ed,' he called, 'Eddie, it's me, Elliot. Can you hear me?'

But the spell had broken. Raphael had reappeared. He seemed to be under intense, almost intolerable, nervous strain. He had aged again rapidly; he was no longer the young man Elliot had known. As Raphael's eyes focused to look at Elliot, he frowned, questioningly, bewildered. With great effort, Elliot tried to regain his composure. He pulled a handkerchief out of his pocket, and under the pretence of blowing his nose, wiped away his tears. For a long while he sat there, the silence draping itself around him. He felt stunned, almost nauseous, the same way he'd felt when told that Ed had died. He wanted to just go on sitting there; no, he wanted Raphael to start writing again. He wanted Ed back.

It was Raphael who broke the silence.

'Was it all right?' he asked. He sounded confused.

'Yes, it was … fine.' Elliot's mouth was dry. He swallowed. What had just happened here? It was as though he had just been watching some theatre play too surreal for him to understand. He became aware of his patient staring at him. He cleared his throat.

'Are you – are you feeling all right?' he asked.

Raphael nodded. 'I think so. My head hurts. May I have a glass of water?'

Elliot got up and poured him a glass from a decanter on the window sill.

'Raphael, do you remember what happened?' he asked as he handed him the water, attempting to control the tremble in his hand. Raphael seemed drained, exhausted.

'Not very much. As I tried to explain to you last time, it is like remembering a dream. The mood; it was sad, as if…' He hesitated. 'Were you ever lost as a child?'

Elliot nodded.

'Yes, like that. Lost, and sad. With the panic rising in your throat, but still trying to be brave. And I remember thinking of snow. But I have a headache now.'

Elliot returned to his seat behind the desk. From

beyond the walled yard outside, a fire engine pealed out an emergency; a clamour of urgent yells suggested a fire somewhere nearby.

'Why – how did you stop?' Elliot wanted to know.

'I don't know,' he answered desperately. 'Dr. Taverley, is it how they say? Do I become another person?'

Elliot couldn't – wouldn't – answer this question. Instead he said quietly, 'I will need you to come to another session. Soon. You must go home and rest; I will see you here again in the new year.'

Raphael rose a few inches from his chair, hovering there for a moment as if unsure whether this was his cue to leave.

'You can go now, Raphael. Go home and rest. Come back in two weeks' time.'

Raphael straightened up. 'Thank you, Dr. Taverley.'

When Raphael finally left, Elliot lay down on the couch to rest his eyes, but was so overcome with tiredness and emotion that he fell asleep there and then, and only awoke at eight the next morning. Still half-asleep, he reached instinctively for his notebook and pencil, but the remnants of his dreams – vivid though they had been – had already fled. He was midway through a yawn when the full recollection of last night's incident suddenly assailed him, and with it, a hit of adrenaline to his system, accelerating his heartbeat until it was no more than a series of fluttering spasms. He closed his eyes and steadied himself, breathing slowly, until the palpitations had passed. He got up from the couch and walked over to the desk, floating almost, in a dream he knew was no dream. Two sheets of paper lay side-by-side on the desk – one genuine, one a forgery – and only by the creases in one of the sheets could Elliot tell which one had been written by Ed.

THREE

There had, of course, been warning signs. Over the past two years since the headaches began, Elliot had become sensitised to the announcement of pain's imminent arrival: a tattoo of twinges just behind the eyebrows; the staccato growing in sharpness throughout the day with relentless intensity. The pain began to howl, scraping at the underside of his skull, bleeding into his eyes. Elliot lifted the balls of his thumbs to his temples and began to apply gentle, circular pressure. His eyelids flickered with the pain, and he felt the familiar nausea blossom in his stomach. He sat paralysed in his chair, leaning forward, afraid of sudden movement; conscious now only of the acid pounding in his head and the brilliant flashes of light that stung his eyes beneath their lids. The buzz from the electric heater was drilling a hole straight into his brain, siphoning off any sense of time passing. He was concentrating hard on not vomiting. His breathing became increasingly shallow, until he felt dizzy from lack of oxygen.

Then gradually, lazily, deliciously, the pain began to wane, surging up in one final crashing wave before fading completely. He inhaled deeply, bracing himself, preparing to expose his eyes to the light. As he exhaled, he tentatively lifted his lids. The room was almost completely dark. He had lost an hour, maybe two. Blinking several times to confirm that the pain had really gone, he reached across to switch the desk light on.

With a *click* the room came into focus. Still propped

up against the desk, Elliot looked at his watch. It was shortly after five. That meant he had only lost fifty minutes, not as much as he'd feared. At that moment the doorbell rang and he remembered that Helena had said she wanted to bring him some poetry she had been working on recently. She tended towards tremendous impatience and had claimed that it couldn't wait until after Christmas.

'Gosh, you look awful, darling,' she said when he opened the door to her. She stepped forward to give him a hug.

'Just a headache,' he told her, responding grate-fully to her embrace by rubbing her gently between the shoulder blades.

'Are you all right? Shall I come back later?' she asked.

'No, no, do come in. I'm fine now.' He began to help her out of her coat. Helena kissed him on the cheek and handed him a large envelope.

'Tell me what you think,' she said. 'And be honest. You know I cannot abide sycophants.'

Elliot looked at the envelope in his hand. He didn't know the first thing about poetry, but Helena insisted that she valued his opinion above all others.

'You really do look awful,' she said again, walking through to the living room and taking a seat next to the fireplace. She shivered. 'And it's cold in here. Would you mind lighting a fire?'

Taking this as a hint that she planned to stay a whi-le, Elliot obliged. Helena sat and watched wordlessly as he knelt down in front of the fireplace and set about building a kindling pyramid.

'You've been working too hard,' Helena said finally, as the warmth gradually began to spread through the room. Elliot took a seat on the sofa facing her.

'Possibly,' he said.

She stood up and took a seat next to him, tucking her feet under her legs and leaning into him.

'You know, I'm sure Charles would grant you a couple of weeks off, if you asked,' she said. Charles Beaumont was an old friend of Helena's parents'; Elliot had met and fallen in love with Helena at a hospital summer fund-raising ball eighteen months ago.

Of that evening – which had initially promised to become a tedious small-talk affair with various wealthy, and accordingly self-righteous, potential donors – Elliot could recall largely two things: the first was a sense of unanticipated delight that he had been seated opposite a keen-eyed, attractive brunette who, judging from the cut-glass ashtray in front of her brimming with lipstick-covered stubs, appeared to be a chain-smoker. This young woman was – unsurprisingly to Elliot – the centre of attention for much of the evening, entertaining those at the table with amusing stories whose content he had long since forgotten, until someone present warned the others to be on their best behaviour or risk featuring in one of her poems. There ensued eager calls for her to recite one, but she just shook her head and waved the requests away. But then her dinner companion, a wide-faced man named Carter (a distant cousin of Helena's, Elliot was later pleased to discover), boomed at her, 'Come now, Helena, treat us to one of those little rhymes or verses you're so fond of making up!'

And this is the second thing Elliot could recall: the raw sting of humiliation in Helena's expression; no anger at this cloddish put-down; instead, a look of dread that she had just been found out; publicly revealed as a fraud; that the poetry she crafted and tended so painstakingly was nothing more than an amateurish assortment of little rhymes and verses worth reciting merely for an evening's amusement.

And this expression on her face touched him deeply, and he heard himself saying, in a voice that seemed almost alien to himself, as he had hardly spoken all evening, 'I would very much like to read your poetry,' and then this young beautiful woman looked at him and smiled.

It was this act of impromptu chivalry, Helena told him later, that had sparked her interest in him. Elliot had proposed to her two months after they began courting and had never quite got over his surprise that she had agreed to marry him. Yet now he knew to gauge a certain pause of hers, a certain glance in his direction, as a request for his assurance; that despite her eloquence and spirit and beauty she was as fragile as anyone he knew; and it made him feel indescribably happy that he was the one she needed assurance from.

He stroked the nape of her neck. 'Time off wouldn't solve this particular problem,' he said.

Helena looked up at him. 'What problem?'

'Oh, nothing. I – ' He stopped and leaned forward. He felt a gentle throbbing just behind his eyes, a vestigial flutter of pain.

'What's bothering you, Elliot? I wish you would tell

me. I do worry about you sometimes, working in that – place,' she said quietly.

'Mental illness is not contagious, if that's what concerns you,' he said abruptly, and regretted his tone immediately.

Helena didn't reply. Fearing he had poisoned the mood and wanting to let Helena know that he was grateful for her concern, he gave her an account of how the Russian had become Ed in his office the previous evening. Naturally, he did not mention the man's name.

'It sounds quite improbable,' was her first reaction. 'Of course, I'm not suggesting for a moment that you're making it up, but are you *sure* it was Ed? I mean, isn't there a tiny possibility that this man just reminds you of your brother, and you got somehow caught up in the situation?'

This was the same thought that had robbed Elliot of his sleep: had he just been deceiving himself? Had the whole episode been the result of some kind of inadvertent auto-suggestion? Or, more disturbingly, had he fallen prey to an elaborate hoax? He had spent the whole day trying to analyse the experience with detached reason, cold hard intellect, scientific objectivity. Of course, to a bystander, the whole episode sounded ridiculously improbable. But Elliot felt as sure about Ed's reappearance as he had ever been sure of anything his whole life.

'You'll have to take my word for it,' he said.

'Fair enough,' she replied softly. She rose and left the room, returning with a bottle of wine. She handed it to him to uncork and sat down in the armchair opposite him. The fire blazed healthily in the hearth.

'But what about the writing?' she persisted. 'As an expert, he may well have detected a degree of fear or distress, or even just homesickness in a letter from the trenches. I'm not speaking from experience, obviously, but fighting on the front line must have been unimaginably distressing! The sheer terror of it all, not to mention the misery and hopelessness. Surely – in terms of graphology – these emotions came out in Ed's handwriting. Who's to say that you aren't the victim of a swindle, that your "patient" isn't merely mimicking, quite consciously, the characteristics he deciphers from the writing?'

'I don't know whether I should be offended by that,' Elliot said, prying the cork deftly from the bottle.

'Oh, don't be like that,' she replied, 'I'm not undermining your professional judgement, I just want to know how *you* know that this isn't the case. Come on, Elliot, don't sulk just because I'm taking an interest in your work. I care, I really do. You just have to admit that this takes some believing, don't you?'

'There's no denying that it sounds extraordinary, but that's the business I'm in. The fact that the human psyche is extraordinary is the reason I do what I do.' He realised that he was sounding defensive again. 'But I understand your doubts. He may be an impostor. Believe me, I've thought of nothing else since it happened.' He turned to look into the fire. 'You know, Ed wouldn't touch chocolate when he returned from the War. The same person who, as a child, ate so much chocolate one Christmas Day that he vomited, and then asked for more. Or, what about this: he was terribly afraid of water as a child, and when he was ten, our father got him to swim across an icy stream one February on the promise of a Cadbury's bar. The fact that this man knew of a reason for Ed's sudden aversion to chocolate can't be explained by an unusual talent for cheap fairground mimicry.'

'But there must be some logical explanation!' Helena exclaimed. 'You call yourself a scientist, for goodness' sake. This all sounds positively paranormal. Explain to me how it's possible!'

'I'm not quite sure myself,' Elliot said quietly. He sighed and took a sip of wine. 'All I know is that it has something to do with the link between graphology and the unconscious. Something crucial. Something I'm missing so far.' He looked across at Helena to find her staring at him intently.

He continued. 'What I'm trying to say is that unconscious fears or desires, which have been repressed – in other words, forbidden entry to the conscious – often reveal themselves as somatic complaints such as insomnia or hysteria. I saw the war churn out countless men who, despite having no physical injuries, couldn't see or smell or taste properly.'

'But surely these are extremes,' Helena argued.

'Yes, you're right. But take your sister's housekeeper, whose chewed fingernails undoubtedly indicate displaced aggression, or your cousin, who giggles uncontrollably and covers her ears at the mere mention of anything remotely sexual. These are not extremes. They are the typical psycho-somatic manifestations that affect us all. And yet this is all that graphology claims to be: the spontaneous graphical expression of nervous impulses that originate in the brain, and are controlled, or guided, by the unconscious.'

'So when I put pen to paper, I have to be afraid of my hidden neuroses spilling onto the page?' she asked.

'Well,' he said and smiled. For the first time that day he was feeling mildly cheerful. 'I wouldn't go so far as to call them neuroses. Idiosyncrasies, let's say. Seriously though, your personality does find expression in your writing. The significance of scientific graphology for psycho-analysis is that in handwriting, there is nowhere for the unconscious to hide. Intentionally or not, a person's fundamental psychological make-up surfaces every time he puts pen to paper.'

'Yes, yes, but what about your patient, where's the connection to his transformations?' Helena was, as always, fully engaged in the discussion.

'Patience, please, I'll come to that shortly. But first, let me give you an example. Or rather, show you.' He stood up and crossed the room. Underneath the drawing room window stood a Vizagapatam Davenport – a piece that his father had brought back from India as an anniversary gift for his wife at a time when their marriage was still untroubled. It was ornately inlaid with ivory birds and gilt-decorated flower scrolls within chequered and feathered ebony and ivory banding. The recess was enclosed by folding doors, which opened to reveal five drawers and pigeon-holes. It was chipped in places, probably as a result of the transcontinental transport, and very striking. Elliot found it almost too elaborate, and it certainly dominated the room, but Helena – admittedly more conversant than Elliot as to what was *en vogue* – would not let him even consider selling it.

The house was crammed full with such things: items that had been of enormous sentimental value to his parents, but that left Elliot with a feeling of morbidity.

He opened one of the small drawers on the left-hand side of the Davenport, and removed a small folder containing several sheets of paper.

'God, the suspense is killing me!' Helena exclaimed, half-rising from her chair in anticipation. 'What have you got there?'

'Yes, this will do,' he said, leafing through the papers and selecting one apparently at random. He handed it to Helena.

'A letter,' she said, sounding unimpressed. She scanned it briefly.

'Just ignore the content...'

'Well, that won't be too difficult, given that I don't speak German.'

'Even better,' he replied. 'You won't be distracted by the subject matter. Now, have a good look. You need to focus on the individual words, but also take into account the way in which the space is utilised. Can you see the tightness in the writing, the meticulous attention to detail?' He walked around the back of the sofa and leant over her shoulder. She nodded.

'The middle-zone letters,' he pointed to the 'e's, 'r's and 'o's in the greeting '*Sehr geehrter Kollege*', 'are all of even size, and in balanced proportion to the understrokes and upper strokes. Look, here the 'g' travels down as much as the 'h' travels upward. In graphological theory, the three zones, upper, middle and lower, can be interpreted in relation to a man's psychic energy. Whether mind-body-spirit or Id-Ego-Superego, whatever you want to call it, this reflects the tripartite nature of man's psyche. Can you see? The writer of this letter has his personality in balance.'

'Yes, I follow that. It makes sense when you put it like that. You can't really imagine somebody who's emotionally disturbed writing so neatly, can you? What does this mean, when the writing slants to the right? I only ask because my writing does that, too.'

'It usually indicates extroversion.' He smiled and kissed her on the cheek. 'You're hardly an introvert, now, are you?'

'Hardly,' she said, smiling back at him. Elliot walked back around the sofa, stopping to add some logs to the fire on the way.

'I only wanted to give you a brief impression of what graphology is about. A comprehensive assessment would involve taking into account the whole, not just individual word shapes and direction.' He held his hand out for the letter, but Helena had obviously not finished, and tapped his outstretched hand down gently.

'We'll have to do this with my writing,' she said, 'so I know you're not just making it all up to impress me. How do I know what you've said about this person is actually true?'

'Turn the page over. You see the signature? Its shape and fluidity are in harmony with the text. This symbolises a high degree of self-knowledge, a person who is aware of his individuality. No need for ostentatious self-presentation.'

Helena turned the letter over, and gave a little gasp

of surprise.

'C.J. Jung! You crafty devil!'

'I wrote to him after attending one of his lectures,' Elliot explained. 'This was his response. It's no coincidence that this letter was written by the man who first described the concept of individuation.' Helena raised her eyebrows in query.

'Refers to the integration of conscious and unconscious functions of the mind, when the interaction between them is in perfect accord. To become what we are capable of, we have to explore the unconscious aspects of our personality, both the personal unconscious and the collective unconscious.'

Helena yawned. 'I think I follow, but I'm getting bored of this theorising now. This patient of yours, what's the story? And in layman's terms, please,' she said.

Over a second bottle of wine – both of them having lost all track of time – Elliot proceeded to share with Helena his tentative thoughts on Raphael's condition. He was still so confused by what had happened last night that he hoped, perhaps unrealistically, that a neutral listener might provide some fresh insight.

'I suspect that this man reads and interprets the writing presented to him, much as I have just demonstrated to you. He does this with extraordinary speed and precision, but as he has had no formal training, I assume that he operates on intuition, or is unusually sensitive to the symbolism of the written word. What happens after that, I can only speculate.'

'The transformations, you mean?' she asked.

'Yes. It's as if he absorbs the writer's psyche while he writes, and, from what he has read, develops a separate personality,' he said. 'Somehow, he managed to re-create Ed from his writing.' He swallowed hard.

'But how do you explain this?'

Elliot spread his arms out wide, lifting his shoulders in an exaggerated shrug.

'Well, the unconscious can't be studied directly, but can only be inferred from a person's behaviour, or dreams, or projective techniques like graphology. If we take the writing as a projection, or reflection, of a collective unconscious, then...' he stopped, shaking his head. His cheeks burned with the heat from the fire, which had now reached a full blaze. He fixed his profound, slightly intoxicated gaze on Helena. 'Do you think it is possible that he has access to – I'm not sure how to describe it – a universal store of human experience? If there is some global psychological amalgamation, a collection of living histories, then perhaps this man has found a way to tap into it, and then uses it to reconstruct individual identities. In this sense, graphology is merely the key.'

'I'll tell you what I think is possible.' She leaned into him and put her arms around him tenderly. 'I think it's possible that you've had too much to drink, my dear. Come on, it's late, you'd better call me a cab.'

The following day, Elliot headed east to meet his friend Stanislav. The long tram ride took him down East India Dock Road, past recreation grounds, tree-planted churchyards, public baths, convenience stores and council offices; a fine wide road leading to the docks and the romantic promise of far-flung places. It was only when Elliot disembarked and turned off the main road into a tight network of dingy side streets, running at right angles from the main thoroughfare, that he encountered the rows of boarding houses that rented out rooms to the poor; filthy, stinking, overcrowded, overpriced hovels. It was an urban wilderness, brimming with people of all creeds and colours. Poverty was all they had in common.

'A different world' was how Elliot had once described it to Helena. 'Decaying, but somehow not defeated.'

He spotted Stanislav standing in the doorway of a squalid, grey building – identical to the squalid, grey buildings adjoining it – entertaining a group of four or five children with a magic trick involving a coin and a handkerchief. The children, enthralled and enchanted as one, squealed their pleasure in a language Elliot didn't recognise. As always, he marvelled at children's ability not to let the brutal realities of life overshadow small, seemingly trivial delights.

Stanislav rented a room at the top of the house; Elliot had visited him in his lodgings several times, and each time had returned home in need of a bath. He told himself that this feeling wasn't due to an inherited squeamishness of the "working classes"; the need to wash away the stench of poverty and desperation that clung inexorably to his clothes, his hair, his skin. Rather, he attributed his revulsion of such living conditions to the conditions themselves, not to those who had little choice but to endure them. Elliot had often considered offering Stanislav a room in his own house, where he had moved back to after his mother had died, and which was ridiculously large for one person, but he knew that such an offer would offend his friend.

Stanislav caught sight of Elliot and slowly raised a hand in greeting, his mouth opening into a gradual smile. His movements were unhurried and thoughtful; this man did nothing accidentally or by half measures. He was Elliot's closest friend, a forty-year-old Pole, tall and thin, with coarse black hair, comically lopsided features, and arched eyebrows that seemed to swoop downwards before joining in a V-shape just above the bridge of his nose. Despite his obvious lack of physical beauty, everyone he met became ever so slightly infatuated with his unassuming gentility. As Elliot approached, he could see how exhausted his friend looked. He worked twelve-hour shifts as a day labourer putting down new tracks for the extension of the Underground on the Northern Line.

The children drifted away sulking and reluctant as Elliot approached, not bothering to hide their displeasure at having lost their magician.

'*Dzien dobry, przyjaciel,*' Stanislav said, taking Elliot's right hand in his and shaking it with as much warmth as his freezing hand could apparently muster.

'Hello, Stanislav.'

'Thank you for coming. Have you brought everything with you?' He pointed at Elliot's bag.

'Yes. Lead the way.'

As they walked down the street, Stanislav gave Elliot an account of the patient they were on their way to see. He was a thirty-five-year old Ukrainian, very sick, who had arrived in England only weeks before, having escaped some of the worst fighting of the civil war.

'He and his family are illegally here, that's why I called you. They arrived at the docks last month and haven't strayed any further west,' Stanislav explained.

This part of the borough formed an ethnic continent of its own: Poles who had stayed in London following their release from the prisoner-of-war camps in Alexandra Palace and Feltham; Ukrainians, Russians and Albanians fleeing from civil war, militias, pogroms and genocide. The London slums, Elliot knew from Stanislav, seemed heaven compared to what they had left behind.

'No help from the Salvation Army?' he asked. 'They'd turn a blind eye to his immigrant status, I'm sure.'

'They're frightened, Elliot. They don't trust anyone in uniform. It doesn't matter what uniform that is.'

'I understand. What's wrong with the man? Any idea?'

'"Inside trouble" is all the wife can tell me.'

Cancer, Elliot thought. *That's what they call cancer.* Consumption was known as "chest trouble". Flimsy veils for unspeakable truths.

'Do they speak English?'

'He can't speak at all; her English is rudimentary. But that's what I'm here for.'

Elliot and Stanislav arrived at a narrow, two-storey terrace. The windows that hadn't been smashed and boarded up were held in place precariously by rotting frames. The stench of sulphur, faeces and decaying food was as typical to the place as the lugubrious buildings. A woman came to greet them at the door holding a handkerchief across her mouth and nose. It was a smell one could never get used to.

The small basement room, which housed the invalid, his wife and their four children, had one grimy window set up high in the street-facing wall. There was barely any light to speak of, most of it coming from a fire in the grate that had been lit to dry some laundry. Stockings, aprons and greying nightshirts in various sizes hung on cords stretched across the room. The wife of the sick man pointed to the wet garments and said something in rapid Ukrainian.

'Washing day,' Stanislav translated. The woman shrugged her shoulders apologetically. She was obviously uncomfortable in Elliot's presence, and he felt suddenly self-conscious in his well-tailored, unsoiled coat and suit. He walked across the cramped room to a narrow bed underneath the window, where the woman's husband lay rasping in agony. The man was shockingly thin; his face a skeletal mask of torment mixed with the kind of fatigue that accompanies such pain. Elliot opened his doctor's bag and took his time examining the man, although he knew the diagnosis from the moment he had looked in the man's mouth.

'He has cancer of the throat,' Elliot said, when he finished his examination. 'He's dying. There's nothing more I can do for him. Look –' he continued, as he saw the face of the wife crumple in despair. 'I'll leave him some morphine for the pain, but you must make sure that it doesn't get around that I'm handing out medicines like this randomly.' He turned to Stanislav. 'Make sure she understands.'

Stanislav nodded. Elliot left to wash his hands.

'Thank you, Elliot,' Stanislav said later, as they walked down the main road towards the tram stop.

'Don't mention it. I'm sorry I couldn't do more.'

'You did all you could. When you left, she told me that he has become too exhausted even to scream at the pain he feels. She thanks you for your kindness.'

'And yours. How many people here have you helped? You are their voice, and I think it's scandalous that you don't use your skills in a more official capacity. Go to the Borough Council, they're sure to have a position for someone with your qualifications. Besides, translators aren't badly paid.'

'I have work, Elliot.'

'It's a shameful waste of your education, and your talents.'

'So you keep telling me. But this is my life – for now, at least. If I can endure it, why can't you?'

Elliot did not respond. It was an old argument and one that he knew he would never win. Stanislav was too obstinate, too *proud* for that. In any case, Elliot half-guessed that Stanislav had already tried to gain employment more suited to his qualifications; but he remained a foreigner, and that meant he was condemned to taking whatever work he could find, which as a rule meant some form of unskilled labour.

They walked in silence for a while, passing by a crowded public house and stepping aside to avoid being urinated on by a drunk who was emptying his bladder with uncertain aim at a lamp-post. In the window of the adjacent wigmaker's, a menorah cradled six lit candles. Elliot declined his friend's offer of a cigarette; his lungs were thick with the yellow, sulphurous fog that had descended on the city.

Stanislav lit up himself and said, 'And your lovely fiancee, I trust she is well?'

'Yes. We're travelling to Brighton next month for her parents' wedding anniversary. They're planning a big party.'

'You don't sound too happy about that.'

'Oh, no, I don't mean to sound unenthusiastic. Helena's family are very charming, but their lifestyle is one of – how should I put it? – they spare no expense. And a part of me is always reminded of the contrast to this.' He stopped and spread out his arms.

'Ah, Elliot, others are responsible for this reality. You will never be happy if you feel guilty about every injustice in the world. And you will not change it. What you did today for that sick man, *that* changes the world.'

Elliot laughed. 'You're sounding more philosophical than usual this evening, Stanislav.'

'You can blame Luljeta. She is driving me insane with her theologising. Every day, it is "God is everywhere. We haven't been everywhere to prove He isn't there. Therefore, He exists!", or "If God does not exist, then where do atheists like you come from?" And she wonders why I do not marry her!'

'But otherwise things are going well?' Elliot asked.

'One day good, one day bad. But as I always say, my friend, if the nights are good, who cares about the days?' And he winked at Elliot.

Elliot smiled back. It was this tempestuous relationship that kept Stanislav in London, and he was grateful for it. A sudden jolt of pain in his head made him groan involuntarily.

'Are you not feeling well?' Stanislav asked.

'A stone in my shoe,' Elliot answered, making a show of taking off his shoe and shaking out an imaginary pebble. If he ignored the warning of a headache, perhaps it would go away. Across the road, a Salvation Army band played *Good King Wenceslas* in dubious harmony, a cardboard sign informing passers-by that they were collecting for amputees. The silence between the two men resumed, but this time each man knew what the other was thinking. Stanislav was the first to break the silence.

'It has been a year now, has it not?'

'A year since his suicide, yes. I – I meant to visit the cemetery the other day, but other things intruded.'

'I'm glad they did. Elliot –' Stanislav laid his arm on Elliot's. 'It is a time of sadness, I know, but do you think it's wise to go there at all? Can you not just let things rest, let the past be the past?'

'You're talking to a psycho-analyst, Stanislav,' he said, smiling grimly. 'The past doesn't rest. I want to find some peace, but –' he couldn't prevent his voice from cracking. He cleared his throat and his breath froze in the air. 'My father ... Ed ... I don't think I will ever find any peace.'

He knew it sounded stupid, irrational, but if anyone understood, it would be Stanislav, without whom he could never have grieved for his brother. In the distance, they heard the clunking of the approaching tram. It was time to part.

'Just promise me you will look after yourself,' Stanislav said. 'Enjoy your Christmas. And give my regards to Helena. Think of what you have, not what you have lost.'

Metal screeched on metal as the tram came to a stop in front of them. Stanislav dropped his cigarette and crushed it under his foot. He and Elliot embraced.

'I'll be fine,' Elliot told him softly. As he stepped up onto the sideboard, he turned and looked down at Stanislav. A shimmer of yellow light from a street lamp illuminated the left side of his friend's face. For a moment, it cancelled the asymmetry of his features, making him look almost handsome.

'Promise me you will be careful, Elliot Taverley. *Dobranoc*,' Stanislav said, and walked off, with as definite a sense of purpose as always.

Four

Elliot leant forward and handed his fare to the driver.

'Keep the change,' he said, and smiled in the young driver's direction, but without looking at him, almost as an afterthought.

'You all right, mister?' the driver asked, attempting to turn around fully in order to face Elliot. His ill-fitting tweed jacket made this an awkward endeavour. Elliot, who was busy struggling to open the car door with his left hand while trying not to crush the bunch of flowers he held in his right, looked up in surprise. They hadn't spoken all the way from Pimlico to Kensal Green; Elliot deep in thought, the driver in concentration as he negotiated the icy roads. Only once had they had a near crash – turning into Kensington High Street, the cab had barely missed colliding with a bus that couldn't stop – but even then, the driver hadn't spoken, just inhaled sharply, and then mumbled some expletives under his breath. But now he smiled at Elliot, and it crossed his mind that he must look as bad as he felt; several sleepless nights were all it took to have that effect on him. The young man spoke again.

'Recent loss, is it?' He nodded towards Elliot's flowers, and then to the cemetery. He didn't wait for an answer. 'Sad places, these. Got three little 'uns over at Tower 'amlets.'

'I'm sorry,' Elliot said, and meant it. They sat in silence for a few minutes, each rehearsing a private, poignant memory. Then, in wordless agreement, their encounter was over, and Elliot stepped out of the car. He watched the black shiny cab drive slowly along the road, until it turned the corner and was out of sight.

Elliot entered the cemetery and headed south. Apart from the cold blue sky, the cemetery was monochrome: the grass bluish-white with frost, and the gravestones grey. The flowers Elliot carried with him were white cactus dahlias – his mother's favourites – delicate, pale green stems bearing with astonishing strength explosive bursts of thin white petals.

It was early on Christmas Eve, not yet nine o'clock, and there weren't many people about. The air was cold and windless, and the sharp early-morning sun was beginning to burn up the mists that hung low among the tombstones. The heavy silence was broken only by an occasional twig snapping behind Elliot. Once or twice he turned around, thinking there was someone behind him, but saw nothing. He was reminded how much he hated coming here: his childish fears of death and ghosts and ghouls resurfaced at every visit.

Two thin, muscular gravediggers passed him, tipping their frayed caps in professional condolence; a young woman dressed in black glided past him as if in a world of her own. A well-dressed young man sat kneeling in front of a tombstone, weeping loudly and unselfconsciously. Atop the large tombstone sat a beautiful young angel, with wings so exquisitely hewn they looked to be made of real feathers. The young man looked wretched. The angel, in contrast, seemed elated, as she crouched on her heels in a flowing gown: arms stretched out and upwards, palms facing the sky, in expectation of some celestial benevolence. In her vulnerability, she looked like a child asking to be picked up. From the greenish moss that had begun to collect in the folds of the angel's stony dress and the creases in her wings, Elliot could tell that this wasn't a new tomb. As he walked past the mourner, he tried to make out the inscription on the stone, but the lettering had become so encrusted with old grime and dirt that he could only read part of the name, but not a date. *Maisie Cav... R.I.P.* was all he could discern. Elliot was sorry he couldn't see when she had died. The tombstone looked like it was at least twenty years old, unlike the man's grief, which seemed agonisingly fresh.

Could grief really last that long? Was it something one could ever recover from? As Elliot walked further south through the cemetery, the man's sobs faded gradually from earshot. Perhaps it was the emptiness of the cemetery that made the man's sadness more tangible, his sorrow more public. Elliot had preferred to mourn in private, out of view of others. He hadn't been ashamed of his feelings, but had struggled with the confines imposed on him by others' expectations. There were acceptable, and unacceptable, ways of grieving. He recalled that when Ed died, he had felt guilty for infringing on his parents' grief. *Unnatural*, the term so overused by sympathetic bystanders, *it's unnatural for the child to die before the parent*, and so Elliot's parents staked a more powerful claim to grief than he was ever permitted. He had only lost a brother, not an eldest son. Worse still, he had had to inform his parents of Ed's death, and so his duty as messenger had in effect usurped his privilege to mourn. For many months, Elliot had been compelled to suppress his own grief, while his mother refused to leave her bed, rising only at the dead of night to wander the house, sobbing quietly and incessantly. His father became a voluntary mute, consuming bottle after bottle of Scotch until the pain-blindness set in. Elliot had withered while watching his parents almost indulgently nurse their pain.

Ed's death had left him feeling broken and he never wanted to feel that way again, but the meeting with Raphael had so easily reopened the scars he thought had healed long ago. It troubled him. He had told himself that the visit to his parents' graves was long overdue, something he had been meaning to do for quite some time. But he knew that he was in fact looking for redemption, a release from his guilt. He wanted to find comfort in the abject notion that his parents – like Ed – were at rest. In a better, more peaceful place. Only a year had passed since his father's death, and Elliot knew that it would take far longer – perhaps forever – for that terrible memory to fade.

A tiny brown sparrow swooped low in front of him, startling him. He stepped off the gravel path onto the grass on his left. As he did so, he heard another sound behind him. It was the briefest of sounds, an echo of his own footsteps. Was somebody following him? He froze, holding his breath, straining to listen if the sound would repeat itself. Nothing. Just the rush of blood in his ears. Then, when he couldn't hold his breath any longer, he released a lungful of air, which instantly became a cloud of frozen white vapour. He breathed in again, this time through his mouth, trying to make as little noise as possible. The coldness of the air hit the back of his throat, forcing him to suppress a cough. He was still fixed in the same position: in midstride, right leg before left, arms bent at the elbow and slightly away from the body to retain his balance; the bunch of dahlias shivering in the wind, their delicate stems slowly being crushed by a cold-reddened hand; only his eyes moving, darting from left to right as he fought to suppress the anxiety that was escalating fast. *Don't be such a fool,* he told himself, over and over. There were no ghosts or ghouls here, just monuments to the memory of those who were loved, and who were lost. There was nothing to be afraid of. He would have to turn around very soon, or he would stay in this position forever, petrified by his own irrational terror. Elliot felt the thumping in his chest subside as his breathing regained some depth. Tiny droplets of sweat had formed on his forehead; he took out his handkerchief and wiped them off.

Twenty yards ahead, surrounded by a congregation of grey sandstone crosses mounted on grubby, mottled plinths, he could make out his parents' gravestones: small, rounded arch Nabresina headstones, much paler and cleaner than those around them. He walked across the frozen ground, carefully steering clear of the other graves, his footsteps making satisfying crunching sounds as the frigid blades of grass yielded to his weight. He stopped in front of his parents' final resting place, crouched down and removed his hat. The two white gravestones, touching in their simplicity, were inscribed with the names and lifetimes of those who lay beneath:

George Arthur Taverley
12th April 1851 – 21st December 1919
R.I.P.
Amelia Rose Carmichael Taverley
21st November 1860 – 2nd August 1920
R.I.P.

Elliot placed the dahlias on his mother's side, pleased that the white of the petals matched the paleness of the stone. He shivered, and then wrapped his arms around himself in a wasted attempt to console himself. In truth, he had known all along that he wouldn't find forgiveness here. It was too late for that. And so, shaking his head, he stood up and left.

Elliot used the quiet hours over Christmas to work at home on a draft of his *Handbook*. He had good reason to be pleased with himself. It had been a laborious process, and now, after months of hard work, he had almost completed his technical scheme for the psychological analysis of handwriting. His *Handbook of Scientific Graphology: A Guide for the Analysis of Handwriting in Psycho-Pathological Practice* lay neatly typed and stacked atop the usual proliferation of paperwork that covered the surface of his desk. It contained twenty pages of technical advice, procedures, recommendations; everything a clinician would need to conduct a detailed analysis of a patient's handwriting in relation to their particular disorder.

The first part of the booklet, and the easiest part

for Elliot to write, dealt with the examination of the physiological features of writing: *Speed* ("Do the t-strokes show prolongation; are the i-dots accurately placed?"), *Spacing* ("Overall use of the space; size of margins, etc."), *Continuation* ("Existence of frequent interruptions; words running into one another"), *Pressure* ("Variations in pressure; peculiarities in emphasis"), *Connections* ("Are the connections angular/garland/arcade?"), *Orientation* ("Is the writing slanted? If so, does it slope forward/backward?"), and finally, *Form.* ("Attention to detail: Negligently placed diacritics; incomplete loops and letters. Is the writing legible?").

This was all fairly standard, uncontroversial stuff, following the conventions of the European graphologists Crepieux-Jamin, Pulver and Saudek. But the main body of Elliot's work, the essence of his efforts, had taken months of observation, research and experimentation. *The Psycho-Pathological Interpretation of the Physiological Features of Writing.* This was the work with which he hoped he would impress his critics and silence his doubters. This section contained a comprehensive treatise of the psycho-dynamics of graphology, and went far beyond colourful descriptions of an individual's personality. Rather than merely illustrate links between writing and character – for instance, taking ascending hairlines as indicative of an aggressive disposition – Elliot had proposed a detailed system of grapho-diagnostics, which, if applied correctly, would result in a definitive graphological synthesis offering diagnosis and proposed therapeutic techniques best suited for the patient on the basis of his handwriting.

He flicked through the pages, weighing them up in

his hand. His work was achingly close to completion, but there was still something missing; something small, but significant. The *Handbook* needed a case study, something to give his theory some objective validation. Would it be worth showing to Beaumont without it? In truth, Elliot was slightly disappointed that his ideas hadn't fallen on more fruitful ground since he began work at the Chapel a year ago. The clinic was a world away from Elliot's previous position at Canning Town Asylum. The asylum had been a pitiful excuse for a mental hospital, nineteenth-century in its wretchedness, where Elliot was charged with the care of the female patients, some of whom were violently insane. He had quickly discovered that women's mental disorders were more than likely to be associated with poverty, malnutrition and overwork, not to mention frequent pregnancies and motherhood, and were not easily curable with the use of heavy sedatives or electric shocks.

The opportunity to work at the Chapel had been more than welcome. It was just unfortunate that for all his forward-thinking, progressive rhetoric, Beaumont seemed unwilling to even *consider* a technique as promising as graphology. Elliot knew that it was a good piece of work; well-structured, convincingly argued. All it needed was a case study. And it was good fortune that such a case had knocked on his office door a week ago – Elliot was sure of it. All he needed to do now was to define precisely the nature of Raphael's disorder, then he could apply the therapeutic techniques he had developed and – hopefully – the man would be cured.

He decided he would speak with Beaumont about

it as soon as the Chapel opened again in January. Of course, he would have to make a very good argument: when it came to new cases, Chapel policy dictated that patients were treated by specialists wherever possible. Elliot was also painfully aware that there were more senior, and more conservative, colleagues than himself, who had previously dealt with cases of multiple personality disorder. But given the circumstances, surely he was the perfect candidate for the job! If he could get Beaumont to read his *Handbook* without prejudice, before coming to a final decision, Beaumont would surely let him treat Raphael.

He had just got up to add some logs to the fire when the doorbell rang. Surprised, and mildly annoyed at being disturbed, he went to the front door and opened it. Two dark-haired children, their mother fussing anxiously with their collars, looked up at him. Behind them stood Stanislav, a look of sincere apology on his face. The woman brushed past the children and took Elliot in a surprisingly strong embrace.

'Merry Christmas, Elliot! May God bless you!'

Elliot looked down at her and smiled. 'Well, Merry Christmas to you too, Luljeta.'

'I am sorry, Elliot,' said Stanislav earnestly. 'I made the mistake of telling her that you were spending Christmas alone and she insisted we pay you a visit. I told her you wouldn't want to be disturbed, but she wouldn't listen to me.' He stepped forward and took Elliot's hand. 'She never does,' he added. Luljeta loosened her embrace and scowled at Stanislav. She was from Albania, and everything Stanislav was not: capricious, lusty and impulsive. And Catholic.

She disagreed with everything Stanislav said, and vice versa, but they were fiercely attached to one another. When Elliot thought of the two of them together, it was always with surprised amusement at how this small, dark, curvaceous woman revealed a side to his best friend that remained elusive to all others.

'If you only ever talk nonsense, don't be surprised that I don't listen,' she said. 'Nobody wants to be alone on Boxing Day. Anton, Kristaq, wipe your shoes before you go in. And you, Stanislav.'

The boys, and Stanislav, did as they were told. They all settled in the drawing room, Luljeta and her sons on the sofa, Elliot and Stanislav in the two armchairs either side of the fireplace.

'Mama, why has this man got no Christmas in his house?' Anton whispered to his mother, casting uncertain glances at Elliot with large, dark eyes. Luljeta blushed slightly.

'What have I told you, Anton? What matters is that Christmas *is* special in your heart. Christmas is special in your heart, isn't it, Elliot?'

'Of course.' Elliot looked around the cheerless room and made a solemn promise to himself to make more of an effort next year. It wouldn't do to be pitied by children.

The boys became restless very quickly, fidgeting on the couch, impatient to expend their childish energy. Elliot could tell that it was taking incredible effort for them to sit still.

'Would you like to go and have a look around the house?' he asked.

They looked at their mother, imploring her silently to say yes, terrified she might say no. Luljeta lowered her eyelids in slow assent and off they ran.

Elliot smiled. 'I finally get to meet them,' he said. 'How old are they now?'

'Kristaq is seven, Anton five,' Luljeta answered, instinctively tracing a large cross from forehead to breast and shoulder to shoulder.

'That wards off the evil spirits,' Stanislav said laconically. Luljeta slapped him across the arm.

'Do not make fun of my religion,' she said crossly. 'If you don't go to hell, it is only because I pray for you also.'

It wasn't long before they heard a scuffle in the hall, followed by a thud and a squeal. Luljeta rolled her eyes and got up. 'I *begged* them to behave themselves,' she muttered as she went to see what the two were up to.

Stanislav laughed quietly and took a roll-up from his shirt pocket – he always rolled three cigarettes at once, forever fearful he would run out at an inopportune moment – and lit up.

'I apologise again for the disruption,' he began, but Elliot cut him off with a wave of his hand.

'Don't apologise,' he said. 'It was a welcome interruption. I can get so caught up in my work sometimes, that I forget what pleasures there are out there. Honestly, it's wonderful seeing you and Luljeta. And the boys.'

'I am glad. It is not good for you to be alone so much. Too much time –' he tapped the side of his head, 'to think.'

Luljeta entered the room with a self-satisfied look

on her face, making a gesture of wiping imaginary dust off her hands.

'There. They will be quiet for a while. Sugarbread and the whip,' she said cryptically. 'Or as they say in English, "the carrot and the stick". A good mother finds the right balance.'

Whatever the balance Luljeta had found, it seemed to work. The boys stayed quiet and out of sight for the next hour, while the adults sat and talked. Elliot produced a bottle of Chardonnay, much to the delight of Luljeta, who loved – but could not afford – French wine. It took only two glasses of wine for her to become even more loquacious than usual. Even Stanislav put aside his characteristic earnestness and for once made no mention of the blossoming sweatshop economy in and around Cable Street or the disturbing levels of police corruption in Bethnal Green.

'The boys have adopted a stray dog,' he began, 'a limping mongrel they found lying near the tramlines. They have named it Charlie, after the actor, because of the funny way the dog walks, with the limping paw splayed out to the side. I haven't the heart to tell them the dog's a bitch.'

They all laughed. Then Luljeta said, 'It's all very well the boys having a pet dog, but I can hardly feed the two of them well enough, let alone a stray mongrel.'

'We'll manage,' Stanislav said gently, 'and it is nice for the boys to have a pet, something that is theirs alone. They don't have much else.'

'I agree,' said Elliot. 'I used to have a dog, a terrier called Raffles. A business partner of my father's gave him to me as a birthday gift. He quickly became my best friend. In fact, I remember Raffles being my first patient; I used to try out all sorts of medical "techniques" on the poor animal. I think I even fastened a splint onto his hind leg once, after I had become convinced he had sustained a fracture.'

Luljeta laughed and said, 'Was this before or after you qualified as a doctor?'

'Very funny,' he replied. 'No, Raffles died when I was nine.'

'What happened?' she asked.

Elliot took a sip of wine. He had a clear memory of the day Raffles died. It was during the summer holidays; he and Ed were back from school and making the most of their short-lived freedom. That day, the day of the accident, however, Ed had been severely reprimanded by their father for an unauthorised excursion to a music hall the previous afternoon, and was now disallowed from leaving the house for the rest of the week. He was understandably sullen, and chose to take his anger out on his younger brother. It was nothing serious, just some teasing and play-fighting that was rougher than necessary. Elliot had become increasingly irritated by his brother's behaviour throughout the day, and come the late-afternoon, had retreated to his bedroom to play with his collection of toy soldiers. It was a hot day; Elliot remembered that his mother had opened all of the windows in the house, in the hope that a non-existent breeze would counteract the oppressive humidity. Through the open window he heard Ed say to his mother:

– *I'm going into the garden to play.*

– *But you know what your father said. You're not to leave the house.*

– *Well, for one thing, he's not here to stop me, and for another, he meant I wasn't allowed "out". As in out there.*

Elliot imagined him pointing to beyond the garden fence.

– *Very well, but make sure to be back in before he comes home.*

– *Whatever you say, Mother.*

Elliot returned to his game. He had set up a pretend military hospital at the side of the battlefield, where his wounded soldiers – toys that had become broken and battered with overuse – were treated for their injuries. He needed some nurses, but knew instinctively it would be impossible to ask his mother to buy him some dolls. Suddenly, he heard a noise from outside, a high-pitched howl that pierced his heart, and knew immediately that something had happened to Raffles. He ran to the window, panic-stricken, but the part of the garden he could see from his room looked empty. He almost fell as he ran down the tall stairs, trying to keep back his tears, telling himself that he couldn't be certain that it had been Raffles, but knowing deep down that he would always recognise his own pet's distress. As he flew through the French window that led into the garden, he almost keeled over at the sight that presented itself to him. Raffles lay on the terrace in an odd, supine position; his legs splayed out to the sides to reveal a pair of gardening shears embedded in his soft, white, furry belly. Elliot couldn't recall whether he had actually vomited at the sight, or whether he had just heaved, but he felt sick to the stomach.

Suddenly, Ed was standing behind him – he hadn't

heard him come up to him – and said:

– *God, that looks nasty. What happened? Do you think we should try and pull the shears out?*

Elliot stood immobile, paralysed by the sight of his lifeless pet. His mother came running out of the house and put her hands over her mouth in alarm.

– *Raffles, oh God, what happened?*

Ed turned to her and shrugged.

– *I have no idea, Mother. I was indoors, talking to you, wasn't I? Raffles must have, I don't know, fallen on the shears or something. Isn't that right, Mother?*

– *What, Ed?*

– *I said, I've just been inside talking to you. Elliot thinks I killed his dog.*

Elliot looked up at his brother in horror. He was upset and confused. He caught his mother looking at Ed with an expression he couldn't read. She whispered:

– *No, no. You wouldn't, you couldn't.*

Then she stepped forward and took Elliot in her arms.

– *It'll be all right, darling. Don't cry. I'm sure Raffles is in a better place now. Come now, let's go inside. I'll get someone to take care of him.*

When their father returned from work that evening, she gave him an account of how Raffles must have jumped from the garden wall and fallen onto the shears, which had been left unattended since the gardener's last visit. Their father acknowledged the news silently, and after that, the incident was never mentioned again.

'Elliot?' It was Stanislav. 'You were telling us how

your dog died.'

'Oh, he ... he had an accident. I remember I cried for days and refused to go back to school. I had to go, of course, but it was dreadful.' He drew on his cigarette. 'Perhaps you shouldn't let the boys get too attached to their stray, after all.'

They sat in silence for a while. Then Luljeta said brightly, 'I still haven't met your fiancee, Elliot. Why are you hiding her; is there something terribly wrong with her that I mustn't find out?'

This made Elliot smile. He was sure that Helena and Luljeta would get on.

'She's always so busy,' he said. 'I usually only get to see her when she tries to introduce me into "Society" – supper parties, picnics, luncheons and that sort of thing. Without much success, I have to say.'

Luljeta gazed at the ceiling and said dreamily, 'Oh, I think I would love to attend such parties. They must be so much fun.'

'You don't know what you're talking about, woman,' Stanislav said. 'Nothing but a bunch of empty-headed, superficial snobs, who have no sense of principle or social responsibility. Present company and their fiancees excepted, of course.'

But before Luljeta could respond to this diatribe, the carriage clock on the mantelpiece chimed seven o'clock. Anton and Kristaq poked their heads through the door. Luljeta nodded, and they came in and took a seat either side of their mother. Anton, the younger one, laid his head on her breast as she stroked his hair. He yawned, setting off a chain reaction of yawns around the room.

'I would invite you to stay for supper,' Elliot said after a while, 'but I'm afraid it would consist of pickled beetroot and leftover trifle.' The boys pulled faces of disgust. Theirs were Mediterranean palates.

'Then come back with us and eat. Luljeta would love to cook for you,' Stanislav said. 'She is a real talent in the kitchen,' he added, leaning over and squeezing her thigh gently. She rewarded him with a big smile.

'Thanks, but no,' said Elliot. 'I still have some case notes to write up.'

'Too much work, my friend. Do they not give you any time off at that clinic of yours?'

'Actually, the clinic is closed for patients over the holidays, but this is an urgent case. I don't like to leave it until January; some patients can be ... fragile.'

'Well then, my philanthropic friend, we must go.' He rose from his chair and picked up Anton, who could barely keep his eyes open. Elliot fetched their coats and hats.

'Thank you for coming,' he said to Stanislav, and to the boys he said, 'You have been most well-behaved. Proper little gentlemen.'

Kristaq beamed at him; Anton had fallen asleep on Stanislav's broad shoulder, a thin silvery bubble of saliva expanding and contracting between his full lips as he breathed. As Elliot helped Luljeta into her coat, he pressed some coins into her hand.

'This is no weather to be taking the long way home,' he said quietly. 'The boys are tired.'

Luljeta reddened slightly, her olive skin turning to

cinnamon momentarily. 'Thank you, and God bless you,' she whispered.

FIVE

Elliot arrived at the Chapel in good time for the first staff meeting after the Christmas break. The high-ceilinged conference room was the largest room in the building, and even then could barely accommodate the twenty-five staff who worked at the clinic. Elliot took a seat next to Shepherd, who briefly acknowledged Elliot's presence before turning back to leer blatantly at the nurses, paying particular attention to the younger ones who wore their skirts slightly higher up the calf than their senior colleagues. To Elliot's left, the Chapel's most recent addition, a young Cambridge graduate named Dr. Benjamin Eastleigh, was passionately defending the views of Sylvia Pankhurst, who had recently been arrested for inciting the dock workers to go on strike. He was interrupted as the doors to the room opened and Charles Beaumont strode in.

'Morning, gentlemen,' he said, walking to the head of the large oval table and taking his seat. 'Ladies,' he added, nodding in the direction of the nurses and administrators who sat at the other end of the room, like spectators to a show. There was no room for them at the table.

'We'll make this a short meeting, shall we?' he began. 'I'm sure you've all got things to take care of following our time off over Christmas. I take it you've all read today's *Times*.' He held the newspaper up and read out the headline. *Psycho-analysts' sex teaching – Call for inquiry.* Well, not a first, but nonetheless nasty and potentially damaging. Some quack in Leeds caught with his pants down. I needn't remind you all that I do not approve of your giving any comments to the press in relation to such matters.'

A swell of murmurs rose and fell around the room. Elliot hadn't had time to read the morning paper, but such stories weren't new and appeared at regular intervals in the press. Every now and again, having failed to unearth some sex scandal involving politicians, minor aristocrats or other celebrities, the press would turn hungrily to the Freudian dogma of sensuo-sexual conflict. It was almost boring in its predictability, Elliot found, although the distinction between "quacks caught with their pants down" and genuine psycho-analytic treatment was rarely made by journalists.

Unfortunately, however, the Chapel's very existence stood and fell on its reputation. Relying exclusively on private funding – a large proportion coming from the Catholic Church – it was crucial that the institution steered well clear of any sort of scandal. So much so that romantic entanglements between members of staff were not merely frowned upon; they were strictly prohibited. Elliot owed his own position there to a doctor becoming engaged to one of the nurses. By his own admission, Beaumont had put up a fight with the funding bodies on their behalf, but in the end had been forced to dismiss the man and his fiancee. Thus, such a press article was not to be taken lightly.

Beaumont concluded the meeting fairly rapidly after this; a brief mention of patients who had successfully completed therapy, and the allocation of new patients beginning therapy in the New Year to the doctors. With an exchange of general pleasantries, the staff returned to their duties.

Elliot's office was on the ground floor at the end of a long cheerless corridor. Although small, the room's redeeming feature was the French window that opened onto a tiny, but picturesque, walled backyard. His was the only room in the building with access to the back; a door that had led once from the corridor to the outside was now wholly covered in spring-flowering clematis, so that from March until June, Elliot could see an explosion of tiny yellow flowers from his office window.

Weeks before his mother died, she had paid him a reluctant visit here, and had been won over by the garden. She had made no secret of her disapproval of Elliot's chosen career – or rather, his career change from physician to psycho-analyst. Elliot often wondered whether she harboured a secret fear that lunacy might be contagious in some way; that working with the insane, or mentally unbalanced, would rub off on him. He knew that his parents would rather have had him follow in Ed's footsteps. A military career; now that was a suitable choice for a gentleman, one that had been denied his father George, who had a dystrophic left leg as a result of having contracted polio as a child. His leg had caused him great suffering – though more psychological than physical, Elliot believed – and was more than likely the reason for his heavy drinking. Yet despite his physical affliction, George Taverley had been a man of enviable mental prowess and had enjoyed a hugely successful career in London as a barrister.

Amelia Taverley had jealously mothered her children, occasionally quelling a boisterousness in Ed that his father had encouraged, while not quite managing to withstand his impulsive charm. Elliot, as the younger son, had received a cool tenderness from his mother, and had realised early on that what most pleased her about him was his quiescence. Thus, it had been out of character for Elliot to stick to his guns regarding his career choice, opposing his parents' wishes and resisting their expectations. It had been a major personal triumph for him, but this, strangely, had seemed to go unnoticed by them. At times he wasn't sure whether he would ever have been able to fulfil their expectations, or whether they even *had* expectations of him. Ed, who had never shown much interest in Elliot's work, was the one of whom everything had been expected; but he had been broad-shouldered and strong, and had always risen to the challenge. Now Elliot was left to develop and fulfil his own expectations.

A tapping at the door. It opened slowly and Nurse Robinson poked her head through, taking care not to knock her cap against the frame.

'Yes?' said Elliot, looking up. The air in his office was stifling.

'Jenny's here.' Nurse Robinson looked over her shoulder, and then back at Elliot. 'And her father,' she added after the briefest hesitation.

'Give me a minute, won't you? I'll just tidy up a bit.' He waved his hand across the confusion on his desk, giving the impression that he had been preoccupied with the patient notes in front of him.

If Nurse Robinson had noticed anything different,

she didn't let on. In her usual restrained tone she said, 'Certainly, doctor. Let me know when you're ready for her.'

'Thanks.'

Elliot sighed as he began ploughing through the piles on his desk. It took a minute or so to find Jenny's file. He opened it and skim-read the first page. Not for the first time he cringed at the scrawniness of his own handwriting. It seemed to be getting more illegible all the time. *Jenny Wilson... DoB 18th June, 1903... hysteria... traumatic neurosis???... responsive to free association...*

The patient, Jenny Wilson, was a young girl who had been displaying symptoms of hysteria twelve months ago. Two general practitioners, a brief spell in an asylum, and several sessions of electroshock therapy later, she had arrived in Elliot's care, frightened, sullen and apathetic. According to her GP's file, she was a "hopeless case". Elliot was more optimistic than that. No child could ever be labelled "hopeless".

He opened one side of the French window and inhaled the fresh air gratefully. The yard was uninspiring and lifeless at this time of year; evergreens were notoriously difficult to grow in the shade, and the crocuses, those heralds of springtime, hadn't yet dared to stick their heads above the soil. The sharp, wintry air suddenly made Elliot cough. He stepped back inside and shut the door, taking pleasure in the warmth that had seemed so oppressive just minutes earlier. There was another knock on the door. It opened a fraction.

'Dr. Taverley, I'm afraid they're getting a bit impatient. Are you ready for Jenny yet?' asked Nurse Robinson.

'Yes, yes, send her in.'

It turned out to be a tedious, lacklustre session. Jenny's father, a factory foreman who reminded Elliot of some unsavoury Dickens' character, intervened constantly, reprimanding his daughter whenever she failed to answer Elliot's questions quickly enough, or in a loud enough voice. Reluctantly, yet realising he wasn't going to make any progress today, Elliot brought the session to a close early, suggesting to Wilson that Jenny might be coming down with a cold and that she should return when she was feeling better. He wanted to add, 'And there's no need for you to come,' but he feared Wilson might take offence, or even act on his threat – one he had made in the past on several occasions – to terminate Jenny's treatment at the Chapel entirely.

As soon as Jenny and her father had left, Elliot opened and closed his mouth wide to release the tension in his jaw. Then he went back to his desk and began with a half-hearted attempt to sort out the mess there.

Nurse Robinson knocked lightly and entered.

'Has Jenny left already? That was a short session,' she remarked.

'Don't ask.'

'Her father?'

Elliot sighed. 'Yes, I'm afraid so.'

'I'm sure you're doing a good job – with Jenny, I mean.'

Elliot looked at her quizzically.

'Those scratch marks she had on her arms the first few times she came, well, they've disappeared completely. That's some progress.'

Elliot nodded without conviction.

She continued, 'You know, with some of these patients, you just want to take them in your arms and scoop them up out of their misery.'

Elliot smiled. 'Exactly.'

She turned to leave.

'Nurse Robinson?'

'Yes.'

'Thank you.'

'You're welcome, doctor.'

Elliot saw two more patients that afternoon – a 14-year old kleptomaniac, and a middle-aged woman recovering from a nervous breakdown following a string of miscarriages – and was exhausted when his working day finally drew to a close. He had just finished writing up the clinical notes as case reports, when he became aware of a presence in the room, right at the edge of his vision. Startled, he stood up, and saw a figure standing in the shadows by the door. In the gloom, Elliot could only make out the slight frame.

'Dr. Taverley, is everything all right?' It was Nurse Robinson.

'Can't you knock before entering?' Elliot asked tersely, wondering how long she had been standing there. He hadn't heard the door open or shut.

'I did,' she replied calmly, her voice betraying no reaction to Elliot's sharpness. 'There was no answer, so I came in to see that everything was all right.'

Elliot frowned. He said, 'I'm sorry, I didn't hear you. I've been busy.' He gestured towards the papers still strewn all over his desk.

Nurse Robinson took a step forward as if wanting to start to tidy up, but Elliot rose from his seat. 'Thank you, but that won't be necessary. I'm just a little messy, that's all.'

'I wish you would let me file your papers properly,' she said, straightening up and adjusting the waistband on her apron.

Elliot cleared his throat. 'Never mind that now,' he said to Nurse Robinson as she continued to stare at the sheets lying scattered on the floor.

'What can I do for you?' he added in a softer tone.

Nurse Robinson gave him a look he couldn't read and said, 'I hate to bother you with this, but I was wondering if – well, if you'd had an opportunity to look at that letter I gave you.'

Elliot put his hand up to his forehead. He had, of course, forgotten all about it. At that moment, the letter was lying on his desk at home, amidst the other bits of paperwork he meant to get to when he had the time.

'Gosh, Nurse Robinson, I am so dreadfully sorry. I took it home to look at during Christmas, but to be honest, it completely slipped my mind.'

Nurse Robinson took a sharp intake of breath, then smoothed down the front of her apron with both hands. If she was angry, or disappointed, she wasn't letting it show.

'Well then, never mind,' she said brightly.

'Please accept my apologies,' Elliot insisted. 'I will look at the letter first thing tomorrow.'

Nurse Robinson nodded.

'I give you my word,' Elliot added.

'Very well,' she answered. 'Thank you.'

It was frustration Elliot felt, not relief, when he finally clo-sed his office door that evening. First Jenny, and then his forgotten promise to Nurse Robinson. But mostly, he felt ashamed and angry with himself for putting her in such an awkward position. However, it couldn't be helped now. He would just have to find some way to make it up to her.

As he made his way down the corridor, he noticed light coming from the director's office several doors down from his own. As usual, Charles Beaumont would be the last to leave. Elliot knew that Beaumont, a widower for some eight years now, delighted in discussing interesting cases with whichever colleague happened to be around at such a late hour. As a rule, Elliot found such discussions rather stimulating, and a useful opportunity to find out more about the treatment methods currently employed by his colleagues. Tonight, however, he was in no mood for such discussion, but before he could lighten his tread to make his presence less conspicuous, the door opened wide and Beaumont stood there, almost filling the doorway en-tirely with his large frame. He smiled generously as Elliot approached.

'A word, Dr. Taverley?'

Six

Charles Beaumont was the kind of man one had to try very hard to dislike. He was, in Elliot's opinion, the ideal psycho-analyst. A natural listener, he was capable of extracting a person's most concealed thoughts, feelings and qualities; gently, surreptitiously, probing the darkest corners and blind alleyways of people's minds without giving the slightest impression that he judged what he found. This gift led some to believe that he possessed the supernatural ability to read one's thoughts. He was also extremely handsome, with thick silver hair that shimmered when he ran his fingers through it, and deep crow's-feet that branched outward from the corners of his eyes to his lower jaw, suggesting a playful optimism that belied his sixty-something years. His good looks assured him the adoration of the female staff, but a few of the other doctors regarded him with muted suspicion, as though such a dazzling personality were too much for just one man. Elliot didn't share these sentiments; he preferred to trust his gut feeling that Beaumont was a genuinely decent man.

Elliot knew from his colleagues that Beaumont had held a senior position at Craiglockhart during the war, and had single-handedly set up the Chapel shortly after the armistice. He never talked about his time at Craiglockhart, but unlike others who had dealt with the horrifying effects of shell-shock, Beaumont seemed oddly untouched by what he had experienced there. Elliot often wondered whether his optimism was a veneer, or whether he really could close his mind selectively to the past. Elliot had spent six months in a casualty clearing station in France in 1917, and even now had occasional nightmares that tended to revolve around severed limbs and bloody stumps. It had, in fact, been his wartime experiences that had triggered a lasting interest in the human psyche. He hadn't long completed his medical studies when he volunteered to join the Red Cross in France in response to the urgent call for doctors. Posted to a casualty clearing station in Crouay, near Amiens, in the spring of 1916, he had very soon realised – with a growing sense of disquiet – that his duties consisted of patching up the wounded as best he could so that they could be sent back to the front as soon as possible. He felt like no more than some kind of mechanic; except that the men he was 'repairing' were not mere machines, but that underneath the skin and bone and tendon and muscle lay something intangible, something that distinguished man from machine, something that was both precious and fragile.

Over the next few months, his disillusionment at the futility of his job, coupled with an increasing contempt for those who so indifferently ordered war-fatigued men into battle time and time again, had developed slowly into a deep-rooted pacifism. More than once he came dangerously close to committing offences that might well have had him court-martialled had he been a regular medical officer. One night in September, following a twenty-hour shift, Elliot found himself treating a very young soldier for what was obviously a self-inflicted wound. He had come across these quite often, but had never diagnosed them as such. Any man willing to mutilate himself – in some cases risking permanent physical damage – suggested to Elliot a level of desperation that rendered the man unfit for battle. On this particular occasion, however, he was being assisted by an eager young subaltern, who immediately recognised a bullet wound to the foot for what it was: an attempt to avoid being sent back to the front line. An argument ensued between him and Elliot, Elliot insisting that, as the qualified physician, he had the final say on any diagnosis and the subaltern accusing him of assisting a would-be deserter. However, before things came to a head, a stray shell exploded nearby, causing the resuscitation tent they were working in to collapse, leaving Elliot with several broken ribs and a ticket home.

He spent his convalescence studying for the recently established Cambridge Diploma in Psychological Medicine, which he successfully completed a year later, and began his first job as a psychologist at the Canning Town Asylum. Ten months on, in the summer following the end of the War, he had been offered a position at the Chapel.

'Come in, sit down,' Beaumont said as Elliot entered his office. He took Elliot's hat and coat and dropped them over the back of a chair, before taking a seat behind his desk. On the mantelpiece behind him stood an assortment of Christmas cards, amateurishly decorated with straw stars and ribbon; given to him, presumably, by his grandchildren.

Beaumont rummaged around in a desk drawer before producing a bottle of Scotch.

'Drink?' he asked, holding out the bottle and raising his eyebrows mischievously, as though he were offering a very special, yet illicit, treat.

'No thanks,' Elliot said, remembering his recent migraine.

Beaumont replaced the bottle in the drawer without pouring a drink for himself. 'Shepherd can't get enough of the stuff,' he said with a sudden bark of a laugh. He was referring to their eminent American colleague with bad breath and an appetite for very young nurses. 'Came over here to escape Prohibition, malicious gossip has it. Prohibition indeed! Now there's a prime example of trying to slay Hydra. It'll never last, though, mark my words.'

Elliot didn't respond. It was typical of Beaumont to flit from topic to topic like a crazed butterfly, and trying to keep up with him would merely have left Elliot feeling drowsier than he did already. He lit a cigarette and waited for Beaumont's mind to settle.

Although the office was large, it seemed an appropriate size to accommodate the director's imposing physical presence. Elliot looked around the walls of the office and noted the artwork that hung there. To the uninitiated, the collection of pictures looked like something belonging to some schizophrenic art collector: scraps of paper with scratchy charcoal sketches hung next to huge, paint-splattered canvas, most of them inexpertly, seemingly completed carelessly. This was part of a therapeutic technique used by Beaumont, who encouraged even the most talentless patients to express their feelings in art. Although there was no single theme running through the pictures, they all exuded an acute sense of desperation. Elliot found them discomfiting.

'Fascinating, aren't they?' Beaumont said.

'Quite,' Elliot replied diplomatically.

'They are slightly disturbing, of course, if one doesn't know the hand that drew them, but painting has the most remarkable effect on the patients. Better out than in, eh?' he added and let out a soft chuckle. His gaze dwelt for a while on the watercolour painting of a girl whose own feet had mutated into enormous webbed duck's feet, before travelling in a direct route towards Elliot and settling on his face.

'How's the lovely Helena?' he asked.

'She's very well,' Elliot answered, at that moment wanting nothing more than to be sitting in front of the fireplace with his lovely fiancee, listening to her talk about her day, luncheon with her acquaintances, thoughts on her most recent poetry; anything that would crowd out his tiredness and ruminations on the day's events.

'Well, make sure to give her my regards,' Beaumont said. He tilted his head to one side and smiled at Elliot. 'She's a fine girl. You're a lucky fellow.'

'I know,' Elliot replied.

'Now to more serious matters,' Beaumont continued, changing the subject as effortlessly as throwing a light switch. 'This patient of yours, Mrs Derby.'

'Margaret Derby.'

'Yes, yes. Tell me, Taverley, how is she bearing up? Refresh my memory, won't you? She came to us suffering from pathological anxiety a few months ago, I seem to recall. Any progress there?'

'Actually, I'm tending towards a diagnosis of manic

depression. But we're making fairly good progress.' He paused. 'In fact, we're becoming far less reliant on supportive techniques.'

Beaumont smiled. 'You are an ardent advocate of projective methods, aren't you?' he said.

'Not unlike yourself,' Elliot answered, gesturing towards the pictures on the wall. Despite his tiredness, he was feeling more and more relaxed. It felt good to be talking.

'You asked her to produce a painting?' Beaumont sounded surprised and thrilled at the same time.

'No, I –' Elliot hesitated. 'I got her to write about herself.' It seemed an opportunity to mention it.

'Write down her recollections, you mean? Is that not a bit cumbersome? From what I know of Mrs Derby, she is not particularly well-educated. Surely you would agree that free association works best when patients can express themselves as effortlessly as possible.'

Elliot shifted in his seat. 'I'm not talking about free association. I let her write about *herself*. I believe her disorder – the *root* of her anxiety – will manifest itself in her handwriting. You see – '

'We may be a developing discipline, Taverley,' Beaumont interrupted calmly, leaning back in his chair and steepling his fingers in an upright position in front of him, 'but we should be well advised to steer clear of the distractions of pseudo-sciences, as modern and alluring as they may appear.'

'But the whole *point* of projective techniques is that they reveal unconscious anxieties and complexes that are blocked by some ego defence mechanism. Psycho-graphology, script analysis, whatever you want to call it, does exactly that! There may be a lack of empirical support, I'll grant you that, but here at the *Chapel* – ' he emphasised the word with as much reverence as he fancied he could get away with, 'here of all places it would be ideal to embark on a new, promising therapeutic approach. You want empirical support, then give me the opportunity to gather it!'

'I can't allow you to use your patients as guinea pigs.'

'But how is it different to what you do? Getting your patients to scrawl their neuroses onto canvas?'

For a second, Beaumont looked like he had been slapped across the face. Then he said steadily, 'Come now, Taverley. This sounds dangerously close to religious fervour.'

Elliot checked himself. He hadn't meant to appear rude or unprofessional. It was his frustration speaking more than anything. He had noted – not without a modest sense of self-satisfaction – the number of graphology practices that had sprung up recently around the city, offering document examination, handwriting analysis and identity screening for businesses, both in London and abroad. The growing popular appeal of graphology was undeniable. If only he could persuade someone like Beaumont, then – who knew? – it might revolutionise the whole discipline of psychology. And perhaps it was as good a time as any to mention Raphael. He needed to tread carefully if he didn't want to throw this chance away.

'I apologise –' he said hurriedly, in what he hoped was a more measured tone, 'if that sounded arrogant. But the technique I'm proposing goes further than mere projection. It goes beyond diagnosis to the actual treatment of patients.'

'I'm intrigued. How so?' Beaumont asked. His tone was sincere.

Elliot jumped at the opportunity. He began, 'I'm sure you're aware of the –' but was rudely interrupted by the loud, aggressive *chirp-chirp* of the telephone on Beaumont's desk.

'I do apologise, but I must answer this call. But please – ', Beaumont said, as Elliot rose to leave, 'stay where you are. I won't be long.'

As Beaumont began a hushed conversation on the telephone, Elliot's mind jumped back ten years, to the occasion when he had first learned of the link between pathology and handwriting. He had been a visiting medical student at the renowned Charite Hospital in Berlin before the War. Elliot's tutor at the hospital had been Professor Heinrich Niermann, a distinguished cardiologist, who had made a name for himself by pushing the boundaries of conventional medicine to their extremes. He was as maligned by his peers as he was respected. One morning, while accompanying Niermann on his rounds, Elliot had witnessed him diagnosing heart disease in a patient merely from his handwriting.

'This man suffers from cardiac arrhythmia,' Niermann had boomed at the eager assembly of white-coated student doctors, waving a fleshy hand in the direction of some unfortunate patient. He held up a piece of paper with his other hand. Elliot could make out a few lines of script.

'Here, the patient's handwriting – the greatest diagnostic tool you shall ever encounter!'

The gaggle of students pushed closer to get a better look at the writing, while Niermann continued his lecture. He spoke louder than necessary, which gave others the impression that he was slightly hard of hearing. His students learned early on – often to their cost – that this was not the case.

'Imagine the blood pulsating through the body,' he roared, 'all the way from the heart to the writing hand. The rhythm of the handwriting will become necessarily disrupted – as seen in the breaks and riffs in the flow, the unevenly pulled understrokes – if the writer is suffering from a weak heart.'

It had been remarkable to witness, and ever since he had progressed from physical medicine to psychology, Elliot had become convinced that this should be put to use in his work with mental illness. He had seen how a physiological pathology finds expression in handwriting; why not *psychological* pathologies? His thesis was simple, if unorthodox: he believed that the modification of handwriting to form a perfect balance between conscious and unconscious was the unique contribution graphology could make to psycho-analysis.

Beaumont finished his call and replaced the earpiece on its hook.

'My daughter,' he explained. 'Apparently I forgot that I'd been invited to dinner. I'll have to make amends tomorrow, I think. But please, Taverley, do continue where you left off.'

'If handwriting uncovers the projection of personality disorders – '

'That's quite an assumption.'

'Well, no more so than Rorschach's ink-blots. But all right then, *assuming* a neurosis is projected into handwriting, then, well, perhaps it can work the other way around.'

'I don't quite follow.'

'If I could work with a patient to change neurotic indications in his handwriting, then perhaps ...'

'Yes?'

'Then that might have a beneficial, perhaps even *cathartic* effect on the patient.' Elliot would have loved to mention his plans for Raphael at this point, but he felt he had backed himself into a corner. He would need to bide his time. Instead he said, 'I'm currently working on a handbook, an exposition of my ideas that you might find useful to read – when it's finished.'

He trailed off, hoping this latter part of his speech had not sounded as feeble to Beaumont as it had to himself.

Beaumont did not respond immediately. Instead, he breathed in deeply, exhaling with the slightest trace of a disappointed sigh. The silence congealed the air between them, and Elliot's fatigue returned in a single, uncompromising surge. It was all he could do to keep his eyes from falling shut there and then. Beaumont also looked exhausted. When he spoke again, his customary baritone was hushed, almost lethargic.

'I like you, Taverley. I believe you have a very promising career ahead of you, and – more importantly – that you possess a genuine ability to help others, to *heal* others.

But if I've learned anything in all my years as a doctor, it is that it is not enough to cure the sick. One must cure them with methods that have been endorsed, accepted, *understood* by the community. Now, let me share something with you.'

He got up out of his chair and walked over to face a smudgy charcoal drawing of a giant snake greedily consuming what looked like a foetus. He turned back to look at Elliot.

'I haven't told this story to many people. It isn't something I'm proud of, but I think it might help you gain some ... *perspective.* I had a patient once – it must have been, oh, almost twenty years ago – who came to me shortly after suffering a nervous breakdown. She was young, and attractive, and I recall how impressed I was at her willingness to cooperate. I guided her through the usual therapy – memory recovery, dream interpretation – and her progress was truly remarkable. In fact, she was such an exemplary patient that I remember feeling slightly regretful that her speedy recovery would mean the end of our sessions together. Then, one day, she confessed to me that she had fallen in love with me. Oh, I know, it was merely a case of transference. Anyway, the rational, objective part of me knew that these feelings of love she had bestowed on me more legitimately belonged to another. But the other part of me, the man who had been married to the same woman for eighteen years, was flattered and – I'm ashamed to admit it – had developed reciprocal feelings. It was as simple, and as narcissistic, as that. I'm happy to say that I didn't act on my feelings towards her, but I struggled with them for some time, to the extent that I even found myself questioning Freud's theory on transference. The end result was that I realised I could no longer help the young woman, and she was forced to seek help elsewhere and begin her therapy afresh.

'So …what I am trying to say – in a ridiculously round-about way – is that we are all prone to barking up the wrong tree on occasion. The *desire* for something to be true can quickly lead to a muddled mess. And forgive me for saying so, Taverley, but your thesis sounds muddled, to say the least.'

He paused, letting this final comment sink in. In the brief silence that followed, Elliot tried to think of a suitable rejoinder, but failed. He felt acutely disappointed that he hadn't used this opportunity to do his theory justice.

'Listen,' Beaumont continued after a few minutes. 'I hope you don't see me as the kind of man who is hostile to new ideas – surely you know me better than that – but I feel we must tread very, very carefully in these matters. There are cretins up and down the country dabbling in psycho-analysis as though it were some sort of party trick. Amateur Freudians wherever you look! They don't understand the damage they can do.' He shook his head and, for a moment, looked very old.

'I'll tell you what; if you are committed to this –' he hesitated, then smiled, 'this *approach*, then follow it up in terms of private study. Indeed, I would encourage it! Let me know what books you need and I'll see to it that they are ordered for the library. But I must insist that you continue to treat your patients with methods we know to be valid. As much as I hate to say this, we are obliged – within reason

– to dance to the tune of the piper that pays us. If the press gets a whiff of anything remotely *hocus pocus*, we'll lose our funding in the blink of an eye. It's a devil explaining to these committees that we're not a collection of sex-mad charlatans. It takes only one negative headline to rob us of our public assistance funds, let alone the private donations. So no experimenting with our patients, Taverley. Are we agreed?'

Elliot nodded, more in resignation than agreement. What choice did he have?

On his way home that evening, Elliot went over the conversation in his mind. It had been an odd exchange with Beaumont, and he couldn't quite decide whether he'd been flattered or duped. Beaumont's story had certainly impressed him; not the story itself, but the readiness with which Beaumont had confided in him. What rankled with him, though, was the fact that Beaumont had missed the point. It was true that no one was immune to becoming too involved with a patient, but that had precious little to do with scientific aspirations. And that was what his aspirations were: scientific, not emotional. He felt annoyed at having been compelled, coerced almost, into making a promise he was reluctant to keep.

He strode to the end of Chapelford Lane, past the black scrawny trees that lined the street, and then turned into a narrow, unlit alley; a short cut to Gordon Street. But on the positive side, he reflected, Beaumont had given his express encouragement for him to continue his research, albeit privately. As he picked up the pace of his walk, he cast off his doubts. He would postpone registering Raphael at the clinic, just for the time being, just until he knew what he was dealing with. Surely, when he had tangible results to show, Beaumont wouldn't hesitate to let him continue treatment. It wasn't an ideal solution, by any means; but after all, Beaumont wasn't the manipulative type, he was merely becoming more conformist and less adventurous with age. Perhaps that was how he would end up himself, one day. A cold blast of air funnelled down the alley, pushing him forward, causing his coat to flap about around his legs. He sniffed. It was time he got home; it was cold and he was tired. He turned right into Euston Square, heading for the station. He would take a taxi home.

A single black taxicab stood waiting at the rank outside the station. As Elliot settled onto the cold leather seat at the back of the cab, he gave the address to the driver and closed his eyes. He only intended to rest them, but fell asleep immediately and woke only as the car turned into the nocturnal, affluent hush of Grosvenor Road.

He entered the large, Victorian town house that was his home and stopped briefly in the dim hallway, wondering whether he was still hungry enough to want to bother with the effort of eating. He decided he wasn't, dumped his coat and hat over the banister and went straight up the stairs. *Up the wooden hill to bed.* His mother's words, followed by his and Ed's squeals of delight as she had chased them laughing up the stairs. These stairs. Tall and steep. Grand, his father had called them. Elliot was now, of course, big enough to take them three steps at a time, but he could recall a time when conquering the grand stairs had been effortful. He remembered the occasion when the newly laid stair carpet had come loose, and he had slid down the stairs; a terrifying, dizzying descent, landing at the bottom with bruised, swollen knees. He was six at the time, and small for his age. He had lain crumpled at the foot of the stairs, stunned and winded, waiting for the shock to subside and his tears to come, giving them time to gather behind his eyes. And in the moment before his little body surrendered to ululation, he had seen Ed, eleven years old and twice his size, standing, grinning, at the top of the stairs. It seemed odd to be remembering this now, when he had so much else on his mind. He shook his head free of the memory, and entered the bedroom. It was completely dark, except for a thin sliver of moonlight that sliced the curtain in two. He undressed without much care, dropping his clothes and leaving them where they fell.

SEVEN

Elliot sat in a pub just off Chapelford Lane greedily consuming a plate of roast beef sandwiches. He was expecting Raphael in his office at eight o'clock; Beaumont would be at his daughter's house for dinner, and Elliot's other colleagues were unlikely to stay at work much past six. He had hardly eaten anything all day – Mrs Blake was on a two-day visit to her sister in Luton, and his own attempts at cooking had failed miserably. Throughout the course of the day he had managed somehow to burn three batches of toast, left a pan of potatoes to boil dry, and sprinkled salt rather than sugar on Mrs Blake's blancmange, rendering it completely inedible.

Elliot had spent the day at home. The doctors at the Chapel were granted one day off every fortnight in order to work through patient files and paperwork. It was one of the more disagreeable conditions set forth by the funding bodies that they receive regular written reports on all that took place there, and Beaumont had generously released the doctors from their therapeutic duties twice a month to fulfil this requirement.

That morning, however, instead of composing comprehensive reports on Jenny Wilson and Margaret Derby, Elliot sat down at his desk with the intention of fulfilling his promise to Nurse Robinson. It was a bit of an empty compromise, really, because his mind kept leaping ahead to the evening's meeting with Raphael, but he knew he would have to keep himself busy if he didn't want to spend the day looking at the clock, watching the minutes peel off, one by one. And it wouldn't be fair on his patients if he drafted their reports perfunctorily.

He had trouble locating the letter at first – his desk was an incoherent depository of files, stethoscope, inkwell and ashtray. A twisted green cloth cord that ran across the desk was the only indication that somewhere, underneath all the clutter, was a telephone. If anybody had asked him about it, he would have said it symbolised a busy mind, but he knew that, in truth, it reflected his inclination to want to tackle too many tasks at once, often resulting in few things getting accomplished at all.

He finally found the letter, which was wedged beneath a copy of *Journal of Nervous and Mental Disease*, and extracted it with growing interest. With the busyness of recent weeks, he hadn't really had time to fully contemplate Nurse Robinson's request. A gentleman courting her sister, and a letter that appeared to shed some doubt on his intentions. It seemed such an intimate request. Elliot was surprised that Nurse Robinson, a woman of whose personal life he knew so little, other than that she was married but living in separation from her husband, would have approached him in this way. He took the letter out of its envelope and began to read:

> *My love,*
> *Your words to me yesterday are still ringing sadly in my ears, and will continue to do so until you replace them with sweeter ones. No, I do not believe that fate has cast us in a state of hopelessness and that we must accept in complete passivity these*

unfortunate circumstances.

    – redacted –

    How I wish you could share my convictions that the future is bright! And how melancholy my heart to think that you wish to surrender to unhappiness.

    – redacted –

    My love, my life, I beg you to reconsider your words. I ask merely for faith and patience – two of the many virtues I know that you possess.

    I remain forever,

    – redacted –

Elliot read through the letter twice and then reached out for a pencil and notebook. He placed the letter in front of him. His initial thoughts – content aside – were that this had been written under a large amount of emotional strain. He ran his fingers over the underside of the page to check for grooves and ridges on the paper, confirming his first impression that there were indeed many variations in pressure. The words in the second sentence, and particularly in the final paragraph, showed a heightened level of anxiety in the i-dots that flew to the right in an upward stem.

Great care had been taken with the legibility; the writer seemed to have taken his time and Elliot doubted whether this was the first draft. He was sure that, under other circumstances, this man's writing would look very different to the untrained eye. So, for example, in places, the script was disconnected, as though the writer was taking great care, yet at times would fall back on connected, thread-like formations. These, Elliot presumed, constituted his "natural" handwriting.

Something was bothering him about the first sentence, but he examined it twice and couldn't put his finger on it. He decided to return to it once he had completed the assessment. The writing in the second paragraph was at odds with the certainty in the content: despite the use of an exclamation mark, the extended cautionary strokes at the beginning of the letters revealed that this man was not at all convinced that the future was bright. Elliot would have liked to have been in a position to promise Nurse Robinson a happy ending for her sister – he presumed from the content that she had become involved with a married man – but at least he could tell her that the man's intentions were honest: there was no sinuous base line or stabs through oval-shaped letters. Rather, the writing showed clarity and simplicity, despite evidence of anxiousness and a certain amount of loneliness on the part of the writer.

It took him a good hour until he was happy that he had extracted all he could from this sample. Although he appreciated the sister's desire to keep the identity anonymous, Elliot thought it a great shame that the writer's signature had been deleted. A man's signature had unique significance in the science of graphology, or rather, in the psychological interpretation of graphology; unsurprisingly, Elliot concluded, as the writing of one's own name was a direct, external projection of one's self-image, on whose assumption of uniqueness legal systems all over the world stood and fell. It was a shame that it had been deleted.

And then, suddenly, Elliot knew why. He returned

to the first sentence, where the word "ears" now seemed to jump right off the page. He carefully examined the remaining script, but no, this was the only word beginning with "e". And this letter – or rather, the way in which the "e" was different from all the other "e's" – betrayed the writer's identity. The use of a Greek-style ε at the beginning of a word and never in the middle or at the end of words was a characteristic whose psychological meaning escaped Elliot – and yet it was an idiosyncrasy he had only ever come across once. Elliot knew, he was almost *certain*, who had drafted this letter.

At first, Elliot was downright astonished that Nurse Robinson had given him this letter to see at all. Had she so little trust in his abilities as a graphologist that she thought he wouldn't recognise the writing? But then again, he himself had made the connection almost accidentally. It was glaringly obvious that this wasn't the man's usual handwriting, so Nurse Robinson might well have presumed that Elliot wouldn't make the match. And besides, Elliot was reluctant to judge her motives. He knew nothing of the circumstances that had led her to place this matter in his hands. Now, more than ever, he was sure that greater forces must have driven her to overcome any trepidation she may have felt in coming to him with this request.

Having discovered the truth, however, he was left in somewhat of a dilemma: should he tell her that he knew who had written the letter? Or should he feign ignorance and just present her with his assessment? On the one hand, he wouldn't want to intrude on an already delicate situation, but then again, a small part of him – he supposed this was professional pride – felt that he shouldn't patronise her and let her know exactly what conclusions he had reached as a result of his comprehensive graphological examination.

He would have to give this matter more consideration before he came to a decision. Then his stomach growled and he suddenly remembered the potatoes he had put on the stove to boil.

An hour before his meeting with Raphael, Elliot decided to stop off in the pub, no longer able to ignore the gnawing hunger in his stomach. He ordered a plate of sandwiches, then another, chewing hastily and distractedly on the gristle and tendon that passed for roast beef in these parts. He finished the last of the sandwiches on his plate, and from his table in the corner, gestured to the barman to pull him another pint. It was only then that he became aware how crowded the place had become. Bodies formed small clusters in all corners of the pub, and the noise had grown from a sedate buzz, disturbed only by the occasional customer's shout to the barman, to an animated concert of sound: talking, laughing, arguing, cursing. The air was full with the warm, yeasty smell of exhaled beer fumes. A group of young men began to sing noisily as someone hammered out some tunes on the piano in the corner. But the noise did not bother Elliot. His mind was buzzing, a kaleidoscope of questions, half-formed hypotheses, tentative suppositions and conjectures about Raphael; no more than an incoherent assortment of ideas. His earlier sense of bewilderment had turned into fascination; a fascination tinged with the euphoria any scientist feels on the verge of some amazing discovery.

He had made a conscious decision to put any thoughts of his brother out of his mind; any emotional entanglement would be a distraction, and as far as he was concerned, the two things needn't necessarily be connected. He intended to take a cerebral approach to the problem.

The hasty research on multiple personality disorder he had busied himself with during the last few days had thrown up more questions than it had answered. On reading the literature, it had become immediately apparent that there was no single definition of the disorder. In fact, much of the research literature was concerned not with case studies, but with disputes over the genuineness of the condition. For some clinicians, the vast number of patients with multiple personality was evidence enough for its existence; others, notably Freud himself, held the opinion that the influence of a subtly persuasive therapist was enough to trigger the putative symptoms of the disorder. The level of animosity between the believers and non-believers was astonishing.

Elliot had no intention of letting himself be swayed by such emotive arguments. He would treat this patient – who himself had not claimed to be a multiple – with an open mind and reach any conclusion based on the hard evidence. As he thought of his patient, he tried hard to imagine what it must feel like to slide from one personality to another. Did one lose one's sense of integrity, the compelling sense of one's own unique existence? Perhaps dissociative states existed on a continuum, rather than an all-or-nothing basis. Yes, surely that was a possibility. Familiar phrases sprang to his mind; how often had he heard a wife complain: *He is not the same man I married.* When was the last time he had commented on a bibulous colleague: *He is a different person when he's had a drink?* And not forgetting: *I'm not myself today.* His excitement at the prospect of seeing Raphael again grew.

He lifted his left hand to check for the time, and a naked wrist stared back at him; he realised he must have left his watch at home. He got up, in a hurry now, and pushed through the crowds of drinkers to catch a glimpse of the grandfather clock that he knew stood to the right of the entrance. It was three minutes to eight. Cursing quietly to himself, he elbowed his way to the hatstand, shaking his head in the direction of an irritated barman, grabbed his coat and hat and stepped out into a cold fog. For a split second, the transition from hot to cold, coupled with the beer he had consumed too quickly, made him lose his bearings, and he had to think hard about whether to turn left or right. A second later, he had turned in the right direction, and began to walk quickly through the fog towards the clinic. Now and again he broke into a trot, but felt too self-conscious running, with his hat firmly pressed to his head with his left hand, and his coat flapping about on his right arm.

The Lane was almost deserted; only the lamp-posts and the sharp silhouettes of the naked trees making the streets look busier than they really were. Although it wasn't far, he was out of breath by the time he reached the clinic, and he just missed bumping into a tall man in a long heavy overcoat.

'Good evening, Dr. Taverley,' the man said, holding his arm out to steady Elliot as he nearly fell backward in surprise.

'Raphael!' he exclaimed.

'We have an appointment,' Raphael said softly.

'Yes, yes,' Elliot replied. With every pant a short burst of frozen breath appeared before him. 'I was just ... a bite to eat ... eight o'clock, isn't it?'

'It is cold, no?'

'Very. Let's go inside.'

Elliot held open the large oak door, and followed Raphael in. He waved at Tanner sitting behind the porter's desk, but he was – as always – consumed by his crossword puzzle. So much for vigilance, Elliot thought wryly.

Once inside Elliot's office, they both took off their hats and coats. The room was completely dark. Elliot switched on the two mismatched table lamps he had in the room, one on his desk, one on a small mahogany side table that stood under the window, then the electric heater. The heater emitted an instant wave of warmth, carrying on its breath the faint smell of burning. Drawing first one curtain, and then the other, he turned and saw that Raphael was standing at the doorway, waiting to be invited to sit down. He looked healthy, much better than he had a few days ago.

Elliot had gained enough breath back to comfortably light a cigarette. He offered one to Raphael, who gratefully accepted, and then gestured for his patient to take a seat. As Elliot relaxed in the armchair opposite, he became aware that he felt quite invigorated. The cold fresh air had done him good. He smiled at Raphael, and they sat in silence for a few moments, smoking. Elliot stubbed out his cigarette in the ashtray.

'What I would like to discuss with you is the nature

of your condition,' he began. 'In order for me to make a comprehensive diagnosis and offer you proper treatment, I need to discover more about you, your troubles, the concerns you are conscious of, and those you keep secret from yourself. This will involve talking candidly about your dreams, and your memories.' He paused, leaning forward. 'Personal things. Do you understand?'

'Yes, Dr. Taverley,' Raphael answered. 'I am not afraid.'

'I will be quite open with you, Raphael: it may – at some point – become necessary to initiate another transformation.'

Raphael's eyes widened.

'We must find out as much as possible about the personae that emerge during such transformations, see what they may have in common. You must understand, Raphael, that your condition is extremely rare. I realise that it is not easy for you, that it distresses you to dissociate. But,' he held his gaze, 'you can trust me. We will work together to make you well again. I have your interests at heart.'

Raphael dropped his eyes to the floor. He sighed heavily, and then lifted his head.

'Very well, I'll do what you ask of me,' he said. He looked anxious, apprehensive, like somebody sitting open-mouthed on a dentist's chair, helpless and vulnerable, anticipating the inevitable pain. Elliot leant further forward and put his hand on Raphael's.

'It'll be all right,' he assured him. He twisted around in his chair to reach behind him for a file that lay on his desk. It was light blue and bore the initials '*J.W.*' If Elliot was going to devise a schedule for treatment, he would need to formally diagnose Raphael, find out how knowledgeable he was about his disorder, and most importantly, the role played by the writing preceding the dissociations.

'To begin with, I'd like you to tell me a little about what you – *if* you can see something when you read another person's handwriting,' he said to Raphael. He pulled a sheet of paper out of the file; it was a treatment consent form signed by Jenny Wilson's father.

'Look,' he said, holding the sheet out in front of him. Raphael hesitated. Elliot understood.

'No,' he said, smiling, 'I'm not going to ask you to copy anything down. No dissociations tonight. I just want you to have a look at this signature, see if you can tell me anything about the person who wrote it.'

Raphael took the page out of his hand. Elliot could tell that it would take some time before his patient fully trusted him, and he would have to tread carefully. Trust, he knew, was the most valuable tool that the analyst had access to, the most slippery and fragile of commodities. The idea behind his request to Raphael was quite straightforward: he wanted to find out if his patient actually possessed any graphological abilities, but at the same time offer up a portion of control in their relationship, let the patient inform the doctor.

As Raphael looked down at the sheet of paper, he nodded. He spoke purposefully.

'I see a man who is angry, who has a desire to dominate and coerce. He is the father of many children, and struggles with this.'

Elliot's first thought was that he had given Raphael something with Wilson's personal details on it, and he could have kicked himself. How stupid!

'May I see it, please?' he asked.

Raphael leant forward and handed Elliot the paper, pointing to the signature as though the man's paternity were self-evident. Elliot scanned the page. It was a standard form of consent, neatly typed, with a short paragraph informing the parent of the proposed treatment, and a line beneath which stood: *Signature of Legal Guardian.* Above the line, the dark, angular, crude signature of Jenny's father, Gregory Wilson. No hint that this was the father of more than one child. But perhaps Raphael had noticed the reference to the requirement for a parent's permission prior to treatment, and made the reasonable inference that a man with uneducated handwriting was likely to have several children. Elliot asked him if he could tell him more. Raphael obliged.

'You can see clearly the variation in pressure in the strokes. How the initials 'G' and 'W' almost cut into the paper, and tower over the letters that follow. I think –' he paused, looking up at Elliot, 'that this is a man who has much unwanted responsibility, and a temper that *boom...*' he drew the image with his hands, '...explodes! His writing shows that he fights a lot with himself. The aggressive but unfulfilled understrokes, the uneven placing of his name on the line. I pity him. But I don't like him.'

Elliot was astonished at how knowledgeably Raphael spoke. 'Why do you dislike him? Because of his temper?' he asked.

'No, he has secrets. Cruel secrets.'

'How can you tell?'

There was a pause as Raphael shifted on his chair, evidently looking for the right words to explain. Not for the first time Elliot wondered at the apparent inconsistency in Raphael's grasp of the English language: at times, he was surprisingly fluent; at others, he struggled to find the easiest words. Perhaps this had some significance; Elliot made a mental note to look into this at some point.

Raphael continued. 'It is not easy to explain. A man in whose writing the letter "e" begins to close and becomes ... what is the word? ... eyeless, then you can be sure that he has something to hide. But I see this afterwards, you know? First I see the secret, then I see the "e". When I am reading a script, I see not just lines and scribbles on a piece of paper. The writing comes alive. I believe that a man weaves his life, his desires, his worries and his secrets into his writing. Every knot and emphasis, every stroke and flourish tells its own story. When I read, it is like hearing an orchestra play: first, as when the instruments are being tuned, everything seems discordant, I can only make out fragments; slivers of energy; ebbs and flow of emotion. Slowly, gradually, the symphony begins, and the histories of the writer that once lay dormant on a sheet of paper are pieced together and come to life. I *see*, I *feel* the writer. After a few minutes of this I can tell if the writer is a man or a woman, old or young, brutal or gentle, kind or dangerous.' He rubbed his chin with his hand. 'I have read that there are systems and codes for how to do this.'

'You are speaking of graphology? Of handwriting

analysis?'

'Yes, that is what I have heard it called. But I would not call what I do *analysis*. I do not analyse or dissect what is written down; on the contrary, I bring together what I see.'

He interlocked his fingers to emphasise his point. What he had just told Elliot was nothing short of remarkable. Elliot had studied graphology for several years and prided himself on connections he had made – in theory and practice – to psycho-analytic understanding. Yet here was this man, with no formal instruction, who was guided by what seemed to be mere intuition. And who, to Elliot's astonishment, was more accurate in his assessment than he himself could ever hope to be.

'When did you first realise that you could see through people's handwriting in this way?' Elliot asked.

'I can't be sure, I have always, please forgive me if I sound foolish, I always believed that everyone does this. I soon discovered, however, that it was not something everyone does naturally. It was a surprise to me to learn that some people cannot see anything in handwriting! So, I suppose I have always seen handwriting as a way of knowing a man.'

'Well, Raphael, I can tell you now that your assessment seems remarkably accurate. This signature is of a man with several children, who is prone to losing his temper, as far as I can tell. However, I have no proof that he has secrets.'

'I understand that it is hard for you to believe, and I do not expect you to take my word for it, but I am confident of what I know about this man from his signature. I had not realised that you were putting me to the test.' He sat back in his chair. For a brief moment, his expression changed to one of dejection, and Elliot hastened to reassure him.

'I am sorry if that is what you think, Raphael. I can only stress that it is important that I know as much about this matter as possible. You see, from what we know thus far, the writing seems to play a part in your condition. I can't be certain whether it acts as a mere trigger, whether other circumstances may induce a transformation equally effectively, but it is important that I get as full a picture as possible.'

Raphael seemed to accept this rationale. He leant forward again, resting his forearms on his knees, palms together, so that his fingertips almost touched Elliot's. 'What is my condition, Dr. Taverley?' he asked.

Elliot took a deep breath. In his experience, the sharing of the diagnosis with the patient could be either distressing or cathartic. For some, the knowledge that their illness was not merely imagined but real, in every painful, stigmatic detail, could serve almost as a cure; for others, a diagnosis could be the confirmation of their darkest fears. As a rule, Elliot had some inkling of how the patient would respond to a diagnosis; but with Raphael, he was uncertain. He spoke slowly.

'I believe you are suffering from a condition known as multiple personality disorder. Some people call it split personality. When you experience a transformation, such as when you came to see me the last time, another personality emerges, a personality that is completely different from who you, Raphael, believe yourself to be. Your voice, your demeanour: all these things undergo a fundamental change. I am convinced that this is also what happened when your friends were making fun of your... accident.'

Raphael sat upright in his chair, looking at him intently, silently.

Elliot continued. 'I need to find out where these personalities come from, perhaps whether they are a product of self-hypnosis, induced during childhood. Sometimes, patients form these personalities, or alter egos, as a kind of protection from psychological harm. We will need to investigate whether you had experiences that occurred when you were younger that you felt you could not tolerate or cope with in any other way.'

'You said my condition was extremely rare.'

'Yes, I have read of cases of multiple personality in which the transitions among identities are triggered by stress, sometimes physical, more often psychological. But in your case, it seems to be the writing that triggers the transition. I will be open with you, Raphael, I am not quite sure why.'

Elliot was taking a gamble in this situation, laying his cards on the table. He had read that with multiples there was always the possibility that the host personality was the controller, one who had full knowledge of the other personalities. In such cases, telling the host of the therapist's full intentions could be dangerous. It was not uncommon for such a patient to use this information to manipulate situations, to deliberately hide or minimise symptoms. However, Elliot also knew that this kind of behaviour was most likely observed in patients who were obviously attention-seeking, and he was reluctant to include Raphael among them. He was not sure of what response to expect, but he was taken aback by Raphael's reaction.

Without hesitation, as though he were offering Elliot another cup of tea, he said, 'There is something else I can do.'

'What do you mean?' Elliot asked, puzzled.

'I can create the handwriting of a person if I know some things about them. Not copy, create.'

'You mean, without ever having seen a sample of their handwriting?'

'Yes. If I know their writing, I know their personality. I explained this to you. But it works the other way around. If I know who they are, what they are like, I can tell how they write.'

'I'm surprised you haven't mentioned this to me before,' Elliot said.

'You want to help me, I am sure, I can feel it. Then I will tell you all I can about the writing,' he answered.

'May I put this to the test?' Elliot asked, smiling.

'Certainly.'

Elliot's thoughts were racing. He hadn't expected this, and his stomach churned with the excitement at what this experiment might yield. His promise to Beaumont was completely forgotten; he felt almost giddy as he deliberated whose writing he could choose. After the incident with Ed, he couldn't risk exposing his emotional vulnerability again. On the other hand, it would have to be somebody he knew well enough to describe in detail. It would have to be Helena. He smiled as her name came to mind – she would be delighted.

'Would you reconstruct someone's signature for me?' he asked, trying hard to conceal his excitement.

'Yes, of course.'

'How much detail do you need?'

'The sex is not so important, but the age can tell me a lot. And the character. Is this person good or mean? Is he – or she – stubborn, warm-hearted, shy, or perhaps self-important? Also...' he hesitated.

'What, anything else?'

'No; I'm not sure. It may be possible for me to tell you the person's name, if you show me a photograph. But I cannot promise.'

'Very well, I shall describe to you a young lady I know. I can show you her picture, but I find it difficult to believe that you will be able to tell me her name – unless you know her.'

He reached into his inside pocket and retrieved a photograph of Helena from his wallet. It had been taken last summer, while they were on a day trip to Stratford-up-on-Avon, unchaperoned by the fortuitous occurrence of Helena's sister Cassandra having fallen ill with a stomach bug. It must have been taken only a day or two before Elliot was called home from work to spend the last hours with his dying mother. In the photograph, Helena sat on the river bank, looking directly into the lens, as self-assured as always. She looked beautiful. She was leaning back on her tanned, bare arms, laughing at the camera, showing the tiny gap between her front teeth. Her hair had lightened in the sun to become a nutty brown – impossible to tell in the picture, but fixed firmly in his memory – a colour to match the freckles that appeared across her nose and upper cheeks. Elliot wondered, not for the first time, why Helena, like many of her peers, spent so much time and effort concealing her natural beauty. It had been their first time out of London together, and Elliot remembered how impressed he had been by her lack of worries. He had never before met anyone with a more carefree nature. Funny, really; it had taken him quite some time to adjust to her relentless optimism, but he had now come to appreciate it, even to rely on it.

When Elliot had told Helena that his mother was dying, she seemed almost confused, as though she were surprised that such bad things happened in real life. She had never before lost a loved one, not even a pet rabbit – the innocence of one who had never grieved – and had wandered around bewildered, like a spoiled child who had been told "no" for the first time. When his mother finally died, days later, in the bed she had shared with her husband for forty-eight years, Elliot had felt he had to show strength, organise his feelings, his grief, while Helena wept openly, as if on his behalf. They were closer then than they had ever been, fused by this interdependence of emotion.

He described to Raphael the Helena he knew and loved: her passion for life and people, for causes both just and dubious; the confidence of someone born into privilege, but with more modesty than most of her upper-class peers; her creativity; her short attention span, her impatience. He must have talked for about fifteen minutes; Raphael listened patiently, attentively, his head to one side. When Elliot finally handed him the photograph, he glanced at it and smiled.

'She is beautiful. May I have a pen?'

Elliot held one out to him. With a shy smile, Raphael took the pen and strode over to the desk. On a sheet of notepaper that lay there, he wrote swiftly and effortlessly

Helena Margaret Rickman

If Elliot never before understood the phrase "I caught my breath", he did now. It was more than he could ever have expected. He felt dizzy, light-headed. He snatched up the piece of paper from the desk and stared at it. Raphael had created a perfect facsimile! A signature Elliot had analysed himself, and in which he now recognised the proud independence of spirit in the even letter spacing; the optimistic forward slant, reaching out to embrace all that life has to offer; the untidiness of a hand impatient to finish. Raphael had duplicated every detail, from the slightly misplaced i-dot to Helena's convention of signing with her full name. What was he to make of this? With the notepaper in his hand, he looked at Raphael, tracing his face for signs of contempt, the contempt a swindler feels for his dupe. At that moment that was exactly what Elliot feared. Yet a part of him wanted Raphael to laugh in his face and tell him it was all part of an elaborate hoax; that he and Helena and Beaumont had dreamed it up together as a practical joke. It would have been a perverse relief: at least then everything he knew, all that he believed in, would still make sense.

But Raphael was now looking back at him, silently, innocently. Elliot lost his patience.

'How is it you know her name, man?' he demanded.

'How? But I explained to you –,' Raphael began.

Elliot interrupted him. 'How can you know this? Her name. Her full name. There is no way, absolutely no way you could know this, unless –,' he paused, a disquieting suspicion – shapeless still, but troubling – growing inside him.

'What else do you know about me?' he asked angrily.

'About you? I know very little. That you are a doctor. That you said you could help me. I don't understand…' He trailed off.

'You must know something!' Elliot shouted suddenly and waved the paper in Raphael's face.

Raphael flinched.

'I'm sorry, Dr. Taverley. I'm sorry I have made you angry. I should leave now.' He got to his feet.

Elliot noticed that the man was shaking. His anger subsided as quickly as it had erupted and was replaced by a sense of shame. He had been so eager for his patient to perform some sort of circus trick, and now he was punishing the man for obliging. He had never acted so unprofessionally in his entire life.

'Raphael. Listen to me,' he said quietly. He stood up. 'I think we have talked enough for today. You should come back and see me again, say –' he flicked through his desk diary, 'on the twenty-fourth. Then we shall begin therapy.'

Raphael nodded and picked up his coat. He looked at Elliot.

'Therapy. Yes,' he said and walked to the door.

Elliot watched him leave the office, then glanced at the crumpled piece of paper with Helena's signature. This was beyond multiple personality disorder. But there had to be a perfectly sane explanation for all that he had witnessed. If he put his mind to it, he would find it out.

Eight

It was just after two o'clock when Elliot arrived outside Helena's apartment in Eaton Mews in a taxicab. He had hailed a cab for the short journey, and had surprised himself by hoping it would turn out to be the young man who had driven him to the cemetery. The route from his house to Helena's was within walking distance, but he was taking two heavy suitcases with him to Brighton, and besides, the sky looked heavy with rain. He had had to pack several days' attire for his stay; from formal tailcoat and perfectly starched white shirts to Oxford bags and golfing trousers, he had a wardrobe to suit any occasion.

He helped the driver unload his bags, paid him, and asked him to return at three o'clock to take him to Euston Station. Their train for Brighton was leaving just after half past three, and Elliot wanted to make sure of getting there in plenty of time. When the driver had left, Elliot stood outside the building for a while, enjoying a cigarette before he went inside. The apartment Helena shared with her sister Cassandra and brother-in-law Frederick was in the new Kensington House building in Eaton Mews. The development was a swish, upmarket affair; an English imitation of New York living, boasting iced running water and a staff of communal servants.

He was finally forced to step inside when the clouds fulfilled their promise and released the rain. A big, heavy raindrop landed with precision on the end of his cigarette, extinguishing the glow with a disappointing hiss. He flicked the sodden stub into the bushes, and gestured to the waiting doorman to help him carry his bags inside. As he stepped into the foyer, he couldn't help but feel overwhelmed by the unadulterated opulence of the building's interior. As grand as Kensington House appeared on the outside, with its glazed facade that gave the appearance of a single floor-less expanse, it was no match for the jewel that lay on the inside. Elliot placed his suitcases on the pale limestone floor, and taking off his hat – in unconscious reverence perhaps – stood in the middle of the foyer, feeling small, almost insignificant against the foyer's expansiveness. He reacted this way every time he came here. He liked to think it was in disapproval of this shameless shrine to excessive wealth; however, it was equally possible that he was, much like every other mortal, succumbing to the magnificence in design and brilliance in construction. The walls of the entrance hall were clad in pale pink marble and the floor in cream-coloured limestone. A giant staircase swept invitingly up the left-hand side of the foyer, surpassed in splendour only by the embellishments on the doors of the lift: a fantastic, dreamlike pattern in inlaid brass and mahogany, seducing the visitor to enter and ascend electrically, rather than on foot. The balustrades, columns and door surrounds were made of translucent moulded glass, and huge vertical sections of chromed steel and mirror glass panelling sliced Elliot's reflection into long, thin slivers around the foyer. It was both breathtaking and nauseating.

Elliot stooped to pick up the bags and carry them across to the lift. As he bent down, he could smell the freshly polished floor. He wondered briefly how many hours the cleaning staff would have to work to maintain the foyer's gleaming, lustrous appearance. The mirror glass alone must take hours to clean. His thoughts were interrupted by a friendly, melodious *ping* that sounded the lift's arrival. The upward-pointing triangle above the lift door lit up as the doors glided open, and Elliot stepped in, the sudden electric hum of the lift's ascent echoing the whirring inside his head.

Helena opened the door a second after the doorbell chimed out his arrival, making him assume that she'd been waiting impatiently for him to arrive. She was wearing a dark green travel suit: a tubular bodice that draped straight down to a dropped waist, then ballooned out very slightly before tapering at a five-inch fur border just above her ankles. A long pleat ran up the side of her skirt, accentuating her slenderness and hinting at the length of her legs that the dropped waistline might otherwise have concealed. The matching jacket that hung casually over the side of a chair had a fur-lined collar and cuffs. Effortlessly elegant as usual, Elliot thought.

'Darling!' she exclaimed, hugging him enthusiastically before turning back to the maid, who was busy trying to force shut a large steamer trunk. Two bloated suitcases already stood by the front door.

'I'm so excited about the new house,' Helena said, helping the maid snap shut the locks on her trunk and throwing Elliot an occasional frantic look over her shoulder. He guessed that she had packed and repacked her cases at least ten times during the past week, and was now worried that she might have forgotten some indispensable item.

'It sounds marvellous from what Mummy's described

– *very* modern. They had the most wonderful architect, can't think of his name right now, who let Mummy have lots of say in the design. She says she's absolutely exhausted from it all, but I'm sure she's exaggerating, as usual. Have you remembered to pack your golfing trousers? Daddy's planning to take all the boys out for a game on Sunday, won't that be fun?' She stepped back from the trunk and pursed her lips. 'Now, have I got everything? Martha, are you sure we packed my shoes? You know, the red silk ones.' Without waiting for an answer, she knelt down – with difficulty, as the designer of her outfit had had elegance, rather than practicality, in mind – and unsnapped the trunk. 'Shall I just make sure?'

Elliot smiled at Martha, who threw her hands up in exasperation. He bent over and gently pushed the lid of the case shut. 'It won't have been worth packing anything if we miss the train,' he said.

Helena sprang up and nodded. 'Yes, you're right. I'm just so *excited!*' She threw her arms around his neck again and kissed him on the cheek.

'Come on, Helena, you're making Martha blush,' he said, winking at the maid. Helena's spiritedness was infectious.

In the cab on the way to the station, Helena continued to talk about the weekend ahead, while Elliot found his mind drifting back to the Chapel and to Raphael. He wasn't a dishonest man, and his initial decision to treat the man secretly without registering him first had begun to torment him. Certainly, if the price he had to pay for clandestine meetings was the constant preoccupation with the man, perhaps it was time to put his curiosity and pride aside and ask Beaumont, or one of his other colleagues, for advice. Yet Elliot couldn't help but picture Helena's signature, and the effortlessness with which Raphael had written it. Though he hated to think it, it was all too possible that he was out of his depth.

The rain continued to pour from the clouds. But if he continued to see Raphael unofficially, he thought, he might have an opportunity to discover something that the others – Beaumont particularly – might never even consider. What if he could show that a connection existed between writing and the unconscious? What if a man's handwriting could make the psyche tangible, in a way that dream analysis and Rorschach never could? He would be vindicated and his approach would have to be taken seriously. The cabbie started up the engine again and the car pulled away slowly. Elliot sat back in his seat. He knew he was running the risk of losing his position at the Chapel; but if he registered the man officially, that might mean having to sit back while some other doctor continued his treatment with some frustratingly orthodox technique. He sighed in frustration. He would give himself this weekend to come to a final decision.

Beside him, Helena was still talking ten to the dozen, describing to Elliot the various relatives he would be meeting in Brighton, their individual foibles and status within the family. He in turn was doing a good job of concealing his pensiveness, making a convincing show of attentive listening as she chattered away.

'So Tom, he's Sibylla's latest conquest; I've only met him once, but he seems a bit of a squib. Is that a really horrid thing to say? Anyway, you tell me what you think when you've met him. And, oh, how could I forget, then there's John.' She rolled her eyes. 'Well, actually, it's Father John, he's a Catholic priest. I'm not quite sure where he fits in, Mummy's side somewhere, I think his brother married one of Mummy's cousins or something, but he's a real...' she lowered her voice and cupped her mouth with her right hand, looking to see that the driver couldn't hear her, '... *arse*. He always turns up at these occasions, even when no one's invited him. So be warned.'

Elliot's thoughts broke away from Raphael for a minute, and he laughed out loud. Helena very rarely swore – despite her attempts to behave like a cosmopolite, using bad language was always a real effort for her. In many ways, Helena was charmingly old-fashioned, a trait that clashed startlingly with her modernity in other aspects of her life. Her cheeks flushed as she realised that he was laughing at her.

'Well, I'm glad something's cheered you up, you miserable so-and-so,' she said. This time, it was Elliot's turn to blush. He obviously hadn't hidden his distraction as well as he'd thought.

The taxi pulled up at the rank, and the driver called for a porter. As the luggage was wheeled off to the baggage car, Elliot and Helena hurried to find the First Class carriage on the train. Although the platform was partially covered, the wind whipped the rain with such force that it lashed them horizontally. They were drenched by the time

127

they got on-board. The carriage wasn't full, and, although they had a choice of several empty compartments, they decided to spend the journey in the dining car. Elliot paid little attention to the fact that the carriage had recently been refurbished, but Helena took pleasure in stroking the padded benches that were lavishly upholstered in burgundy velvet. They removed their soaking wet coats, handing them to the steward, and sat facing each other either side of the table. The lighting in the carriage was muted, and so although it was only mid-afternoon, it seemed to be much later in the day. Outside in the gloom, Elliot watched a handful of sparrows sheltering from the wind behind a brick wall. Funny, he had never seen birds shivering before. But in this weather, flight was impossible. He was glad to be where it was cosy and warm. The only thing inside this luxurious shell that hinted at the unpleasantness outside was the smell of wet wool that had begun to emanate from the passengers' coats, which hung from brass hooks at the end of the car. The rain bounced off the window panes, relentlessly, as though it were trying to break through the glass. A moment later, the rain had turned to hail, determined to carry out its threat of shattering the windows. The stationmaster's whistle blew, sounding thin and frail through the wind and the hammering of ice on glass, and the train began to crawl out of the station. Elliot settled back for the ride.

He had eaten earlier, and declined the menu offered to him by the steward. Helena, not wanting to eat alone, followed suit and ordered tea and biscuits instead. Then she pulled a pack of cards from her handbag and handed it to Elliot. He and Helena often played cards; her favourite was bezique. As Elliot shuffled the cards, he became aware of a slight but discernible ache just behind his eyes. He stopped what he was doing and closed his eyes, feeling around for the tell-tale signs of migraine. He had developed the ability to trace the inside of his skull for the whisper of pain, a whisper that could lead to a crescendo within minutes. Nothing. He opened his eyes again. But instead of relief, he felt a sudden anger that his constant fear of this affliction could so brutally disrupt even the most mundane actions. He brought the cards together too forcefully; rather than interleaving, the two piles of cards struck one another, bending precariously, before jumping out of his hands. Several of them went flying under Elliot's side of the table. He bent down and retrieved them, his head colliding with the edge of the table on the way up.

'For Christ's sake!' he murmured, gathering the cards together.

Helena stretched across the table to rub his head.

'That's the first thing you've said for a while,' she said. 'I thought you might've taken a vow of silence.'

'What?'

'I said you're very quiet today.' She drew her arm back. 'I hope you'll cheer up before we get there.'

'I'm sorry, I've just got a lot on my mind.' He gathered up the remaining cards from the table and tidied them into a pile.

'Helena,' he said after a moment, 'do you know a man called Raphael Najevski?'

Helena frowned. 'Najevski. Hmm. Doesn't sound familiar. Who is he? Where would I know him from?'

'Oh, nowhere. Just somebody I met recently. He mentioned the name Rickman and I thought he might be talking about your family.'

'Well, it doesn't ring a bell. Sorry.'

'I must have been mistaken then. Come on, then, let's see if we can finish this game before we reach Brighton.' He attempted a smile and handed Helena the pack of cards to cut. She cut the higher card, the queen of hearts. She dealt – three, two, three – and then placed the seventeenth card face-up on the table. Seven of spades.

'My lucky day,' she said, and nodded in the direction of the pad and pencil, indicating to Elliot to write down her score. He did so. Ten points. They played in silence for the next ten minutes, until the steward, whose uniform stylishly matched the maroon and cream livery of the carriage, glided towards them with a tray of tea and biscuits, professionally immune to the swaying and jerking of the train. Helena smiled her thanks at him, and then put her cards down to pour out the tea. Elliot's hand circled the biscuit platter in indecision before picking up a piece of chocolate-covered shortbread. As he took a bite, Helena broke the silence again.

'It's not your parents, is it?' she asked. 'I mean, there's nothing troubling you, is there?'

It took a second for Elliot to register what she was saying. He swallowed what he was chewing.

'What do you mean?'

'You went to the cemetery a few weeks ago. I should have come with you.'

'No, no, it's nothing to do with that. It's … no, it's

silly. C'mon, let's finish this game.'

He gestured for her to pick up her hand. But she ignored him.

'Well, something's troubling you, and I want to know what it is. If you don't tell me now, it'll be on your mind all weekend, and that's not fair.'

Elliot felt guilty. He knew that he would continue to brood over his patient until they returned to London. But he was concerned that the bizarre episode with her signature might disturb her, so instead he began to tell her about his indecision over whether to register his new patient at the Chapel.

'I don't see why you wouldn't be able to continue as his doctor,' she said, when he had finished. 'Anyway, you saw him first. Finders keepers, and all that.'

'But that isn't the way the Chapel operates. One shouldn't just reserve the interesting cases for oneself. It belittles the other patients' suffering.'

Helena shook her head in disagreement. 'Your colleagues would do exactly the same, given the chance,' she said. 'You have just as much right, and expertise, to treat the patient. If you ran a private practice, and he had money, you wouldn't hesitate for a moment.'

'Well, perhaps. But I can't shake off the feeling that it seems dishonest,' he replied, frowning.

'I love that about you.'

'My dishonesty?'

'Your integrity, you fool.' And she laughed, reaching across the table for a sugar cube. It made a contented plopping sound as she dropped it into her cup. She stirred her tea thoughtfully. After a short while she said quietly, '*The fragile spirit / beautiful – yet / dislocated.*'

'Sorry?' Elliot asked.

'Oh, nothing. It's a poem I'm working on. It just popped into my head.'

'You must let me hear it when it's finished.'

She smiled at him. 'You'll be the first, I promise. I haven't quite got there yet; parts of it still sound so... affected, you know?'

Elliot smiled, taking her hand and squeezing it gently. Helena was anything but affected. She often spoke before she thought, it was true, but that saved him the trouble of having to read between the lines. How different his parents' relationship had been! Years of unspoken resentment and bitterness towards each another; feelings they prolonged and cultivated like priceless orchids, nurturing them until they were fully matured, and until finally the relationship couldn't function without them. Those Sunday lunches when he and Ed were children – the stilted conversations and even more painful silences. *This beef has seen better days* from their father, knowing his wife had slaved over the roast on a hot summer's day to show that she was just as good a cook as Mrs Blake; her response *Do you really think you should, dear?*, when he opened a second bottle of claret. Gestures and half-remarks whose contents Elliot hadn't quite understood, but whose meanings were glaringly transparent. Occasionally, rarely, some goofy behaviour from Ed had managed to snatch a smile from them, liberating them temporarily from their discontent; offering them in a shared laugh a fugitive glimpse into a parallel life in which they were free from the mutual enmity that – paradoxically – held their marriage together. It was an ability Elliot had admired in his brother, but never managed to emulate.

Helena gathered up her cards, smiling to herself. Elliot played his card, and waited for Helena to respond. But instead of playing her card, she banged her fist on the table.

'Damn!'

'That's your second profanity today. Not your lucky day after all, eh?'

'No, no. I mean, not that. I just remembered something.'

'What?'

'I forgot to bring the charm bracelet you gave me for Christmas.'

'Oh.'

'And I so wanted to wear it tomorrow,' she said. 'I know the others would have thought it so sweet of you.'

Helena was referring to her three other sisters, Cassandra, Sybilla and Maia. Helena was the youngest of the four flamboyant women, the contradictory offspring of two unusually diffident but loving parents. The term "overwhelmed" never seemed more fitting to Elliot than when he first saw this couple in the presence of their children. Goodness knows how they had raised them safely to adulthood.

'Never mind, I'm sure they'll be pleased just to see you again,' Elliot said. 'Come on, at this rate we'll never get this game finished.'

He played a card, just as Helena began to slide under the table.

'What's the matter?' he asked.

'Behind you. No, don't look! It's Lady Maxime. Oh please, please, please, don't come over here.'

Elliot turned and looked. It was an involuntary reaction. Several seats behind him was Lady Maxime Waterford, a young aristocrat, well-known on the London social scene. Although they had never been formally introduced, Elliot recognised her instantly: a twelve-foot-high photographic image of her face stared down at the traffic in Piccadilly Circus, encouraging the passers-by to mix their cocktails with Gordon's Gin. Her status as an aristocrat made her a darling of the advertising world, and she was feted in the popular press for her ostensible glamour and celebrity.

'Oh God,' Helena groaned, as Lady Maxime spotted them and made an immediate beeline for their table. She appeared a lot plumper than Elliot recalled from her photograph; perhaps she belonged to that unfortunate group of modern women who were not naturally slender, and were subsequently in a constant battle to maintain the malnourished shape that seemed so fashionable. The fact that the shift dress she wore had no discernible waistline did her no favours.

'Sweetie, what an adorable coincidence!' she called, arms outstretched.

'Yes, isn't it just,' said Helena, grimacing.

'So, who's this then?' Lady Maxime asked, with a little upper-body shimmy in Elliot's direction.

He opened his mouth to speak.

'No, don't tell me,' she cried, clapping her hands together and bouncing up and down on her heels, like an oddly overgrown schoolgirl. 'I know who you are, Helena's mentioned you before. I never forget a name. Daddy says I have a memory like an elephant.'

Under the table, Elliot gave Helena a gentle, precautionary kick on the shin.

'It's Elliot, isn't it?' she said, evidently pleased with herself and her elephantine memory. 'I'm Maxime, but call me Max.'

'Yes, Elliot Taverley. How do you do?' he said, shaking her outstretched hand.

'How do you do?' she replied with a small curtsey and the impeccable manners of a debutante. She turned to Helena.

'I haven't seen you for ages. Not since before Christmas, am I right? So, what have you been up to, darling? I didn't see you at any of the Christmas do's, did I?'

'Elliot and I have been keeping ourselves to ourselves.'

'Oh, how romantic, just the two of you.'

'Yes, I suppose so.'

Elliot pretended to look out of the train window into the pitch-black darkness. He was actually watching Helena's reflection, wondering how long it would be before she ran out of patience and told Lady Max to get lost. Her eyebrows, thin and tapered, rose and fell in impatience, and her dark red lipstick began to fade as she chewed her lower lip in irritation. After a while, Elliot's thoughts began to loiter around the impending weekend, and Lady Max's meaningless chatter merged with the rattling of the train, until it became one continuous hum. He had only met Helena's parents twice before; the first time when he and

Helena had announced their engagement, and then again a short time later when Helena moved to London. They had appeared to be a lot happier than Elliot's mother had been with what seemed to everyone else a speedy engagement; not because they believed any woman over the age of twenty-two should be grateful for a willing suitor, far from it, but because they seemed to support their children in whatever choices they made. He was looking forward to meeting them again.

The train suddenly slowed, and then came to a full halt. There was an abrupt hush in the carriage, as the passengers looked out of the windows to see what had brought the train to a standstill. Helena let her head fall back onto the plump headrest, and began drumming her fingers on the window ledge. Her nails made a pleasant clacking sound against the wood. Elliot checked the time. They still had at least an hour of the train journey to go. Abruptly, Lady Max turned her attention to Elliot.

'You aren't by any chance –' she asked, dropping onto the seat beside him. Then, 'No, you look nothing like him.'

'Like whom?' Helena asked, her curiosity now apparently stronger than her dislike of the woman.

'Well, I was just wondering if he's related to someone I used to know. Ed Taverley. Gorgeous fellow, a right one for the ladies. This is going back a few years, though; he's probably got himself a wife and ten kids by now. Used to be at all the parties, when he was on leave, that is. He joined up quite early on.' She shrugged. 'I just thought, Taverley, might be some relation.'

'He was Elliot's brother,' Helena said, suddenly animated. 'I'm right, aren't I, darling?' She looked at Elliot.

'It certainly sounds like him,' he said. It was a while since he had run into a mutual acquaintance – other than Stanislav, of course – and this capricious socialite was just the kind of acquaintance Ed would have had. She was a bit on the plump side, though, not quite Ed's type.

'Well, what a coincidence!' Lady Max said, beaming. 'What's he up to these days? How many of those ten kids does he have?'

Helena glanced at Elliot. Lady Max caught the look. 'What? He hasn't been a naughty boy, has he?'

'No, he died,' Elliot said, matter-of-factly.

'Oh.'

The steward passed by slowly carrying an assortment of pastries, cakes and eclairs. Lady Max looked longingly at the plate, and her indecision was painfully evident. Courtesy, of course, dictated a certain propriety; indulging in sweets immediately after hearing of the death of a friend was no way to behave. Elliot felt almost sorry for her as she continued to stare at the plate.

'Please, go ahead,' he said gallantly.

'Are you sure?' she asked. Her hand went out for a chocolate eclair, wavered for a second over the plate, then plunged down and swooped before she could change her mind again.

'Please accept my sincere condolences,' she managed to utter before the eclair slid into her mouth. Elliot acknowledged her sentiments with a nod.

'So, what was he like? Ed, I mean,' Helena asked, when Lady Max had wiped the corners of her mouth with a napkin.

'I'm sure Elliot's told you all about him, hasn't he?'

Helena gave Elliot a cautious look. He raised his left shoulder and let it drop. It was only natural that she would want to know.

'Well, of course,' Helena lied. 'But I'd love to hear about him from someone else who knew him.'

'He was so funny, always had people laughing. Although –' she stopped and wrinkled her nose. 'He was a bit *scary* sometimes. No offence,' she said to Elliot. 'I don't mean downright *nasty* or anything, but sometimes you weren't sure whether he was joking or being serious. You know what he was like, Elliot. Sometimes you didn't know –' she stopped and shrugged her shoulders.

'What?' Helena persisted.

'Well, for instance, it was the way he would compliment the plain girls. With the pretty ones, his intentions were quite obvious, but it was just the way he'd say something like, *You're quite something, aren't you?* to a girl who was anything but beautiful. He'd come right up close to your face, well, *her* face, and say it. And it was something in his tone ... oh, I don't know.' She seemed to have run out of words. After a pensive moment she resumed. 'You would've had to be there. And then there was this one time, when ... oh, how should I explain? Well, as you know, Elliot,' she looked at him briefly, her tone more chirpy, 'his proper name was Edward, but everyone called him Ed. Anyway, one day we were at a party and this girl he had come with, Alice, got a bit tipsy and started calling him Teddy. It was *Teddy this* and *Teddy that*, and he kept saying *Don't call me that*, but she didn't stop; in fact, I think she was enjoying getting a rise out of him. Everyone was laughing, because she was teasing him and squealing hysterically, and he was running around the room trying to catch her, and then he somehow managed to trip her up, and she fell quite hard against a table. I'm sure he didn't mean to hurt her, but she had split open her eyebrow and was bleeding, and he bent over to help her up and said, *You see, bad things happen to people who call me Teddy*, and sort of smiled, and she looked terrified for a moment, but then he laughed and everyone realised he was just joking.'

'Was she all right?' Helena asked, evidently concerned.

'Oh yes, it looked worse than it was. She cheered up after a drink, but I don't think she ever called him Teddy again.' She looked down at the table. 'You know what he was like, Elliot,' she repeated. 'A bit boisterous, but a good sort.'

Elliot stirred his tea, breaking up the dark film that had formed on the liquid's surface. It was odd, hearing this story; echoes of the life of the man who still blazed so intensely in his memory. He was surprised at how easy it was to sit back and listen to someone else tell stories about Ed, and yet not being able to find the words himself. Perhaps, it occurred to him, perhaps it was coming close to the time when he would no longer be required to guard his memory – their shared history – so possessively. He owed it to Helena to let her in.

Someone called Lady Max's name from the other end of the dining car.

'Well, I'd love to stay and chat, but I've got to go.' She blew Helena and Elliot a kiss and then got up and tottered away.

The train started to move again, at first in a series of small, jerking spasms that made what was left of the tea slosh over the sides of the cups, until it finally gathered speed and settled into its familiar, undulating rhythm. A few long minutes passed, as Helena wiped the tea-sodden playing cards dry. The steward came to clear their table, apologising for the interruption to their journey.

'Fancy that,' Helena said a moment later. 'Her knowing Ed, I mean.'

'It's a small world.'

'Everything all right?'

'A bit tired, that's all. That woman.' He smiled without conviction. 'She sucked the life out of me.'

Helena smiled back. 'Listen, you're obviously in no mood to chat, so you won't mind if I read my book.'

'I'm sorry for being such a poor travel companion.'

'Don't worry. I won't hold it against you. But you must promise to make up for it in Brighton, all right? No Mr Grumpy, just relax for a change.' She stretched out her hand. 'Deal?'

Elliot took her hand, but instead of shaking it, turned it up towards his face and, leaning forward, kissed her palm. 'Deal.'

NINE

When the train finally pulled into Brighton Station, it was thirty minutes behind schedule. As Elliot and Helena clambered down from the train onto the platform, they were spotted immediately by Helena's sisters. True to form, they had arrived with no less than three motorcars full of friends, all eager to begin celebrating. Helena was soon swallowed by the crowd of greeters, leaving Elliot standing on the outside. He knew only a few of them by name, and felt a little out of place, not sure whether to join in or stay back. He decided on the latter, and went to instruct the porter with their luggage. Helena's gang had begun to move towards the exit. Beyond a set of iron gates, he could see what he assumed were the cars that would be taking them to the house. When he had tipped the porter and pointed out where the bags should go, he stopped to light a cigarette. Above him, a giant railway clock told him with precise mechanical clunks that it was six o'clock. He leaned against a tall black post that seemed to be holding up a whole section of the arched roof, and inhaled, savouring the sharpness of the smoke as it hit the back of his throat.

The rain had followed them from London, but the tall iron and glass station roof was keeping him dry for the time being, and the air was noticeably milder here. Presently, a man came and stood beside Elliot, nodding his greeting and lighting a pipe that he pulled out of a pocket. It was Helena's father. The two men stood in silence for a while, both concentrating on the stationmaster who was busy readying the train for departure. Helena's father, Henry Rickman, was an unlikely magnate: a very quiet, pensively attractive man, who had founded a company twenty years earlier specialising in the manufacture of engineering models and – Henry's private passion – model railway engines. The company, moderately successful during its early years, had taken on war work, and had made enormous profits as a result. Henry was a man who carried good luck around with him everywhere; Elliot had been warned not to play cards with him.

'Good journey, was it?' he asked Elliot after a while.

'Fine, thanks. Just a short delay outside Crawley.'

'That's good.'

'How's Julia?'

'Very well, thank you. Busy with the house, of course, but she's been looking forward to seeing Helena.'

'Yes, I can imagine.'

Elliot finished his cigarette. He liked Henry very much; like Stanislav, Henry used words sparingly. Elliot felt there was a certain honesty about quiet people. One could always be sure that they meant what they said. He heard someone calling his name, and turned to see a beaming Helena waving him over to the group of friends who were standing under the glass canopy at the entrance to the station.

'Come on,' she called to him. 'I need to introduce you.'

He walked over to the group with Henry beside him, and smiled and shook hands with about fifteen different people, while Helena proceeded with a roll-call of names and nicknames; far too many for Elliot to retain.

As they walked out through the black gateposts at the entrance, Henry said to him, 'Did you know that these,' he pointed at the gateposts, 'are actually the original gun barrels from Brighton's Napoleonic gun battery?'

'No, I didn't.' Elliot said, shaking his head.

Someone, whose name Elliot had already forgotten, shouted, 'Don't admit that, he'll never let you marry Helena!'

The gang laughed. Someone else chipped in, 'Hey, Elliot, ask Henry for a tour of the locomotive sheds and marshalling yards! That'll buy you some favours. He'd let you marry all his daughters.' More laughter.

Henry looked at Elliot. 'They all think I'm obsessed with the railway.' He smiled, and then added more quietly, 'Perhaps I am.'

The three-car convoy drove at breakneck speed from the station, with the passengers singing songs from some light opera Elliot was unfamiliar with. He was relieved when the twenty-minute drive was over, and they arrived safely at the house. As the cars came to a standstill, the passengers spilled out of the vehicles onto the driveway. A very young maid, perhaps the same age as Elliot's patient Jenny, ushered them indoors anxiously, and was soon drowning in a pile of cashmere coats and silken shawls thrown at her by the incoming guests. As she carried the garments away across the hall, Elliot watched her furtively rub her cheek against the velvet wrap that lay on top of the pile. The expression on her face was a story of longing and envy and stifled hope. He didn't look away quickly enough, and she caught him watching her. She blushed furiously, and then hurried away through doors that were meant for servants only.

There was no formal dinner that evening; a buffet had been laid on, allowing for casual plates-on-knees dining. Helena gave an entertaining rendering of their meeting with Lady Maxime to laughter and applause: her imitation of Lady Max's nasal, high-pitched *darling, sweetie, how aaaare you?*, and the clumsy gesturing that accompanied everything she said was especially well-received. A young man whom Elliot vaguely recognised from a London club sat at the piano and hammered out his whole – limited – repertoire of popular songs. What was intended as a precursor to tomorrow's celebrations had now become a full-scale party.

Elliot didn't feel much like celebrating; he was tired and headachy, but had found a bottle of good brandy. He helped himself to the buffet, more to line his stomach than to satisfy any real hunger, and found a quiet spot near the window in the drawing room. When he had finished eating, and had his empty plate scooped out of his lap by a member of the unobtrusive staff, he sat back in his chair, a strongly geometric piece of furniture that would have caused his own parents to tut and frown in disapproval. It was made from tubular steel and black leather, and had the appearance of an oversized black bun, perched on short metal legs, with two fat, curved sausages placed one on top of the other to create back- and armrests. It was more comfortable to sit in than it looked.

Glancing around the room, a tribute to contemporaneity and good taste, an angry weariness began to spread through Elliot at the thought of the furnishings that cluttered his own home in Pimlico. He disliked them, but had never felt quite ready to discard them, as though he would be betraying his parents' memory if he did so. And yet there was nothing comforting about retaining such memories. On the contrary, the furniture represented an eloquent reminder of all that was flawed. It was all very well rationalising furniture; he could run through the arguments in his head: they were essentially items of practical use, his mother's dressing table, his father's wardrobes; a few of them of some financial value; inanimate, functional objects. Sofas and sideboards had no history out of context, no meaning, no soul. The problem was that they were prime targets for transference. His father's large oak bureau, for example, wasn't really oppressive; in truth, Elliot had displaced his infantile fears onto it because it had housed the cane his father had used on him and Ed. But he still caught himself flinching inwardly at times when he had to open the bureau. He couldn't transcend such base psychological processes just because he was aware of them, even believed to understand them. He made a sudden resolution to rid the house of the furniture on his return.

The people who had been standing just in front of Elliot's chair chatting and laughing gradually dispersed, and Elliot could see across the room to where Helena sat with her parents. He had lost count of how many brandies he had drunk, but knew from the weight of his head that it was probably too many. Through swollen eyelids he watched as Helena pulled a piece of paper out of her small handbag, and began reading from it to her parents. He wondered which one of her poems it was. She was sitting wedged between Henry and Julia on a white sofa, looking younger than ever, like a little girl in her Sunday best. Her mother's hand rested gently on her daughter's thigh, and as she read, her parents glanced at each other occasionally and smiled, an ancient smile that carried more meaning than any onlooker could imagine. Elliot felt a peculiar mixture of pride and envy – or was it jealousy? – as he watched them silently. The whole picture was one of finely diffused intimacy and private love. He longed deeply for some part of that.

'Elliot!'

It was an unfamiliar voice behind him. 'Elliot Taverley, is that you?'

He tried to turn around. It was difficult; in this chair, there was no leverage, all smooth curves and sleek leather. But there was no need; the woman who had addressed him came and stood in front of him. She was fairly old, in her late sixties, he guessed, not very tall but straight-backed, with a sun-tanned face covered in a web of fine wrinkles. Her very white hair had been piled carefully, elegantly, on top of her head. As she smiled at him, her lips parted slightly, and Elliot could see something red on her front teeth. For a split second, he thought she might have been punched in the face and not noticed she was bleeding, but on closer inspection, he could see that it was the crimson lipstick she wore on her lips that had rubbed off on her teeth. He made to stand up, but she waved him down.

'Elliot. I was sure it was you. As soon as we arrived I said to Andrew, "Look, that's George and Amelia's son," but he wasn't sure. So anyway, what a coincidence! And you're the one who's snagged the beautiful Helena. Lucky you! Oh, and I was so sad to read about your parents. It was pretty much one after the other, God bless their souls, wasn't it? It must have been so difficult for Amelia, losing George like that. But then, since Ed's death … I suppose they never really recovered, did they? Not fully, I mean.'

The woman had been joined by a small, wiry man with a huge black moustache, whom Elliot presumed was Andrew.

'It is Elliot Taverley, Andrew. What did I say? What did I tell you?'

Andrew opened his mouth, shut it again, and grunted. His wife carried on talking.

'And he's getting married to Helena, isn't that just wonderful!'

Elliot stood up. He felt self-conscious being talked down to like this. His legs wobbled briefly on the way up, and for a moment he thought he might have to sit down again, but he steadied himself – with difficulty – on one of the soft fat sausages on his chair. He was confused. He knew he was drunk, or close to it, but he could have sworn that he had never seen these people before in his life. He frowned, struggling to appear more sober than he felt.

'I'm sorry,' he began, increasingly bewildered at the fact that nothing, but nothing at all, was triggered in his memory as he looked at these people. He rubbed the side of his face with his hand. 'I'm not sure … I mean … have we been, um, introduced?'

It sounded stupid, and he knew it. Of course they must have been introduced; these people obviously knew his family. He made another attempt to revive the alcohol-sodden brain cells. No. Still nothing. His confusion must have shone through in his face. The woman elbowed her husband in the ribs, more forcefully than necessary, Elliot thought, and said in an exaggerated whisper, 'Bless him, he doesn't remember us.' And then to Elliot, 'All right, I'll put you out of your misery. But it isn't very gentlemanly to be so forgetful, mind you. Isabel Griffiths.'

She held out the back of her hand for Elliot to kiss. He obliged. 'And this, of course, is my husband Andrew.' Isabel nodded to her husband to shake Elliot's hand.

'You must think me terribly rude, Mrs Griffiths,' Elliot said, shaking Andrew's hand, which was rather limp. 'But to be frank, I can't remember where we met. You knew my parents?'

'Goodness me, Elliot, you have a terrible memory! It's a while back since we last saw each other, but surely we're not that unmemorable! Christmas '17. Andrew and I were back from India, and we stayed with your parents over Christmas. Ed was home from France, so handsome in his uniform, wasn't he? I can't recall what you were doing at the time, something virtuous, no doubt, and we all had a wonderful holiday! You remember now, don't you?'

Elliot didn't remember. Christmas 1917. That was just over three years ago. Had his parents had visitors that year? He would have remembered visitors from India, surely; his father was always going on about the place. And as for Ed being home for Christmas, he had no recollection at all. The warmth in the room was oppressive. Elliot inhaled deeply to feed his brain with some oxygen. He was sweating, and his shirt was sticking uncomfortably to his back, but it would have been bad-mannered to remove his jacket. The Griffiths were staring at him, expecting, no, demanding recognition. But the void in his memory was palpable. He could feel the frayed edges on either side of the memory gap – vague recollections of his mother's sixtieth birthday that November, a bout of chickenpox he had had, caught from one of his patients, in the January. It was as though the episode had been violently and arbitrarily ripped out of his consciousness. He wanted more detail from Mrs Griffiths: a description of the weather, the presents, the food, anything that might initiate some recollection. But he could hardly do that. They would think him mad, or rude, or both. He would have to bluff it. He rolled his eyes into the back of his head, and clucking his tongue as though he had just remembered, he said, 'Yes, yes, of course, Mr and Mrs Griffiths. From India.'

He took his handkerchief out of his pocket and patted his forehead. Andrew Griffiths wordlessly offered him a cigarette, which he took. He was desperate for another brandy.

'That's right,' Mrs Griffiths continued, obviously delighted to have found someone to talk to. 'No one's that forgetful, are they?'

'Are you still out there? India, I mean.' Elliot felt obliged to make an effort at conversation, as atonement for not having recognised them. But apparently, this was the wrong thing to say. She looked at her husband, who looked at the floor.

'No. We've been back for a year now. Well, the

climate wasn't really conducive to Andrew's health, was it, darling? Mmm?' She patted her husband on the arm. Elliot began to wonder whether the man chose not to say much, or whether he really was incapable of speech. Perhaps he thought that his wife did enough talking for the two of them.

'And India isn't what it used to be, anyway.' She pursed her lips in contempt, and gave Elliot a look to suggest that he were somehow to blame for the erosion of the high standards of Englishness in the Empire. The conversation had reached its natural end, Elliot thought. He glanced over to where Helena and her parents had been sharing their happy family moment. Julia and Henry had gone, and Helena sat, or rather lounged, on the sofa: legs up, shoes off, one arm on the armrest, the other casually draped over the curve of her hip, looking very grown-up again. She smiled at him, then frowned in the direction of the Griffiths couple, whose backs were turned to her, then looked back enquiringly at Elliot. Elliot shrugged his shoulders and shook his head. He turned to make his excuses to the Griffiths, but when he looked back, Helena had gone.

It was past three in the morning by the time Elliot went upstairs to his room, and he was suffering the premature onset of a hangover. His room was one of two small spare bedrooms at the very top of the house. Although he felt exhausted, it was another hour at least before he fell asleep, kept awake by several party diehards and their sporadic outbursts of laughter, which emanated from the room directly below his. A group of younger guests, apparently evicted from the ground floor, had moved the party into one of the larger first-floor guest rooms.

Whether due to his inebriation, or just his general tiredness, Elliot became gradually filled by a lazy, comforting melancholy. If, now and again, he thought with a nuance of self-pity, he could just let go of all pretence of contentment and emotional resilience, then he could retain a healthy psychological equilibrium. It was like an exercise in autogenic therapy, an ego defence mechanism. Besides, no one, barring Helena perhaps, could be happy all of the time. Tonight, for example. Although he enjoyed the loud, vibrant, joyful company of Helena's family, it wasn't the same as when he was alone with her. She anchored him, while at the same time giving so much of herself to others. Was that an intrinsic quality unique to Helena, or something her parents had carefully nurtured in her? And if the latter, what had his parents nurtured in him? Downstairs, someone had turned on the gramophone. The song, that was once a full orchestra, was now condensed to a tinny, nasal whine, that penetrated the ceiling into his room.

He turned onto his back, and then, encountering more resistance than expected, kicked the blankets out from where they had been tightly folded under the mattress. His legs explored their newfound freedom beneath the sheets. The bed was icy cold where his body hadn't warmed it. Almost at once he wished he were back under tightly tucked blankets, safely cocooned. He wondered whether marrying Helena would really give him that feeling, that sense of belonging he yearned for and that she took for granted. That unconditional, multilayered love that radiates between those who truly belong together. She was so perfect; sometimes the thought of her caressed a part of his soul that was almost too sensitive to touch.

The small sash window rattled in its frame, and he felt the draught in spite of the heavy velvet curtain. He turned onto his right side. The bed sagged in the middle, which was very uncomfortable; the mattress certainly wasn't as new as the bedlinen. Despite his physical tiredness, he found that holding his eyelids shut cost more effort than keeping them open. It was frustrating. Perhaps he could fall asleep with his eyes open? It was dark enough in the room. For no apparent reason he suddenly thought of Lady Max. His heartbeat quickened just thinking about her having known Ed. What were the odds? But she excited his mind as inexplicably as she had entered … He dozed off and woke again. He could hear the last of the revellers finally turn in. A door fell shut somewhere, and the house was suddenly silent, apart from the sound of distant snoring and the hissing of one or two insomniac cats outside. Finally, his thoughts drifted back to London, to the Chapel, to Nurse Robinson, to Raphael. Already, he had forgotten his promise to himself not to ruminate over his impending decision. But perhaps now was the best time to think things through. He hoped that the decision would make itself, if only he approached it logically, rationally … And then he was asleep; or rather, in that hypnagogic state between waking and sleeping, when the dreamer, paralysed and impotent, must witness that which the unconscious chooses to expose.

TEN

Late the next morning, Elliot climbed stiffly out of bed, rubbing his left shoulder and hip. Although he reckoned he'd had six or seven hours' sleep, he felt physically drained. He was hung-over and in need of a glass of water. He noticed the warmth in the room immediately: the small gas fire on the opposite wall had been lit, and the cramped room already felt quite cosy. He drew back the curtains. The tiny attic room window was fairly high up and set in a particularly deep reveal, forcing him to stand to get a view of anything more than the sky, and making him feel like a prisoner in some children's adventure story.

He opened the window, desperate to find out if the air was as fresh as it looked, and in poured the sound of high-pitched screams and laughter – the jubilant, frenzied shrieks only excitable children can produce, denoting the kind of acute excitement that can flip over into equally heightened despair at a moment's notice. Directly beneath his attic room window, he saw Maia's children in the garden, two boys and three girls, playing catch with one of the boys' shoes. The eldest child, a girl of about ten, was using her height advantage to keep the shoe from its owner. Judging by his facial expression, the boy was very close to tears, but with grim determination kept a rigid smile on his face as he leapt, short arms flailing, for his shoe. The tall girl must have noticed his anguish, for a moment later she let her arm drop and returned the shoe to him. The other children crowded around him as he sat on the grass to put it on and even helped him tie his shoelace. Elliot couldn't help but smile at this act of childish compassion.

He yawned and stretched, mentally debating whether to get back into bed for half an hour, or to get dressed. His stomach made the decision for him: it hadn't been properly filled the evening before, and was now growling its discontent. Elliot contemplated briefly the thought of a full English breakfast, and hurried to get ready, hoping there would still be some food left for him downstairs. But first he needed a shave. Next to the fire stood a wooden washstand with a basin and a jug of water. Elliot had no recollection of it from the night before. He tested the water in the jug with his hand; it was still lukewarm. One of the servants must have brought it up not long ago, while he was still asleep. He peered reluctantly into the mirror that hung above the washstand, and stroked his overnight growth with a cupped hand. He didn't look as bad as he had feared. His eyes weren't as bloodshot as expected, his grey irises were clear, and he looked generally well-slept. He stuck his tongue out and inspected it, paying close attention to its texture, the fine fissures around the edges, and the shades of greyish-yellow fur that stuck to the back. Nothing to be concerned about. He lathered the soap, and began shaving the coarse, dark stubble from his cheeks and throat.

He would never be described as handsome, certainly not in the way Ed had been; but he wasn't particularly unattractive either. Nothing was out of place, or horribly distorted; his nose, though longish, was in proportion to the rest of his face; the dark eyebrows were fairly bushy, but at least his eyes weren't set too close together; his lips were neither narrow nor fleshy. He pulled his lips back to reveal a set of teeth rooted in pink gums, slightly crowded at the front, but a healthy shade of ivory. Overall, he was quite unremarkable. What bothered him most about his appearance was the gauntness of his face, the way his cheeks looked as though they were being perpetually sucked in, making him look chronically undernourished. But then again, Helena must have seen something in him that she liked, and that was all that really mattered.

He finished shaving and patted his face dry. A long way off, he heard the children being called in for their lunch. It must be later than he had presumed. Why had nobody thought to wake him? He got dressed in a hurry, and then dashed down the two flights of stairs, taking just enough care not to fall. When he arrived in the breakfast room, he was relieved to see that breakfast was still being served. Julia Rickman was standing at the door, in a green silk, kimono-style robe, and greeted him with a soft "Good morning," as he entered the room. She was a woman of seemingly effortless elegance, slim and graceful, with pale, almost translucent skin that was remarkably unlined; silky blonde hair; a soft, dark pink, sensual mouth; and untroubled light blue eyes. From what he had seen of her home so far, Elliot could see how the house had been designed to reflect her lightness, her femininity, and understated beauty. The breakfast room was a case in point. The long, rectangular room was as airy and spacious as his bedroom was cramped, with long, south-facing windows that led through a set of French doors into the garden. Geometric sideboards had been placed on either side of the room, offering up a variety of breakfast dishes in elegant silver bowls: steaming kippers; eggs, fried and scrambled; crisp sausages; saffron kedgeree, and white china pots of tea and coffee.

The room was still fairly full, but Elliot spotted Helena immediately. She was having an animated conversation with the young man sitting beside her, only very lightly made-up, with a touch of rouge to pink her cheeks. Her short black hair, which she painstakingly straightened when back in London, had returned to its natural state of soft, girlish curls. Her beauty was perhaps less flawless than her mother's, but to Elliot, this made her somehow more honest and more attainable. When he had helped himself to a plate of eggs and toast, he went over and sat down next to her. She leant in towards him and kissed him on the cheek.

'Sleep well?'

'Yes, eventually.' As if to prove his point, he stifled an oncoming yawn.

'Oh, by the way –' Helena half-turned in her chair towards the young man on her right. 'This is Tom. Tom, this is Elliot.'

'How do you do?'

'Nice to meet you.' They shook hands. Tom had a pleasant handshake; his hand was firm and dry and big-knuckled. He had ash-blond hair that flopped forward in a fringe, affording him, it seemed, a convenient curtain behind which to hide his light green eyes.

'Tom came with Sybilla,' Helena explained. 'She's still in bed, apparently. I was just telling Tom about the other week, when you analysed Jung's handwriting. He doesn't seem convinced ...'

Tom blushed; his face turned a pale pink with deep red mottles. 'I wasn't being disrespectful, I just said that many a theory was founded on the so-called science of phrenology several decades ago, and that it seems to me that graphology may be criticised along similar lines.'

Elliot dropped his head until his chin was almost touching his chest. Then he took a deep breath and looked back up at Tom.

'I understand your scepticism, Tom, but I would call that a false analogy. Surely you must appreciate that the analysis of a person's handwriting is more valid than the interpretation of cranial lumps and bumps. I would point out that in terms of empirical validity, graphology has nothing in common with nineteenth-century pseudo-science. It's all a matter of insight, really. Forgive me for saying so, but your ignorance is based on widespread misconceptions.'

Tom turned even redder, and by the movement of muscle around his jaw, Elliot could see that he had laid into him more than was justified. Even Helena looked embarrassed, probably wishing she'd never mentioned Tom's comments to Elliot in the first place. She put her hand on Elliot's and squeezed gently.

'You know, it'd be awfully good fun if you'd do someone's handwriting tonight!'

Tom agreed. 'Yes, we'd get people to write out a poem or something, and Elliot would have to guess whose writing it was! That would be one hell of a party trick.'

'Go on, darling, what do you think? It was so impressive when you did it the other day. Do it for me?'

Elliot looked down at his plate. The scrambled eggs

– pale yellow with flecks of black pepper – looked back at him. A long thin rectangle of light moved almost imperceptibly across the table; its outline sharp and distinct, then blurred, until the rectangle disappeared completely as the sun stepped momentarily behind a curtain of frantic cloud. The wind was gusting audibly, and Elliot wondered if there was a storm brewing. This wasn't what he'd expected when he got up this morning. For him, a graphological analysis involved the slow, laborious task of scrutinising every inch of the writing for major and minor patterns of script. He had to gauge whether certain traits appeared consistently or erratically; make judgements regarding the harmony, rhythm, tension, dynamism. He had been showing off to Helena with Jung's letter; he'd carried out a comprehensive analysis on it a long time before he had shown it to her, and now she was making him out to be some kind of entertainer.

'Look, Helena, I can't do that. Really. I'm just not comfortable doing that kind of thing in front of a crowd.' He lowered his voice so that Tom would only be able to hear if he moved forward noticeably. 'And anyway, it could damage my reputation. Imagine if there happened to be someone here tonight who knows me, or anyone at the Chapel, and they saw me using graphology as a party trick. I'd lose any chance I had of legitimising it as a therapeutic technique. You understand, don't you?'

He hoped she would; she had been looking forward to the party for weeks, and he didn't want to be the one who spoiled it for her. She pushed her lower lip forward and then pulled her shoulders up and down quickly, as if shrugging off her disappointment.

"Course I do,' she said, smiling. 'Come on, eat up, there's lots to do before tonight.'

The rest of the day hurried by in the blur of activity and noise of frantic preparations for the evening's celebrations. There were angry voices coming from the kitchen – Julia had hired outside caterers for the first time, much to the chagrin of the cook; the children were running amok, intoxicated with excitement, as well as with furtive sips taken from a half bottle of sherry the oldest girl had found in the drawing room; servants were struggling with the mountain of luggage that had grown in the hall; and Helena and her sisters, who had volunteered to prepare the dining room for the dinner that evening, were engaged in loud, apparently hilarious, discussions about silverware and seating arrangements.

In the afternoon, Elliot decided to take sanctuary in the library. As he entered the room, whose door was tucked away, almost hidden, beneath the grand staircase, the tension he'd felt all day began to dissipate. The room was noticeably more masculine than the rest of the house, the tall space kept low by a ceiling of dark, closely-spaced joists, and sections of oak panelling on the walls above the solid bookshelves. Two heavy leather armchairs faced each other in sober consensus across an oriental rug; the room's only compromise to modernism was the angular, black marble fireplace, which despite being set back in the corner warmed the room nicely. It was a very calm space, and the thick studded door kept out all audible trace of the mayhem outside. Elliot browsed the shelves for something to read. He was pleasantly surprised to find a copy of Fabian Essays in Socialism, among the many books on railways: Our Iron Roads, by Frederick S. Williams; Stockton to Darlington, 1821-1863 by R.B. Montgomery; George Stephenson: the Greatest Victorian, by William Papen; and even an engineer's operation manual. The occasional Dickens or Woolf appeared on the shelves, most likely a concession to Helena's tastes, he thought. The classification of the books was not immediately apparent; the books were not sorted alphabetically, or even according to subject matter. It was only when Elliot stepped back from the bookcase to get a better look at the higher shelves that he realised that the books had been sorted according to size and colour of binding. He laughed to himself. There was no ambiguity of intentions here, just another sacrifice made to the integrity of design.

He was about to choose a book with which to sit down and read, when he heard a soft coughing behind him. He spun around and saw Henry standing by a small, low-set window. He was wearing some kind of dressing-gown, and clutched his pipe in his right hand.

'I didn't see you there,' Elliot said, almost in confession. He was startled, mentally retracing his actions since he entered the room a few minutes ago, trying to recall whether he had done something that might look odd to an onlooker. He was fairly sure he hadn't done anything strange, but the feeling of self-consciousness lingered. 'I thought the room was empty.'

'I gathered that,' Henry replied. He nodded towards the bookcase. 'Please, be my guest. I'm sure you'll find something of interest.'

'Thanks.' Elliot turned back to the books and grabbed one at random. Henry gestured for him to take a seat in one of the leather chairs, and Elliot complied. For a while, the two men remained in silence; Henry browsing the shelves, pipe in hand, Elliot on his chair, pretending to read *Karachi to Khyber: Railways of the Raj*, wondering how long he would have to sit here before he could make a polite retreat. After a long ten minutes, Henry turned, paused, and said, 'Did you know that to enable passengers to verify that they were not being overcharged, railways had to place mileposts alongside their routes, with intermediate posts every quarter of a mile, because fares were calculated to the nearest farthing?'

Elliot looked up in surprise. He looked briefly over his shoulder to check whether Henry was addressing him, or someone else in the room. No; still just the two of them were there. 'I didn't know that.'

'Yes, that's often the way, in my experience. Enforced integrity – corporate or otherwise – is better than no integrity at all. Wouldn't you agree?'

It wasn't so much a question as an invitation to concur.

'I suppose so.' Elliot answered quickly, without really thinking about what he was agreeing with. Had he thought about it, he would have argued that enforced integrity is a contradiction in terms; that moral uprightness comes willingly or not at all. But he wasn't quite sure of Henry's intentions, and didn't want to offend. Outside the library window the wind was blowing more forcefully, whipping several scrawny branches of forsythia in syncopated rhythm against the window pane. Henry didn't seem to notice, or at least, he didn't make any attempt to raise his voice beyond the noise.

'Integrity, honesty, these are important attributes. Your father, he was a barrister, Helena tells me.'

Elliot raised his eyebrows at the sudden change of subject, but answered all the same. 'Yes, but he passed away not long ago. Both my parents did.' Was it just him, or was this conversation as contrived as it felt? He crossed and then uncrossed his legs.

'Mmm. I'm very sorry.' Henry said. 'Any brothers or sisters?'

'A brother, Edward. But he died two years ago.' It sounded macabre, almost comic. His closest family members dropping like flies. There was an odd, funereal tension in the room, and it was all Elliot could do to prevent himself from breaking into a nervous laugh. He bit down on his lower lip and waited for some response from Henry. There was none. Instead, Henry lit his pipe in deep concentration. The grey smoke that curled through the air to hover just below the ceiling matched the colour of his hair. His eyes narrowed as the smoke drifted past his face, accentuating the lines that ran from the outer corner of his eyes down his cheeks to the side of his face. Just then, a black rain cloud passed over the sun, throwing the dark room into even darker shadow. For a brief moment, all of Henry's sophistication and dignity were suspended, and he looked like nothing more than a haggard old man. But the moment passed, as did the rain cloud, and the golden light

spilled back into the room. When the pipe was lit to his satisfaction, he exhaled, his eyes resting on Elliot, thoughtful,
scrutinising. The forsythia branches were still tapping on
the glass, as though asking to be let in.

'Let me be honest with you, Elliot. I like you. I am
pleased that Helena has chosen someone like you to marry. You seem to possess a good amount of decency. But
I must tell you: I am suspicious of people with no family
ties. I feel that can give them a licence to ...' he paused,
evidently searching for the right word. 'Let's just say they
have less to lose. A man with no family is free to do as he
wishes, without consideration for others' needs or desires,
and with no one to hold him accountable. Family, on the
other hand, can be a terrible burden. So much dependence,
so much expectation –' he broke off, and turned away to
relight his pipe.

The silence was lengthy and pointed. Elliot felt that
he'd been caught off guard; he wasn't sure if this was the
obligatory father-of-the-bride speech, a monologue during
which he was expected to sit quietly and take note. Perhaps
Henry was waiting for him to speak. It was tricky, and puz-
zling. He watched Henry's back, and began to count silently
in his head. If Henry hadn't said anything by the time he
got to thirty, he would make his excuses and leave. Twenty-five, twenty-six, twenty-seven ... But Henry turned back
to face Elliot and continued.

'It's all a matter of give and take, I suppose. A well-
worn philosophy, but true nonetheless. Incidentally, I'm
pleased that you don't ridicule me for sharing those snippets
of railway trivia – unless you do it behind my back.'

'No, no, of course not.' It was like being in the head-master's office. Elliot wasn't quite sure whether he was be-ing admonished or praised, but either way, he was feeling increasingly uncomfortable. He sat up straight in his chair. 'Listen, Henry –' he began, but Henry, pipe in mouth, held up his hand to interrupt him. He puffed on his pipe several times, the thick, swirling smoke briefly obscuring his face.

'Please, let me finish. This is not an attempt to belittle you, or intimidate you. I expect you to understand this. You want to marry Helena; I want her to be happy. I want you to know that I will be erecting milestones to safeguard her happiness. You will love, encourage and support her. You will never neglect her, hurt her, or give her reason to be afraid of you. It is not an easy task; it will take effort. You will carry the burden, but you will reap the rewards. You will be where I am now. I am offering you a family, Elliot, but think hard before you accept.'

He sat down. He had finished his monologue. There was something vaguely threatening about what he had said, and it occurred to Elliot how he had misjudged the man, how seriously vulnerable first impressions were to distor-tion. Henry wasn't a thoughtful, reticent gentleman; he was a shrewd businessman, not shy, but fiercely protective of what was his. His speech had made Elliot feel uncomfort-able; not because of its content, which was, in a way, flat-tering, but because Elliot couldn't shake off the feeling that he had been so effortlessly probed. Was he really that trans-parent, or was this a speech Henry would have given to any prospective son-in-law? He thought about how to phrase a pertinent question that wouldn't make his uncertainty too obvious, but there was a sudden stillness in the room, and Elliot understood that it was now time for him to leave.

It was with great relief that he closed the library door behind him. The noise in the house had risen to a clamour: it struck him in the face and made him feel dizzy after the dark calm in the library. That suited him fine. He wanted to immerse himself in the goings-on, join in the activities, and not think about that odd exchange with Henry. Julia and Cassandra were discussing with the exasperated house-keeper where to accommodate some unexpected overnight guests; Helena and Maia were busy in the dining room with some last-minute flower arranging; the children, still intox-icated, but more subdued than earlier, were squabbling qui-etly in the drawing room. Helena spotted him, and waved excitedly.

'What do you think?' she shouted through cupped hands, before gesturing with outspread arms to the space around her. Elliot was impressed. They had managed to transform the entire ground floor into what resembled an oriental food bazaar. In this impressive space, the women had created intimate dining areas with eight small round ta-bles, each seating six guests, and elaborate drapes and fabric room dividers around each table. It was all very stylish and opulent, and tonight, he was determined to put his politics aside and indulge in the luxuries of the very rich, if only for Helena's sake. He smiled to her and nodded his approval.

Looking past the tables through to the conservatory, Elliot could see a long, cherrywood dining table, the kind used for formal dinners at which guests could only converse politely with those sitting next to them or directly opposite, so that one's evening could be either appalling or delightful, depending on one's immediate neighbour. He was thankful that the Rickmans were not the kind of family to insist on such formalities. Indeed, on this occasion, the dining table had been converted into a gift repository: it was heaving under the weight of countless stunningly wrapped parcels, large and small; some of them belated birthday gifts for Maia, the others anniversary presents for Julia and Henry. Earlier in the day, Elliot had watched as the sheer abundance and unattainability of the gifts had caused upset among the children: amid loud sobbing and gentle pleading (the children), and open bribes and veiled threats (the nursemaids), the area around the table had been declared strictly out-of-bounds to anyone under the age of twelve. With a tiny flash of bitterness, Elliot realised that he had never received as many presents in a whole lifetime, let alone on one occasion. He shook himself, at once startled and embarrassed by his petty envy. How could he begrudge anyone their birthday presents? It must be the effects of that peculiar conversation with Henry. It had left him feeling confused; he hadn't enjoyed being spoken to like that, like a child who has smashed a neighbour's window. He turned to go upstairs and get dressed for dinner, forcing a smile at Helena as he passed her on the stairs. She called him back, kissed him softly on the mouth, and handed him a small yet perfectly formed red rose. He shrugged, with a trace of annoyance, but she just whispered in his ear "For your buttonhole", and skipped lightly back down the stairs to join her sister.

ELEVEN

Elliot's earlier predictions about the weather were borne out. As the evening approached, the rain clouds lost interest in their game of hide and seek with the sun and moved in with alarming speed, covering the sky with a low-lying cushion of dark grey. When the first guests – those that were not staying overnight – began to arrive, the storm burst through and nobody was spared a drenching.

Very few guests had turned down the invitation to the party, which was above all an opportunity to satisfy their curiosity and have a good look at the new house. Elliot got himself a glass of milk from the kitchen – with last night in mind, he had decided not to start drinking too early in the evening – and shuffled about the drawing room, introducing himself now and again to those who appeared interested enough to know who he was, waiting to be seated for dinner and resisting the temptation to fill up on canapes. The maids, he noticed, were dressed in different, upgraded versions of their regular uniforms: the black skirts were longer, and appeared more fitted, and the white waist-level aprons had noticeably more lace than the ones they had been wearing the night before. He looked out for the young maid he had embarrassed yesterday, hoping he would be able to make amends somehow, perhaps by being especially friendly. He had put the encounter with Henry out of his mind, and was looking forward to a pleasant evening. In fact, he was feeling more relaxed than he had been for a long time; London, the Chapel, his caseload - all seemed at a safe distance now. It would do him good, this weekend. Someone began playing the piano in the drawing room, and it was with a definite sense of optimism that he sauntered, almost danced, towards the music.

As he entered the drawing room, he heard laughter from the other side of the room; unmistakably Helena. He looked across, and saw her standing in front of the huge Salome marble fireplace, sharing a private joke with her sister Cassandra. She wore a blood red silk dress with a hip-level waistline and a black fringe that reached well below her knee, with a black velvet choker and jet earrings. Maia must have helped curl her bobbed hair, so that a single dark brown lock fell forward on either side of her face, framing it perfectly. Elliot strolled over to her, smiling, only now noticing that the buttonhole rose she had instructed him to wear matched her dress perfectly. How foolish his earlier thoughts seemed now! She took hold of his hand and squeezed it, leaning forward to kiss him. She tasted faintly of cinnamon and red wine. Before he could tell her how beautiful she looked, a large hand grabbed his shoulder and spun him around.

'Dr. Taverley, I presume.' The man standing in front of Elliot wore a heavy, full-length cassock, which, judging by its smell, hadn't been washed since the man's ordination. He was red-faced and fat, and had the fleshiest ear lobes Elliot had ever seen.

'How do you do?' Elliot replied, offering his hand.

'It's a pleasure, I'm sure. John Roper, Father John; I suppose you've heard all about me?'

The arse, Elliot thought, thinking back to Helena's

description of him in the taxi, but replied much more diplomatically, 'Yes, this and that.'

'Good, good,' Roper said, pulling his big lips back over his teeth in a smile. The whiteness of his dog collar made his teeth appear all the more yellow. The crowd had begun to move towards the areas where dinner was being served. As guests discovered the seating arrangements, little cries of marvellous, how bijou!, and so clever, Julia, were heard, as everybody decided where, and with whom, they were going to sit for dinner. Elliot reacted too slowly. John Roper had taken Helena's elbow and guided her to a table near one of the tall windows. A white sari adorned with silver embroidery had been suspended from the ceiling like a huge sail, partially obscuring the table from the view of the other tables. As Elliot took a seat beside her, Helena looked at him apologetically. He shrugged. Roper sat to the right of Helena; to Elliot's left sat Mr and Mrs Evans, a quiet, middle-aged couple from Wales, and to the right of Roper sat a young ginger-haired man, Nigel, who was obviously infatuated with Helena and hung on every one of her words.

'So what do you specialise in, doctor?' the priest asked, breathing whisky fumes into Elliot's face. Although his speech was perceptibly slurred, he gave the impression of one who was experienced in dinner-party conversation, even when intoxicated. Not unlike his own father, Elliot thought, although that was where the similarity ended.

His father had been scrupulous about his personal hygiene, for one thing, but also adamantly anti-religious. Elliot had vivid memories of the occasion his father had taken him and Ed to a Catholic mass, to demonstrate to them the "undignified absurdity of the human worship of imaginary deities". Elliot was seven years old, and Ed was twelve, and they had set off one morning, with empty, grumbling stomachs, to enter the local church, a building they had up to this point ignored for as long as he could remember. Despite his father's subsequent systematic and contemptuous dissection of the mass, Elliot's overriding sensation had been one of awe: the strangeness of the place; the exotic, overwhelming scent of incense that made him want to sneeze; the reverential echo, which amplified every sound, every movement; the austerity of the cold, hard pews, and the even harder kneeling stools; the waxy smell of wood polish that crept up his nose when his face came close to the pew in front; the intimidating, angry man in a black and purple robe who stood at the altar with his back to the congregation and spoke in a language Elliot had yet to encounter in school. But above all, he was taken aback by the behaviour of the worshippers, who knew every detail of the rituals off by heart, a synchrony of genuflections and chanting and head bowing. It was almost beautiful; it was undoubtedly impressive. But even at seven years of age, he knew better than to share his thoughts with his father, who held the view that religion encouraged the ignorant and unenlightened, and was therefore a danger to a healthy society.

'I specialise in psycho-analysis,' Elliot said, as a waitress set down the hors d'oeuvres: thinly-sliced veal on a bed of sliced lemons with a tuna dressing. 'But I'm not sure this is an appropriate topic for the dinner table.' He looked down at the vitello tonnato on his plate, hoping his comment would suffice to end the conversation before it started. A vain hope.

'Freudian, eh?' The priest drained his glass.

Elliot was hungry, and in no mood for this sort of conversation. 'Not exactly,' he answered, but remained unheard.

'Well, I'm telling you this now: as far as I'm concerned, the human soul is no business of yours. Psycho-analysis indeed. It's disgusting!' This was emphasised with a fist on the table. Mrs Evans gave a little gasp of surprise. 'Sons wanting to have sex with their mothers? The whole idea is repellent to anyone with an ounce of Christian morals.'

Elliot sighed, and, knowing he might regret it later, waved one of the staff over to pour him a large glass of wine.

'It's quite a dilemma, isn't it?' Mr Evans said suddenly. The other diners turned to look at him.

'Mmm? What's that you're saying, man?' Roper asked.

Evans looked slightly embarrassed, as though he had just been thinking out loud and hadn't meant to draw attention to himself. Then he said quietly, 'The dilemma of the Church in the modern age. Psychology is encroaching directly on what has, for the longest time, been the strict concern of the Church. When you think about it, the psyche, the essence of man, hitherto elusive, is now becoming tangible. And tangible through science, not religion.'

He spoke softly, enunciating his words precisely as if to test their meaning on his tongue before releasing them to his listeners. His wife smiled knowingly beside him.

'I quite agree,' Elliot said. In spite of his conviction that religion was little more than institutionalised superstition, he wasn't entirely unsympathetic towards the Church's dilemma with regard to psychology in general, and psycho-analysis in particular. Of course, it wasn't the first time in history that science had threatened to rock the foundations of religion – but, as far as he was aware, religion had survived more or less intact.

Evans continued, his tone still modest, but more assertive than before. 'But the truly irreconcilable difference between psychology and religion is even more fundamental.' He paused, thereby ensuring himself of the full attention of his listeners. Perhaps he was a teacher by profession, Elliot thought.

'You see, psychologists – if they carry out their work seriously and competently – aim to work themselves redundant.'

'Please explain,' Helena said, wiping the corners of her mouth with a starched white napkin. She was obviously enjoying the discussion.

'Yes, do,' Nigel added, obviously eager to find some point of agreement with Helena.

'The analyst's goal is to guide the patient into self-reliance, to be no longer dependent on therapy or the therapist. The priest, on the other hand,' Evans nodded towards Roper, 'will never be in that position. Thanks to the concept of original sin, he is kept in perpetual employment. The construction of original sin not as an act, but as a state, a permanent privation, is quite ingenious. Try as he might, the believer will never be truly free from sin, and from guilt.'

Elliot smiled. It wasn't often that he came across a kindred spirit outside of work, and such an eloquent one at that.

'But then along came Freud,' Evans continued, 'and offered us an elegant, demystified, scientific explanation of the innate tendency to evil in terms of the unconscious, the Id. What is now to become of these priests and vicars, and the power they wield over their flocks, once they are no longer the keepers of souls, once they lose their supreme authority in matters of faith and morals?'

All heads turned to look at Roper, who sat shovelling a forkful of pale pink tuna into his mouth, breathing heavily through a red-veined nose. He looked up at Evans with disdain, but then continued eating.

'Your apprehension is understandable, Father John,' Evans concluded. His wife gave his hand a gentle squeeze.

'That was a very interesting – and articulate – lecture, if I may say so,' Elliot said warmly as the main course arrived. 'Do you have a background in psychology?'

Evans shook his head. 'Sadly, no. No formal credentials, if that's what you mean. It is a ... a personal interest. I believe that we have experienced a trauma – a collective trauma – as a result of this meaningless war. It is essential that we determine our own recovery, rather than leaving it in the hands of –' he gestured towards Roper, who was now too drunk to notice what was going on around him. 'You see, my son, our son –' he broke off, his hands trembling slightly as he picked up his knife and fork.

'Our son was about to enter the seminary when he was called up by the Army four years ago. Now he sits in his bedroom in Cardiff and can't remember his own name, let alone recognise his parents,' his wife said. 'He's been like ever since he came home. Godless.' Her voice was hard and devoid of emotion. It occurred to Elliot that she had long since learned to function beyond grief.

'I'm sorry,' he said, realising at that moment that they had no use for his sympathy. He looked at Helena, who was close to tears.

'No, I'm sorry,' Evans said. 'I didn't mean to spoil your evening.' He excused himself and left the table, quickly followed by his wife. They didn't return for the rest of the meal, and the others were left to finish in a despondent, uncomfortable silence.

After dinner came the obligatory speeches, toasting Julia and Henry's long and happy marriage, with belated birthday wishes for Maia, followed by the unwrapping of presents. Elliot took the opportunity to excuse himself and seek some fresh air. He made his way swiftly through the crowded room to where a set of French doors opened into the gardens. He stepped outside and shut the doors behind him, hoping he would be able to enjoy some peace and quiet before someone else had the same idea. The storm had run its course, leaving behind a clear, inky-velvet sky, pinpricked with stars. It was cold, but after several hours of sharing the same smoky atmosphere with fifty others, the air felt fresh and crisp, and with every breath he felt more invigorated. He tugged at his bowtie, alleviating the tightness he felt around his neck. The moon was plump and bright, so radiant that it was hard to believe that it was not a source of light itself. So nice to be out of London, he thought, to be able to see beyond the smoke screen that filtered out the sun by day and veiled the stars at night. He stood on the patio with his back to the house and basked in the expanse of the grounds, gazing out at the generous lawn in front of him, which sprawled from hues of greeny-grey into blackness.

It hadn't been his conscious intention to go for a walk, but the gravel path that led off the semicircular patio into the darkness of the gardens seemed too inviting to resist. He walked for a while, following the path until it reached its destination – a small white summer house, as fresh and new as the main building. In contrast to the main house, however, this little structure was quite plain, and very charming. Elliot tried the handle on the glass door, expecting it to be locked. To his surprise, and delight, the door opened, and he stepped inside. The summer house comprised one main room and a small kitchenette in the back. The room was empty, aside from some builder's rubble scattered on the floor. It seemed colder in here than outside, but Elliot decided to stay for a cigarette and flipped over a wooden crate to sit on.

He was grateful for the quiet, and began to reflect on how his life might change once he and Helena were married. They would, of course, remain in London, but the Rickmans were a very close, stable, almost clannish family, who expected any outsider joining their tight circle to adapt to their way of doing things. His conversation with Henry had certainly reinforced this impression. Elliot didn't really mind now; he laughed quietly to himself at his earlier irritation at Henry's attitude. The man had been slightly sanctimonious, that was true, but he hadn't meant any harm. No, Elliot didn't mind changing his ways, if that was what it took, in order to be with Helena. He could almost hear his mother's critical tut-tutting at the thought of any action that might upset the precarious social balance that gave individuals their role and meaning. His mother had opposed the vote for women, and had certainly believed Helena's independent lifestyle to be potentially corrupting, if not outright immoral. If women began to act like men, well, what role would there be for men to play? To her mind, the purpose of gender hierarchy was unambiguous; women's suffrage was the beginning of the decay of social harmony. She had warmed to Helena eventually, though, and Elliot suspected that she had privately hoped that he and Helena would settle down, once married, to become a nice, traditional couple.

His father hadn't really known Helena – he had never shown much interest in Elliot's private affairs. He had met Helena briefly at the same fund-raiser where Elliot had first been introduced to her, but that had been only several months before his death, during which there never seemed to be an appropriate opportunity for a second meeting. Elliot was sure his father would have come around to liking her, eventually. And Ed ... For the first time ever, Elliot wondered how Ed and Helena would have got along. She was certainly his type – in fact, come to think of it, they were really rather alike in many ways: attractive, confident, charismatic. The qualities he had admired, envied, in his brother were the same qualities that had attracted him to Helena. He shifted uncomfortably on his makeshift seat.

What would a Freudian make of that? He shook his head and lit another cigarette, even though his tongue already felt unpleasantly leathery from too much smoking. No, it was much simpler than that: Helena and Ed shared characteristics that were universally attractive, and that was why he had fallen in love with her, not because of some warped psycho-sexual displacement. Besides, beyond their similarities lay a whole raft of differences. Helena, for instance, possessed a benevolence that touched everything she did, in spite of her apparent frivolity. But Ed, he had a fierceness about him, a passion that had sometimes threatened to spill over into malice. Elliot took a last drag on his cigarette as he returned in his memory to occasions where Ed had seemed just to pull back from the brink of brutality. Then suddenly, unexpectedly, Elliot had the disturbing vision of Ed and Helena making love, forcefully, violently – and for the shortest time, he felt glad, and secure, that Ed was no longer alive. He let his cigarette drop to the floor, and crushed it carefully under his shoe.

Leaving the summer house, he gently closed the door behind him, hoping he would have an opportunity to return when the summer had arrived. He began to make his way back down the path towards the house. From where he was approaching, he could see the details, both subtle and prominent, that made the Rickmans' house an architectural delight. It was a cool, white building, which seemed to have been designed with the intention of creating a stark, tangible division between notions of masculinity and femininity. Already, Elliot had noticed the differences inside the house between Julia's areas – the reception rooms, the kitchen

– and Henry's areas – the library, the smoking room. The interior design portrayed a dynamic equilibrium between austerity and playfulness, sobriety and fantasy, asceticism and eroticism. These differences were echoed on the exterior of the house's main wing. All over the facade, graceful curves battled it out with blunt, unmoulded blocks; the rectilinear but brutally understated entrance was contrasted with elaborate carving elsewhere on the stonework.

In contrast, the service wing was noticeably less sophisticated in design. It had been conceived, Elliot presumed, to reflect the Rickmans' ideal of what hired help should be: practical, unambitious, and attracting as little attention as possible. In fact, as he stood staring up at the dark service wing, one window on the first-floor unexpectedly stood out from the others, as someone in the room switched a light on. Elliot watched as that someone walked backwards and forwards across the room, and then towards the window. At first, he could only make out from the person's square shoulders and large build that it was a man, and he thought back to the Rickmans' staff, curious to know if he'd seen the man among the serving staff earlier tonight. As he searched his memory for recognition, he slowly became aware that the man was looking towards him; at least, from where Elliot stood, roughly fifty yards away from the house, it appeared as though the person was looking directly at him. Elliot looked away hurriedly. His curiosity had got the better of him yesterday, when he had invaded the young maid's private moment. He didn't want to feel guilty of that again. He waited for what seemed like a decent amount of time, perhaps half a minute or so, and then glanced back at the window. It was a natural reaction, he told himself – if the man in the window was actually watching him then he had every right to stare back. Indeed, the light was still on, and the man was still there.

Then suddenly, the world around him dropped away into blackness. The muffled sound of piano music danced in waves through the French doors of the drawing room into the garden, across the wet lawn, into Elliot's ear, and played out its acoustic rhythm on his ear drum. But Elliot didn't hear it; just like he didn't feel the damp, oozing from the sodden grass through his shoe leather, turning his feet cold and clammy; didn't smell the acrid remains of the cold smoke coming from a minor fire that had just been extinguished behind the kitchen: didn't taste the stale strand of tobacco from his last cigarette that was still lodged in his back teeth. Every one of his senses dead. With the exception of his sight; his vision tunnelled in a rush of dizzying velocity all the way to the face of the man staring back at him through the window, a face he recognised, a face unmistakably familiar. It was Raphael.

Twelve

When he was a young boy, Elliot suffered regularly from night terrors; those nocturnal episodes of private wretchedness that lasted minutes but felt never-ending. One such evening, his mother had tucked him tenderly into bed, bending over him to place goodnight kisses on his tentatively closed eyelids, smelling of warm milk and lavender soap, hush-a-ba-bairn; Elliot with a smile on his little face and his head on a soft white cloud of a pillow, as his fragile, immature mind briefly relived the excitements of the day gone by: the intense thrill of flying, as Ed swung him around by one arm and a leg; the acute misery of sore, smarting, grazed hands and knees when Ed couldn't hold him any longer and he fell; until finally, he was asleep.

BOOM! He was woken up by the noise. It was coming from underneath his bed, a sonorous pervasive bass of a noise, relentlessly expanding, growing into an indefinable presence with its own terrifying rhythm, boom-ba-boom-ba-boom, increasing in intensity and volume and nearness, and then spiralling into a frenzy above him. His eyes were wide open now, his pupils the only part of him he could move; the room was pitch-black, but he could see everything clearly. Behind his head, at the end of the bed, he felt it, watching him with intense interest, making the noise swirl faster and faster above his body until the noise-helix began to descend, very slowly, before landing on his chest, crushing the air out of his lungs until he couldn't breathe; he was panicking, trying to shift his arms and legs, but he couldn't move. He wanted to scream for help, wanted his lavender-smelling mother to come and save him from it, make it go away but he couldn't open his mouth; he was breathing rapidly through his nose, trying to get more air into his lungs, he was dizzy; and the terror was unbearable, he was so afraid, convinced he was going to die ... until, overwhelmed with dread, anxiety, fear, he passed out.

In the Rickmans' garden, a veil of blue clouds shrouded the moon, colouring the darkness purple. The wind had subsided; the resulting stillness in the garden was almost intolerable. Then the music from the piano started up again, an optimistic, jazzy tune, bouncing intrusively into the heavy silence. Elliot stood completely motionless on the path, reliving every night terror from his childhood. For the longest time he was unable to move, his eyes fixed on the window, Raphael gazing back down at him. He felt the crushing weight on his chest, the violent sensation of asphyxia; he heard the deafening roar of noise coming from somewhere behind him, smothering the jazz piano; but worst of all was the total paralysis. And then ... then suddenly he was running, sprinting, through the cold, black air, barely aware of the sound his footsteps were making as they tore through the gravel; the thoughts in his head like shards of glass, tearing, cutting, bloodying; excruciating like no headache he had ever experienced. That face in the window; the soft, vulnerable stare. It was him. Why was he there? What did he want? The distance to the house was short – fifty yards perhaps – but the path stretched out infinitely ahead of him ... seemed to increase the faster he ran. His legs were heavy;

the adrenalin was coagulating the blood in his body, turning it into a thick, sticky syrup. He ran and ran; confusion and anger blossoming with every stride.

The cold air stung his wet eyes, making him blink furiously. His nose was running badly, but he had no time to get his handkerchief out. He wiped his nose with the back of his hand. Finally, he reached the house, out of breath and stretched out his arms to open the French doors. He grabbed the handles and wrenched the doors towards him and the warmth of the room punched him in the face. He momentarily lost his bearings, crashing into an empty table and upsetting a bottle of wine. He gathered himself quickly, oblivious to the stares and whispers of the other dinner guests ('Drunk, do you think?'; 'Isn't that Helena's chap?') and weaved his way past the tables and chairs, across the dining room into the hall. The black and white chequered floor tiles in the hallway seemed to dance in front of his eyes, so he lifted his gaze and focused on the broad wooden uprights that were spaced out evenly along the walls in order to retain his balance. Helena was standing by the main staircase, talking to Cassandra. As he lurched towards the stairs, she held an arm out to him.

'Elliot, I was wondering where you'd got to. Are you all right? You look terrible.'

Elliot brushed her arm off him; he didn't see her, didn't hear her, didn't stop. Up the stairs, two, three steps at a time ... his lungs begging for mercy. Where was the service wing from here, left or right? Turn right ... down the landing. Helena was running after him, calling him.

'Elliot, what's the matter?' Louder. 'ELLIOT!!'

This time he heard her. Needed to say something, tell her something. Opened his mouth, momentarily afraid he wouldn't be able to speak. But the words came out in bursts; rasping, hoarse, 'I saw him, I have to find him. He's here somewhere.'

Another door. Yes, another corridor; dark, shabby, this was it, the servants' part of the house. Four doors on his right, two on his left. Which one to try? Which room looks out to the back? Never mind, try them all. First door. Locked. Come back to this one. Next one, a broom cupboard. More shouting.

'ELLIOT! You can't go in there! What's the matter with you?' Crying. More people, more shouting.

'Hey, what's going on?'

'Get this lunatic out of here!'

The third door. Dark; a bed; two children asleep, two little bodies under a blanket, breathing in synchrony. The next room. Empty. He was sweating and panting from the physical exertion. He was swallowing great gulps of air. Every muscle in his body was tensed, in anticipation of ... what? What would he do when he found him? Strike him? Talk to him? He didn't know. But, anyway, he would have to find him first. Across the corridor, two more rooms. A laundry room, the sharp smell of soap powder and sodium bicarbonate; another bedroom, dark, empty. Back to the locked room ... yes, Raphael must have locked himself in here, in the hope that he wouldn't be found. I've got you now, Elliot thought, the tears still streaming down his face. Hands were snatching at him, grabbing him, as he threw the weight of his body against the door. His whole body jarred, he heard the sound of wood splitting, but the door didn't give. Elliot didn't feel the pain in his shoulder as he tried to throw himself at the door a second time. But arms were holding him back now, restraining him, strong arms, around his waist, one around his throat, Helena screaming, 'Elliot, talk to me! Elliot, what's the matter?'

Why were they trying to stop him opening the door? Why were they hiding Raphael?

'Get your bloody hands off me!' he yelled, snot and saliva spraying from his nose and mouth, writhing in a grip so tight he thought it would crush his spine. 'Let me go! I know he's in there! Why are you hiding him?'

The grip around his throat tightened; he could feel his windpipe closing. His face was turning bright red. He gasped for air. Helena's voice came again, frantic, desperate.

'Let him go! You're strangling him! He can't breathe!'

The arm loosened, Elliot took great thirsty gulps of air. He'd lost the fight. He was at their mercy. His tense, taut body suddenly relaxed; his shoulders slumped, his legs jelly. The arms that had restrained him now struggled to support him, to keep him on his feet. He closed his eyes, and let his head drop forward. The two men either side of him, the ones who had restrained him – Tom to the left, one of the Rickmans' menservants on his right – were now holding Elliot between them; his arms were draped around their shoulders; they were carrying him like some wounded comrade, staggering beneath his dead weight.

All around him was suddenly quiet, hushed. A familiar smell close to him, a gentle whisper in his ear, 'Elliot, darling, it's me. It's all right, everything's fine. Let's sit you down.'

And he heard Helena requesting that someone bring a chair for him. Only as he sat down did he open his eyes again. A crowd had gathered in the narrow corridor. A few of the people standing to the front of the crowd shuffled uncomfortably as he looked up in their direction. Others who were at the back struggled to get a better view, craning their necks, standing on tiptoes, whispering to one another. Elliot saw Julia placating the housekeeper, who was now noisily complaining about the intrusion into the service wing. Julia stood, palms pressed together as if in prayer, listening to the protest, nodding in assent, calmly assuring the woman that everyone would be asked to leave immediately. She glanced at Elliot; their eyes met, and she shook her head at him, a movement so small it was scarcely noticeable, but full of contempt and repressed anger. She turned away, and with outstretched arms began shooing the crowd away, back through the shabby corridor, back to the splendour of the main wing of the house. Not for one minute did she lose her composure; always the perfect hostess.

Helena was kneeling, sitting on her heels, in front of Elliot. Her small, slender hands rested on his knees. She looked red-eyed, frightened, beyond comprehension. She didn't speak, but merely looked up at him, blinking rapidly to prevent herself from crying any more. He could see from the movement of her throat that she was finding it hard to swallow. After a while, she turned her head to the side and laid it on Elliot's lap. He lifted one trembling hand and began to stroke her hair. I'm sorry, he mouthed, knowing that these words were not enough. Someone prodded Helena's shoulder. It was Henry.

'Get up, you silly girl. I want to have a word with this lunatic.'

Looking too upset to argue, Helena got to her feet and walked into her mother's arms. Henry looked down at Elliot.

'What the hell do you think you are playing at?' he said. The words came out through clenched teeth; clipped and precise. He didn't shout; he controlled his rage admirably. Elliot said nothing.

'Answer me – what is going on?'

Elliot couldn't think beyond the locked door. He needed to look inside, make it real, show everyone – including himself – that he wasn't mad. Raphael was there, a few feet away, behind the door. When he spoke, his voice was shaking.

'He's … in there.' He pointed to the door.

'Who's in there?'

'Raphael. He's a … a patient of mine. I saw him from outside. He was looking at me through the window.'

'Christ, have you had too much to drink, man? There's nobody in there. It's locked.'

'He must have locked himself in.' Elliot got up and went to the door. He turned to Henry, pleading. 'Just let me have a look. Please.'

Tom stood next to Henry, looking extremely uncomfortable. He had his hands thrust into his pockets, and shifted from one foot onto the other. His head was bent, and his hair hung down in his face, strands of blond sticking to the sweat. One of his shirt buttons was undone; it must have come loose in the struggle.

He said, 'I say, let's just go back downstairs, have a brandy. What do you say?'

'No, it's all right, Tom,' said Henry. 'We'll unlock the door, have a look inside. If he wants to make a fool of himself, I'm not going to stop him.'

He walked over to the housekeeper and took the key from her. Elliot's heart started racing as Henry put the key in the lock and turned it. He wanted to position the men around the door in case Raphael tried to make a run for it, but he realised this would be an impossible request. The key clicked in the lock; Henry stood aside to let Elliot open the door. As he turned the cold metal knob, he felt sweat from his forehead drip into his eyes. His breathing was shallow, his blood pounded in his ears. He took one look at Helena, who stood at Julia's side, biting her lip. She looked terrified. Of him? He didn't want to think about that. It was an unbearable thought. He pushed the door wide open, and stepped inside. The room was empty; completely bare except for a dustsheet that covered the wooden floor, a metal bucket with dried-up paint, and a ladder, leaning against the window. Helena came and stood beside him, talking at him, saying things he didn't want to hear, like 'You must have imagined it, darling,' or, 'You're tired, you've been working too hard,' and, 'It could have happened to any of us.'

But he didn't really hear any of it; he only imagined that was what she'd be saying. He was still overcome by the shock, the realisation that he might be going mad, losing his mind, turning into one of those lamentable lunatics who sit naked in small dark rooms smelling of their own excrement and tearing at their hair until it comes out in clumps in their hands. And there in that small room, while others around him deliberated how he could have mistaken the ladder for a person, that it was perfectly feasible, that such tricks of the light happened all the time, Elliot sat down and cried for his sanity.

Elliot and Helena sat side-by-side on the bed in his attic bedroom. It was very late, and dark outside. They hadn't switched on the light, but the gas fire was lit, secreting a low hiss and glow of orange light. They sat, barely touching, heads bent, with the slight awkwardness of a courting couple who find themselves on their own for the first time. Elliot was the first to speak, his voice oddly calm in the dull silence.

'What did your father say?'

Helena shrugged and shook her head, every movement tired, unhurried. She said, 'He wasn't impressed. But I told him about your work, how you sometimes get more involved with your patients than you should. I told him that this was a good thing; an indication of your commitment to your profession. I'm not sure he understands. But what he does understand is that I love you, and that I want to marry you regardless.'

'Are you sure about that?'

'Of course.' She smiled, taking his hand in hers. For a moment, she just stared at it, as though contemplating every line, every crease of his skin. Her smile faded into a frown.

'And another thing.'

'What?'

'He, um, he wants me to go to New York with him next week; he's giving a series of lectures over there.'

'For how long?'

'A month, maybe two.'

'Do you want to go?' His voice was strained. He cleared his throat.

'I suppose I ought to. After tonight. It doesn't mean ...'

'What?'

Her chin was trembling. She was trying not to cry.

'It doesn't mean that I don't love you. I just ... I have loyalties to them, too, you know. My family. Just because I'm with you doesn't mean they're any less important to me.'

Elliot's heart lurched at the realisation that he had so badly upset her. He forced as much brightness into his voice as he could.

'Helena, I know that. I want you be happy. I know how much they mean to you. Seeing you this weekend, with your sisters; it showed me how happy they make you. I suppose I felt a bit left out. Jealous, if you like.'

She slipped her arm around his, and pressed up against him. 'You must never feel jealous, Elliot. I chose you, don't you see? I didn't choose them, they just happen to be my family. But I chose you, because you are a good man. And I want to be with you. Always.'

He rested his head against hers, looking into the fire, not blinking until the warmth pricked his eyes and they filled with water. He sat there with Helena for a long time, in silence, their synchronised heartbeats and the hissing from the gas fire the only sounds in the room. Finally, Elliot broke the silence.

'I want … I need to tell you something.'

'What?'

'It's about my brother.'

'Ed.' Helena turned her head to look at him. Individual strands of her hair shone copper in the orange light. Elliot nodded.

'He died in the war, didn't he?' she said.

'No. It was after that.'

'But I thought – he was in the Army? I don't understand.'

'He was in the Army, but he died shortly after the war ended. Helena –' He looked away. His next words came out in a whisper.

'I was responsible for his death.'

Helena cupped her hand over her mouth, eyes wide with sorrow, with disbelief. Elliot reached across, and gently took her hand. He never wanted to lose her. He kissed her palm.

'I wanted you to know,' he whispered into her hand.

'Tell me what happened.'

And he told her his story.

THIRTEEN

'The armistice was two days old when my parents received word from Ed that he wouldn't be returning home from France with his regiment. In a short telegram, Ed informed our parents that he had been seconded by the War Office to the Allied Expeditionary Force in North Russia. He would be serving a three-month tour of duty there, and looked forward to returning home in time for spring. I can't begin to describe the effect the news had on my parents. My mother in particular; she took it so badly, it was as though Ed had been killed in the war. Her anguish was so profound, so forceful, it was frightening, and both my father and I became seriously concerned about her mental state. I was working at the asylum at the time, and it was disturbing to witness my own mother unravelling in such a way, gradually but inexorably.'

'During the first few days, we simply left her alone to cry, thinking she just needed to recover from the shock. She wept for days, stopping only when she had fallen asleep with exhaustion, and we thought it was a mother's natural response. It was when she stopped eating that we couldn't ignore her condition any longer and decided that something had to be done. My father blamed the War Office, but I was never completely sure that Ed didn't volunteer to go – there was something about the cheeriness of the telegram, an undertone of misplaced zeal, as if he hadn't had quite enough of his share of adventure. I don't know; it's always easier to interpret the ambiguous with the benefit of hindsight...

Anyway, something had to be done, and one night, just before succumbing to a sedative-induced sleep, my mother pleaded with me to go and get him back. I know that it was something she'd been brooding over for days.'

'I agreed readily; but my real reason for wanting to go was another. You see, throughout the war, Ed had always been an avid letter writer. I received letters from him on a regular basis for years, sometimes at weekly intervals, at other times I wouldn't hear anything for months and then suddenly receive a whole batch of ten or twelve. It all depended on the reliability of the postal service in whatever place Ed happened to be at the time. His letters were eternally cheerful – he was just that kind of man – and it was always a relief to hear that he was all right. But about six months before the telegram came, I began to notice something in his letters that gave me serious cause for concern.'

'It wasn't the content; he usually wrote about the small daily matters of life on the front line: the poor food, the lice, the sense of comradeship. Things that weren't likely to be censured. He was a good soldier and that life seemed to suit him well. But then I began to detect a sense of ... desperation in his writing. His script had started to become oddly dislocated – unconnected letters in the middle of a word, for example – with the capital letters sometimes grand and ostentatious, sometimes minute and almost illegible. I won't go into all that here, but I knew I wasn't imagining it. By then, I had studied graphology fairly extensively and was very sensitive to these things. In addition, I was – still am – treating men who had lost their minds as a result

of their experiences in the trenches. For months, I became almost obsessed with analysing his letters, hoping I had
read something into his handwriting that wasn't there, but
the closer I looked, the more apparent his mental instability
became in the gross conflict within the writing. As letter after letter arrived, I began comparing these symptoms with
the scripts from some of my patients, and a horrible pattern
began to emerge: the fluctuations in Ed's writing matched
with those found in patients who had attempted suicide.'

'I knew then that I had to go and see for myself
whether Ed really was on the brink of a breakdown. I didn't
tell my parents of my concerns; I don't think my mother
would have been able to stand it. I made some enquiries,
and as luck – or misfortune, depending on how you see it –
would have it, there was a Red Cross relief delegation due
to go to Northern Russia the following week. They were
desperate for medical staff – the 'flu and all that – so I had no
trouble getting a place in the delegation. Everything seemed
to be going like clockwork; I had just enough time to arrange for a colleague to stand in for me at the asylum, organise my travel documents and have some clothes made that
would stand up to the freezing conditions they had out there, and so forth. It's funny, really, if my preparations hadn't
gone as smoothly as they did, if there hadn't been a relief delegation heading out at that time, if I hadn't managed to secure a place, any number of things, everything might have
turned out so differently. The White Sea begins to freeze
over in November, and it stays ice-bound until May; if I
hadn't gone at that precise moment, I would have had to
wait for months, or else would have had to travel overland,

which would have taken weeks. Either way, Ed would have probably completed his tour of duty and returned home. But I wasn't to know – I could never have known that he wouldn't come home. I have to keep telling myself that. At the time, I felt an overwhelming sense of compulsion, as if nothing could have stopped me; I went so far as to make an impassioned promise to my mother that I would not return without Ed. I can't count the times I wished that I'd never made that promise.

'I set off on the train to Dundee the following week, arriving there in the early hours of the morning. The weather was atrocious, I can remember it clearly. Everything was rain-soaked and gloomy; it was as though all colour had been sucked out of the place, leaving behind a washed-out palette of greys. And the rain, it was the kind of fine, freezing rain that falls silently and soaks you through before you know it. I remember feeling cold. Can you imagine that! I thought that a Scottish November day could be classed as cold. Had I known what was to come, I think I would have enjoyed the sensation of inhaling without fearing my lungs had turned to ice, would have enjoyed the relative freedom of movement unrestricted by layers upon layers of clothing.

'Our ship was the HMS Humber, the last ship to set sail that winter, taking British and French troops to join the Allied forces in Russia. We left Dundee in convoy, with two destroyers as escort. A group of Canadian Mennonites had boarded the ship with me, also heading to Russia for relief work. We were the only civilians on-board, and spent most of the journey from Dundee to Murmansk in each other's company. The Mennonites were a pleasant bunch;

four men, two of them with their wives, and a young girl, about eighteen, who was the niece of one of the couples. I didn't hold much with their religious beliefs, but they were so genuine, so sincere in their principles, that it was very hard not to like them. Besides, although we came to it from completely different directions, we had our pacifism in common, something which was painfully apparent to the naval officers on-board. The men – the sailors and soldiers – were friendly, though; I think many of them had had enough by now, and desperately wanted to get home. Whoever had dreamt up the North Russian campaign evidently hadn't spent much time in the trenches. The sense of battle fatigue was written in every man's face.

'I shared a cabin with one of the Mennonites, Alvin Castle, who had brought his wife Dorothy, and his niece Grace, with him. We were due to pick up a further civilian passenger, a translator, in Murmansk, who was to share the cabin with us until our final destination. I wasn't looking forward to that; the cabin already seemed squalid and cramped. It was very small, measuring only about eight foot long and six foot across. Alvin and I had a bunk each, which was preferable to hammocks, but the beds were narrow and hard. There were metal steam pipes running through the cabin, right above my bunk, which, due to the cold outside, were constantly sweating. The noise of the engines never quite concealed the relentless drip-drip-drip of the condensation on the metal floor.

'There was little to do during the day. Our movements on-board were heavily restricted. We ate in the same cabin as the officers; apart from that, we had access to the troop deck, which was always crowded, brimming with sea-sick men. More often than not I was one of them. I regretted early on not bringing more books, as reading became the only way of passing the time. Alvin was an agreeable companion, though, and very talkative, which went a long way to relieve the tedium of the voyage. It was a thoroughly miserable journey. When we finally reached Murmansk, I was in a pretty dreadful state. My stomach hadn't settled since we left Dundee, and I was feeling quite weak from the constant nausea. I would have liked to disembark there and then, but Alvin persuaded me to stay on-board, showing me on his map that it was only a matter of a day or two before we arrived in Archangel. How wrong he was! It was, in fact, another seven long days before we finally reached our destination. We were docked in Murmansk for several hours, while provisions were restocked and the ship was refuelled. Alvin went to land with his compatriots, Martin and Jakob, while this was happening, but I decided to stay in my cabin, fearing that if I went with them, I wouldn't want to board the ship again. I must have fallen asleep; the next thing I knew we had pulled out to sea and I had missed my chance of disembarking. I stayed in my bunk and rested, dipping in and out of sleep. It's amazing how exhausting boredom can be. When I got up the next morning, I saw that the third bunk in our cabin was now occupied. I knew it must be the translator who had been expected to board in Murmansk. He lay facing the wall, almost completely covered by his blankets, tufts of thick black hair sticking out at the top. Alvin was already up, and I decided to leave the man sleeping. In fact, I didn't get the opportunity to speak to him for another couple of days – mainly due to the fact that he kept himself to himself. As I recall, he spent most of his time reading, but he struck me from the outset as sullen. Only Alvin's young niece, Grace, seemed unusually attracted to him, and was able to engage him in conversation for hours at a time.

'For the next two days we sailed steadily through the Barents Sea, in the company of a Russian ice-breaker, the Svaitogor. The waters were much calmer than I had expected, and I began to feel more at ease. Perhaps I'd just found my sea legs. Anyway, we were making a good run until we began to sail around Cape Gorodizki, about two hundred miles from Archangel. There we encountered the severe, and inevitable, drop in temperature. I was on the troop deck, getting some air, when I first noticed the ice on the water. It appeared at first like a thin film on the surface, moving gently in rhythm with the waves, breaking up when the sea got rougher, but it became noticeably thicker as the ship continued southwards. The Svaitogor was sailing ahead of us, creating a water corridor for the Humber to pass through between the thickening ice. The scenery was breathtaking in its desolation. The sky was a permanent steel-grey, and the water that was still ice-free was dark and troubled. It seemed such an uninhabitable place, and yet there were dozens, maybe hundreds of seals nearby, flapping about on the carpet of ice, diving into the icy water, oblivious to the freezing temperatures. Every now and again, I caught a glimpse of a seal swimming underwater alongside the ship; a sleek, black torpedo propelling itself past us at amazing speed. After an hour or so, it was clear that parts of the ice, floating in broken, grubby fragments around the ship, were up to seven foot thick. The two ships appeared tiny in the vast, icy bleakness of our surroundings, and for a while, I was anxious that we might have set sail too late, and become trapped in the ice for good. Everything was overpowered by the cold; all other thoughts, matters, concerns, were suspended. The struggle to keep warm became an obsession. I was no longer hungry, tired or bored; the only thing I felt was cold.'

'I was woken up the next morning by an enormous crashing noise. Alvin was thrown clear of his bunk, and I hit my head quite painfully on the wall. We had hit yet another block of ice refusing to yield to the bulk of the ship. It was unbelievably frustrating. We were making very little progress. The sailors seemed blissfully unaffected, but the soldiers were getting just as restless as we were. There were rumours of fighting going on in the men's quarters below deck. The officers discussed it over dinner, some arguing for the identification and court-martialling of troublemakers, if only to make an example of them to deter others; but I assume the unrest was due to the fact that the soldiers weren't used to these levels of claustrophobic inactivity. This became the main topic at the dinner table for two days, and there were palpable, albeit unspoken, fears of mutiny among the officers. I had a few days to ponder the implications of a possible uprising for the civilians on-board, but then the officers' concerns were allayed, as the men got the relief they desired – in a display of barbarity I shall never forget.'

'The Svaitogor had been ploughing ahead of us through the ice field at an agonisingly slow pace. And the noise was incredible, especially at night. I don't know about the sailors, whether it was something they were used to, but for us, sleep was virtually impossible. We either had to endure the grinding, creaking sounds of the ice breaking up around us – at times it was a low, moaning noise, as though the ice were in distress, complaining softly, persistently, at being fractured – or else put up with the noise of the ship slowly becoming encased with ice when the ice-breaker had steamed too far ahead, and the sea between us had closed up again. It was terrifying when this happened. Then it was the ship's turn to suffer, shrieking and groaning under the pressure of the surrounding ice; it was as if the sea were trying to squeeze her, crush her to pieces. My Canadian friends were usually to be found huddled in prayer when we became ice-bound like this, and I admit that, on occasion, I wished I could have joined them. The translator stayed in his cabin throughout; his miserable demeanour would have done little to cheer me up, anyway.

'After three days of moving at a snail's pace, both the Humber and the Svaitogor were stuck hard and fast in the ice. News of what was going on trickled down very slowly and unreliably to our group; we were hardly considered a priority on-board when it came to sharing information. But as I understood it, two further ice-breakers were wirelessed to come from Archangel and release us from the ice field. There was nothing for it but to sit around, waiting, waiting. It was during this time that the officers on-board decided to give the men the opportunity to relieve their boredom – and transfer any hostility that may have been directed at them – by organising a seal hunt.

'It began as a group of some twelve men clambered over the side of the ship onto the ice, carrying ropes and tools. The seals seemed bemused by our presence; they clearly didn't sense any threat at all. Some of the men in the group appeared hesitant, but there were a few sailors who evidently knew what they were doing, and they were quite deliberate in their actions; the entrapment and slaying of the animals was quick, clinical, dispassionate. It seemed a straightforward process: once a particular seal had been targeted, one man would approach it from the front, talking to it, cajoling it, as though he were talking to his pet dog, head nodding, hands patting thighs, with a friendly, affable tone of voice, 'Come on, boy, here, come on'. Remarkably, a seal would respond to this, rising to stand on its hind flippers, moving awkwardly across the ice, and watching the man with an air of genial confusion. While the front man was distracting the seal in this way, a second man would come from behind and smash it over the skull with some blunt instrument – a belaying-pin, a rifle butt, a hammer – stunning the creature into unconsciousness, before slitting its throat. The whole episode lasted only a few minutes. Finally, a loop of rope would be slipped around the animal's tail, and the men would drag the carcass – often still heaving in sporadic, violent convulsions – back to the ship. I must admit that the first few times I watched this impeccably choreographed sequence from the deck of the ship I felt little pity for the animals; they seemed incredibly foolish to be so trusting. Other seals watched their friends, their relatives, being lured and slaughtered, one after the other, and yet each one was duped as easily as the one before, except perhaps that the initial air of geniality turned into a look of momentary indecision, a split second before the seal's skull was bashed in. Although I didn't find it pleasant to watch, it didn't seem particularly cruel to me; just a primitive, natural ritual that had been played out innumerable times throughout history. But this was only during the first few killings, when the hunters showed little discernible emotion in what they were doing. Then the massacre started.'

Elliot stood up and walked over to the window. Outside, the grounds lay in muted darkness, the black sky disturbed only by the unsteady, hesitant shimmer of a remote luminous speck. Elliot wondered whether the star was dying, its final remnants of light spluttering down towards Earth in fits of brilliance. Looking down across the garden, he could just about make out the small white summer house behind the silver birches, at the end of the gravel path. It seemed a lifetime ago that he had sat in the summer house contemplating his future life with Helena. But it had been only hours earlier. Now here he was, narrating a story from his past, and yet, it felt as if that person travelling towards Russia were different somehow, fundamentally distinct from the one he was now. He shivered with the sudden realisation that what he felt was a lack of cohesion, of historical continuity, as though Elliot Taverley, 1918, was not merely a younger version of Elliot Taverley, 1921, but a completely separate person. He wrapped his arms around himself and continued the story.

'It was twenty minutes or so before the other men began to join in. Those who had stood by at first, watching, had decided that it was now their turn. They came together in predatory pairs, impatiently, ineptly stalking the seals, most of which had now achieved some kind of under- standing of the ruthless gravity of their situation. Sounds of snarling and hissing flew across the ice, some seals ma- naging to escape by diving into breathing-holes, or by hi- ding in snowdrifts. But their attempts at flight only made the hunters more determined. It was unbelievably violent. More and more men climbed down the ladders on the hull eager to take part. At one point there must have been close to a hundred men on the ice. Sometimes they only managed to injure an animal, concussing it and then half-heartedly stabbing it, before moving onto the next one, like crazed piece-workers. Countless wounded seals lay in the snow, bleeding profusely, a few of them attempting to shift their heavy bodies towards the water. Other men preferred to concentrate on one seal at a time, hacking away frantically at already dead animals, until all that remained were bloody scraps of flesh and blubber. A cacophony of soft moaning and high-pitched whining sliced through the coarse chee- ring of the men. Before long, smears of blood, like giant crimson ribbons, traced a pattern of lines criss-crossing the ice field back to the ship. The limp grey bodies were pi- led up on the deck. Steam was rising from the fresh blood, which had spilled out onto the deck, causing men to slip and slide about. After a while I couldn't watch any more and decided to go back to my cabin. I couldn't stay on deck; the air seemed thick with the warm, fetid smell of blood, and the cries from the half-killed creatures left on the ice were too much to stomach. As I turned to go, I heard a voice behind me.

– What will they do now with their appetite for blood, for killing? Now that the war has turned them into animals.

'It was the translator. He stood at my shoulder, staring straight ahead at the bloody carnage, his eyes reflecting a scene of suffering that reached far beyond the events taking place on the ice. I didn't want to leave him standing there alone, and, although I badly wanted a cigarette, I stood next to him for a while, in silence, watching the men deal the final death blows to the seals that hadn't been killed outright on the first attempt. It must have been the thud thud thud of stick on skull that finally got the better of my stomach, and I leaned over the side of the ship and retched. The contents of my guts were half-frozen before they hit the ice. The translator came forward and put his hand on my back. When I was sure that my stomach had settled, I looked up at him and smiled apologetically. He smiled back at me, holding out a handkerchief for me to wipe my mouth on. When he spoke, his voice was assured, and oddly comforting.

– Are you all right?

'His accent was audible but light, and he spoke English effortlessly.

– Yes.

– Will you need a doctor?

– Actually, I am a doctor. I shouldn't really get squeamish at the sight of blood.

– If you are anything like me, then it is not the blood that makes you sick, but man's eagerness to spill it.

'He was right, of course. What made me sick was the unadulterated pleasure the hunters had derived from killing those defenceless creatures. Is there a truer measure of compassion than the way one treats animals? It was reassuring that I wasn't the only one here who felt this way. I held out my hand, or rather, my glove.

– Elliot Taverley. Pleased to meet you.

'He was wearing an enormous fur hat, very similar to my own, which came down over his forehead to his eyes. A thick woollen scarf was wrapped around his neck and the lower half of his face, so that it was difficult to make out any particular facial features. I could tell, however, that his face was gaunt, with quite protuberant cheekbones, and that the left eye was set slightly higher than the right. On the bridge of his nose, just below the fur hat, I could see that his eyebrows joined in the middle.'

'Stan!' Helena exclaimed. 'That's where you met Stan! I never knew. I thought you'd met in London.'

Elliot turned towards her, shaking his head.

'No, we met on the way to Russia.'

'You never told me that,' she said. She spoke barely above a whisper, yet Elliot could clearly detect her sadness that he had withheld this from her all this time.

'I'm sorry,' he said, 'truly, I am. I left you under that assumption because to tell you the truth would have meant telling you all … this.'

'You should have trusted me,' Helena said.

Elliot glanced back out of the window. 'I know,' he said quietly, to himself as much as to Helena.

'I shan't pretend to imagine how painful this must

be,' she said. 'And I'm pleased you are trusting me now.'

A moment's silence fell between them. Then Helena said, 'So, what happened when you got there? Did Stan know Ed?'

Elliot gestured to her to pass him his cigarette case that lay next to her on the bed. She felt for the case and picked it up, not taking her eyes off him for a moment.

'Yes, they did meet. But –' He paused to light a cigarette. A curl of smoke drifted into his eye, causing him to blink furiously. He rubbed both his eyes with a thumb and forefinger. He felt unbelievably tired now.

'But what?' Helena asked.

'They didn't really get on.'

Elliot suddenly felt hot, the atmosphere was cloying, stagnant; his words were cushioned, echoless in the dull airlessness of the room. He needed to open the window, needed to breathe fresh air. The frame was stubborn, it took as much strength as he had to push it up, but then, the wind poured in, clean and eloquent, momentarily subduing the mean-spirited throbbing that had started behind his temples. He stared out into the darkness, unseeingly, recovering his memories. Behind him, Helena shivered.

'Anyway, after the two ice-breakers reached us, we just sailed away, leaving dozens of bloodied cadavers behind. It was a short day's journey through the bay and into Archangel. After we disembarked, I said my goodbyes to Alvin and his friends, and they left the port travelling south across the bay. They were heading for a place called Vologda – where some of the fiercest fighting had taken place. Apparently, there were hundreds of destitute civilians there and the Mennonites were part of a relief mission aimed at clearing up the human debris. I worried about them, particularly about Dorothy and Grace. In my experience, some men will use the suspension of civilised practices as an excuse to exert power over the vulnerable. During the war, when I was in France, some of my colleagues reported treating dozens of women who had been savagely beaten or raped – not just by the Germans, the enemy, but by French and British soldiers. It sometimes made me wonder what we were fighting for. So as for Alvin and his fellow travellers, well, I admired their commitment, but I don't believe they knew what they were letting themselves in for. Although, to be honest, I didn't give them another moment's thought until much later on. As I waved them away I had more pressing things on my mind. I heard later that they'd been found shot dead about two hundred miles south of Archangel. The men and Dorothy, that is. Grace was never found.

'I knew from one of the officers I had spoken to on-board that Ed was in the General Staff at the Force's headquarters in Archangel. I had to report to the head of the Red Cross mission first, an affable American named Mitchell Walker, to discuss my duties. It turned out that one of the nearby field hospitals was desperately understaffed following an outbreak of influenza, and so I agreed to stand in for a week, until at least a couple of the Army doctors had recovered. When I had completed the necessary formalities, I set about locating Ed. I was so excited, I hadn't spoken to him for such a long time, and here I was, so close to seeing him again!

'He was always a very imposing man, physically.' Elliot stopped briefly as he involuntarily recalled the mental image he'd had earlier of Ed and Helena together, but managing to shake it off while the image was still amorphous, before it acquired too much definition. 'I recognised him immediately. He was standing outside a large wooden house – the whole town seemed to be one vast sprawl of wooden structures – giving orders to some unfortunate subaltern, who appeared to be hard of hearing. When Ed looked up and spotted me, he started grinning and held both his arms out to greet me. In his thick fur coat and hat he had grown to a giant. Ed was an extremely handsome man; his attractiveness lay not only in his enviably flawless features – thick, black hair; sharp blue eyes – but in his grandeur. He had broad shoulders, a strong jaw, all the things that make one think of majesty.

'I didn't get an opportunity to speak with him properly, not straight away. I was called on to attend to some sick officers almost immediately. A part of me hoped that I had been completely misguided; that I had merely read something into his handwriting. Looking back, that seems so unrealistic, so naive. Ed just assumed that as I'd come with the rest of the "do-gooders", as he called them, it was a lucky coincidence that I'd been sent to Archangel. It always surprised me how he never seemed to see further than his own nose.

'During the day I was kept busy in the hospital; in the evenings I'd join Ed and Stanislav in the officers' mess. It was proving impossible to speak with him quietly, for me to make some sort of assessment of his mental state. One of the more noticeable changes in him, however, was the amount he drank. Like my father, he'd always been fond of a drink, but here it seemed he was completely drunk every night within an hour of sitting down to dinner. He would sit in his chair, talking to himself, laughing at phantom jokes, answering imagined salutes. It all served to reinforce my concerns. I was glad of Stanislav's company, though, as Ed's conversation tended to become unintelligible after about nine o'clock. The other thing I noticed about him was his physical health, or lack of it. He looked bloated; his skin was greyish, not the tanned complexion he'd always had, at home and in France. Like I said, there was a wave of 'flu going around, and I thought he might be at risk of contracting it. I told him of the symptoms, the warning signs, and advised him to be careful, but he just said he felt as strong as ever. He must have paid me some attention though, because I did hear that he had excused himself from some recce expedition in the south on the grounds that he felt under the weather.

'After a week I decided I couldn't procrastinate any longer. So one night, I took him to one side before dinner at the entrance to the mess hall – I needed to speak to him before he got paralytic, he already had a whisky in his hand – and told him straight out that I was worried about him. I had to speak up; the hall was loud and busy with officers arriving for dinner, gentlemen of war in smart uniforms dripping with ponderous medals, and shining boots with bright burnished spurs. I almost shouted in his ear, wincing at the disproportionate loudness of my own voice in relation to the gravity of my concerns. My carefully prepared words sounded terribly inadequate all of a sudden; I had come with the intention of gently probing him for signs of psychological instability, but the atmosphere, the sense of urgency that had suddenly assailed me made me forget all that.

– You're not well, Ed. I can see it. We need to get out of here, talk about it. Your letters, I can tell. You have to talk to me about it.

'At first he didn't speak, just stared down at his drink, swirling the ice around until it clinked off the side of the glass. I watched his face for a reaction, saw the muscles tighten across his jaw as he clenched his teeth. Then he tilted his head up and flashed a smile at me, a private smile, a smile that was just for me, a smile from our youth, full of generosity and conspiratorial promise, a smile that said, I won't tell if you don't, but with an underlying shade of ... what? Mischief? Menace? A second later the smile was gone; replaced by a peculiar look of concern.

– You're not well? That's too bad. Well, make sure to get checked over. There are a few good docs here I can recommend. He looked around for a steward to refill his drink. I'll get you a name first thing in the morning. And then, nudging me in the ribs, he smiled again and added, Don't tell me it's something you picked up from a certain type of lady. Elliot, you old dog, I never knew you had it in you!

'The noises in the background were louder now. Dinner was being served. The baritone of all-male conversation droned through the swing doors to where we were standing in the cold foyer. Murmurs and chuckles mixed with the tinkling of glasses and the scraping of cutlery on china. I frowned at Ed. He had obviously misunderstood me. I told him again.

– I know the signs, Ed, you must get help. If not from me, then from someone else.

He took a great gulp from his glass.

– I have no idea what you're talking about, Elliot. Look at me, I'm fine!

He slapped his chest, not caring about spilling his drink, and a strange, nasty smile came over his face. He leant forward and said:

– Look at me, little brother. I'm a man!

We both knew what he meant. He was referring to the fact that he had seduced – if not physically, then emotionally – every single girl I had ever expressed an interest in. Once, just once, I'd challenged him about it. I must have been sixteen and deeply in love with this girl, and Ed – twenty years old, handsome, an adult – had started flirting with her, paying her compliments, until she decided she would rather walk out with him. When I demanded an explanation from him, he explained in no uncertain terms that he was the man out of the two of us, the real man; that regardless of what I did or felt, I would never quite measure up to him.

It was when he mentioned it again at this moment that I relived all that pain and humiliation.

– Yes, I'm the man here, he said.

He glanced over my shoulder and winked at a pretty barishna who'd just come in, presumably looking for work in the kitchens. It was an innocuous act, one I'd witnessed countless times before; Ed, the eternal ladies' man. He was attractive to women, and he knew it. But here, now, when I had come all that way, had suffered months of worry, only because I cared about him ... with that little wink, that tiny, transient gesture, he'd trivialised everything: my concerns; my competence, as a doctor and as a man; my presence here – everything torn into insignificance with a blink of his eye. The next thing I knew I was shouting at him, screaming; I wanted to fight him, hurt him like he'd hurt me.

– What's the matter with you? Don't you understand what I'm doing here? There's something wrong with you! You've become another person, there is a part of you in-side that has experienced more than it can cope with. I've seen it with my own eyes. In your letters, your writing is so ... fractured, I knew at once that there was something the matter with you. And now, to see you here, like this ... You're SICK, Ed! You are a sick man. You need help. Before it's too late!

'I went on like that for a while. I couldn't stop myself. It startled him, but only for a second. Then he grabbed my arm and dragged me out of the mess, around the back, into an alley, away from the street lights. He was hurting my arm, bruising, crushing it with his huge hand, and I knew I wouldn't stand a chance in a fist fight against him. When we reached the back of the building, stopping near the entrance to the kitchen, he let go, hitting my arm away in disgust. There were piles of snow heaped up against the side of the building, stained yellow with urine. Ed drew his face to-wards mine, the tips of our noses almost touching. His bre-ath hit my face in sour waves. His eyes were dark; he was very close now, but the alley was unlit, and I couldn't make out his expression. But I could see that he was trembling. When he spoke, he didn't bother veiling his contempt.

– You fucking weakling! Do you really think that psycho-babble is going to work on me? Look at my hands; here, look! Do you know what I've done with them? No, you have no fucking idea, do you? I've had to shoot my own men, for Christ's sake! Men who've lain dying with their fucking guts hanging out, screaming like stuck pigs, begging me to put them out of their misery! He banged his fist on his chest, and then suddenly turned to hit the side of the wooden building. When he pulled his hand away I could see that the wood had splintered and cracked. His knuckles were bleeding. I was torn between wanting to hurt him and needing to comfort him.

– You're just saying that now, because you're angry. That's not really you, Ed, and that's why I'm here. Please, let us talk, not like this, quietly. I'm sorry if I've belittled your experiences, I really am. But ...

– You have no fucking idea, do you?

'He spat this last sentence out, and then walked off. That made me so angry, him turning his back on me like that. I shouted at him, vile, hateful things, but he didn't look back. I didn't know I would never see him again. I ...' Elliot broke off. This was the first time he had told this story to anyone. Telling it was making it real again. He looked down at his hands and saw that his finger was bleeding where he'd torn off a hangnail. A perfect drop of red clung to his skin. He quickly put the finger in his mouth and sucked on it. The taste was metallic, rusty.

'If we hadn't argued, if I hadn't told him what a selfish, arrogant fool he was being, he would have stayed there, at headquarters, instead of volunteering for that stupid mission.' His voice wavered; he cleared his throat. Before he could go on, Helena spoke, her voice cautious, the note of alarm thinly disguised.

'What happened? I mean, how did he die? Did he...?' She left her question unfinished.

'He must have reported for the expedition early the next morning. He was due to return the day after, but nobody noticed that he had gone missing – some British soldier, a young boy, had been shot in town the night before, and the authorities were busy dealing with that – and I assumed he was just avoiding me. They found him five days later. It was estimated that he had been dead for three days before they found his body, about eighty miles south of Archangel, on the edge of a wood his battalion had been using as cover. Half of his face was missing. They reckoned his head had been bashed in with a rifle butt. Probably some savage Bolshevik, they said. When they told me he was dead, I went into shock. I have no real recollection of what happened after that. Nothing I can relate to you in words, anyway. Perhaps it was the shock, or grief, or guilt, that made me repress those memories. All I know is that Stanislav somehow got me back to London. And then I had to tell my parents. It was the hardest thing I'd ever done.' His voice was just a whisper now. 'I never told them what really happened. They would have despised me.'

'But it wasn't your fault.'

'He wouldn't have gone off if we hadn't fought, I know that. He was so angry, like I'd never seen him before.

I knew what kind of state he was in, and yet I lost control of myself. And I shouted at him that I hated him, hated him, for what he had done to me. That was the last thing he ever heard me say.' He was gripping the window sill with both hands, his fingernails digging into the soft white wood. It was hurting but he didn't care. He wanted it to hurt. His disgust at himself came bubbling back to the surface, his wretchedness, his shame, his inadequacy. All he'd done was let his petty jealousies get the better of him, churned up the troubles of the past. The only thing his parents had ever asked of him – Ed's safe return – and he'd failed. Miserably. A quiet rain washed in on the wind through the open window onto Elliot's face, so that it was soon impossible to tell whether his face was wet from rain or tears.

'It's all right, Elliot, it's all right,' Helena said, and he went and sat beside her, took the offer of her embrace, and buried his face in the fragrant spot between her head and shoulder that smelt so warm and perfumy, while she gently, tenderly, stroked the nape of his neck.

FOURTEEN

Elliot arrived at the morning meeting just before it was due to start. He was feeling slightly nervous that one of his colleagues would have heard about the incident in Brighton, and had taken three days off after returning to London, stating a vague "illness in the family" as the reason for his absence. It was a tenuous excuse, of course, and he wasn't sure at all how many people here knew he had no family to speak of. He sat down quietly, trying not to draw too much attention to himself, but was soon addressed by the man on his right.

'Nice to have you back, old boy.'

It was William Attrill, an endocrinologist at the Chapel, whispering into his ear. His words carried a spray of fine spittle, and so, without thinking, Elliot's hand went up to wipe his ear after the man had spoken. Elliot didn't particularly like him; Attrill was known as a malicious gossip and Elliot felt disheartened to be sitting next to him of all people on his first day back at work. Attrill opened his mouth to speak again, but was interrupted as Beaumont came into the room.

'Good morning, everyone,' he said, walking to the head of the table and taking his seat. Elliot kept his head down, eyes glued to the notepad in front of him. If he could get through the meeting without anyone making a big fuss about his return, so much the better. It wasn't to be; Charles Beaumont didn't miss a trick.

'Taverley! So nice of you to join us again. Hope

everything's ... all right?'

The slight pause between 'everything's' and 'all right' was loaded enough for Elliot to recognise that Beaumont had heard what had happened in Brighton. He sighed. Well, it was a small world: what did he expect?

'Fine. Everything's fine,' he said with more conviction than he felt, not daring to look around the table, sensing that all eyes were fixed on him. The air in the room was hot and dry. Someone should open the window, he thought. He felt the sweat gather on his forehead and on the back of his neck. Soon it would appear in dark flecks under his armpits and down his spine. This was exactly what he had dreaded. These were his colleagues, experts in all aspects of the human condition. If he wasn't careful, they would spot his state of mind a mile away. The heavy tweed of his jacket was trapping the heat in next to his skin, making him itch like mad. Nobody spoke. Were they waiting for him to say something? Only one or two solitary coughs, some papers were needlessly shuffled about with a hint of impatience. Finally, Beaumont put him out of his misery.

'Good, good to hear. Now, what have we got? Let's see ...' He ran his finger down the sheet in front of him. Cases were reviewed at these meetings at regular monthly intervals, unless they were proving particularly problematic, in which case the individual doctors would bring them up for discussion. 'Dr. Shepherd, your patient, James Bull. How's it going? Any progress?'

Shepherd proceeded to give a lengthy discourse on how his young patient's self-hatred was based on feelings of inferiority and alienation. He evidently felt that his methods were superior to those of any others, and continued to laud their virtues for a further twenty minutes, plodding obstinately through his colleagues' stifled yawns and restless shuffling. Finally, Beaumont seized on a pause, and brought Shepherd's monotonous droning to an end.

'Thank you, Dr. Shepherd. I'm sure we're all looking forward to your next oration in a month's time.' All heads, including Elliot's, turned as one in Beaumont's direction, trying to confirm the hint of sarcasm they thought they'd detected. As usual, it was impossible to tell. Beaumont continued. 'Now, Taverley, I believe you're still treating young Jenny Wilson. What was it – ?' He consulted his notes. 'Ah, yes, hysteria. Quite an unresponsive patient, I seem to recall. So, what can you tell us about Jenny's progress, Dr. Taverley?'

All eyes were back on Elliot, as his empty stomach twisted and tightened. What an idiot he was! He had completely forgotten that today was his turn to discuss Jenny. He hadn't even thought of bringing the case notes. He lit a cigarette, placing his elbows firmly on the table in a pre-emptive attempt to control his hands, should they decide to start shaking. It was taking him an alarmingly long time to think of what to say. He needed to play for time somehow. Then, into the fierce silence came a woman's voice: 'Dr. Beaumont, I have Jenny's file.'

It was Nurse Robinson, standing at the back of the room, a small white figure of resilient austerity, in her hands the blue folder containing Jenny's notes. Elliot looked at her. Her eyes flicked in his direction, resting briefly, tellingly, on him, and then back to Beaumont. Elliot could have jumped up and kissed her. Beaumont looked at her over the top of his glasses. 'You have the file?'

'Yes, I've had it for a while, I'm afraid. Dr. Taverley asked me to type up his most recent notes – they were quite comprehensive – but with his handwriting being what it is –'

There was a low chuckle from around the table. '… or should I say, doctors' handwriting being what it is –' The chuckle was now taken up by the nurses at the back of the room. '– it is taking me forever to complete. I had forgotten that Dr. Taverley needed the notes for today's meeting. I'm awfully sorry.'

She sat down, her posture as starched as her uniform. It was clear that she did not fear confrontation. Elliot was made to think of the letter she had given him – and the secret it contained. He decided to speak to her about it as soon as possible.

'Well thank you, Nurse Robinson,' Beaumont said. 'We'll discuss Jenny next week.'

Elliot nodded, making some noises of assent. For the next thirty minutes, various other cases were discussed, but Elliot paid them little attention. Finally, Beaumont called the meeting to a close.

'Right. Well, if there's nothing else?' He spread his hands out. 'No? Thank you very much, gents, that'll be all.'

He stood up to go, signalling his permission for the others to leave. First the administrators and nurses, then the doctors began to leave the room, filtering slowly through the doors behind Elliot's chair. Elliot tried to back his chair up, but a bottleneck had formed behind him, and he was temporarily hemmed in. He could feel Beaumont's eyes on him. He knew Beaumont wanted to speak with him privately, and he wasn't in the mood. A space gradually cleared behind his chair, and he was able to stand up. He turned to his right, away from Beaumont's gaze. But he felt the man's stare at the back of his head, and he felt the pull of Beaumont willing him to turn around. This was stupid, he told himself, there's no avoiding it. So instead of following Attrill out of the door, he turned back and squared up to Beaumont, who just at that moment began to speak.

'Dr. Taverley. A word, please?' He stepped closer to stand next to Elliot, and then, unexpectedly, placed his arm around Elliot's shoulder. Elliot was startled by this show of familiarity, and tensed, trying hard to conceal his discomfort. Beaumont held him even closer, squeezing Elliot's shoulder with a large, strong hand. They stood like that for a while, in this awkward embrace. Eventually Beaumont spoke.

'Life ... work ... it can get on top of us sometimes. It happens to the best of us occasionally. My advice to you is not to get too involved with patients. I admire commitment; hell, if there were no commitment, this place would have closed its doors long before they opened! But you've got to learn when to let go, when it's time to rest this –' he rapped his head with his knuckles, '– and this.' He patted the left side of his chest with an open palm. 'Listen, man, if there's anything I can do, let me know. We're all in this together.'

This gesture of concern made Elliot feel oddly emotional. He suddenly felt a strong urge to come clean with

Beaumont, tell him exactly what had happened in Brighton, how he had come face-to-face with the terror of his own insanity, but had survived. The room had cleared. They were all alone. A confession, perhaps that was what he needed.

'The thing is, Dr. Beaumont –'

'Charles.'

'Charles.' It was something about saying his name, the way it felt on his tongue, somehow contrived. Nobody – nobody that he knew of at the Chapel, anyway – nobody called the clinical director by any other name than Dr. Beaumont. And now, for no reason he could think of, Beaumont was offering Elliot his first name. Something didn't seem right. Perhaps this was an attempt at manipulation. Perhaps Beaumont wanted some excuse to demand Elliot's resignation. Perhaps he wanted him out. Beaumont was an experienced psycho-analyst; surely he was aware of the psychological power of the confessor. The cleanser, the absolver. The more Elliot thought about it, the more wary he felt at this pseudo-paternal posturing. He would be damned if he confessed to Beaumont! He made his voice sound clear and strong.

'The thing is, I feel perfectly fine. I had some trouble at home, some ... difficulties that required my attention, that's all. I apologise if I didn't seem myself today. It won't happen again, I can assure you.'

Beaumont let his arm drop and shrugged his shoulders, making his rejection, his disappointment, seem awfully real.

'Well, in that case, Taverley, I'll be frank. I won't claim to know the exact nature of your, shall we say, troubles, but it's evidently distracting you from your work. Under the circumstances, I don't think it wouldn't be wise for you to continue with such a demanding caseload. I shall look through the list of patients you currently have and perhaps –' he sighed, 'perhaps we can see about referring some of your patients to Eastleigh. He's certainly made a promising start here. You'll continue to treat Jenny – it would be counter-productive to switch her to another analyst at this point – and perhaps Mrs Derby and that young fellow, Burns.'

Elliot couldn't believe what he was hearing. He was torn between humiliation and rage. Beaumont continued, his voice subdued but firm.

'In our profession, we carry an enormous responsibility. We have talked about this before, Taverley. This is no reflection on your competence as a doctor, but to do justice to your patients, you must be all there. I would have advised you to take some time off, but too much time to think wouldn't do you much good, either. Just slow down for a while, that's all I'm saying.'

He folded his arms across his chest. Elliot hurriedly gathered up his notebook and pen from the aggressively polished conference table, and left the room.

From behind the closed door to Nurse Robinson's small office, Elliot could hear the sound of typing. He passed by quickly and headed for his own office; he was certainly in no mood now to discuss Beaumont's letter with her. He let himself in and closed the door. The room was dark and cold, but instead of switching the light on, he remained facing the closed door, resting his forehead there and feeling the damp warmth of his breath on the wood. Then he heard a sound behind him. Some slight movement, shuffling, but definitely inside his office. He spun round and reached out for the light switch.

The room lit up and Elliot found himself looking straight at Raphael, who was sitting in the armchair closest to the window. He was wearing his heavy overcoat.

'How the hell did you get into my office?' Elliot asked, shouted almost. The sudden memory of the man's face in the window in Brighton made his heart ricochet inside his chest.

Raphael looked past Elliot towards the door – as if to give the obvious answer to this question – and then back at Elliot.

'I came to see you,' he said.

'You –' Elliot began tightly. Then he stopped. Over the past three days, he had thought of little else but the vision, apparition, hallucination – for what else could it have been? – of Raphael in Brighton. For a moment, his heart thumping and his breathing ragged, he had to suppress the urge to rush over and take the man by the shoulders, shake him hard until he released every last thing about himself that was leading Elliot to question his sanity. But only for a moment. Instead, he crossed the room to stand behind his desk. He knew that if he didn't manage to control his alarm, he might well end up humiliating himself in front of his patient. He took a few deep breaths, feeling his nostrils flaring with the effort, but then felt himself relax as he realised that his alarm may well be taken for justifiable outrage. After all, the man had entered his office without permission.

He said, 'You have an appointment for Monday. Perhaps I didn't make myself clear the last time we met, but under no circumstances can you just turn up here without an appointment.'

His voice was low and shaky. He must avoid a scene at any cost. Beaumont had showed just moments earlier that he was beginning to question Elliot's competence, and things were complicated enough without clandestine meetings with unregistered patients. Elliot looked at Raphael, awaiting his reaction. None came, at least, none that might have been cause for concern. Raphael merely bowed his head and sunk further into his chair. Elliot let out a deep breath. But how to get the man off the premises without being seen? Elliot went back over to the door.

'Wait here,' he instructed, opened the door and stepped out into the corridor. A series of naked, yellow light bulbs hung like ugly, shrivelled Chinese lanterns from black cables along the length of the corridor's ceiling, swinging gently to and fro in the cold draught. At the far end, closest to the Chapel entrance, a couple of white-uniformed orderlies stood chatting. The clacking of Nurse Robinson's typewriter was still audible from behind the closed door.

Elliot stepped back inside his office. Raphael had got to his feet and stood looking at the floor.

'You need to go now,' Elliot said. 'I'll escort you out.'

He held out his arm. Raphael took a few slow steps towards him. He opened his mouth as if to speak, but then closed it again.

'I'm sorry,' Elliot heard himself say. 'I'll see you

on Monday. Now, please, I have a lot of work to be getting on with.'

He let Raphael step through the door ahead of him and walked beside him down the corridor towards the exit, all the while mentally rehearsing his explanation for the man's presence (a stranger who had wandered into the clinic in desperate hope of immediate treatment, perhaps), in case he ran into one of his colleagues, or even worse, Beaumont. But they met no one. Even the orderlies had left. Once out on the pavement, Elliot let his hand rest on Raphael's arm.

'Monday,' he said. 'Only four more days. Then you can come and see me.'

Raphael nodded without speaking, then pulled the collar of his coat up and walked off. Elliot stood and watched until he had disappeared around the corner, and then re-entered the clinic.

He barely had five minutes to recover from Raphael's startling visit when Nurse Robinson knocked on his door and came in.

'Jenny's here,' she said, stepping forward and placing a file on his desk. She paused, and then said in a quiet tone, 'I was wondering if I should make a start on typing up Mrs Derby's notes.' She folded her hands in front of her.

'I – ' Elliot flushed as he remembered this morning's meeting. 'Nurse Robinson, this morning, it was – '

She shook her head and smiled. 'Least said,' she interrupted.

'Very well,' Elliot said. 'Show her in.' And in a

much lower voice he added, 'I don't suppose he's going to wait outside?'

She pulled down the corners of her mouth and shook her head. She opened the door fully, and let in Jenny and her father.

'Come in, Jenny,' Elliot said, trying to force a smile that seemed as genuine and warm as possible. Jenny's fair hair hung down on either side of her thin face. She had a yellowish-grey, unhealthy-looking pallor. Her father, in contrast, was red-faced and overweight.

'Mr Wilson.' Elliot stretched out his hand. That was the only time Elliot intended to acknowledge the man's presence. They shook hands: Wilson with an unusually limp handshake for a man of his obvious physical strength.

'Please lie down, Jenny, make yourself comfortable.' He guided her to the couch, and then sat in the chair behind his desk, facing towards the door. Wilson sat in an armchair beside the couch, jealously guarding his daughter with his huge body.

'Now, how have you been, Jenny?'

'I'm all right, thank you.' It was a thin, reedy voice.

'Did you have a nice Christmas? I bet it was exciting.'

There was no answer.

'Go on, say something,' her father growled, poking his daughter roughly on the shoulder. Elliot saw her wince. He shook his head; this was not a promising start to the session.

'Please, Mr Wilson, that's enough,' he said. 'It's up to Jenny whether she wants to answer any of my questions.

It's important that she knows that. And I must ask you not to interrupt.'

Wilson sat back on his chair, folding his arms in defiance and resting them on his bloated abdomen. His mouth was twisted, and his breathing was heavy. Here was a man trying very hard to control his temper, Elliot thought. In a different setting, Wilson would not be far away from using physical violence to put his point across. Elliot would have to tread carefully with the man.

'Now, let's see.' He turned a page in Jenny's file. 'What were we talking about last time? Oh yes. Have you had any more of those nightmares you told me about?'

'No. Yes. I don't know.'

'Have you had a go at writing down the nightmares?'

'I forgot.'

This was the usual tone at the beginning of their sessions. She was brusque; not an easy girl to like. It took a long time for her to warm up.

'Well, could you write it down for me now?' Elliot asked.

'S'ppose.'

He sighed in exasperation, despite himself. These were the most difficult kinds of patients: either monosyllabic like Jenny or loquacious like Mrs Derby, his depressive. Neither was optimal for psycho-analysis, but it was always easier to ask someone to shut up than to get someone to speak. He got up and fetched a chair from the far side of his office and placed it at the desk opposite his chair. Then he took a sheet of paper and a pencil and handed it to Jenny.

'You'll be more comfortable writing here,' he said.

Jenny shot a quick glance at her father, but then did as Elliot asked. Mr Wilson leaned forward in his armchair, gripping the armrests with both hands.

'Just write what comes into your head,' Elliot said to Jenny. 'And don't worry about spelling mistakes.' He gave her a smile that she didn't return. Elliot watched her make her first hesitant scribbles, huddled over the paper as if she were guarding her most precious possession, and then walked over to the window. There wasn't much to look at in the yard, but Elliot didn't want Jenny to feel as though she were being invigilated. Writing must flow freely, that was the key. Another thing to mention to Beaumont, he thought. Script analysis was a unique way of getting to an uncommunicative patient. He would make a note of that.

He realised with a stinging twinge of conscience that his mind was wandering. He looked back at Jenny, who had placed the pencil and paper in front of her. From where he stood, he could see that half the page was covered in her small handwriting.

'Thank you, Jenny,' he said, coming forward and picking up the sheet of paper. 'I'll keep this here, and perhaps we can talk about it the next time.'

Jenny nodded without looking up.

'Right, very well,' Elliot continued. He sat back down behind his desk. 'Why don't you take a seat in the armchair?'

Jenny stood up and went back to sit next to her father. He had settled back on the chair, arms folded across his belly, and was breathing noisily through his nose.

'Today I thought we'd talk about your mother again,' Elliot said.

Jenny sniffed quietly. Was this emotion, or just the onset of another cold? He paused, anticipating a reaction from her father. Nothing. He continued.

'Jenny, I'd like you to think back. Think very hard. What's the very first thing you can remember about your mother?'

Elliot could hear her breathing become more rapid, then slowing down, settling on a gentle rhythm.

'Baby.'

'Baby? Do you remember being a baby?'

'No. I remember Mum with a baby. She was all … round … and happy, in bed with a baby. She let me in the bed next to her, and she smelled all funny, but I stayed there, with her and the baby. I was only little.'

'How old are you now, Jenny?'

'Seventeen.'

'Quite grown up, then.'

'Mmm.'

'You said you remember your mum being happy.'

'Yeah, really happy; not sad, like usual.'

'Like usual?'

Out of the corner of his eye, Elliot could see Wilson stirring, like a lion ready to pounce.

Jenny didn't answer.

'You said …' Elliot hesitated. 'You said your mum was sad, usually.'

'Yeah, most of the time. But specially just before –' She stopped, sniffed again.

'Just before what, Jenny?'

Another pause.

'Just before she died?' he asked. The last few words had come out in a hurry, faster than he had intended. He heard an intake of breath as Jenny opened her mouth to answer, but it was too late. Wilson pounced.

'What's the matter with you, doctor?' he shouted. 'These are stupid questions! You know how old the girl is; why are you asking her? This isn't going to make her better. Can't you give her something for when she has one of her turns? She frightens the other children when she's like that. Think about them!'

Elliot was fighting hard not to lose his temper. He realised that he was still feeling somewhat shaken by Rafael's sudden appearance in his office earlier, and for the second time that day, had to repress an impulse to just let his emotions wreak havoc.

'Mr Wilson, you are being extremely unhelpful. I have explained to you before that your disrupting the sessions in this way will not help your daughter. On the contrary, it will make it exceptionally difficult to achieve any kind of improvement in Jenny's condition.'

'But all this gibberish about her mum being sad: how's that helping her?'

Jenny was perched on the edge of her chair, her legs barely touching the ground, shoulders hunched, picking the skin from around her nails. Elliot was furious with himself. He had tried too much, too soon. It would be a long, tedious way to Jenny's recovery at this rate. He placed the file on his desk.

'Jenny, would you mind waiting outside?' he asked. 'We're finished for today. I just want a quick word with your dad.'

Jenny slid off the chair and walked over to the door. Without turning around, she said, 'Sorry'.

'Never mind, Jenny, it's not your fault,' Elliot said. 'Next time, we'll talk about what you wrote for me today, eh?'

She nodded, almost imperceptibly, and stepped out, closing the door behind her.

'Mr Wilson.' Elliot leaned forward and sighed. Tilting his head to one side, he said, 'We both want the same for Jenny, don't we?'

'Yes, but...'

'She's not well, and I believe I can help her get better. But she needs your help, too. You mustn't keep interfering like that. I know what I'm doing, believe me. This is a therapeutic technique that has been shown to work for exactly the kind of problem that Jenny has. There's nothing for you or her to be afraid, or embarrassed, of.'

Wilson looked uncomfortable in his chair.

'All right,' he said, reluctantly. 'I'll keep my mouth shut, then. But no talking about...' his knuckles grew white as he gripped the edges of the armrests, '...you know what.'

'I'm not sure what you've heard about psycho-analysis, Mr Wilson, but it seems to me that you are worried about, how shall I put it, some kind of moral corruption of your daughter,' Elliot responded calmly. 'That is not my intention, believe me. I do not aim to introduce sex as a topic of analysis, but I cannot rule it out. If Jenny decides that it's something she wishes to talk about –'

'NO!' Wilson barked. 'I will not have my girl talking about things like that. It's disgusting. I'll have someone else sort it out.' He got up to leave. 'Them doctors, at the asylum, they had other ideas.'

'You can't be serious.' Elliot jumped up.

'Try me,' he snarled. 'I'm her father. You don't go anywhere near my daughter unless I say so.'

It was clear that the man wasn't bluffing. And Elliot knew that Wilson was right; without the father's permission there was very little he could do for Jenny. The only authority he had as her doctor was to have her sectioned, should he fear she was a danger to herself or others, but that would mean her being committed to the exact place he wanted to protect her from. Wilson folded his arms across his chest.

'I'll tell you what, doctor. I'll keep bringing Jenny in to see you if we can come to an arrangement.'

'What kind of arrangement?' Elliot asked.

'You won't talk to Jenny about – those sorts of things. Anything else, fine. I read the papers, you know, I'm not some stupid oaf you can talk down your nose to. I know what goes on in places like this.' He waved his hand around the room, and jabbed his finger in the direction of the couch. 'I wouldn't be bringing her here if I didn't have to. But, see, the others need her. Since their mum died, she's the only one they have.'

Although the man's manner did not invite compassion, Elliot's heart went out to the girl and her siblings. He doubted whether she would survive another spell at the asylum. In any case, if her complaint was the result of a lack of maternal affection in childhood as he suspected, then the omission of the topic of sexuality from the therapeutic process would probably do no harm. He saw little alternative.

'All right, Mr Wilson, I will avoid any reference to sexual matters when I talk to Jenny. Should I feel, however, that this impedes her progress, then we will have to talk again. Is that clear?'

'Right. Well then, I think that'll do,' Wilson said, giving Elliot a smile so smug that Elliot could have punched him. 'We'll be back next week. Same time as always?'

'Yes.'

Elliot opened the door for Wilson and just about refrained from slamming it behind him. He wasn't sure whether to direct his anger at types like Wilson or at the irresponsible journalism that provided fodder for such paranoia. A swell of exhaustion rose up inside him, compelling him to grab onto the door handle to keep his balance. He felt frustrated and exhausted; too tired at least to make any notes on the session. And what would there be to write, anyway? One step forward, two steps back.

There was a light tapping at the door and Elliot released the handle and took a step back. It was Nurse Robinson. She took one look at Elliot and raised her eyebrows.

'You look terrible, Dr. Taverley. I'll make you a cup of tea, shall I?' she said quietly, before turning to leave. 'Oh, and you've got your next patient in twenty minutes; enough time to get your things in order, perhaps?'

She closed the door behind her. Elliot walked over to his desk, dutifully straightened the patient files on his desk, but without enthusiasm, and got his coat. He then left his office to inform Nurse Robinson that he was unwell and would be taking the rest of the day off.

FIFTEEN

Helena was in great spirits when she arrived, considering it was the first time she had seen Elliot since Brighton. He had been somewhat nervous about seeing her again, while at the same time counting the hours until she was back in his arms. Leaving Brighton had been a shameful experience – he, the emotional cripple, and Helena, his very own Florence Nightingale, sneaking out of the house, *bei Nacht und Nebel,* while everyone else was still sleeping off their hangovers. But then they'd had to face Helena's parents. Helena had talked her father into lending Elliot a car, plus driver, to take him back to London. She was marvellous, behaving as though Elliot's actions had been perfectly normal; that he was overworked, nothing more; showing no outward signs of worry or alarm; helping carry his distress, his humiliation, and making him feel that it really was all right, that in her eyes he had lost nothing. She had been forced to give a promise to accompany her father to New York in order to be spared her parent's disapproval. Yet how was she to know that he wouldn't suddenly turn again, run riot like some crazed lunatic? The truth was that she didn't; he didn't even know that.

So it was a great relief to see her jumping out of the taxicab at his front door, as brightly as though nothing had happened. Now that things were out in the open, he had no desire to speak about it again. He was pleased to see that she seemed to feel the same way.

'Elliot,' she called, running up the steps and embracing him. 'How are you? Did you get back to London all right?'

'Yes. And you? How was your journey?'

'Fine. Well, I drove back with Cassie and Fred, so fine is perhaps an exaggeration. But I got back safe and sound last night and have been dying to see you.' Then, with a changed voice she said, 'Are you really all right?'

'Yes, perfectly all right. Are you staying for supper?' he asked, to change the subject. 'Stanislav is coming, and I think Mrs Blake made a shepherd's pie.'

Helena looked suddenly thoughtful, but then said cheerfully, 'Sounds great. I'd better give Cassandra a bell, though, and let her know I won't be back till later.'

'Good idea.' He didn't ask whether this was a condition set by her father.

They went inside and Elliot helped her out of her coat. Then they went into the kitchen to see what the housekeeper had prepared for Elliot's lunch. Helena walked ahead of him, leaving a fragrant trail on the air for him to inhale – a dry, musky perfume with touches of sandalwood and cloves. He controlled a sudden impulse to take hold of her, consume her, never let her go. She read his thoughts.

'Hey,' she said softly, turning her body into his so that he had no option but to embrace her. 'You should let me cook for you sometimes. I'm no match for Mrs Blake, but it'll be good practice for when we're married.'

'That would be nice,' he answered, loving her so strongly at that moment that he startled himself.

'I haven't seen Stan in quite a while. How is he?' she asked, extracting herself from his arms.

'He came to see me on Boxing Day, didn't I tell you? With Luljeta and her boys. They're all doing well,' Elliot answered. Her scented warmth lingered on his chest for the shortest time. He followed her into the kitchen, where they hunted for and then located Mrs Blake's shepherd's pie on the sideboard. It was barely warm enough to eat, but that didn't stop Helena from plunging her finger through the creamy-golden potato crust to scoop up a fingerful of gooey filling. As she licked her finger, some of the filling escaped and dripped down her chin onto her silk blouse.

'Blast!' she said, looking down as the gravy was slowly absorbed into the delicate fabric. And then, with a wide smile, 'I'm such a pig!'

Elliot looked at her and laughed. She was perfect.

The doorbell rang as Helena was upstairs, looking for one of Elliot's shirts to wear. Her blouse had been left to soak in the large kitchen sink in a bath of cold water and bicarbonate of soda. In the drawing room, Elliot looked up at the ceiling and followed her footsteps with his gaze, as she roamed around his dressing room, no doubt tearing through the wardrobes and drawers – oblivious to Mrs Blake's painstaking attempts at orderliness – upsetting regimented piles of linen, discarding trousers and socks, relegating handkerchiefs and neckties to the floor. His eyes rested near the corner of the room; she had stopped moving, had probably found what she was looking for. He felt a sudden twinge of excitement as he pictured her standing in front of one of the heavy Victorian wardrobes, wearing the champagne camisole he had once glimpsed her in that delicately skimmed her breasts, hips and buttocks; burying her face in the shirt she'd chosen to wear; smelling it – a ritual she performed every time she wore something new – before slipping it on, and then wading out of the room through a sea of clothes a foot deep. Perhaps the mess wasn't a bad thing. It would give him an excuse to sort through the mass of clothing that inhabited the room, compel him to finally separate his own clothes from his father's; clothes that had remained unworn and untouched during the last year, becoming musty and moth-eaten. A dead man's clothes. Elliot had no more use for them.

The doorbell rang again, startling him out of his thoughts. He hurried to the front door, mildly irritated that he couldn't just go upstairs right now and make love to a half-naked Helena before asking her to help him sort out his clothes, and his life. The door, which jammed during the cold, damp winter months, opened reluctantly. He tugged at it in annoyance, but smiled the moment he recognised his friend.

'Come in, come in,' he said, but Stanislav was already inside, his left arm around Elliot's shoulder, giving him a gentle, familiar squeeze.

'Good evening, przyjaciel,' Stanislav said. 'I hope you are well?'

'Not bad,' Elliot answered, smiling. He took his friend's overcoat and cap. Stanislav had obviously come straight from work; his fingernails were filthy, and he smelled of grease and sweat.

'You look tired,' Stanislav continued. 'I am pleased to see you are not working, for a change.'

Elliot made no comment. He saw no reason to

worry his friend unduly with a report of what had happened in Brighton.

'Hi Stan,' said Helena, cheerfully, as they came into the drawing room. She was standing by the fire, dressed in a pale blue shirt: the first three buttons undone to reveal a soft, peachy – unfashionable – cleavage. Her beige skirt barely covered her knees, down to which she had rolled her honey-coloured stockings for comfort. Elliot's arousal returned momentarily as he acknowledged how she was dressed, but it thankfully abated just as quickly.

'You've arrived just in time for supper,' she continued, heading out of the room. 'Do sit down. And we're having shepherd's pie. Now, I must just go and make a telephone call.'

Her voice trailed off as she went into the hall.

'She will make you a good wife,' Stanislav said. 'I am pleased that she found you. When will it be – June, no?'

Elliot gestured for Stanislav to take a seat. 'Have you come tonight to discuss my wedding?' he asked, smiling.

Stanislav threw his hands up. 'No, no,' he said, sounding horrified.

'But come now, you are to be the best man,' Elliot continued, enjoying his friend's obvious discomfort. 'There are plenty of duties involved, you know, like –'

'Stop there, Elliot, or I shall refuse to attend,' Stanislav interrupted. 'I am sure that a family such as Helena's will be planning the happy occasion down to the last detail, no?'

'Thank God,' Elliot said, and both men laughed.

After a moment's silence, Stanislav said, 'But it shall be a far more modest occasion when you are my best man.'

Elliot looked at his friend and suddenly understood. 'Do you mean –? Are you and Luljeta –?'

Stanislav glanced towards the door and lowered his voice. 'Slow down. I have not yet proposed,' he said. 'But yes, I intend to make an honest woman of her.' He smiled. 'If she will have me.'

Elliot waved away this last comment.

'What wonderful news!' he said. Indeed, it was the best news he had heard in a while. He got up and went to shake his friend's hand. Stanislav looked slightly embarrassed, but could not, it seemed, suppress a large grin.

'When are you going to propose?' Elliot asked as he sat down again.

Stanislav sighed heavily. 'It is not just Luljeta, but her boys, too. This will mean a true responsibility towards them.'

Before he could explain what he meant, Helena came in.

'Cassandra knows I'm staying for a while,' she said. 'Are you two as hungry as I am?'

Stanislav nodded.

'Starving,' Elliot added.

'Well then,' said Helena. 'I'll go and see if I can heat up this pie without causing a major fire.' She winked at Elliot and left.

Elliot lit a cigarette. 'What do you mean, responsibility?' he asked. 'You take this responsibility as seriously as you can already.'

'But when I marry Luljeta, I will be their father,' Stanislav replied. 'And they will look up to me and see – what?' He held up his filthy hands. 'A cheap labourer.' He shook his head.

'Then let me make some enquiries on your behalf,' Elliot said, trying not to sound too eager. 'There is far more suitable work in London for a man with your skills. I'm sure that Helena's father could –' He stopped as he realised that he was making a promise he might not be able to keep.

'No, Elliot. Please. I do not wish to be the beneficiary of a rich man's favour. I will find other work myself. If, as you never tire of telling me, there is such work to be had, then I should not fail. If not, then –'

'Then you would rather let your pride get in the way of your happiness – and that of Luljeta and her sons,' Elliot said. He shook his head. 'Christ! You can be so stubborn at times.'

Before Stanislav could comment on this, Helena popped her head through the door, bringing with her the delicious smell of meat and gravy. 'Dinner's up, boys,' she said and went ahead to the dining room.

Stanislav rose from his chair. 'I trust you will say nothing of this to Helena,' he said, 'not until I have asked Luljeta.'

'Of course,' Elliot said and stubbed out his cigarette. 'But she'll kill me when she finds out I didn't tell her immediately, of course.'

'Life is full of risks, my friend,' Stanislav replied. He took a deep breath and smiled. 'But now we must eat.'

After Stanislav had left, Elliot and Helena sat in the drawing room listening to the gramophone. It was a recording of a song played by a Dixieland band that Elliot had never heard of, something Helena had bought for him on a whim one afternoon while they were shopping in Oxford Street. The tune was pleasant enough, but Elliot wasn't really in the mood for something so jazzy. He would rather have listened to a classical piece. Haydn, perhaps, or Chopin.

Helena sat across from him, legs tucked beneath her, her hand tapping in rhythm to the music. She was staring into the fire, apparently deep in thought. Elliot wondered what time she had arranged with Cassandra to be home. Would it be like this from now on, he wondered, Helena asking her older sister's permission before she could meet with him? Well, it was only a matter of months before they were married; then things would return to normal.

'So you didn't tell Stan?' Helena said suddenly, in a tone that suggested they were picking up a conversation they had just left off.

'Tell him what?'

'You know. What happened on Saturday.'

Helena's question irritated Elliot. He was tired, and frustrated that Stanislav continued to be so unreasonably obstinate in refusing his help. The last thing he felt like doing now was to discuss any events relating to what happened in Brighton, not when they were sitting here so peacefully. He said, 'There's nothing to tell. Can't we just –'

'I'm sorry,' she said, with a trace of impatience in her voice. 'You tell him everything else. I just assumed –' She left her sentence unfinished.

'Assumed what? And what do you mean, I tell him everything else? He's my closest friend. I thought you of all people would have some understanding of that.'

'I thought I was your closest friend,' she said quietly.

'You know what I meant,' Elliot said. He felt weary. He had long suspected – although Helena would never have acknowledged this outright – that she was jealous of his friendship with Stanislav. She was right, in a sense; he did usually share things with Stanislav. He shouldn't have reacted like that, but just now, he was tired; tired of putting others' feelings before his own. Why should he always be the one to compromise, the one to make sure that everybody else was fine, happy, contented? Surely it was about time that others took his needs into account.

Helena sighed and stretched out her legs in front of her. 'It's late,' she said, avoiding Elliot's eye. 'Perhaps you should call me a taxicab.'

The night was relentlessly long, interspersed only with short bursts of sleep which were filled with bizarre and disturbing dreams. Elliot went to work the next day feeling exhausted. He saw two patients in the morning, but plodded through the sessions almost automatically. He felt as though he were in a daze; felt as though he had been hit hard on the head with a blunt object and feared he would be assailed by a migraine at any moment. Finally, after lunch, his head cleared, but his restlessness grew. Raphael was due in his office at three o'clock. During the long waking hours in the night, Elliot had resigned himself to the fact that it

was futile to try and hide the man from Beaumont any longer. Futile and exhausting. At around four o'clock in the
morning, as he lay in bed listening to the wind shrieking
down the street outside like some asthmatic fury, making
the window panes rattle in their frames and forcing in icy
wisps of air through the heavy curtains, he decided that
following his next session with Raphael – whatever that
might bring – he would inform Beaumont. He might tweak
the truth here or there: there was no need to let Beaumont
know the extent of Raphael's disorder, his transformations
– not yet anyway. But he knew that once the truth was out,
he would feel much better for it. He must have fallen asleep
eventually, because the next time he opened his eyes, the
room was no longer pitch-black, but instead a bland, cre-
puscular grey.

There was a knock on his office door, bringing Elliot back to the present with a start. He checked the time.
It was almost half past three, half an hour past the agreed
time. What could have held Raphael up, he wondered? He
shifted patient files from the left to the right of his desk and
back again. There was barely half an hour until he was due
to see his next patient. He would have to tell Raphael that
punctuality was essential.

He closed the journal that still lay in front of him
and placed it in the desk drawer before calling, 'Come in.'

The door opened and Nurse Robinson came in.

'Mrs Derby is here early,' she said.

'Mrs Derby?' asked Elliot, momentarily confused.
He had been expecting her to announce Raphael's arrival
and now had to sort his thoughts. He pushed his careful-

ly worded explanation for Raphael's visit to the back of his mind.

'Yes,' Nurse Robinson answered. 'Her appointment is for four o'clock.'

'Yes, yes, I know,' said Elliot.

'She's quite happy to wait, though.'

'Thank you,' Elliot said. He looked over to the door, which stood slightly ajar. 'Would you mind closing the door and taking a seat for a moment?' he asked. He might as well use the time to discuss his analysis of the letter she had given him. He owed her as much – and if Raphael arrived now, then he would just have to wait until Elliot had time.

Nurse Robinson looked a little surprised, but heeded his request. She appeared uncomfortably out of place on the chair normally reserved for his patients and looked at him expectantly. Elliot opened his desk drawer and extracted her letter. Seeing this, Nurse Robinson let out a little cough.

'Oh,' she said.

Elliot took the letter out of the envelope and placed in in front of him. 'I have completed the analysis,' he began. 'It wasn't a very large handwriting sample, but I feel confident in telling you that the writer of this letter is honest in his intentions.'

Nurse Robinson said nothing, but she was clenching her hands together tightly, and Elliot had the impression that she was doing this to prevent them from shaking.

'I'm not entirely sure how much further detail you require,' he said. He hoped she would come out and tell him herself who had written the letter. He wasn't prepared – yet

– to let her know that he knew the truth.

'As much detail as you have, Dr. Taverley,' she responded. 'Perhaps something about his, um, character.'

'I shall gladly let you have my notes, of course,' he said. 'But overall, in terms of character, this man appears to be intelligent and ambitious. I would think he could be described as large-spirited, although his script also reveals a tendency towards extravagance. But I will be honest with you, Nurse Robinson. I have reason to doubt that this is the man's, let us say, natural handwriting.'

Nurse Robinson eye's widened.

'Many features of the writing suggest that he was under a fair amount of emotional strain when he wrote this letter,' Elliot continued. 'This must be taken into account with anything I tell you. In the absence of further context I cannot tell the reasons for the man's tension. But presumably your sister will understand why. Also – ' he hesitated,

'Yes?'

'Also, it would have been very useful for me – for anyone compiling a graphological assessment – if I could have analysed the writer's signature.' He waited for her reaction. Nurse Robinson looked up at the ceiling and then bowed her head. Elliot thought she might have her eyes closed, but couldn't be sure. Then she said something, whispered it, so quietly that he didn't catch it.

'I adopt a holistic approach in the analysis of scripts,' he said. 'And – '

'You know,' she said suddenly. She shook her head several times with her eyes shut. 'You know. Oh, how could I have been so foolish?' She stood up and looked at him. 'I'm sorry, Dr. Taverley, I'm sorry. Please forgive me.' She held out a shaking hand for the letter and was evidently fighting off tears. 'Please let us forget this conversation.'

Elliot also rose from his chair and leaned forward, resting his hands on the desk. 'Sit down, Nurse Robinson. Please.'

She slumped back down on her chair and began chewing on her lower lip, which soon turned a dark, bruised pink.

Elliot took a deep breath and sat down. 'First of all,' he began, 'I can assure you that I will treat this matter in the utmost confidence. You needn't fear that anyone else will know about this. Is that clear?'

She nodded wretchedly.

'Good. Now, to be frank, I am more than a little surprised that you entrusted me with this, rather than commissioning a private graphological practice. Surely it must have occurred to you that I might recognise Dr. Beaumont's handwriting.'

Nurse Robinson sighed audibly, as though relieved that the truth had finally been spoken aloud.

'Of course I considered that,' she said quietly. 'But I don't have the funds. I –' She wrung her hands together. 'I hoped that because he writes so differently, so … neatly, here, that you wouldn't be able to tell.' These last few words came out in a whisper. 'I was a fool.'

'Please, don't feel foolish,' Elliot said. 'Now, you may tell your sister –'

Nurse Robinson let out a groan, then covered her face with her hands and began to sob. Elliot rose quickly from his chair and went to place his hand on her shoulder. He was both surprised and moved by this show of emotion. After a minute, Nurse Robinson stopped crying. She took a starched white handkerchief from her pocket and patted her face dry.

'I have no sister,' she said in a low voice. Elliot withdrew his hand from her shoulder.

'It is me,' she continued, and the emotion in her voice had completely disappeared. 'I am the addressee. Dr. Beaumont and I –' she swallowed. 'My husband refuses to grant me a divorce, you see. Although he has not been living with me for years. He chooses to make his own life a living hell with drink, yet he refuses to let me carve out a little happiness for myself.' Her chin began to tremble, but she sniffed and repressed the tears. 'Chapel policy prevents Charles and I from being together. Yet he tells me that he will find a way, goodness knows how, and that I should be patient, that –' She stopped talking, as though it were too painful to continue.

'And you wished to know if he believes his own assurances,' Elliot said.

She nodded.

Elliot went back to his side of the desk. He picked up the letter. It made sense, now, the tone she had used in the Chapel meeting, a tone no one would have otherwise dared to use towards Beaumont. Elliot felt touched and helpless. He felt his earlier irritation towards the man dissolve. Each had his own cross to bear, it seemed. And yet he couldn't bring himself to let Nurse Robinson know that the man's handwriting did indeed betray his apparent convictions.

'In that case,' he said, 'I can tell you that the results of my analysis suggest that he holds nothing but love and affection for you.'

Nurse Robinson blushed and patted her face again with the handkerchief.

'And if Dr. Beaumont says that he will find a solution for this – let us say, predicament – then you may rest assured that he speaks the truth.'

Nurse Robinson stood up. 'I am truly in your debt, Dr. Taverley,' she said.

Elliot shook his head. 'No, please. I feel honoured by your trust in me.' He held out the letter for her to take. 'I think it's time to show Mrs Derby in,' he said.

Sixteen

Three weeks after Helena had left for New York with her father, Elliot sat in a shadowy corner of The King's Arms on Hooper Road, waiting for Stanislav to arrive. Outside, the weather was bleak and inert; the clouds hung dark and low in the sky, invoking claustrophobia in a city already overcrowded. He had put off seeing his friend for weeks, worried that Stanislav would notice the change in him: the edginess, the exhaustion, the dark purple rings he wore under his eyes as the result of incessant migraines. His "episode" – this was how he'd started referring to the incident in Brighton – had left a mark on him; so much so, that he had begun to feel its effects in everything he did. Despite his attempts at self-analysis, despite his insistence to himself that all that had happened had some logical, psycho-dynamic explanation, he couldn't shake off a vertiginous feeling of panic.

With Helena away, he felt vulnerable, intensely lonely, and frightened that when she returned from America she wouldn't be returning to him. His unauthorised absences at work hadn't gone unnoticed, either. But with only a handful of patients left, he saw no reason to sit around in his office all day, drudging through the paperwork the administrators at the Chapel should have been dealing with. Mrs Derby had made a full recovery, and the young chap Burns, well, if Elliot was honest, the man was suffering from nothing more than mild agoraphobia. A few outings with his hand held would cure the man within a session or two. Jenny's complaint was still somewhat of a mystery, but Elliot had no intention of giving up on her. Her father's constant, inappropriate interruptions made each session drag on in an endless, frustratingly dislocated manner, but Elliot remained convinced that they would get to the core of her disorder sooner or later.

And then there was Raphael. His failure to appear at his last appointment had initially worried, then increasingly irritated Elliot. In fact, he couldn't help but feel that he had been misled by the man as to the seriousness of his condition. If he was suffering so much, then why seek help only to throw the offer of it back in Elliot's face? But as the days, then weeks, had passed by, Elliot had almost put Raphael out of his mind completely.

Then, the day before yesterday, he had received an unexpected note from Raphael, addressed to him at the Chapel, requesting an appointment. Elliot had been in his office, playing around with some expense accounts, wondering how to squeeze them into an already overstretched budget, when Nurse Robinson had come in and handed him an envelope.

'For you, Dr. Taverley.'

He took the envelope from her. He recognised the handwriting immediately and felt a slight thrill of anticipation.

'Who gave you this?' he asked, trying not to sound too keen.

'Someone must have dropped it off at reception. I'm not sure. Is it something important?'

'I – I don't know. Well, thank you.'

Nurse Robinson went to leave but turned as she reached the door. 'Dr. Taverley?' she said, her voice quite soft. If he didn't know her better, he would think she sounded apprehensive.

'Yes?'

'I wouldn't want to intrude on your – well, your personal life. But I was wondering, is everything … all right?'

'What do you mean?' he asked. 'Why shouldn't it be?' Then, in order not to sound too defensive, he added, 'I think I might have a cold coming on.'

'Oh.' She hesitated, then said, 'what I wanted to say is that if you – if you ever want to talk, about work, just knock on my door.'

Elliot gave her a quizzical look.

'I know that I need to talk to someone, every now and again. The other doctors here always have an open ear. But if it was something … I don't know … more personal, then, well, please don't hesitate.' She was blushing as she spoke.

'Thank you, Nurse Robinson,' Elliot said. He felt a rush of tenderness towards her as she went to close the door behind her. 'One more thing,' he called after her.

'Yes?'

'Do you have a first name?'

'Evelyn.'

'Thank you, Evelyn.'

Nurse Robinson closed the door quietly behind herself. Elliot sat pensively for a moment and then remembered the letter in his hand. He opened the envelope. There it was, in black and white, a request for a meeting the following Tuesday. Dr. Taverley, meet with me, at the Chapel, 3 pm, Tuesday, 1st March. No explanation, no reason for failing to attend the last meeting. Curious as he was, Elliot was nonetheless rankled by the use of the imperative: meet with me. As though he had nothing better to do! But then, he thought, perhaps this just denoted a sense of urgency. Whatever the case, he realised he had been spending far too much time alone, and that he needed the voice of reason – Stanislav's voice.

He hadn't been inside the pub since the time he worked at the asylum, and was astonished to see that very little had changed in over three years. It was a very ordinary East End pub, noisy, smelly, drab, but Elliot had spent many hours there with Stanislav, and felt at home as soon as he stepped inside. The pub had low ceilings, the blackened oak beams exposed and ready to meet head-on any man taller than six feet who was unwilling, or unable, to duck. The little light there was in the place came from a couple of tired, naked light bulbs that hung close to the bar, and the glow of a few dispassionate flames in the sooty fireplace. Elliot got himself a pint, and then sat down at one of the unsteady wooden tables close to the fire. It was just after three in the afternoon, and there were only a handful of men in the pub with Elliot. Three elderly cockney men sat in a huddle at a table by the window, red-faced and weary, talking and joking with one another. The landlord was leaning against the bar, complaining loudly to one of his customers about the increasing rent. At the far side of the bar, a nervous, wiry man with a receding chin and a tweed cap sat cradling a pint of warm beer.

Elliot had arrived early, overestimating the time it would take a taxicab to travel across town, and so he just sat, chin on hands, contemplating the mood of his parting from Helena. It was difficult to ignore the extent to which their relationship had been strained by the events in Brighton; however much Helena tried to put a brave face on it, things had changed. Following their argument upon her return to London, there was a tacit agreement that they wouldn't talk about the incident, and so all there was left to talk about, it seemed, were trivial, everyday matters. They talked a lot about the weather, about the mutual acquaintances Helena might meet on the boat to New York, about news items in *The Times*. Their conversations were pleasant, polite, rose-coloured; they didn't argue, there were no attempts to undermine each other's position. They didn't talk about how they felt, or about what would happen when Helena returned from America. The most manifest – but unstated – change in their relationship was that Helena spent no more than an hour or two with Elliot at any one time. There was no longer any physical contact between them, no kisses, no embraces; but every time Elliot inadvertently touched her, or brushed off her, he felt a violent longing rush through him, and he could have screamed. It was almost more than he could bear, but he was terrified of confronting her, speaking out, afraid that she might tell him what he desperately didn't want to hear.

On the day before she was due to leave for New York, she came for a final visit to Elliot's house. Mrs Blake must have let her in on her way out, and so she when entered the drawing room, Elliot was taken by surprise. He put down the paper he'd been reading and looked at her wordlessly. She wore a new dress, in charcoal moire silk with a row of tiny mother-of-pearl buttons running down the front, its bias cut fabric clinging pleasingly to her hips. The outfit made her appear taller, even more poised than usual. Elliot saw immediately that she wore a sense of purpose. He panicked. He opened his mouth to speak, to prevent her from saying whatever it was she had come to say, but no sound came out. His mouth was dry, he swallowed with difficulty. Then, without warning, she stepped out of her shoes, flicking them with her big toe a short way across the room.

'Come on,' she chirped. Her tone was far too cheerful to be genuine, but Elliot's relief washed over such nuances. She hadn't come to tell him she was leaving him. Instead, she came over to where he sat and kissed him on the mouth. It was a firm, confident, but unerotic kiss; a kiss that gave a little, but held much back.

'I've come to help you sort out your stuff,' she continued. 'It's about time we cleared some space here. Swept out the cobwebs, you know?'

Elliot nodded, his elation dampened only by the suspicion that this might be Helena's farewell gift to him; an act of kindness she was bestowing on him in order to assuage her own feelings of guilt for leaving him. If it came to that, to Helena saying goodbye, then he was powerless anyway.

They spent the next four hours sorting through things Elliot's parents had left behind when they died, a lifetime's worth of belongings. They sorted the items, which ranged from the hideous to the striking, into different piles: those who were valuable, like the silver Victorian carriage clock given to Elliot's mother by his grandmother on the occasion of Ed's birth; those that were of lesser value and could be donated to charity; and those items that carried no financial worth, and had only had sentimental value to Elliot's parents. Elliot and Helena worked furiously, without a break, carrying things back and forth, up and down the stairs, emptying cupboards, filling boxes. They worked wordlessly side-by-side, using a system of grunts and nods for communicating with each other, neither of them willing to admit their exhaustion. The last thing they tackled was a huge leather trunk in Elliot's bedroom, which contained an apparently endless supply of trinkets and keepsakes from his parents' marriage that had to be sorted and stored away. Finally, as the daylight outside began to fail, blurring the outlines of the objects indoors, Helena sat down heavily on the bed, and dropped her shoulders in concession to her tiredness.

'I give up,' she said, yawning. She stretched across the bed to switch on the small bedside lamp. It filled the room with a warm, pinkish light. Elliot, kneeling on the floor, put his hand in to retrieve the final objects from the musty depths of the trunk. He pulled his hand out clutching a postcard. It was nineteenth-century pornography, and depicted a plump, semi-naked woman striking a pose so ludicrously tame only Victorians could find it immoral, or even remotely erotic. Elliot sat back on his heels and looked up at Helena.

'I wonder how much this would fetch at auction,' he said neutrally, holding it out in front of him.

'I don't know,' she replied, trying to mirror his solemnity. It was too much for her. It began with a polite little snigger, a few short bursts of breath through the nose, accompanied by a gentle giggle, but before long, she had succumbed to a full, satiated guffaw, a laugh that Elliot couldn't resist sharing. It was a loud, emotional laugh, releasing huge bubbles of tension out of him into the room. He saw tears running down Helena's face. Then their laughter subsided gradually, in synchrony, and the stillness in the room told them what would happen next.

Elliot sat up on his knees and moved forwards, until his chest was touching Helena's knees. She lifted her arms and began to stroke his hair, letting her fingers run through it, firmly, close to his scalp, tracing the contours of his head with her fingertips. Elliot leaned his chest against her legs, placing one hand on either knee, and gently, tentatively, guided them apart. He unclasped her stockings and rolled them gently down her legs, pulling them off over her feet. Then he buried his face between her white thighs. He felt her fingers move down past his ears, down to his shoulders, squeezing, coaxing him up onto the bed. She lay back, her eyes closed, her mouth half-opened ... Aah, her mouth, plump and reddened with desire, waiting for his mouth, his tongue, his kiss. He stood up, pushing the smooth, yielding fabric of her dress up as he rose, up past her thighs, over her hips, her waist. As he stopped to unbutton himself, Helena pulled her dress up over her head. Elliot gazed at the perfection in front of him, and hesitated. For a moment he was paralysed, frightened of her, of what would fill the gap she would leave behind. He wasn't whole without her. She understood; she reached up and took his hand, and pulled it towards her. He lay gently on top of her; he brushed her flushed cheeks with his lips, and then moved to her ear and whispered hoarsely 'I love you, I need you', over and over; until she turned her head to collect his mouth with hers. They kissed thirstily, undoing all of the polite conversations and painful silences of the past few weeks. When he woke up the next morning, there was a small, cold hollow in the mattress beside him. Helena had gone.

Sitting here in his dark corner of the pub, Elliot was filled with a sense of loneliness more acute than he had ever felt before. He sat nursing his beer, becoming aware of a feeling that he was being watched. He looked up to see the thin man with the tweed cap apparently staring at him, but he turned away hurriedly as soon as their eyes met. Elliot looked back down, but a moment later felt the man's stare on him again. He lifted his right hand and put it up to his forehead, covering his eyes, pretending to be in deep contemplation, but instead, opened his fingers a crack so that he could look through them. From this perspective, he could see the man looking in his direction, but he couldn't tell whether the man was actually keeping an eye on him, or whether he just had a particularly unfortunate squint. He was about to go over and ask him what he was up to, but at that moment Stanislav arrived.

Elliot could tell straight away that something was wrong. He hadn't seen his friend for a while, and his appearance had deteriorated considerably since the last time they'd met. Stanislav's clothes hung from his already thin frame as though they were two sizes too large, and the pockets were sagging dejectedly. There were hollows where his cheeks should be, and his eyes were red-rimmed with fatigue. He dragged his right leg heavily behind him. As he caught sight of Elliot, he made a pathetic attempt to disguise his limp.

'Dzien dobry,' Elliot said.

'Czecs, sorry I'm late,' Stanislav replied.

'You look terrible. Sit down. What happened to your leg?'

'Just a small accident; don't worry about it.'

'But you can hardly walk!'

'Walk, yes – work, no,' he replied, easing himself gingerly onto a chair.

'But if you're not working, how are you eating? Did this happen at work? They are legally obliged to pay you maintenance if this accident happened at work.'

'They, who?' Stanislav replied. 'They who select me and hundreds of other hungry men from the docks at five o'clock every morning? Or they who give me the name Joe Smith and tell me not to open my mouth if the police come sniffing about? Or what about they who tell us at the end of the week that we haven't earned the two pounds we were promised and tell us to make do with 30 shillings instead? They who know we are too desperate to complain?'

'I apologise, Stanislav, I wasn't thinking. What can I get you to drink?'

'You are very kind, Elliot, I will have a stout, please.'

Elliot went to the bar and ordered their drinks, trying to curb the worries about his friend. He was outraged at the blatant exploitation of one man by another, and was angry that Stanislav hadn't asked for his help. He brought their drinks back to the table. The pub was filling up steadily, bringing in men filthy and cold, thankful that a long working day was over.

'I ordered us a pie each, just in case you're hungry,' he said, hoping his tone wouldn't betray his concern.

'Yes, thank you,' Stanislav responded, much to Elliot's relief. When the pies arrived, they ate in silence. After they had finished, Elliot asked about his leg again. It seemed too serious to leave unmentioned.

'Have you had your leg examined?' he asked.

Stanislav took a large sip of stout, then sighed. 'Very well, my friend. You have won. I cannot do any physical work with this leg. I am sure it will heal on its own, but that may take several weeks. Luljeta is out of her mind with worry, and there is nothing pleasant about a woman in such a condition. So,' he laid his hands palm down on the table, a rolled up cigarette squeezed between his yellow-stained index and middle fingers. 'You have won. I must humbly ask for your help. I need work – work that occupies my mind rather than my body. And I have not been able to find such work on my own.'

He looked Elliot straight in the eye and Elliot could see how profoundly difficult it was for his friend to be making this request. He realised that he had underestimated the power of pride, yet at the same time felt a guilty twinge of satisfaction that he wasn't alone in having problems.

'I will be very glad to help you, Stanislav,' he said. Then, to change the subject, he added, 'may I take a look at your leg? It might even be a hairline fracture.'

'It will heal.'

'Please.' Elliot wasn't backing down. 'Do you know what might happen if you leave a fracture untreated?'

'Very well, but not here.'

'Good. You will come back home with me tonight and I can examine your leg. All right?'

'Very well, Elliot, I will let you look at my leg, but only if you promise to stop behaving like my mother.'

'Promise.'

Elliot took out a packet of cigarettes and, as usual, offered one to Stanislav. Unusually, Stanislav took one. Elliot lit up, as Stanislav tapped his thoughtfully on the table. The table wobbled ominously, and Elliot's glass almost tipped over, splashing beer over the sides of the grimy glass onto the floor. Stanislav seemed not to notice. Instead, slowly, deliberately, he put the cigarette to his lips and held a lit match to it. As he inhaled, Elliot watched the tip of the cigarette as the intense orange glow flourished, and then retreated behind a cover of grey ash, waiting for the next stream of oxygen before it reappeared in all its glory. He glanced over to the thin man at the bar, who seemed to turn his head away the moment Elliot looked in his direction.

'It's good to see you,' Stanislav said.

'Yes, it's been too long.'

'How is Helena?'

'As far as I know, she's fine. I haven't seen her for a few weeks.'

Stanislav raised his eyebrow.

'No, there's nothing wrong,' Elliot said, hoping he was sounding more confident about that statement than he felt. 'She's gone to New York; her father is giving some lectures over there, and he asked her to go with him. I think it'll be good for her.'

'And you – you feel so lonely that you want to look after your sick friend?'

'You know that's not true, Stanislav.'

Stanislav changed the subject.

'You sounded strange on the telephone. As though you had something urgent to discuss.'

'Did I? That wasn't my intention. I've just had a lot on my mind recently, and I thought you might –'

'Counsel you?'

Elliot smiled. 'I wouldn't have put it like that, but yes, I suppose I'd like your counsel.'

'Shall I put these two chairs together so that you can lie down?' Stanislav asked, pointing at the two empty chairs that stood at their table, the slightest hint of a smile on his lips. 'After all, like the *New Statesman* said, "We are all psycho-analysts now!"'

'If you keep this up, I won't tell you anything,' Elliot said, mildly irritated by the way his friend was making light of his concerns.

Stanislav held up his hand in apology. 'So, what is it, my friend? What can I help you with?'

'It's about a patient.'

'A patient? At the Chapel?'

'Yes. No. Well, it's more than that. It's to do with Ed and this patient of mine who …' Elliot hesitated, trying to order his thoughts. He knew that if he didn't explain it properly, he would sound foolish, he might even let on how unsure he was about his own state of mind. Stanislav seemed to read his thoughts.

'Don't worry how it sounds,' he said, leaning in to-wards Elliot. 'I won't make any judgements before you have told me everything.'

Elliot pulled his chair up to the table. 'I have this patient who dissociates, turns into different people. From what I can tell, it only happens when he writes – when he copies other people's handwriting. The most accurate di-agnosis I can come up with is some rare form of multiple personality disorder.'

'And Ed? You mentioned Ed. I haven't heard you talking about him for a long time.'

Elliot reached for another cigarette. 'I've been think-ing a lot about him recently. The thing is, Ed is one of the personalities displayed by my patient.'

Stanislav's expression hardened. He said after a pause, 'What do you mean?'

Elliot looked away, and then sighed heavily. 'My patient turned into Ed. Look, I know it sounds fantastic, but it's true. It happened. I saw it.' He stubbed out his half-smoked cigarette, pounding it into the ashtray, angry that the tremor in his voice had betrayed his emotion. Stanislav placed his palm on the back of Elliot's hand. His touch was warm but firm.

'It's all right, Elliot, I believe you.' He looked straight at him. 'I wasn't quite sure what you meant, that is all.'

'But I didn't come here just to talk about Ed, anyway.' Elliot continued. 'I made some ... associations between Ed and my patient, but I'm fairly sure I've dealt with them. What I'm unsure about, what I wanted to discuss is the nature of my patient's disorder.'

'What makes you think I can give you any advice on this matter?'

'It's not advice I'm after, just someone with an open mind who can listen to my ideas. I think it might be helpful if I hear my own ideas out loud. Does that make any sense to you?'

'Of course. I'm flattered that you consider me open-minded. But before I start listening, you must get me another drink.'

When Elliot got back to the table with the drinks, Stanislav drank thirstily. He wiped the beery froth from his upper lip.

'So you think this patient has multiple personalities?' he asked.

'From what I've seen, and from what he's told me, I'm leaning towards that diagnosis, yes. But this isn't a classic case of multiple personality. As a rule, a patient suffering from this disorder typically has one or more recurring alters, or separate personalities, who "take over" and temporarily control the person's behaviour. These alters have well-developed, self-contained identities, and may or may not know of each other's existence. In many cases, the different personalities are fundamentally different in attitudes, mannerisms, speech and so forth. One patient, for example, might be honest, kind and industrious in one personality, and violent and destructive in another.'

'Jekyll and Hyde.'

'Well, essentially yes, but that's an oversimplification. I read recently about a case where a woman who had just gone into labour slipped into a different personality, because this one was analgesic – she felt no pain. In fact, this example demonstrates what is generally believed to be the purpose of multiple personalities: to protect the so-called "host" personality from pain or fear. Somewhere – or somebody – for the host to escape to when a situation becomes unbearable.'

'And your patient?'

'That's just it: I can't see the reason for his dissociations. Certainly, the personalities are separate from the host, they have quite distinct characteristics – his transformation into Ed was so convincing, Stanislav, it was as though he had come to life,' he realised he was gripping the side of the table with his hand, 'but I can't see what possible purpose the transformations have. The only case in the psychiatric literature that comes close to mine is that of a young girl who wrote automatically – you know: writing when one's attention is completely distracted – with both hands at the same time. With her left hand, she wrote in a small, flowery, feminine style; with her right hand, the handwriting was crude and masculine. When the girl was asked her name, the left hand wrote the name Elvira Clark, while the right hand claimed to be that of a man named David Avenel. These identities reappeared consistently under those names, but only when the girl was writing.'

A small boy came to clear the plates and glasses from their table, wiping its sticky surface with a stinking rag. Elliot looked at him. Below each of the boy's nostrils, thick globs of greenish-yellow mucus hung in trembling suspension, only to retreat rapidly into the nose every few minutes as he sniffed. Elliot took a clean handkerchief out of his pocket and offered it to the boy, who, misunderstanding the intention of Elliot's gesture, wiped the table dry with it. Laughing quietly, Stanislav ruffled the boy's hair, and pressed a halfpenny into his grimy hand. The boy looked down at Stanislav's offering, then solemnly nodding his approval, pocketed it and moved on to the next table. Stanislav turned back to Elliot.

'So the handwriting made the girl dissociate. And why did she do that?'

'She had witnessed the brutal murder of her mother by her stepfather, and it was thought that she created the "David" personality in order to stand up to any man she found threatening. "Elvira" was the character she slipped into when she was severely depressed: a little girl who lived in a beautiful house with her loving mother.'

'Can you apply a similar analysis to your case?'

'No. The only similarity between the girl and my patient is the writing. I thought at first that her case would give me some insight into my patient's condition. But her dissociations were the reaction to a traumatic experience, and clearly served to fulfil a role. That's what's missing in my case.'

Stanislav sipped his beer thoughtfully.

'And had you ever come across such a patient before?' he asked.

'No. Why?'

'No reason. Carry on.'

Elliot frowned briefly, then rested his elbows on the table. 'So, we have the trigger: the writing.' He held up

his thumb. 'The manifestation: the different personalities.'
Then an index finger. 'But no apparent function. How do
I explain it?' He shrugged his shoulders and dropped his
hands back down to the table. 'The existing psychological
interpretations are inadequate; they're lacking somehow.
They tell us nothing fundamental, nothing about the "self".

Stanislav snorted; but mildly, not derisively. Elliot
drained his glass.

'Seriously, Stanislav, I might be on to something
here. I mean, isn't that what we have here, a collection of
"selves"? Ed, the old woman he talked about, and one or two
others I haven't yet got the details for. Who am I to assume
that my patient is the host, the "real" one? Perhaps there's
a multiplicity of selves, bound together by some unifying
control, a sense of collective agency? You know, like a colony of ants: each ant acts individually, does its own thing,
but at the same time the group of ants seem to be acting as
one, in accordance with some grand masterplan. So is my
patient the real person, the underlying "self", who splits off
into different personae when he writes? Or is he just like
the ant colony, one of many fragmented selves, choosing
one particular identity to present to me?'

'Perhaps he is neither.'

'What do you mean?'

'Have you never heard of "demonic possession"?'

Elliot looked up at his friend in irritation. Demonic
possession?

'You are joking, surely.'

'No, I am serious.' Stanislav scratched the side of his
head. 'Of course I don't mean that your patient is possessed

by demons.'

'Well, that's a relief.'

'What I mean is that you are seeking an explanation for a phenomenon – you call it a disorder – within a framework of psychological understanding: the "self", consciousness, identity. I am merely pointing out that the same phenomenon used to be accounted for in terms of theology: demons, witches and spirits.'

Elliot frowned and shook his head impatiently. 'I'm not quite sure what you mean.'

'Roles. You were talking about roles and their purpose. Aren't we all given roles to play, by our families, our friends, our lovers, by society? We all have many roles, and those roles have many functions. In medieval times, the witches and demons had roles, as did the priests and shamans who exorcised them. These roles were real to those who played them; the demon was real to the possessed, just as your patient's personalities are to him. You, the psycho-analyst, validate the multiplicity with your techniques.'

'I'm not sure that I'm comfortable with your comparison. All I'm concerned with is curing my patient, alleviating his suffering.'

'And your aim is – what? To unify, to synthesise the personalities into one. In other words: to get rid of the demons.'

'But to take your argument to its logical conclusion, then ...'

'... psycho-analysis is merely exorcism by another word.'

Elliot sat back in his chair and laughed. His heart felt

lighter, he wasn't the same man who had walked into the pub earlier that afternoon. He had missed these conversations with Stanislav; conversations that made him question his assumptions, look at everything from a completely new perspective. He may not agree with his friend's point of view, but it was enough that he'd pinpointed the major uncertainty in Raphael's case: the question of the roles the different personalities played in the disorder. If he could define their function, he would be halfway to treating his patient back to health. This question alone would give him much to think about over the next few days; take his mind off Ed, and Helena, and what had happened in Brighton. He swallowed hard; it still felt raw, painful, to think about. His expression changed rapidly: his mouth twisted, and his gaze dropped to the floor.

Stanislav reacted to Elliot's change of demeanour right away. He leaned forward heavily. 'Elliot, this is not like you. What is your concern for this patient that makes you want to risk troubling yourself like this? Can you not refer him to another doctor?'

'In theory, yes. But I don't want to. And anyway, it's complicated.'

'Complicated?'

The noise in the pub was getting louder. Elliot was being jostled repeatedly from behind as the drinkers, with bellies and bladders full with ale, tried to squeeze between his chair and the congested bar in order to get to the stinking urinals in the backyard. The air was stuffy with smoke and heat and busy with noise, and Elliot was beginning to feel a headache rising.

'Well, no one else at the clinic knows I'm treating him,' he admitted.

'Why not?'

'I suppose it was the way the patient came to see me. It was all a little unorthodox – well, more than that. I wasn't sure –'

'– that you weren't being taken for a fool. Is that it?'

'Exactly.'

'When do you next meet with him?'

'He's ... I've scheduled another appointment for next Tuesday. Why do you ask?'

Stanislav didn't answer, but instead reached into his top pocket and retrieved his leather tobacco pouch. He rolled his cigarettes, one, two, three, without a word. Stanislav had always been Elliot's confessor, but also his absolver, and his silence was now inviting Elliot's contrition. He gave in.

'All right, I'll speak to them, and get Raphael formally registered as my patient. But let's get you home; I want to examine that leg.'

Stanislav gave him a wide, uneven smile, and Elliot reciprocated. They had each scored a small victory tonight.

Elliot felt a sharp pain in his temple. He winced.

'Another headache?' Stanislav asked.

'No,' he lied.

A glass smashed on the floor behind him, shattering noisily into a thousand pieces, making him jump. Elliot had had enough for tonight. As they left the pub, he noticed that the man who had been watching him had gone. Elliot hadn't seen him leave, and was momentarily struck by the irrational fear that he might be waiting for him outside. As they stepped out into the dark alley and the disappointingly stale air, Elliot looked around hastily, but there was no small, wiry man lurking in the shadows. All he could see was a handful of Chinese children who should have been in bed long ago, playing smut-faced and shoeless in the gutter; a drunkard, boozed up and prostrate on the pavement; and a man beating the living daylights out of his wife by the light of the electric street lamp.

SEVENTEEN

As Tuesday afternoon arrived, Elliot sat waiting in his office, staring at a piece of paper on his desk. It was a letter written to him by his former tutor Professor Niermann, and Elliot intended to use it for his impending session with Raphael. Two nights ago, he had woken up in the early hours of the morning with the idea that a text written in a foreign language might affect Raphael in a way that could render valuable insights into his condition. From his study of graphology, Elliot knew that on the Continent, originality of handwriting was considered highly desirable, unlike in England, where conformity and systematic self-restraint were expected. What would happen if Raphael wrote in German? Would the writing restrain him, or would it facilitate his transformation? Elliot hypothesised that the expression of individuality in the handwriting should bring about the latter, but he would have to wait and see.

Although the days were stealthily becoming longer than the nights, they still on occasion required artificial illumination. Elliot reached across his desk and switched the lamp on. His pupils contracted as the light carved out its circle of brightness on the desk, tossing disproportionately long shadows across the room. He yawned. To him, the nights seemed longer than ever, and yet they never quite managed to rid him of the weariness that dragged at him lately. He picked up the yellowing paper, recalling his time at the Charite before the War. Niermann had been a commanding, occasionally intimidating personality, but an inspiring teacher, and Elliot had discovered a capacity for learning he never knew he had. He had learned German with remarkable ease – the ease of an uncontaminated and eager mind – and the six-month study visit had been one of his most treasured experiences. The letter he was holding was Niermann's summary of a scientific paper on the accurate registering of heart sounds using a capillary electrometer. Elliot let the letter drop onto his desk, and closed his eyes for a moment. Yes, he'd been a physician once. It seemed so long ago. The memory made him feel strangely tired; recently, all recollection seemed to be having this effect on him, as though there were only a finite number of possible life experiences, and his store was slowly becoming depleted.

The sun shone in suddenly through the French doors, pitching long rectangles of golden light onto the dark floor. Elliot switched the desk lamp off again. He took the last cigarette out of his case and lit up. For the first time in ages, he could see more of the surface of his desk than the bits and pieces that usually covered it. It hadn't been a busy day so far. He had had what seemed like a very promising telephone conversation with a fellow from Hackney Borough Council regarding his promise to Stanislav. He knew the man, Chambers, from years before at the casualty clearing station in France, where Chambers had worked as a stretcher-bearer. He had seemed delighted to hear from Elliot, and appeared confident that finding a position as a translator for a multi-lingual Eastern European at the Council would pose no problem.

Following that, Elliot had eliminated any semblance

of a good mood by writing a ridiculously unctuous letter of gratitude on behalf of the Chapel to some wealthy businessman who had recently made a large donation to Chapel funds, and whiled away the rest of his time leafing through the latest issue of *Psychological Bulletin*. A few of the authors' names he recognised; one of the articles – a treatise on the role of the analyst in iatrogenesis – was written by Beaumont himself. Elliot drew on his cigarette. It was not too long ago when Beaumont would have welcomed Elliot's ideas on such matters; hours spent discussing the complexities of treatment-induced disorders. There was no more of that now. He hadn't had a decent talk with Beaumont for weeks, or with any of his other colleagues, for that matter. Elliot wasn't sure what exactly was being said about him, but they all kept a polite distance, abruptly ending conversations when he entered a room, standing aside to let him pass in the corridor, smiling idiotically at him, as though he were contagious, carrying some transmittable mental disease. He didn't even bother attending the morning meetings any longer. The pretence cost too much effort. He thought about the letter that Nurse Robinson had given him to analyse, and wondered briefly whether there had been any change, or progress, regarding her situation. But he realised that he felt numb to the cares of others.

Elliot stubbed out his cigarette in bored irritation. His *Handbook*, the work he'd spent so much time on, lay beside the telephone, limp and dog-eared. It was pathetic really, the hopes he'd had for it. Whatever gave him the idea that these bits of paper would really persuade the doubters? It would take much more than that to combat bigotry of the magnitude shown by the group of cynics at this institution. What, exactly, had he done to deserve this kind of treatment from his colleagues? He got up and crossed the room to get his notes on Raphael from the filing cabinet. As he got closer to the cabinet he noticed that it looked different somehow, smaller. He had to think hard, but then it came to him: someone had removed the pile of handwriting samples that used to sit on top.

He looked around the room to see if they had been moved to somewhere else in his office, but he couldn't see them anywhere. In fact, all of the surfaces that used to be piled high with his books and papers – mantelpiece, window sill, side tables – were all empty; dusted and polished. If I were paranoid, he thought sardonically, I'd think they were trying to get rid of me. With a slight note of panic, he rifled hurriedly through the filing cabinet, anxious that they might have found Raphael's notes. No, the file was still there. He withdrew it with a sense of relief, and stood tapping it against the open palm of his left hand in contemplation. In his alarm, a thought had occurred to him: What if they did find out about Raphael? It was inevitable that there would be a concerted effort on their behalf for some other doctor to take over his case. Elliot felt a knot tightening in his stomach. When he had first agreed to treat Raphael, it had been out of a sense of duty a doctor feels for his patient. Now, it was so much more than that. If they took Raphael away, it would be disastrous. Raphael's case was what kept him going; it was – in some strange way – his raison d'etre. Suddenly, he felt the walls closing in on him. He quickly crossed the room to the French doors and tore them open, gulping down air.

When the feeling of suffocation had subsided, he stepped back into the room and shut the doors. He checked the time; it was quarter to three. Raphael would be here in fifteen minutes. With a growing sense of purpose, he threw his coat over his arm, concealing the blue file beneath its folds, and strode out of his office. He knocked on the door of the room next to his, opening it without waiting for an answer.

'I'm going out,' he told Nurse Robinson, who looked up in surprise. 'I won't be back in today.'

She nodded with what seemed to Elliot a certain sorrowful comprehension. She said, 'You take care now, Dr. Taverley.'

He closed her door, and taking care not to look too frantic, marched towards the exit. He had plenty of time to head off Raphael in front of the Chapel before the man reported to reception.

It was five to three, and Elliot stood in the Lane watching out for Raphael. It was warm in the sunshine, and Elliot kept his coat off. The lunchtime trade at Evans's had died down, and so the only place Elliot could stand about now without drawing attention to himself was outside the Truth Society, where the proprietor had put out some bookstalls in the hope of attracting customers. Elliot started leafing through a copy of *A Journey to Rome*, ostensibly engrossed in what the author, a certain P.T. Holmes, had got up to in the Vatican. Every few minutes, Elliot looked up, checking that he hadn't been spotted by anyone coming in and out of the Chapel, and making sure Raphael didn't pass by him. He checked his watch again. Three o'clock. He glanced to his left. Fifty yards down the Lane he could see Raphael walking towards him. Elliot's relief was palpable. He grinned despite himself.

A taxicab pulled up at the pavement, just yards away from Elliot. Out of it stepped a tall, handsome man with silver-grey hair. It was Charles Beaumont. Elliot looked away hastily, burying his face in his book. Don't look this way, don't look this way, he chanted under his breath. Looking to the left out of the corner of his eye he could see Raphael coming closer. Had he spotted Elliot? Would he walk straight past him into the Chapel? Elliot's heart was thumping in his chest. A cloud pulled across the sun, snatching the warmth out of the air. The sweat on the back of Elliot's neck turned cold. He shivered, and turned up the collar of his jacket with his free hand. If he put his coat on, Beaumont might see the file and ask about it. A group of schoolgirls streamed by, teeming with suppressed giggles and whispers, a couple of irascible schoolmistresses at the helm. They bustled past Elliot, who stood, stock-still, with his back to them. They were so noisy; they were bound to draw Beaumont's attention to where he stood. The girls passed by. Beaumont was close to him now, really close; as he walked up behind him, Elliot could smell his cologne. He tried hard to control his breathing. He closed his eyes and waited for a tap on the shoulder. He waited for so long that when the tap eventually came, he was almost grateful. His nervous tension cascaded off him like a waterfall. He turned around. A familiar face stared back at him.

'I am here now, Dr. Taverley. I hope you weren't waiting long?'

Raphael.

A sighing noise, like that of a wounded animal, escaped from the back of Elliot's throat. He put his hand over his mouth. He felt caught off guard; this was the face he had seen – thought he had seen – in the window in Brighton. A brief resurgence of the terrifying blur between reality and illusion overcame him. It cost terrific effort to compose himself. He turned quickly to the right. Beaumont wasn't there. He must have failed to spot him. Elliot took his handkerchief out of his trouser pocket and wiped his neck. He turned back to Raphael. He said, 'I'm glad you came.'

Raphael just smiled. Elliot draped his coat, with the file still hidden underneath, over his other arm. He gently took Raphael's elbow and guided him away from the entrance to the Chapel. He wanted to get away before he did get spotted. Raphael lifted his eyebrows.

'We are not going in?' he asked.

'No. We're going somewhere else today.' Elliot paused. Where would they go? Back to Pimlico? He hadn't given it any thought until now. It would have to be his house; there was nowhere else that they would be undisturbed. The house would be empty: Stanislav had fully recovered from his accident – his leg hadn't been broken, just badly bruised and swollen – and he had found new lodgings with Mrs Blake's brother-in-law in Poplar. He was back working on the Underground extension. Helena was still in New York – she had wired him several days ago to tell him that she was busy putting together a portfolio of her work for an American agent she'd been introduced to there. For the first time since they'd met, Elliot had more spare time on his hands than Helena. But now, with the budding prospect of treating Raphael privately, he would stop feeling redundant. Yes, he could hold the sessions in his study. He'd have to tidy up a little first – he didn't let Mrs Blake clean that room any longer, it was his one private sanctum in the whole house – but it should do nicely.

He said, 'I'll be treating you at my home from now on. I have an office there.' He softened his voice. 'If that's all right with you?'

Raphael nodded. 'Yes, Dr. Taverley, I do not object.'

The sun asserted itself once more in the sky, shining white and bulbous against a pale blue. 'Shall we walk?' Elliot asked Raphael. 'It's about half an hour on foot.'

'I think that will be nice.'

Elliot rearranged the furniture in his study to make room for a chaise longue, which Raphael helped him carry in from the drawing room, to serve as a makeshift couch. The large oak desk was pushed closer to the wall; a dozen boxes, which Elliot had filled with Helena before she left for New York, were piled up underneath the window. Elliot stood in the middle of the room with his hands on his hips, surveying the space. It looked nothing like a conventional consulting room; Elliot simply lacked the patience and the inclination to attend to all the details that make a room suitably clinical. There were plenty of his personal items strewn around, but the room would serve its purpose well, he thought. Finally, he crouched down in front of the fireplace and set about lighting the fire. It was pleasantly warm in the outdoor sunshine, but the air inside the room was cold and damp. Raphael stood hesitantly in the door. Elliot waved him in.

'Come in, come in. Sit down. Oh, and close the door, would you?'

Raphael came in and took a seat nearest the window. Elliot blew softly on the little mound of smoking coal in the grate. When he was satisfied that it would stay alight without his assistance, he stood up and turned around, eager to begin the session. Raphael was sitting on the end of the chaise longue, his large, angular frame contrasting with its rounded delicateness. He looked up at Elliot, with the same expression of vulnerable expectation that had weighed on Elliot since the first time they'd met. He was suffering, that was obvious, and the only person who could help him was Elliot. Never mind the circumstances, Elliot was more convinced than ever that their encounter had been fated; that this relationship was meant to be. Fated! How could he explain that to the doctors at the Chapel? Even to Helena, or Stanislav? But he had been touched by fate; he hadn't chosen this path; he felt certain that this was the only path available.

He sat down behind his desk and opened Raphael's file. Niermann's letter lay on top. Now, looking at Raphael, Elliot struggled to recall the significance of getting him to write in German. The theorising seemed irrelevant; the man was all that mattered. It was instinctive, everything he did from now on was on instinct, and for the first time in his life, he felt that he could trust his intuitions, that they

would guide him safely down his path. He held out the letter to Raphael.

'Here, this is what I'd like you to copy.'

Raphael shuffled forward on the chaise longue and
took the letter. He needed no further explanation. He
scanned it briefly and nodded slowly.

'May I sit there please?' He gestured towards Elliot's
chair. Elliot jumped up.

'Certainly. You will need the desk to write on. I'll sit
over here.' And he exchanged places with Raphael. Raphael
settled into his chair and fixed his gaze on Elliot, as if to say
Will you look after me? Elliot nodded.

'Please, begin when you are ready.'

The metamorphosis began even before the pen touched the paper. Raphael's Adam's apple, usually quite pronounced, seemed to retract into his throat, making his neck
appear shorter, his head larger. His eyes widened: no, they
became a different shape, rounder, so that Elliot could see
the whites of the eyes above and below the brown iris. The
man's breathing became slightly asthmatic, as though the
air were scraping at his lungs with every breath. He pulled
his eyebrows down into a frown; not so much in anger as
in contemplation. His shoulders grew broad and rounded.
Raphael's transformation was almost complete. And then:
the words began to spill onto the clean white page, quickly
but not rushed; the impatient i-dots hastening ahead; the
elongated t-bars slashed to the right of their stems; the ele-
vated, idealistic diacritics, perched atop their corresponding
vowels; the surprisingly distinct, meticulous separation of
lines and words. It was only as he began to write that Elliot

noticed the ink smearing from left to right across the page, and he realised that Raphael was holding the pen in his left hand. Raphael was ordinarily right-handed, and yet here he was, wielding the pen with his left hand, as though it were the most natural thing in the world. It was perfectly still in the room now; all Elliot could hear were the seconds ticking by on his watch, and the fire emitting sporadic, irreverent, popping sounds.

Raphael lay the pen down carefully, pedantically, adjusting it to a forty-five degree angle on the page, and then clasped his hands together in front of him. These movements brought back a torrent of recollections to Elliot's mind – a small, dark, stuffy office on the ground floor of a large square building; the dust caught on the golden streamers that spilled in through the tiny windows on a beautiful spring day. Fragments of remembered sounds floated into his mind: harsh onset phonemes; guttural, throaty consonants; pointed vowels; all rearranging themselves into increasingly familiar words and phrases. Elliot is sitting with a group of fellow students, his Kommilitonen, in awed silence, waiting for the huge man with the Kaiser-moustache sitting behind his uncluttered, ordered desk, with his hands clenched and his breathing heavy, to begin speaking. Nobody dares make a sound or meet his eye, desperately trying to avoid being the one singled out for questioning; but to no avail: the huge man leans forward, propping himself on the desk like some giant walrus.

'*Sie, junger Mann! Ja, Sie! Erläutern Sie uns doch bitte den Vorgang der Anastomose der Halsschlagader mit der Aorta.*'

(You, young man! Yes, you! Would you please describe the process of anastomosing the carotid artery with the aorta?)

He was addressing Elliot! His heart started beating rapidly.

'Herr Professor,' he stuttered, at once terrified and thrilled at the possibility he saw opening up before him; that he might be able to interact with one of Raphael's alters. The Professor/Raphael continued.

'Na, wird's denn heute noch? Nein? Sie haben nichts zu sagen? (Well, will we have it today? No? You have nothing to say?) And turning to an invisible audience of receptive students, he said, in a noticeably more benevolent tone, *'Unser englische Freund hat noch viel zu lernen, glaube ich. Wie man, zum Beispiel, den Eindruck erweckt, als hätte man die größte Ahnung, auch wenn man keine Ahnung hat!* (Our English friend has much to learn, I think. For example, how to give the impression that one knows a great deal about something, even when one hasn't a clue!) And he erupted in laughter, a loud, sonorous chuckle that invited everyone in the room to join in.

'Herr Professor, können Sie mich hören?' (Professor, can you hear me?) Elliot asked, desperately wanting the man to acknowledge him. But his attempts came to nothing. The Professor's gaze went right through him; Elliot was completely transparent to him. He was invisible, incorporeal, illusory. For a short, terrifying moment Elliot was overpowered by the sensation that he only existed in his own mind. He held his breath; he was helpless, suspended in this void; and then it was over. He closed his eyes and covered his face with his hands. He didn't see Raphael rising from his

chair, but suddenly felt a large, gentle hand on his shoulder. When he spoke, Raphael's voice was soft and clear.

'I can see you need a rest, Dr. Taverley. I will come again next week, if you wish.'

He left without waiting for an answer.

Elliot continued to sit on the chaise longue for over an hour after Raphael had left. The room grew colder. The fire was dying, a few grey-encrusted embers barely glowing, giving off with reluctance the little heat they had left. Elliot stared into the grate, deciding whether it was worth rekindling the fire. He sat, elbows on knees, with his head in his hands. He was lost.

Four days later, the rain had set in. One of the gutters at the back of the house was broken and had come away from the wall. The water collected there, before spilling over, filthy and stinking of rotting leaves, onto the step below. Mrs Blake's complaints that she couldn't even step outside to pick a bunch of parsley without risking a cold shower grew in frequency and insistence, and so Elliot decided he would have a go at the repair himself. Early that morning, with the help of a tall ladder, he surveyed the damage, but soon realised it wasn't a one-man job. He would need help. He telephoned Stanislav, who agreed to come around as soon as he could.

When he arrived a few hours later, Elliot was feeling unusually exhilarated. Perhaps it was something as simple as the arrival of spring – the air was warm despite the rain, and the small backyard was radiant with the bright yellow of a hundred daffodils – but suddenly life seemed quite clear, fresh, no longer full of perilous complications. Helena had sent him a telegram the day before yesterday letting him know that she was due to arrive back from New York, and, although he hadn't seen her yet, the tone of the wire was conciliatory. It was an intense relief to know that she still wanted to see him. But more than that, he'd finally realised what was missing from his *Handbook*; he was palpably close to identifying the element that would pull everything together, and turn his work into a seminal piece of academic and clinical literature. He would discuss it with Stanislav, get his friend's advice; then he would waste no time in writing it down. It seemed things would be returning to normal. Elliot suddenly felt quite foolish. It was as though he had woken from a troubled sleep only to find that there were no monsters hiding under the bed after all. Stanislav seemed to notice the change in him, too.

'That's quite an embrace, my friend!' he said, as Elliot greeted him at the door. He stepped inside and went to hang up his coat.

'Yes, I'm full of life these days,' Elliot replied. 'So much to do. I must tell you all about it. I've had some very interesting ideas about Raphael; about the psycho-graphological aspects of his disorder.'

'So you are keeping busy? Dobry, good. The last time we spoke you were complaining that your caseload at the Chapel was dwindling.'

'Yes, yes; well, there's a young girl I'm still treating there. I'm seeing her at the Chapel on Monday. But listen,' he waved the thought of Jenny away with his hand. 'Raphael was here the other day, and it was extraordinary!'

Stanislav stopped abruptly. 'He was here?'

'Yes.'

'Since when are you treating patients in your home?'

Elliot was annoyed. In his newfound excitement he'd forgotten about his promise to Stanislav to register Raphael at the Chapel. But in truth, it was no real concern of Stanislav's; Elliot shouldn't have to defend his decision as to how and where to treat his patient. He decided to respond with indifference. 'It seemed the best thing for the patient. A decision made on the basis of my clinical experience.'

They walked through to the kitchen, where Mrs Blake had just made a pot of tea. She nodded a greeting to Stanislav, and then spoke to Elliot.

'I'll be off, then. Gutter'll be fixed when I get back?'

'Yes, Mrs Blake. It'll be good as new, won't it, Stanislav?' Elliot answered, winking at his friend, hoping that this would dissolve the friction that seemed to have emerged between them.

'Well, that's all right then,' Mrs Blake said, and waddled out of the kitchen, mumbling, 'Pity it's taken so long.'

Elliot concentrated on pouring tea for himself and Stanislav. How could he persuade his friend that it was immaterial where he met with Raphael, that the content of the sessions, and what his transformations signified, were all that mattered? The clinical niceties were irrelevant; why was Stanislav so intent on bringing them up all the time? He held out a cup to Stanislav, not wanting to look him in the face. Stanislav took the cup from Elliot, and blew on the hot liquid before taking a sip. Elliot watched him squint as the steam rose into his eyes. After a disquieting, lengthy silence,

Stanislav finally spoke.

'I don't know that this case, this patient, is doing you any good. It's all you seem to care about. Speaking to you as a friend: I'm concerned about you, Elliot.'

'You're concerned about me?' Elliot echoed in amusement. What a ridiculous idea! What was Stanislav thinking? 'Well, there's no need to be, I can assure you. On the contrary; after the last meeting I had with Raphael ...' He paused, trying to think of the right description. 'It was cathartic! I haven't felt this way since – since before Russia.'

His voice faltered as he said it. He had just blurted it out, without any thought, but yes, it was true! Before Russia; that was the last time he'd felt this untroubled, this free from guilt and shame. His eyes flashed with the thrill of this sensational realisation. 'Do you know what this means, Stanislav?'

His friend rubbed his face, and then looked Elliot straight in the eye.

'Was this man impersonating Ed again?' he asked.

'No. No! It was different; someone else. But that's not the point.'

Why didn't he understand? This was a revelation – years of desperate wretchedness, self-chastisement – all washed away. Stanislav should feel happy for him.

Instead, Stanislav sighed heavily, and put his cup on the counter.

'It's stopped raining. Let's go and see about fixing that drainpipe,' he said quietly.

It became apparent very soon that Elliot had bought the wrong type of bracket for the guttering. With expert hands, Stanislav made several attempts to mount the bracket, but it was no use. He immediately volunteered to go and fetch a new bracket, but Elliot insisted on going himself. Neither of the men had spoken any more than was absolutely necessary since they'd started work on the guttering, and Elliot was beginning to find the silence disheartening. He reckoned a walk would be useful to clear his mind, and, as he set out towards Lupus Street, the tension caused by Stanislav's surliness began to pour off him. The sun still struggled to burn through the cloud, but the earlier rain had cleaned the streets nicely, clearing the gutters and polishing the cobbles. Even the smell from the river couldn't spoil Elliot's mood. He picked up his pace, pleased to see that the poplars growing near the Embankment were starting to produce buds. Not long to go now, and London's parks and gardens would be in full bloom.

He had walked half a mile or so before he realised that he had forgotten his wallet. He smiled at his absent-mindedness. What better excuse to prolong his walk? He turned back towards the house, his keys jangling playfully in his pocket. He pulled them out as he reached the house. But when he bounded up the steps to the front door, he found it was on the latch. The door opened smoothly and silently. Mrs Blake had finally got around to oiling the hinges, he thought, smiling to himself. He stepped through the hall and turned left to go into his study. Just then, he heard voices coming from the kitchen at the end of the hall. He froze. He heard a woman's voice. Helena! She must have arrived after he left the house. He controlled an impulse to rush down the hall, and stood instead with his hand on the doorknob to his study, motionless. Then came Stanislav's voice: deep, resonant. Elliot remained where he was for a few moments, the rest of his senses dulling in order to sharpen his hearing. Any notion of reason was being replaced by raw instinct. After a minute or two, he began to creep down the hall towards the kitchen, trying to make as little noise as possible. The kitchen door stood slightly ajar. He didn't want them to know he was there; at first, he wasn't sure why. As he drew closer to the kitchen door he understood. Even if he couldn't make out the individual words, there was something strange, something conspiratorial about the tenor of their conversation. He was certain they were talking about him. When he had come as far as he could without running the risk of being discovered, he crouched down behind a low shoe cupboard that stood a foot away from the kitchen door in a small recess below the stairs. He crouched and listened. He caught the tail-end of Helena's sentence.

'... didn't tell you what happened in Brighton?'

'No.'

A pause.

'He, um, well, he had ...' her voice trailed off inaudibly. She must have turned away from the door. Elliot closed his eyes.

Stanislav said, 'I didn't know that.'

'Yes. It was awful.'

'So you believe it is a good idea to –'

She interrupted him. 'It's the only thing I can think of. Otherwise, who knows where it'll end?'

Elliot tightened his fists. A nauseating mixture of humiliation, guilt and anger rose inside him, transporting him back to when he was eight years old; except then, he had sat at the top of the stairs, an accidental eavesdropper, listening to his parents talking about him. He'd woken up during the night, hot and frightened, for the third or fourth time, spooked by a nightmare that refused to go away. It was the night before he was due to leave for boarding school for the first time. He came out onto the landing, in search of the usual comfort and reassurance from his mother. The upstairs was dark, only a flicker of gaslight coming from the downstairs hall. He stopped as he heard a voice drifting up the stairs. For reasons he couldn't now remember, he decided not to go downstairs, but instead, to sit down at the top of the stairs and listen. It was his mother's voice.

'… only a boy, George.'

Then his father spoke. His voice was thick with drink.

'He's starting school tomorrow, for Christ's sake! How d'you think it's going to look when he's up in the middle of the night, sucking his thumb and asking for Mummy?'

'George, please. You'll wake him.'

'Don't bloody George me!'

A clink followed by a quiet sloshing sound. He was topping up his whisky from the decanter. Elliot bit down on his lip as he imagined his father standing with a glass of amber liquid in one hand, the other hand resting on his brown bureau. That bureau. 'And pissing the bed. What eight-year-old boy pisses the bed? He needs his face rubbed in it, that's what he needs. You know, Amelia, Ed's done bloody well at that school. He doesn't deserve to have a (inaudible) like that up there, ruining his reputation.'

Then his mother's voice, thin and unsteady. 'It's not his fault he's so … well, not like Ed. Some children are like that. He's only a –'

'He's a bloody runt, that's what he is.'

Elliot's cheeks were burning. He rocked backwards and forwards. He was such a silly, silly boy. He pinched his arm until it hurt. And again. And again. Until his eyes were stinging with tears. There. Now he had something to cry about.

And now, twenty years later, he was sitting beneath those same stairs, listening to the two people closest to him conspiring against him. He pulled the corners of his mouth down and pressed his lips firmly together. A glob of phlegm had gathered at the back of his throat. He felt an irresistible urge to clear his throat, but had to make do with swallowing repeatedly. It didn't do any good. His fingernails were digging into his kneecaps, and his buttocks were beginning to go numb. He wasn't sure how much longer he would be able to stay in this position. The stench of cold sweat rose into his nostrils. Helena was still speaking.

'And Mrs Blake said that she heard voices coming from his study. As though he were talking to himself.'

The interfering old witch, Elliot thought. She must have been trying to eavesdrop when Raphael was here. Gossip-mongering, just because he wouldn't let her in the room to snoop about.

'And then when Charles mentioned it, I realised it must be serious. But I just wanted to run it past you first, Stan. You know him so well. What do you think we should do?'

More low, inaudible mumbling. Elliot leant forward, his eyes wide open now, cupping his ear towards the door. Charles? She didn't mean Beaumont, did she? He thought hard. Yes, of course, Beaumont was a friend of the Rickmans'. How stupid of him to forget.

'And the patient he claims he saw in Brighton was called Raphael?' It was Stanislav.

'Yes. Why?'

Elliot couldn't make out the answer. He thought he heard Stanislav mention Luljeta, but couldn't be sure. Helena's voice again.

'Well, I don't know what to make of that. But I'm meeting Charles for lunch today. Speaking of which, I have to be off now, I'm afraid, or I'll be late. But …' She hesitated. 'I wouldn't mention it to Elliot, though. He knows I arrived back yesterday, but I haven't seen him yet. I'll telephone him later today, perhaps.'

Elliot pictured Stanislav nodding his assent. Moments later, Helena came striding out of the kitchen, heading straight for the front door, her heels clacking loudly on the tiled floor. Elliot could smell the warm patchouli that trailed behind her. He pressed himself against the wall as far as he could, hardly daring to breathe. If she turned around now she would be looking straight at him. But she just pulled her green cloche hat down further onto her head, stopping briefly to check her reflection in the mirror that hung near the door, and stepped out.

EIGHTEEN

Sick – Chapel
Frog – Green
Voyage – Tears
Cold – Pain
Bread – Butter
Friend – Surrender
Head – Broken
Fear – Helena
Window – Ed

Fifty-four stimulus words in total. Fifty-four responses. The instructions were simple. "Answer as quickly as possible the first word that occurs to your mind." Elliot had used word association before, but in the past, he had always acted as operator and never as test person, and certainly never as both simultaneously. He had constructed a set of stimulus cards – one word on each card – and was writing a response word each time he turned a card face upwards. He drew the top card with his left hand, read it, and without further thought, wrote his response with his right. His office was dark except for the circle of light that came from the desk lamp.

When he had finished, he turned the last of the stimulus cards face down and dropped his pencil onto the desk. He pumped his right hand several times to alleviate the cramp and encourage circulation. He shivered; it was cold in the room. Spring had briefly regressed back to winter, and the cold was reaching in through any crack or crevice it could find. The window glass was laced with ice. He got up from behind his desk and went to close the curtains. His footsteps echoed on the hard floor. The room was almost bare; Elliot was left with a desk and chair, and a despondent, dilapidated armchair that presumably none of his colleagues had wanted. Through the French doors he could see that the yard was dipped in blue-grey shadow, and black around the edges. He quickly drew the curtains, shivering again as he bent down to switch the heater on. His clothes were loose on him; perhaps he was becoming increasingly sensitive to the cold.

He went and sat back in his chair and stared at the list of words he'd generated. What else could he do? If he couldn't trust his friend or lover, then he would have to rely on himself. An overriding sensation of insignificance rose up through his body, lodging briefly in the back of his throat, causing him to gag. He took a sip of water and forced himself back to his list, hoping it would tell him something. He turned over the pile of stimulus word cards so that the first word sat on top. Working his way through the stimuli and the responses he'd given, he discarded the obvious associations: ink – black; frog – green; bread – butter; sick – Chapel. The remaining twenty cards he sorted into two piles: responses that appeared ambiguous; and responses that were completely obscure. He looked at the first pile. Head – Broken. Perhaps not so ambiguous. That probably referred to his migraines. Fear – Helena; it was momentarily painful, but the idea that she might no longer love him was the worst fear of all. He crossed the word out on the card. Voyage – Tears. Slightly more tricky, but after a minute or so the association stirred a memory; one he'd put away a long time ago, but a resilient one nonetheless. He remembered a scene from when he was eleven or twelve, when he had been told that his parents and Ed were going to India for six months, and that he would be staying behind in school. He had cried for days.

Voices in the corridor. Elliot sat very still, hoping nobody would come in. He had a session scheduled with Jenny late that afternoon; he didn't want to be disturbed before that. The voices travelled slowly down the corridor. Elliot exhaled gratefully. He moved on to the list of obscure associations, the ones that he knew to be the most meaningful, the ones that indicated that a deeper layer of psychological content had been tapped. He swallowed. A sudden, searing fear swelled inside him, running through him like lava, scorching his guts. Was this how his patients felt when he confronted them with their complexes? He closed his eyes. That didn't matter now. He took a deep breath, putting out the fire inside. His stomach churned. Perhaps he'd only fuelled the fire. He opened his eyes and looked at the words. Friend – Surrender. What did that signify? Surrender, that meant admitting defeat, giving in, giving up. Was he giving up on his friendship with Stanislav? Or was he afraid that Stanislav was giving up the friendship with Elliot? Unconditional surrender – a military term. Perhaps that was how he now construed the relationship – in terms of war. His mouth twisted. They had betrayed him. Stanislav, Helena. Why? If he hadn't overheard them yesterday, he might never have found out. How long had they been deceiving him? He cleared his throat and looked across his desk for the cigarette box. It was gone. Shaking his head, he reached into his jacket for his silver case. His mouth was dry, his lips cracked. He took another sip of water and then lit a cigarette.

His eyes dropped to the next word pair.

Window – Ed.

He stared at the two words for a while, opening his mind as far as he could.

Window – Ed.

Nothing. Perhaps he was trying too hard. One word at a time, then. Window: what could this mean? Some kind of opening, perhaps; an entrance, a threshold. Window pane, glass, transparency; one could look through a window. To the unconscious? Was that what this association represented: that Ed was somehow the access to his unconscious dilemmas? He stubbed out his cigarette, burning the tip of his index finger on the embers. He grimaced, and put his finger in his mouth and sucked on it. This explanation was unsatisfactory; it was too simple, too contrived. He was overanalysing. Thinking back to the task, he recalled that he'd generated the association with surprising speed. And yet, there wasn't a straightforward connection between the two words, like "bread" and "butter". The short reaction time must therefore itself have some meaning. There had to be a preformed psychological connection between the concepts "window" and "Ed". A profound connection. Slowly, a tugging began in his mind, as though the recollection was being gradually, painfully dragged to the surface. His heart was thumping uncomfortably in his chest. It felt as though he were riding downhill on a bicycle: travelling at a frightening speed but unable to stop pedalling. He clutched the sides of his desk.

Window – Ed.

Looking through a window – watching Ed.

Pedalling faster and faster.

In the dark, looking through a window, crouching down – watching Ed.

Downhill, all the way.

Looking in, from outside, in through the scullery window – Ed in his uniform, no, his jacket is off, he's sweating despite the freezing cold.

Still gathering momentum.

From inside the house, Christmas carols, laughing, cheering, "Isabel, sing 'The Holly and the Ivy,' there's a girl!"; Elliot outside in the cold, looking in, not taking his eyes off the action in the scullery – a black dress with white lace apron; a white leg, no, two legs, either side of Ed's waist; stockings torn, the skin marbled, tinged with blue, kicking the air.

At breathless speed now.

Elliot's fist tightening around the neck of the wine bottle he'd gone out to fetch; looking, watching, hearing – a whimper, a soft, muted plea; Ed's hand pressed tightly over her mouth; her eyes staring straight at Elliot, imploring, penetrating; Ed moaning, deliciously, triumphantly, his legs trembling slightly; then stepping away from the girl, away from the countertop, fastening his trousers before tossing her some coins and leaving the room.

Elliot barely managed to run to the French doors and

wrench them open before throwing up the contents of his stomach. For the next hour, he sat on the cold concrete step with his head in his hands, tasting the bile of shame in his mouth.

Jenny arrived late, as usual. Elliot had heard them walking up the corridor, the sound of two of her footsteps echoing every one of her father's as she struggled to keep pace. Elliot had waited for them at the door, watching, taking in the couple's striking physical asymmetry – his weight and bulk exaggerating her smallness and frailty. She entered the room behind her father, as meek and sullen as ever. Elliot invited her to sit in the battered armchair. She obeyed, pulling her dark blue dress down over her knees as far as it would go. The dress was made of some coarse woollen fabric, and billowed around her tiny frame. The chair swallowed her.

'You been robbed or something?' Wilson asked, looking around the room in irritation. He looked, and smelt, like he had been drinking. 'Where am I supposed to sit? It's not –'

Elliot interrupted him. He'd spent the last hour rehearsing his confrontation with the man.

'I think, Mr Wilson, that you should wait outside. You'll find plenty of seats there.'

Wilson swayed briefly back and forth on his heels, threatening to topple over completely, but then gathered himself. He held out a finger at Elliot. 'You don't forget what we talked about,' he said, 'what we agreed.'

Elliot looked towards Jenny, who sat silently in the

giant chair. She was staring straight ahead. He turned back to Wilson and held his stare.

'I haven't forgotten, but I've decided that it isn't in Jenny's best interest to let her father determine suitable topics for therapy. Frankly, Mr Wilson, I'm not convinced you really want your daughter to get better.'

'Right, well,' he said, his mouth twisting in defiance. He marched over to Jenny and grabbed her wrist violently. 'We'll be leaving then.'

Elliot moved quickly to the door and blocked the way. He was shaking: with apprehension, with anger.

'Mr Wilson.' He pressed the words out one by one, slowly, carefully, savouring each one as it rolled off his tongue. 'You have, by law, a parental responsibility for the welfare of your daughter,' he said, as calmly as he could. 'If I feel you cannot – or will not – take this responsibility seriously, then I will be forced to act in loco parentis.'

Wilson sniffed. 'In loco what?'

'You take her out of my office, and I'll call the social worker.'

On hearing those words, Wilson's head jerked backwards. He screwed up his eyes several times, apparently deciding whether to put Elliot to the test. He inhaled deeply, pushing his chest out. For a moment, Elliot feared the man might strike him. But instead, he exhaled and released Jenny's wrist, flinging it down roughly. She continued to stare into space, displaying no reaction to what was taking place.

'In that case, I think you'd better leave the room. I'll call you when we've finished,' Elliot said. He turned and opened the door, holding it open for Wilson to leave, hoping desperately that his bluff would work. It did. Wilson glowered at him for a moment, but eventually acquiesced.

When Elliot had closed the door behind Wilson, he turned to Jenny. Folding his arms, he tilted his head to one side and observed her for a while. He would have to tell her that this was the last time he would be treating her; that after today, somebody else would take over his job, trying to uncover the origin of her neurosis. This morning he had found a note on his desk, from Beaumont, requesting a meeting regarding Jenny, his last remaining patient. Elliot knew what this meant. His position at the Chapel was no longer tenable; it hadn't been for a while. He was being asked to leave, and he would be glad to. It was only a matter of getting his letter of resignation in before they demanded it. He didn't want to give them the satisfaction of knowing they'd driven him out of the place. The thought that Helena might have conspired with Beaumont against him slipped into his mind. He swallowed hard, and then silently rebuked himself for these feelings of self-pity. There were others far worse off than him. He was only sorry that he hadn't made a better job of helping Jenny. Confronting her father had been his pathetic attempt at making amends.

He perched on the edge of his desk, opposite her, waiting for her to acknowledge him in some way. But she showed no reaction, just remained sitting, motionless, shoulders hunched. She appeared to be shivering slightly.

'Jenny.' Elliot spoke softly. 'Are you warm enough? Would you like me to fetch you a blanket?'

'No thank you,' she said, not looking up. She gripped her knees tightly with small white hands. Elliot could see that her fingernails were so badly bitten that there was only a small pink sliver of nail at the tip of each finger. The surrounding skin was red-raw. Her vulnerability was unsettling. How to get through to her? He had tried projective techniques – word-association, Rorschach – but only with limited success. Even her handwriting sample hadn't thrown up any clues. It was as rigid and opaque as any script he'd come across. Only her profound sadness and self-hatred had surfaced in the small angles and sharp spikes of her middle and upper-zone letters, and the contracted quality of her childish signature. But there was nothing to indicate the source of her neurosis.

Now that her father was out of the room, perhaps he'd have better luck. Or should he try something more – unorthodox? It was his last chance; maybe he could do some good. He had only ever used hypnosis once before on a patient, during his early encounters with psycho-analysis. While it had only been a case of mild claustrophobia, nothing as complex as Jenny's complaint, Elliot had marvelled at the cathartic effect it had had on the patient. But the Chapel – or rather, Beaumont – disapproved of the use of such techniques, claiming them to be ostentatious nonsense, designed to flatter the therapist, but ultimately proving ineffective for the patient. Elliot sighed. Perhaps Beaumont was right; perhaps he should persevere with the orthodox methods. He took a cigarette out of his case, put it in the corner of his mouth, and struck a match. Still Jenny didn't move. Elliot couldn't shake off the impression that she had sealed herself in, was more impenetrable than ever before. His exhaustion suddenly overwhelmed him. He rubbed his face. He owed it to Jenny to make as superior an effort as he could. This was his opportunity to make things right. Would she respond to hypnosis? If nothing came of it, at least he could say he'd tried his best. He stubbed out his cigarette and emptied his glass. Then, filled with sudden resolve, he lifted his chair from behind his desk and placed it opposite Jenny's armchair.

When he had sat down, he said, 'I want you to close your eyes. Shut them tight. Good girl. Now, I'm going to count backwards from ten, and you are going to start feeling very calm and sleepy. Don't worry about anything; just relax. All right?'

'All right.' Her eyes fluttered open and she glanced nervously at the door.

'Your father is just outside. You'll be fine. Now, I want you to lean back in your chair and close your eyes.'

She did as she was told. Her eyelids flickered; whether with trepidation, or with the effort of holding them shut, Elliot couldn't tell. Her whole body was rigid with tension. He would have to be very gentle with her. He began counting backwards, slowly, steadily, until he got down to one. Then, in a series of simple suggestions, he instructed her to relax her whole body. She responded gradually, but graciously. After five or so minutes of this, she sat limp and peaceful in the large chair.

Elliot addressed her. 'How do you feel, Jenny?'

'Mmm...'

'Are you relaxed?'

'Yes. A bit sleepy.'

'You're feeling nice and warm now, aren't you?'

'Yes.'

'Good. Jenny, tell me about your brothers and sisters. What are they like?'

Her eyes relaxed beneath their lids. She smiled. 'They are lovely, doctor. A bit naughty, the little ones are; what when it comes to going to bed and all.' She spoke very slowly, and Elliot was struck by the change in her voice. It was a woman's voice; much stronger and more resonant than the thin, nasal tone he was used to hearing.

'It must be hard work, looking after six children.'

'Yes. I get very – tired.'

'You don't get much chance to rest?'

'No. Except, when the young ones are in school, then I go and work up at Mrs Newham's laundrette in Clark Street. She's very nice – she let's me put my feet up when it's too much. Still pays me like, but lets me rest.'

'That's nice of her.' Elliot was pleased; she was being more cooperative than he'd expected. 'Now, Jenny, I'd like to talk to you about your … about when you're not feeling well. All right?'

'Yes, Dr. Taverley.'

'I'd like you to tell me about the first time you re-member not feeling well.'

Jenny wrapped her arms around her chest. She star-ted breathing rapidly. Elliot leant forward.

'Can you remember the first time it happened?' he asked again. She didn't answer, but instead screwed her face up and began moving about in her chair.

He persisted. 'Jenny, tell me what happened.'

Her eyes flew open, and her lips parted. But she

didn't speak. Small beads of sweat appeared on her upper lip. She looked terrified.

Elliot spoke louder now. 'Jenny.' She didn't appear to hear him. 'Jenny, what's the matter? What can you remember?'

She started shaking violently, as though a massive electric shock were travelling though her body. Elliot grabbed her shoulders to try and keep her still.

'Jenny!' he called, but she stared ahead, still shaking, her pupils dilated. She was pale and sweating. She tried to flick his hands away from her shoulders, but Elliot kept hold of her, anxious that her convulsions might get worse if he let go. Her head began to roll around on her neck, as her breathing became more rapid. She hit out at his chest, feebly, and then started moaning incoherently. Elliot leaned into her, his ear close to her face, trying to make out what she was saying. He could smell her panic.

'Jenny, what is it?' he whispered. 'What's the matter? You're safe. It's me.'

She started muttering; she had stopped shaking and was squirming around on her chair, pulling her knees up to her chest and back down again.

'No. No. I don't want to. Dad. Please. I don't want to. Don't make me. Please. Dad.'

'Make you do what, Jenny? What don't you want to do?'

'No, pleeease. It hurts. I don't like it. I don't want to.'

Suddenly she stopped moving. Elliot let go of her shoulders. Slowly, lethargically, the horrific realisation of what she was saying began to take shape. Jenny inhaled sharply, and stared at the door. Then, without warning, she dropped to her knees. There was a loud cracking sound as her knees hit the floor, but she appeared oblivious to any pain. She lifted her arms up and out, the too-big sleeves sliding smoothly down to her elbows. She turned her head to face the door.

'I'm sorry, Mummy. I didn't mean it. It wasn't my fault,' she cried softly, and her face lost any trace of churlishness, and instead took on an expression of such ingenuous despair that Elliot could barely stop himself from shouting. She looked like a wretched version of the angel he had seen in the cemetery.

'Oh Jenny. I'm so sorry,' he stammered. How could he have been so blind? For months she'd come to his office, in desperate need of help, and he hadn't spotted what now seemed so obvious. Her father's tenacity; his trepidation that Elliot might bring up the subject of sex. No wonder! Elliot ran his fingers through his hair, acknowledging the nausea rising in his stomach while Jenny sat back on her heels and wept silently. He walked over to her and stroked her hair with a trembling hand, whispering a belated, futile apology.

Then suddenly, something inside him snapped. He ran to the door and threw it open. Wilson was sitting on a chair near the door, head leaning back against the wall, asleep, emitting heavy, guttural snores. His large mouth hung open, revealing a thick, fleshy tongue. A gleaming thread of saliva trailed from the corner of his mouth down to his chest. Elliot stared down at the broad, burgundy face, as the anger grew in his stomach, making him sick with rage.

'YOU!' he screamed at Wilson, and the sound hurtled down the corridor and back again. Wilson lifted his head and blinked. He grunted and wiped his mouth with the back of his hand. Elliot didn't give him a chance to prepare. He grabbed the man's ears with both hands and smacked his head into the wall as hard as he could. Wilson's eyes opened wide with pain; Elliot noted the disorientation in his face as he hit his head a second time. It was an unexpectedly quiet sound; a dull, non-resonant thump. Elliot pulled the head further forward in order to hit it even harder against the wall, but he lost his grip on Wilson's greasy hair and over-balanced. A second later, Wilson had brought up his knee into Elliot's groin. He didn't manage to place a perfect blow, and so the pain wasn't as acute as it might have been. It was enough, however, to stun Elliot briefly. As Elliot went to cup his groin with his hands, Wilson threw a fist at the side of his head. This time he met his target, and Elliot felt, and heard, a loud crack as one of his molars fractured. He stepped back, tasting blood in his mouth. He spat the tooth out as Wilson went to punch him again. Instinctively, he whipped his head back and then brought it forward, just as Wilson stepped close enough to deliver a blow to Elliot's stomach. There was a loud crunch, and a burning pain spread through Elliot's skull. His vision surrendered temporarily to a series of silver flashes. He groped blindly for the wall to support him, hoping Wilson felt as dazed as he did. If the man chose to attack now, Elliot stood no chance. As his vision slowly regained clarity, he saw Wilson doubled over, dripping great globules of bright red onto the floor. Wilson looked up at Elliot, snivelling.

'You broke my fucking nose.'

He straightened up, and Elliot tensed, thinking he was coming for him again, but the joint effects of the pain and the alcohol made Wilson stagger from side to side. He sat down heavily on the floor and crossed his legs, head bowed, bleeding into the gap between his legs. Elliot's breathing was laboured; he leaned against the wall, trembling, not taking his eyes off Wilson, and spat blood into his handkerchief. His senses, heightened by the adrenalin-fuelled rage and sharpened into the narrow focus of the fight, slowly began to return to normal. He heard loud, rapid footsteps behind him, and turned to see Beaumont and Attrill running up the corridor towards him, accompanied by one of the Chapel's broad-shouldered orderlies. Nurse Robinson stood at his office door, which was still wide open. Elliot turned his head to look in past her, and saw Jenny lying curled up on the floor; her small body shuddering in occasional spasms. Elliot let himself slide down onto a chair. Jenny was safe now.

Beaumont hid his irritation well. Only the erratic tapping of his foot against the side of his desk gave any hint of his state of mind. Elliot could tell he was furious, but that he was restraining his anger beneath a thick layer of well-rehearsed civility. Elliot crossed and uncrossed his legs, waiting for Beaumont to speak. His jaw had begun to hurt badly; it was swollen and bruised, and it would have been prudent to ice it. But there were other matters to be discussed now. They were in the director's office; Beaumont, Attrill and the orderly, who stood at the door, arms folded over his chest.

It was obvious that he was guarding the exit. What did they think Elliot was going to do in his state? Run away? Start another fight? He grinned to himself, but winced as the muscles contracted painfully in his face. Attrill was smoking one cigarette after the other. He seemed more nervous than Elliot. Beaumont's foot stopped tapping. He leant forward on his elbows, placing his hands together so that his thumb and forefingers shaped a perfect diamond. When he spoke, his tone was slow and deliberate.

'I do not have to explain to you the seriousness of your actions.'

He looked up at Elliot, his dark eyes catching Elliot's and holding them, not wavering in the slightest. The ceiling light threw a harsh, yellow light into the room, drawing long shadows down Beaumont's face and making his skin look sallow. Elliot opened his mouth to speak, but Beaumont held up his hand.

'Before you say anything, Taverley, let me assure you that there are no excuses – absolutely none – for your behaviour this evening. I realise; we all realise,' he nodded in Attrill's direction, 'that you have been under considerable stress lately. But, to come in here, a place of healing, a place where people with the most delicate conditions think they will be safe...' He paused, shaking his head. 'Such gratuitous violence I haven't seen since the war.'

'I had no choice.'

'You're just a violent thug,' Attrill threw in with a sneer. 'You should learn to control yourself, man.'

'You just mind your own business, you son-of-a-bitch,' Elliot snapped. He turned towards Attrill, breathing heavily.

'Now look here, Taverley,' Attrill bleated, half-rising off his seat.

'What? Do you want to fight me?' Elliot shouted, standing up. He wasn't going to be humiliated by this snivelling upstart. He was good for another fight if need be. His chair tipped over and clattered against the wooden floor.

'Gentlemen!' Beaumont's voice filled the room. Even the orderly flinched slightly. 'Remember where you are.'

Elliot bent down to pick up his chair. He sat down, sorry that he'd let Attrill provoke him. Attrill looked like he was about to cry. He lit another cigarette, but then succumbed to a coughing fit. When he finally stopped, Beaumont continued.

'In light of the circumstances surrounding tonight's events, I doubt if Mr Wilson will be pressing charges. However, this is not to say that your actions will go unpunished. I will not make any judgements here. I shall submit your case to the board tomorrow, Dr. Taverley. You will be given the opportunity to put your side of the story forward, and then you will be informed of the board's decision as soon as possible. But you should be under no illusion that the penalty will be nothing if not severe.'

'And Jenny?' Elliot asked, momentarily grief-stricken that his actions had perhaps undermined what he had attempted to achieve.

'She is being looked after. The social worker will arrange for her and her siblings to be taken into care.'

Elliot sighed gratefully. He could think of nothing else to say. His throat was dry and his jaw was throbbing intolerably. He badly wanted a drink of water. Beaumont leant back in his chair.

'You are free to go. Please go home and calm down. You should also have your face seen to. It's probably not as bad as it looks, but it will be sore for a couple of days.'

Elliot got to his feet. The orderly stepped aside and opened the door for him.

'Dr. Taverley.' It was Beaumont.

'Yes?'

'I'm sorry.' It wasn't meant as an apology. Elliot understood.

'Yes. So am I.'

NINETEEN

He first became aware of the words in his dream, floating at the rim of his consciousness: 'Elliot. Elliot.'

It was Helena.

'Are you asleep?' she whispered.

It cost him effort to answer. 'Yes. No… Just resting.'

He could feel her lean over him as he willed his eyes to open. It was no use; they were glued shut. He had fallen asleep on his favourite chair, arms splayed out to either side of the armrests, head resting lopsidedly, awkwardly, on the back. He could smell her: cold, smoky air on her coat; warm, fragrant patchouli underneath. She must have just come from outside. For a moment, he became aware of an ache in his neck, and then slipped back down briefly into the limbo between consciousness and dreams.

'It's really chilly in here,' he heard her saying. 'Why haven't you lit the fire? Come on, darling, we're going out at six.'

She gently tugged his ear lobe, and he woke up fully. She was right; the room was freezing.

'Let's get the heater on,' he said. He got up off his armchair and walked across the room, stretching his stiff limbs, twisting his head from side to side to alleviate the soreness in his neck, then bending down to switch on the electric heater. As he straightened up, Helena wrapped her arms around his back, resting her head on his shoulder. She inhaled his smell deeply.

'It's not like you to sleep during the day,' she murmured. 'You're not getting ill, are you?'

Elliot turned and put his arms around her. She was much smaller than he was, with soft shoulders and a straight back. He had always liked to hold her this way; to feel protective, wrapping his large body around hers, shielding her from any harm. But things had changed now. Did she not feel it, too? He couldn't trust her any more, not completely, not as he used to. He held her for a moment too long.

'What's wrong?' she asked.

He broke off the embrace.

'Nothing, nothing.'

'Your face, it still looks terrible,' she said.

'It's fine. Just a little sore, that's all,' he replied.

She frowned at him, but then smiled affectionately, like a mother who understands when lenience is more effective than scolding.

'Let's stay in tonight. I'll cook something.' She hesitated. 'We'll have a quiet evening together, how does that sound?'

'That sounds fine,' Elliot replied.

Helena placed her open palm very gently on the bruised side of his face and stroked it with her thumb. 'You light the fire, and I'll make a start on dinner,' she said, and then left the room.

Elliot set about lighting a fire in the grate. He used plenty of kindling, and before long, the fire was blazing. For a while, he just sat, crouched down, staring into the flames. It was three days since his fight with Wilson; he hadn't been back to the Chapel since. He knew that the board had met, and assumed that they'd agreed to suspend him. What was the use of going back? They weren't really interested in what he had to say, and he wasn't interested in their sanctimonious lecturing. Helena had fretted a good deal when he told her what had happened, but he put most of that down to the state of his face. He'd managed to convince her that things would turn out for the best. Perhaps he would turn to private practice? He straightened up, his knees cracking as he did so. His time at the Chapel was over. He was surprised at how little it bothered him. The main thing was that he'd helped Jenny. Nobody could deny that. If that was all the good he would ever do, then surely that was better than nothing. And then there was Raphael.

The fire spat a lump of coal onto the hearth rug. It glowed fiercely for a few seconds, scorching a black circle into the rug. Elliot watched as a strong, thin plume of smoke spiralled up into the air before petering out. He looked around him for something with which to scoop the coal back into the fire. On the coffee table lay a society magazine that Helena had brought in. He grabbed it and managed to toss the coal back where it belonged before it did any more damage to the rug. He looked down to inspect it. The scorch mark was barely noticeable. He stamped on it, just to make sure any embers were put out, and went and sat back down in his armchair with the magazine in his hand. He flicked through it absent-mindedly.

On the final pages, just before the advertising page at the back, was a collection of photographs taken at several of London's recent social events. Elliot's eye was caught by a picture taken at some society party of three young women, all dressed in Japanese kimono-style robes with elaborate tapestry designs, posing to the camera with foot-long ivory cigarette holders. The woman in the middle, the chubbiest of the three, was Lady Maxime. Elliot smiled as he read the caption: "Three little maids from school are we". He was about to close the magazine and toss it back onto the table when he saw another photograph below the one of Lady Max, this one far more sober in style. In the picture, a group of five or six men in top hats and tails stood facing forwards, two of them with broad smiles for the camera. Behind them hung a banner, 'Happy New Year, 1921!' Elliot's eyes moved swiftly from the picture to the caption, a strangely familiar sense of bewilderment rising in him. The caption read: "Gentlemen at the Banquet", and beneath it, reading from left to right, were the names and occupations of the men depicted in the image. It was the second man on the left Elliot was interested in. Boris Nevskaja, Russian Businessman. He looked at the picture again – the light wasn't perfect and it was a grainy image – but it was clearly him. It was Raphael.

Elliot got up slowly and walked into the kitchen, where Helena stood buttering a piece of bread. The afternoon sun shone in through the kitchen window, low and bright, illuminating her hair. Elliot looked up and gazed at her for a moment.

'What have you got there?' she asked, looking up briefly before resuming her task.

'This photograph. On the left. The group of men. I –'

Helena reached out and took the magazine out of his hand.

'This one,' Elliot continued distractedly, pointing at

the man in the picture.

Helena took a quick look at the photograph. She nodded. 'Yes, I saw the photograph of Lady Max, looking ridiculous, and then noticed that one,' she said. 'Funny, isn't it?'

Elliot frowned. This wasn't the reaction he'd expected.

'We met him. Don't you remember? At Janet and Marshall's party. Last summer.'

Elliot hesitated and gripped the magazine.

'Come on,' Helena continued, 'you can't have forgotten. You even had a lengthy conversation with him. About handwriting analysis. He had some sort of graphology business.' She tapped the magazine with her hand. 'And afterwards, you told me what an unpleasant man he was. You were complaining that he was very pushy. Ring any bells?'

She stopped, looking at him in expectation, and then started talking again. The words continued to pour out of her mouth – he was sure, because she was moving her lips in that way – but he had stopped hearing what she was saying.

The palms of his hands were moist. He wiped them on his trousers. Beads of sweat forced their way urgently through his skin. He turned and lurched down the hall and into his office. On his desk, he fumbled through a pile of papers, his fingers thick and clumsy. It must be here, surely. He found the note in the lower half of the pile. It was just as he recalled. Dr. Taverley, meet with me, at the Chapel, 3 pm, Tuesday, 1st March. He hadn't imagined it. Helena came up behind him; her tone less friendly now.

'… the matter with you? I really don't like being ignored like that. Elliot!'

She grabbed his arm and spun him around. He held
up the note between forefinger and thumb, triumphantly.

'There! There it is. In black and white! Go on, read
it!' he shouted.

She snatched the sheet off him and inspected it closely. She shrugged dismissively, and then handed it back to
Elliot. 'Well, you're the expert, but I'd say this looks a lot
like your handwriting.'

He took the piece of paper off her angrily, shaking
his head rapidly as though to clear his mind of the torrent of
thoughts that were rushing in. This wasn't his handwriting!
Certainly, it was angular, like his, and the letter spacing was
not very economical, but anyone could see that this wasn't
his writing. What was she talking about?

Helena stepped forward and touched his arm. She
said, 'Look, Elliot, I don't know what's been the matter with
you lately, but you're going to have to fix this. You can't go
on like this.'

He let his arm drop away from her touch. The
thoughts continued to needle his brain. Had he met this
man before?

Helena interrupted his train of thought. 'Please don't
ignore me, Elliot. There's something the matter with you.
Perhaps … oh, I don't know, perhaps you've just been working too hard.' The last few words came out in a whisper.
'Perhaps you just got some things mixed up. I don't know
what to do. You've been so … bad-tempered lately.'

He held the magazine in a fist.

'Look at the state of your face. And now this! I'm worried about you.'

Elliot lost his temper. 'God! What's the matter with everybody? Can't anyone mind their own business?'

He noticed that her chin was trembling. Now she was going to start crying. He watched as she searched her pockets for a handkerchief, tracing the shape of her face with his gaze. Her cheekbones stood out more prominently than he remembered. Perhaps she had lost some weight. Her eyes were heavily made-up. Was this something she'd picked up in America? Well, it didn't suit her. The pink mouth he had always found irresistibly sensual now hung loosely open. It gave her a slightly infantile, dim-witted look. He was beginning to wonder why he had always thought her so attractive. Now she began to cry, and her eye make-up ran down her face, leaving dirty black streaks. He shook his head; this little attempt at manipulation wasn't going to work. He pushed past her to the kitchen. He needed another look at the photograph. Helena called out something, but her words didn't stick. A minute later, just outside the perimeter of his awareness, the front door slammed shut.

Shortly after Helena had left, Elliot set himself the task of getting drunk. He wanted to let the alcohol marinate his brain. He searched the kitchen for something to drink. He opened every cupboard, every drawer. Nothing. He shouted in frustration; a loud, angry roar, which sprang from a deep reservoir inside him and filled the big empty house. There was no answer. Walking out into the hallway, he let his head drop, for the moment resigning himself to a night of sober wretchedness. But then he remembered: there was a bottle of French brandy in the bureau. Feeling refreshed by this thought, he strode into the sitting room with an increasing sense of determination. He paused briefly at the door and flicked the light switch on. The large Victorian chandelier came alight, its heavy crystal prisms splicing the light, which winked and danced provocatively about the room. The imposing bureau stood in a corner of the room, mocking him with torturous recollections of painful, unpredictable beatings. Elliot recalled his father's voice, viscous with menace and drink: Stand still, boy. Hold out your hand. – Whack! – That'll teach you to be insolent. –Whack! – Stop snivelling. – Whack! – Now, turn it over; yes, so I can see your knuckles. – Whack! – Now get out of my sight!

Curling his left hand into a fist, Elliot beat the memory aside, and opened the bureau. He stared inside. It was dark and empty, except for a bottle of cognac, and it reeked of a foul combination of blood and leather. He grabbed the bottle and quickly shut the bureau, promising himself – not for the first time – to dispose of it at the next available opportunity. He lifted the bottle to his mouth and drank, twitching slightly as the alcohol stung his cracked lips. He drank a quarter of the bottle standing up. Then, as the alcohol spread through his blood, diffusing his thoughts and weakening his legs, he let himself fall back onto the sofa. He rested the bottle on his thigh, clutching it with his left hand. He shivered. The fire had burned itself out a while ago, leaving behind a pile of bluish charcoal and white-grey ash. Elliot closed his eyes. The harsh light burned red through his swollen eyelids, and his thoughts came to life. That can't have been Raphael in the photograph. It was an absurd idea; after all, everybody is said to have a doppelgänger somewhere. The man in the picture, this Russian businessman, had a confident air, arrogant almost. The way he had posed for the photographer, looking straight into the camera, straight-backed, with an oddly angular frame – and those eyes. Elliot took another draught from the bottle. His empty stomach lurched in protest. Stanislav would know, he thought suddenly, Stanislav would know where to find Raphael. He would find him and sort this thing out, once and for all.

He levered himself out of his seat, suddenly intent on telephoning his friend, and staggered into the hall. A note lay on the floor in front of him. He hesitated before picking it up, and for a few moments, merely stood and looked at it. The envelope lay white and innocent on the coarse russet rug. Just his name was written in scratchy black ink on the front. He was very drunk; it wasn't long before the nausea would set in. Steadying himself against the wall with one hand, he tried to open the envelope with his other hand. It was no good. He stumbled against the opposite wall, and then slid down to the floor. His legs stretched out in front of him, long and thin, like two oversized matchsticks. He noticed that the fabric around his knees was dirty and worn. He shuddered. It was cold and draughty down here. With both hands free now, he managed to tear open the envelope and pull out the letter. It was very short, only three lines, but the words refused to stand still on the page. Elliot closed his eyes and focused on his breathing. Deep breath in, hold, and out again. When he opened his eyes again and looked down, the words were obligingly static. The letter read:

Dr. Taverley,

Please forgive my brevity; I do not have much time to spare. You have tried to help me, and I thank you for your efforts, but it is now time for me to return home. Perhaps one day you will understand?

Raphael

A violent pain exploded in his head, and Elliot dropped the letter to the floor. He lost consciousness.

TWENTY

The room was dark and cramped. A kerosene gas lamp sitting on a small wooden table in the centre of the room gave off more odour than light, but it was better than sitting in the gloom. The tiny window on the far wall was now a square of black glass, indicating that night had fallen outside. Elliot lay on the lumpy mattress on his side, one arm tucked beneath his head as a makeshift pillow. He was covered by a coarse, grey blanket, and – for additional warmth – a sheepskin coat. His eyes travelled around the small space. A reddish-brown glow seemed to emanate from all the sides of the room, but it was merely the dim gaslight reflecting off the mud-coloured walls. The surface of the walls was unevenly rendered, giving it the appearance of a spongy, padded texture. A square black wood stove stood unlit in the corner. The smell in the room – a biting mixture of urine and camphor – no longer bothered him; the only thing that frightened him now was the dark. The bunk he lay on was narrow and short, so that his feet hung uncomfortably over the end. He had been having recurring nightmares that he was being chased, but couldn't get away because his feet had been amputated. He blinked heavily, rubbing his chin on his shoulder.

He was in Archangel.

The door opened, and Stanislav came in, stamping the snow off his feet. He carried an armful of branches and twigs. Second-rate firewood. He dropped them in a pile on the floor, and began clearing the cold ash out of the wood stove. Elliot watched but didn't move; only his eyes darted back and forth as Stanislav prepared the fire. He worked slowly and methodically, first breaking the driest twigs up into kindling, then piling them up carefully to form a pyramid inside the stove. His fingers were black with ash and red with cold. He hadn't removed his large fur hat, but beneath it, Elliot could see the frost that rimed his eyebrows. When the stove finally began to give off some heat, Stanislav stood up and rubbed his hands together, blowing on his fingers to warm them. He didn't speak. When he lifted his head to look in Elliot's direction, Elliot turned to face the wall.

The next day, Stanislav returned with more firewood and some food. He boiled water for tea, and extracted several lumps of sugar from his filthy coat pocket. Elliot continued to lie on his bunk, watching Stanislav through inflamed eyelids. After a few minutes, Stanislav gestured for Elliot to sit up, and then handed him a bowl of soup. It looked watery and colourless; a greyish liquid with small chunks of white cabbage and shreds of meat floating limply on the surface. Elliot held it close to his face and felt the hot steam rise off it. He shook his head when Stanislav offered him a spoon, and cupped the bowl to his lips instead. The soup was salty, and the cabbage soft and bland. But the meat was strong-tasting, and strangely sweet. Elliot had never tasted anything so delicious in his life. He chewed each scrap of meat until it became liquid in his mouth and he had to swallow.

'Horseflesh,' Stanislav said, placing his bowl down on the floor beside him. Elliot was surprised at how alien his friend's voice sounded. It was only the second time Stanislav had spoken since his arrival in Archangel three days ago. The first time was just after he had arrived and asked Elliot for some money to pay for lodgings and food.

Elliot tried to speak, but his throat felt weak, as though his voice had wasted away from lack of use. Even swallowing was an unbelievable effort. Stanislav seemed to read his thoughts.

He said, 'You don't have to talk to me. It is enough that you listen. For now, anyway.'

He sat back and pulled a small leather pouch from his trouser pocket. He opened it and proceeded to roll three cigarettes. Elliot lay back down and closed his eyes briefly. When he next opened them, Stanislav had gone, and the room was blissfully warm. He realised that he must have been asleep for a while. He got up and went to relieve himself in a battered tin can that stood in the corner, and then looked inside the cooking pot to see if there were any leftovers. A few despondent pieces of pale cabbage stuck to the bottom. Elliot used his fingers as a scoop and fished them out. He licked his fingers greedily, and then went to lie back down. He fell asleep instantly.

Over the next few days, this routine continued. Stanislav came and brought food and fuel, until Elliot slowly felt his strength returning. Every day, Stanislav asked for a little more information about his journey, and he obliged as best he could, but the truth was that most of it was a blur. He had no idea how long it had taken him to get to Archangel; his memory was shot through with flashes of acute pain and a dull, terrifying sense of despair. His only lucid recollection was of the pull; a tangible, physical compulsion that had kept him moving; kept him placing one foot in front of the other; kept him boarding boats and trains; and kept him walking, walking, walking, until his shoes were so badly worn he had to wrap string around them to keep them from falling off. And all the time he thought of Raphael. There was no questioning the need to find him. He felt – no he knew; this was beyond feeling or believing – he knew that Raphael had the answer. Once he found Raphael, then everything would come right. Archangel was the only place he could be.

Stanislav listened patiently and attentively to his account; throwing in an occasional question, now and again requesting some clarification. When Elliot spoke of Raphael, he listened particularly closely, usually in complete silence. Only once did he ask: 'Did you ever talk about Archangel?' but Elliot couldn't remember.

On the fifth day, Stanislav came and brought with him a definite sense of unease. Elliot noticed it immediately in the way he lit the fire and cooked the soup. It took him countless attempts to get a match to light, and then he burned himself twice on the cooking pot. He was noticeably preoccupied. They ate in silence facing each other – Elliot on his bunk, Stanislav on a wooden stool. When they had finished eating, Elliot questioned him directly.

'Is something the matter?' he asked.

Stanislav exhaled heavily and rubbed his eyes. Elliot was suddenly struck by how old his friend looked. Thin strands of white ran through his coarse black hair, and the dark bags of skin under his eyes were not indicators of tiredness, but of the gradual, physical deterioration that comes with age. He felt a sudden rush of tenderness towards him.

'It's all right,' he said softly. 'You needn't be afraid that I'll go to pieces. Whatever it is, you can tell me.'

He reached out and gently patted Stanislav's knee. Stanislav blinked wearily, and picked up the small rucksack that lay beside him on the floor. He reached inside and took something out.

'She wanted me to give you this,' he said, holding out an envelope. Elliot looked at it, and flinched. Helena. He looked away. He wasn't ready for this. Stanislav pushed the letter right under Elliot's nose, making him jerk his head back. 'Look, Elliot, that's the least you can do. You owe it to her to hear what she has to say.'

The gas lamp spluttered indignantly. Elliot continued to look away. Stanislav sat back out of the light, and began to tear open the envelope. His tone was calm but authoritative.

'Well, my friend, if you will not read it quietly, then I will read it aloud.' And in a soft monotone, he began to read:

Dear Elliot,

I can only hope that this letter reaches you safe and well. This is by far the most difficult thing I have ever had to write, and yet, I know that I will get no rest until I have shared my thoughts with you. Over the past few months, you have grown increasingly distant, and, although I could see you clearly, I was – am – frightened that I may never quite reach you again. I am so confused; you have left me behind in a mess. I am not sure what it was that drove you away, but I am terrified that it was something I might have done. I know that I have made demands on you; that I expected you to accept my lifestyle without demur; to defer to my family's peculiarities; to be nice to my undeserving friends. Was I being selfish? Was this asking too much? Is that why you ran away without saying goodbye?

You have been so remote, so unapproachable, recently. At first I thought it had everything to do with Ed's death, you see – the way you told me your story made me realise how much you were suffering. And I kept remembering that Welsh couple, Mr and Mrs Evans; what the War did to their son, and to them, the raw sadness they carried around with them. When you told me about Ed, I was convinced – naively, arrogantly – that I was the one capable of alleviating your pain. But then the night before I left for New York, when we made love – '

Stanislav stopped and looked up. He said, 'Do you want me to continue?'

Elliot reached out and took the letter from him. Stanislav grunted sympathetically and got up out of his chair. He stretched and yawned, his breath freezing instantly on the air, and then went to add the last pieces of wood to the fire. Elliot leaned forward into the light and continued to read. Instinctively, he noted the elegant curl of her garlands, the eloquent fluidity of movement, but also the indicators of her anxiety: the spasmodic pressure, the lack of rhythm in her strokes, the vibrant but controlled energies that ran through the writing like subterranean tremors. He stopped himself, cursing silently.

'– made love, I was so afraid that it would be the last time. I thought you didn't want me any more. You knew I was leaving, and yet you made no attempt to stop me. Do you understand how

much effort it took to keep up the pretence of cheerfulness, when my heart was crying out for you to take me in your arms and comfort me? That morning, I made myself a promise. I told myself that if a single day went by during my stay in America when I didn't think of you, then I would not see you when I returned. How absurd! You were in my thoughts every moment of every day. Nothing I did there seemed real, of any substance, because I hadn't shared it with you.

I must confess that when I got back I even went to meet with Charles Beaumont – you see, I thought you were ill; over-worked. When he told me that you had virtually stopped coming to the clinic, I was frantic with worry. What could I do? And then, when you behaved so strangely, so aggressively, over that photograph in the magazine, I thought that either I was losing my mind, or you had stopped loving me.

The last time we were together I was angry. I was angry that you would not let me know what was wrong. How could I help you if I did not know? My darling, I am sorry. I could see you needed me, and I yet I did nothing. When Stan told me he thought he knew where you might have gone, and that he was going to find you, I cried with relief. I am deeply ashamed that I was ever jealous of your friendship – if he can offer you something that I cannot, then I should be happy that he is your friend. When he finds you and you read this, please tell him that I am forever in his debt.

Elliot, darling, I want you to know that you have held my heart in your hands from the moment I met you. It is fragile. Please do not break it.

Helena

Elliot put the letter down. He screwed up his face as a

deluge of shame and humiliation poured over him. It overwhelmed him. He started trembling violently and didn't
stop even when Stanislav took him in a tight embrace. For
a long time, his friend just sat and held him. When Elliot's
shaking finally subsided, Stanislav helped him into bed, and
murmured in his ear, 'I am sorry. I thought it might help
you.'

When Stanislav left that evening, Elliot curled up on his
bed, pulling the sheepskin coat over his head. The smell was
unpleasant, but the coat was useful in retaining his body
heat. He closed his eyes. It was like being back in school,
when the lights had been switched off in the freezing dor-
mitory, and the claustrophobic darkness had enveloped
him. His mother's face appeared in front of him; the face he
used to stare into for hours when he was a child. She had
porcelain-pale skin and tiny soft blonde hairs that covered
her face, which he could only see if she sat very still and he
looked closely enough. His mother never raised her voice
in anger. Only once, when he was five years old, had he
seen her lose her temper. It was so long ago, and yet he
remembered distinctly how her voice had escalated several
decibels to a screech, making her sound hateful and cruel. It
had distressed him, and he felt guilty that he was the cause
of his mother's transformation into something so ugly.

It was late summer, and Elliot's parents had returned
from a trip to Italy. It was the first time they had taken Ed
abroad with them – Elliot was deemed too young to travel,
and had to stay behind with an aunt whom he hardly knew.
She was a cold, domineering woman; the very opposite of

his mother. Elliot was terrified of her. Time crawled by; every day seemed to last a lifetime, and each day was longer than the day before. His nights were filled with bad dreams. Then, one day, his aunt decided to teach him how to write. Until then, Elliot was hardly able to write his own name, and was childishly content with painting and drawing. But for his aunt this was evidently not enough. She sat him at the dining room table on a tall chair – his feet could barely touch the ground – and laid a blank sheet of paper and a pencil on the table in front of him. Taking his right hand in hers, she began to guide it roughly across the page.

'See, like this.' She drew a capital T, and then took her hand away. 'Now you try it. Go on!'

She had a deep, rasping voice: a voice that carried an implicit threat in its harsh elocution. Elliot obeyed, adequately reproducing the vertical line, but unable to stop the horizontal line dissecting it in the middle. His aunt grabbed his hand.

'No!' she shouted, and proceeded to write the letter with his hand again. She was so close to him, he could smell her skin. It smelled of sour milk. She let go of his hand. 'Try again!'

He tried, but failed. He needed to go to the toilet. The pencil just wouldn't do what he wanted it to.

'Try again,' she repeated. He tried. T T T. The pressure on his bladder was growing. T for Taverley. His fingers were just too thick and clumsy. His aunt lost patience.

'Well, let's try another one.' She wrote a lower case a. 'This is the second letter in your surname: a,' she said, speaking loudly and deliberately, as though Elliot were hard of hearing, or retarded, or both. Elliot looked unhappily down at the letter on the page. It was a tricky one; a cautionary stroke leading up and over a carefully formed oval, ending in a little upward kick. He couldn't remember how she'd drawn it, and he felt too afraid to ask her to write it again.

'Stop squirming about in your seat. Now write the letter. Go on, write it!'

He couldn't hold it any longer. The hot liquid spread around his crotch, saturating the front of his shorts and the chair cushion beneath him. The release was liberating and terrifying at the same time.

'Oh! You *disgusting* little boy!' she roared. Elliot began to cry.

When his parents and Ed returned to collect him, his aunt told them what had happened. Elliot buried his face in his mother's lap, hiding his shame, angry and upset that the joy of reunion was being usurped by tales of his disgrace. His mother stroked his hair, while Ed jumped about triumphantly, whooping, 'Smelly Elliot! Smelly Elliot!'

Elliot, in frustration at this name-calling, began chasing after Ed, screaming for him to stop. They ran into the kitchen; Ed chortling with delight, Elliot behind him, crying with rage. Suddenly, Ed stopped in his tracks. He turned, and gave Elliot a hard, violent punch in the face. Elliot reeled, and fell to the floor with a bump. The pain was dazzling; lights flashed in front of his eyes. He felt stuff dripping from his nose. He put his hand to his face and it came away red. He looked from his hand to his brother in stunned incomprehension. He was too shocked to cry. Ed crouched over him and hissed in his ear, 'You tell anyone

I hit you, and I'll put a pillow over your face when you're asleep. Smelly Elliot.'

The next moment, his mother ran over to them, screeching like a banshee. She grabbed Ed by the scruff of his neck and tossed him to one side with remarkable strength. Her face was twisted, mottled red. It was the first and last time she ever defended Elliot from Ed.

He woke up to a loud banging on the door. Confused by sleep, it took him a moment to orientate himself. He sat up on his bunk, and the icy draught coming through the gap in the door instantly jogged his memory. Some cold light seeped through the window; not strong enough to illuminate the room, but enough to outline the objects in the room in a vague, blurred greyness. The banging continued. Elliot swung his legs over the side of his bunk and wrapped the sheepskin around his shoulders, clasping it around his neck with one hand, while holding his trousers up with the other. They had grown loose on him. He walked towards the door and opened it a fraction. A sudden blast of angry shouting rushed in at him. A woman – in her sixties, fat, dark-haired, ugly – stood at the door, yelling at him unintelligibly and making gestures with her hands that appeared to be anything but polite. Elliot staggered backwards in alarm. What did she want? She continued to rant, and Elliot looked past her to see if there was anyone who might be able to translate, explain to him what was going on, but beyond the covered entrance to his hut he could only see rows of similar, primitive wooden structures, and beyond that, bleakness.

Although he had only ventured out once or twice since his arrival, it seemed to Elliot that much had changed since he had last been in Archangel over two years ago. Gone was the sense of urgency in the town, when it had been the centre of the military operation to ward off the Bolshevik advance. The crude type of hut Elliot was staying in had then housed up to four soldiers at a time; men already beyond their limits, wearily, furiously acting out the futile war games dreamt up by their superiors. Loading and unloading ships, constructing railway lines, transporting weapons to the White Russian front in the south. It had been frenzied and desperate. And always cold, so cold. And now, a ghostly silence seemed to have enveloped the town, disturbed only by the clanking and hammering of shipbuilding taking place in the harbour.

The woman in front of him was still ranting. Bewildered by her aggressive presence, Elliot gestured for her to come in. Perhaps she had mistaken him for someone else. She wore a brown headscarf and a fur coat, and her boots were lined with straw. She was a complete stranger to him. Following his request, she stepped inside, but kept up her hostile address. Her front teeth were missing, and when she spoke, flecks of saliva escaped from her mouth and sprayed Elliot's chest. Although she was much smaller than Elliot, her ferocity intimidated him. He glanced helplessly around the room, wondering if there was something he could give her to make her leave. She began to poke his shoulder painfully with a short, muscular finger. Just as Elliot was cursing himself for inviting her in, Stanislav arrived. He addressed the woman in Russian, and she turned and began shouting at him. Stanislav didn't raise his voice, but spoke with her calmly, reassuringly, until she had stopped talking altogether. He turned to Elliot.

'Her brother is the head of the housing committee. She has come to collect another week's rent. She wants it in advance.'

Elliot nodded, relieved that the situation had been clarified. He took his wallet out of his pocket.

'Of course. How much does she want?'

'Fifty roubles.'

The woman nudged Stanislav in the ribs and said something. It sounded urgent. He said, 'If you do not have that much, she says she will take sugar.'

The woman was leering at Stanislav's greatcoat pocket. He placed a protective hand over it.

'No, no. I have enough,' Elliot said, and handed her the money. She took it with a disappointed grunt, and turned to leave. Just then, Stanislav laid a large hand on her shoulder and spoke quietly into her ear, while she glanced occasionally over at Elliot. She pulled the corners of her mouth down and shook her head vigorously several times.

As soon as she had left, Stanislav said to Elliot, 'I asked her about your patient. Whether she had heard anything.'

'And?'

'No, nothing. She has not seen any strangers arrive here.' He hesitated. 'Besides you.'

He walked over to the bed and sat down. Elliot frowned. It would have been too good to be true if she had known where he was. But, in truth, he wasn't really disheartened. He knew Raphael was here, somewhere. He could feel it. Just because one old woman hadn't seen him – that meant nothing. Now that he was beginning to feel stronger, he could start looking for him. He looked down at his hands. His fingers looked like gnarled twigs. The skin was chapped and dirty, and his knuckles seemed unduly pronounced. Tobacco had stained his fingers a sickly, brownish-yellow, like some five-day-old contusion. He clenched and unclenched his fists several times. He was ready now. It was time. He straightened himself.

'I'm going to find him,' he announced.

Stanislav looked up in concern. 'You will freeze out there,' he said. 'Please, stay here. Just for a few days more. Until you are stronger.'

'I can't wait any longer. I – '

Stanislav rose from the bed and walked over to the door, blocking it with his large body. 'We must talk first.'

Elliot felt a wave of panic surging up from his stomach to his throat. He had to get out. He didn't want to do any talking. He wanted to find Raphael. He swallowed, to try and get rid of the lump in his throat, the lump that was threatening to asphyxiate him. He swallowed again, and again. His breathing was erratic and heavy. He felt dizzy.

Stanislav stepped forward and grabbed his shoulders, just as he thought he was going to collapse. He guided him over to the bed, like a mother would a sleepwalking child, and sat down beside him.

He said, 'So you want to go and find Raphael?'

Elliot nodded dumbly.

'Have you any idea where he might be?'

He shook his head. 'No. But he's close. I can feel it.'

A sudden, angry shaft of sunlight pierced the window, catching Elliot's eye, blinding him momentarily. He closed his eyes and rubbed them with the balls of his hands. When he opened them again, a kaleidoscope of light and colour spiralled jauntily in his line of vision, before slowly subsiding. He felt the mattress move as Stanislav leaned forward heavily.

'Elliot, I want you to do something for me,' he heard him say.

'What is it?'

'I want you to think back. To when Ed died.'

'Why? What's this got to do with Raphael?' He could hear the note of alarm in his own voice. He didn't want to think about that. He'd had to relive it just recently, when he told Helena. Surely Stanislav knew how painful, how raw, this memory was. Why was he doing this to him?

'What's this got to do with Raphael?' he repeated, this time in a whisper.

'Do you think he might know what happened?' Stanislav asked.

'I don't understand.'

'Does he know what happened, here, in Archangel, with you and Ed?'

Elliot ran his fingers through his hair vigorously. His hands wouldn't stop shaking, so he crossed his arms over his chest and put his hands under his armpits to calm them. He tripped over his words. 'No. I – I don't think so. We never talked about that. I don't know what you mean.'

He scratched his beard impatiently, but that just compounded the itch. He needed to have a shave. Yes.

That's what he would do. He would shave, and then he would go out and find Raphael. He smoothed his hair down with both hands. He looked around the room. Water. He'd have to fetch some water and heat it up. He got to his feet. Stanislav pulled him back down effortlessly onto the bunk.

'I think he might know.' His voice was solemn. 'I think Raphael might know what happened to Ed.'

TWENTY-ONE

'You went after him that night.'

Elliot stared at him. He couldn't believe what he was hearing. 'I went after him? No, no, I –' He paused, straining to recall that night in the stinking alley behind the officers' mess.

Stanislav continued, his tone striking a note of insistence. 'I saw you. I heard you and Ed arguing in the foyer, and I came out to see what was going on, just as you were leaving. I saw him grab you.' He looked down at his boots, and lowered his voice. 'I didn't want to intrude, so I stayed where I was. But about ten minutes later, Ed came storming past the mess, with you in pursuit. I stood at the doors, and watched you follow him all the way to the barracks. When you were out of sight, I went back inside.'

'No. That's not right! I would have remembered,' Elliot shouted. He rocked back and forth to control his nerves. The bed creaked in protest. Stanislav put his hand on Elliot's shoulder. He shrugged it off in disgust. It wasn't true. Why was his friend saying that?

'Why are you saying that?'

'I know what I saw, Elliot. I do not lie to you.'

It was no use. Elliot had to get up and walk about. His legs felt unsteady but he couldn't contain the energy that was coursing around his body any longer. He started pacing about. The room seemed to have shrunk. Only two steps to the window. Three steps to the door. He walked to the opposite wall and stopped. He turned swiftly.

'Perhaps you got it wrong, Stanislav. Perhaps it was a different night!'

Yes, that was it. A different night. This had happened years ago; Stanislav's memory was as susceptible to errors as anyone else's.

Stanislav said, 'No Elliot. I remember it clearly. The following day, Ed was gone.'

'Very well then; I went after Ed that night. Where did we go?' Elliot spat the words out in anger, as he tried to suppress the alarming realisation that was crawling up through his consciousness like caustic bile: the realisation that he perhaps he did remember what had happened after Ed left him standing in the alleyway that night.

Stanislav's tone remained frustratingly steady. 'You have to answer that. You have to remember.'

Elliot turned his back on him, and the fierce sunlight flashed in his eyes a second time. At that moment, suddenly and unannounced, Elliot's memory regurgitated the events of that night. The memories spilled out, chattering, twitching, eager to escape, restless and excited after two years' incarceration. Elliot screamed, placing his hands on his ears; an attempt to hold them in. They wouldn't stop coming.

The walls of the room disintegrated, the light disappeared, and the stench of frozen urine crept up his nostrils. He was screaming, shouting, ranting at the man who was walking away from him, down the alley, towards the light of the main street.

'Don't walk away from me!' he screamed. His voice cut through the cold, steely air with precision. 'You come back here, you coward! I hate you!'

Ed strode ahead, ignoring Elliot's shouts. Elliot began to walk after him, but struggled to keep his pace. The ground was frozen solid, and his boots couldn't prevent him from slipping. Half walking, half running, he chased his brother down the road. Ed turned right at the top of the alley. Elliot's pulse raced with determination. He would confront Ed in the mess; he didn't care who saw them. He stumbled and fell, cracking his knee painfully on a rock at the side of the road. He scrambled to his feet. He had reached the top of the alley; on his right, he could see the entrance to the officers' mess, spilling warm, yellow light onto the wintry street. He stopped briefly to catch his breath, with his hands on his thighs. He took a moment to compose himself before he went inside. Ed was drunk; he didn't know what he was saying. He was confused; needed help desperately. But how could he relate this to Ed? Perhaps he should have brought Ed's letters with him, to show his brother how his writing had betrayed the instability of his mind. He needed to convey to Ed the urgency of the matter, convince him of the risk he faced. Ed would understand, he must understand, if only Elliot expressed his concerns rationally, calmly. He straightened up. The fabric of his trousers was stuck to his knee. He peeled it away, wincing as the congealed blood came away from the skin. A group of men passed him from behind, heading for the mess. As he looked up in reaction to their greeting, Elliot saw a tall figure walking away from the mess building, towards a row of blockhouses that lined the main road. The man wasn't wearing a coat; just a thick khaki uniform. It was Ed. He was walking away from the main square, into the quiet backstreets of the town. Elliot ran across the road, shouting his brother's name. Ed stopped and turned.

'Piss off!' he shouted, but Elliot carried on running after him. Two young soldiers walked by, each with a woman on his arm. One of them whispered something to the others that caused great amusement. Elliot ignored them. The streets were unlit, but the full moon bounced off the snow and ice, illuminating the town with an odd, silvery glow. Ed kept walking for about a mile, towards the north of the city, Elliot hastening behind, until they came to a wide expanse – some kind of waste ground with a building, a disused sawmill, on the far side. There was nobody else about. The area was completely desolate. Ed walked across to the building and leant against the wall. Elliot stopped, leaving a good twenty yards between them. The moon cast their shadows across the grey snow. Ed put a cigarette to his lips and lit it. He inhaled, and then held his cigarette up and stared at the glowing tip.

'Leave me in peace,' he said, not looking at Elliot.

Elliot took a few steps closer. His breath froze on the air. The lunar glow gave the surroundings a dreamlike quality.

'Ed,' he said, trying to force an element of calmness into his voice.

'I said: leave me in peace,' Ed repeated.

Elliot walked right up to him and tried to catch his eye. 'Ed, please.'

Ed shot him an angry look.

'Are you deaf?' he asked.

They were both shivering uncontrollably now. Elliot's words came out in a dislocated stammer.

'Th–*this* is not you, Ed. You are n-*not* like this! I'm here t-to help you!'

He curled his frozen fingers around Ed's lapel, but the cold had weakened his muscles and his hand slipped away. Ed snarled. His face grew into a mask of loathing and contempt. Elliot watched him pull a silver hip flask from his pocket and put it to his lips. He drank greedily, his Adam's apple moving up and down in quick, urgent jerks. When he had finished, he threw the empty flask to the ground. It was cushioned by the snow. Elliot bent down to pick it up, but Ed knocked his hand away.

'That was their present to me when I joined up!' he shouted. He laughed out loud, making no attempt to conceal his derision.

Elliot ignored his mockery. He hadn't given up yet. Ed was sick, unbalanced.

'I saw it in your letters, Ed! Your anger, your suffering. As though you were unravelling ... bit by bit. That's why I came to Archangel. I'm here to help you, Ed, because I care about you. I'm here to help you.'

He took a step forward and laid a hand on Ed's arm in conciliation. Ed shrank back as if he had been stung. He turned away. Behind him, to his left, a frozen stream stood waiting, motionless, for spring to arrive. The banks on either side were mounds of untouched snow, which glinted – seductive, insidious – with a million ice crystals. Ed stumbled across to the stream, his boots cruelly defiling the white snow with large, deep footsteps. Elliot went after him. When he got to his side, Ed spoke. His voice was hushed, barely audible.

'Father made me swim across a stream, like this one. I tried to tell him that I didn't want to, that I wasn't a strong swimmer, that I was bloody scared!' He raised his voice. 'But he wouldn't have it. "No son of mine is weak!" he shouted, the sadistic bastard. I wasn't allowed to be weak, or frightened, from the moment I was born. And so I undressed, and climbed into the water, and swam. It was so fucking cold, I thought I was going to die. When I was yards from the far side, my arms stopped moving. They were paralysed with the cold. He just stood there, watching me; he could see that I was struggling, but he didn't move. I was going under; I must have swallowed gallons of that filthy stinking water. And all the time, he had that grin on his face, that heartless, cold-blooded grin. I don't know how I made it to the other side, but when I did, he gave me a pat on the back and a chocolate bar.'

'But, I thought –' Elliot began. His recollection was hazy, incomplete.

'Yeah, well, you thought,' Ed replied, his voice filled with contempt. 'And look at me now,' he slapped his chest, 'I'm just as much of a bastard as he was!'

'But that's not true. You're a decent man, Ed. In spite of him.'

'D'you think?' Ed replied sarcastically. He started walking back to the barracks. Elliot trotted behind.

'But our mother, think of her, Ed. She needs you. Don't make me go back home without you. Please.'

Ed stopped suddenly. He turned to Elliot and put his face up close. He fixed his heavy-lidded gaze on Elliot.

His eyes were bloodshot, and his breath smelt strongly of whisky.

'You just don't get it, do you? You make me sick, with your begging. It's disgusting; it's – demeaning. D'you think I'm such a decent man?'

Elliot was silent. Ed yelled at him. 'Well? Do you?'

Elliot flinched, trying hard not to show any emotion. He didn't want to hear this. This wasn't how it was meant to be. Ed was emotionally unstable; he was traumatised. Elliot needed to help him realise that. He had to be the strong one now. He cleared his throat.

'Ed, listen. I understand you've been through a lot. Sometimes it can be very hard to let go of difficult experiences. The war has had this effect on countless others; it's nothing to be ashamed of. Let me –'

Ed stood up straight, pulling back his shoulders. He seemed to lose his balance, but caught himself before he fell backwards.

'All right, since you won't listen to me, I'll have to show you,' he said. His tone carried no inflection at all.

Elliot suddenly felt the cold as thought it were a brand new sensation. It stung his skin and made his bones ache. He looked at Ed, whose lips were tinged with blue.

'I'm cold,' he said.

Ed ignored him, grabbing his elbow and pushing him ahead, like a policeman escorting a prisoner. Elliot had no choice but to comply. They walked across the compound, past the timber blockhouses, through the town, Elliot struggling to keep up with Ed's giant strides. They finally arrived at a large stone building. A wooden sign announced that this was the military police headquarters. Ed pushed Elliot roughly up against the wall.

'Stay here,' he hissed.

'What – ?' Elliot began, taking a step forward, but Ed shoved him back again.

'Shut up and don't move,' he said, and went into the building. Elliot didn't dare move. The cold was burning now; penetrating his whole body; twisting in a sharp pain just behind his eyes. His nervous system responded by shuddering sporadically, jerking his limbs in violent spasms. He tried to gather his thoughts, but they were also numbed by the cold. He needed to speak to Ed, but he couldn't quite remember what he had planned to say. The cold fogged his mind. He rubbed his face and shivered. He looked around, wondering where Ed was. The street was completely empty. A sense of wretchedness grew inside him, constricting his throat and making him feel nauseous. He crouched down, feeling unbelievably weary now, transfixed by the smoke that rose from the chimney-topped house opposite. It rose gracefully, spiralling upwards in the moonlight, unfurling gradually until it vanished into the air. Elliot struggled to keep his eyes open. He was so tired. If he could just lie down, rest for a while. He placed a hand down onto the ground beside him and pulled it back up sharply. The ground was freezing. He opened his eyes wide. What was he doing? He'd freeze to death if he lay down. But – he was so tired ... If he rested his head against the wall, then he could close his eyes for five minutes, just to take the edge off his tiredness. That would do. Five minutes. His heavy lids fell shut, and a sudden warmth began to spread through his body. His weight was dragging on him; the ground was inviting him to lie down. It was too much to resist. He felt his body sliding to the ground. Then suddenly, a slap to his face, stinging, jerking him back to consciousness.

'You can't sleep here, you fool,' a voice said.

Elliot opened his eyes. It was Ed; he was standing over him, but he had somebody with him; a young man, a youth, barely eighteen. Elliot stood up painfully. His legs were fighting off cramp.

'Who's this?' he asked, looking at the youth. His voice was hoarse. The youth looked nervous; his eyes darted between Ed and Elliot. His face was soft and fine-featured, almost like a girl's. He wore an oversized khaki uniform which was dirty and worn; his collar was turned up against the cold.

'Come with me,' Ed said, grabbing the youth's upper arm. Elliot could tell by the way he flinched that Ed's grip was painfully tight. He saw the black gleam of metal in Ed's belt, but was too tired, too cold, to register it properly. He repeated his question.

'Ed. Who's this?'

The youth opened his mouth to speak, but one look from Ed silenced him. They began to walk in the direction Elliot and Ed had come from. Elliot followed on behind. He spoke louder.

'What's going on, Ed? Where are we going?'

'You'll see.' Ed stopped and stared at Elliot. His eyes were wild. 'And don't forget – you asked for this.'

Elliot's memories poured out. He heard Tanner's voice at the

Chapel: There was no one came past me, I swear. I don't let no one in who's got no business here.

Elliot kept silent as they walked back through the town, through quiet side streets, past grey-weathered houses and timber huts, to the disused sawmill. The town seemed empty; they met nobody on the way. A growing sense of unease settled in Elliot's mind. What was going on? What were they doing here? That boy, hardly old enough to be out of short trousers. What did Ed want with him?

They reached the waste ground. Ed stopped, and spun around, letting go of the youth's arm.

'Kneel down,' he instructed. Elliot's stomach lurched. The youth looked at Elliot, imploringly, but obeyed Ed's command. He was very young, and very thin. Ed began to unbuckle his trouser belt, and proceeded to use it to tie the youth's hands together behind his back. The youth stared at Elliot, panic-stricken, but still made no sound. Elliot shook his head with growing anxiety.

'What are you doing, Ed? What's going on?'

Ed ignored him. The moonlight reflected off his sleek, black hair. He worked quickly, wrapping the belt around the youth's slender wrists, before tightly securing the buckle. Elliot's voice rose to a shout. 'Ed! What's going on? Talk to me!'

Elliot felt his eyelids flutter; he was back in the present.
'You know who he is now, don't you?' Stanislav said.

Ed pulled a handkerchief from his pocket. The boy's eyes

opened wide with terror. Ed leaned over him and began to blindfold him. Elliot couldn't move. A distant rushing noise filled his ears.

Tanner's voice gave way to an image of the room in Brighton, containing nothing but a ladder and bucket.

Ed acted with cool, detached precision. When he had tied the knot behind the boy's head, he straightened up and began to speak. His voice was clipped and authoritative.

Elliot whispered to Stanislav. 'You need to leave now. He'll be here soon. Just once more, that's all.'

> *'I said, you know who he is now, don't you?' Stanislav said.*

'Private Francis Poole, you have been tried before a court martial and found guilty of desertion. You have been sentenced to death by firing squad.'

He pulled the pistol out of the holder on his belt. It shone as sleek and black as Ed's hair.

Henry Rickman's voice came in: Are you drunk? There's nobody in there. An angry Helena: I'd say that looks a lot like your handwriting.

As Ed cocked the gun, the youth jerked his head back. He shrieked, 'No! Please, no!'

'Yes. I know who he is now, Stanislav. I know who he is.'

Elliot ran forward in horror. Ed was placing his pistol on the back of the boy's head. The boy was blubbering now; the lower half of his face a mess of snot and tears. Ed looked up at Elliot.

'He's already been found guilty, Elliot,' he said, with a cold smile. 'That's why we had him locked up. I'm just carrying out the sentence a day early.'

Elliot put his hands to his head. He was finding it hard to breathe.

Mrs Blake outside his study door, listening to him talking to himself. His disbelief at seeing Helena's full signature on a piece of paper reproduced so effortlessly by Raphael...

'Ed.' His voice came out as a whimper. 'Ed, please. I'm begging you. Don't do this.'

'It was Luljeta who told me,' Stanislav murmured.

'Luljeta?'

'She is Catholic. She knows... about these things. Raphael is the archangel who healed the earth when it was defiled by the sins of the fallen angels.'

'You wanted to know what kind of man I am,' screamed Ed. 'Well, this is me.'

'Raphael is your healer.'

Ed pulled the trigger. There was a loud crack, and a cascade of blood and brains spurted out onto the dirty snow. Francis Poole fell to the side, twitching once, before lying perfectly still. There was a jagged hole where his mouth and nose had been a moment earlier. A smell of burning skin filled the air.

Elliot dropped forward onto his knees. He grabbed his stomach and retched. His body was juddering forcefully, with cold, with shock. A grinding, smashing pain entered his head, robbing him of his senses. He became vaguely aware of Ed's voice, talking down at him.

'... as weak as shit. You make me fucking sick.'

He heard a sharp clicking sound behind him as Ed cocked his gun. With tremendous effort, he rose slowly to his feet and turned around. Ed was standing four feet away, his arm raised, the pistol pointing at Elliot's face.

Elliot became aware of a light over Ed's shoulder, near the sawmill. It was the moonlight reflected in a windowpane. He looked into the light, and then stepped out of his body. He walked towards the light. He no longer felt the cold. No harm would come to him now. He turned around. From a distance, he watched as Ed kicked up some snow to cover the blood that stained the ground. He lifted the gun and fired a shot into the air, before bringing the butt down hard on Elliot's head. He placed the gun back in his holster and walked away.

Elliot was back in the room. Stanislav spoke quietly.

'Raphael is you.'

He rose slowly and crossed the room. Standing at the open door, he looked back at Elliot as though he wanted to say something more. But instead, he stepped outside, closing the door carefully behind him. Elliot curled up on his bunk and closed his eyes. The wind had picked up outside, loosening snow from the drifts that lay piled up against the side of his hut and peppering it against the small window pane. Elliot lay very still. For a long while, his mind submitted to the relentless assault of dreams, or memories, he no longer knew and he didn't care. Not now. Now, all he had to do was wait.

When he opened his eyes, Raphael was standing in the doorway. Elliot got up, but his knees trembled so badly he hurriedly sat back down on the bed.

'Where have you been?' he asked.

Raphael put his head to one side. He said, 'I had to leave.'

'Why?'

'It was important that you came to find me. And now you are here.' He walked over slowly and laid his hand on Elliot's shoulder.

'I needed to find you, Raphael, but I didn't know why. Until now.'

Raphael squeezed his shoulder gently, and nodded in the direction of the table. Next to the lamp lay a small pile of paper, and on top of that, Elliot's pen. Elliot pulled the table over to the bed, grimacing at the sound of the legs scraping the stone floor. He picked up a sheet of paper, and his pen, and wrote several lines of text, his heartbeat quickening with every word. When he was finished, he handed it to Raphael.

'Would you copy this for me?' he asked tentatively. His heart was close to exploding in his chest. Raphael look-

ed down at the writing, and then back up at Elliot. He nodded slowly.

'Are you sure that is what you want?'

'Yes, I'm sure.'

Raphael smiled, and bent over the writing, curling
his fingers around the pen. Elliot watched in silence as the
words poured out onto the empty white page: *My name is
Elliot James Taverley ...*

The transformation began. An exquisite feeling of
lucidity unfurled inside him as he and Raphael became one
again – languid and invigorating – so strong that he had to
check his hands to ensure he hadn't become transparent. A
cold draught blew into the room. Elliot smiled. He placed
the pen down carefully, and lay on his back with his hands
resting on either side of him. His breathing slowed, as his
body melted into the mattress. He fell into a dreamless sleep.

EPILOGUE

London, Pimlico, July 1922

The doorbell rings and Elliot jumps out of his chair without a word to the others. He meets Mrs Blake in the hall, but she shoos him back into the drawing room and heads towards the front door. Elliot pauses momentarily to glance up the stairs. He holds still, but can hear nothing. For the hundredth time that day, he feels his heart pounding madly in his chest. Surely there must be some news anytime soon!

Back in the drawing room, he takes a seat opposite Julia and Henry Rickman, but then stands up again almost immediately and begins pacing the floor. Cassandra is talking quietly to her mother, but both women look up when the drawing room door opens. Luljeta comes in with a huge, open-mouthed smile, and then rushes forward to embrace Elliot. Behind her, Stanislav stands holding hands with Kristaq and Anton. He is wearing a tweed suit that makes him appear bulkier than usual; but perhaps he has put on weight. He, too, is grinning at Elliot.

'How are you, my friend?' he asks.

Luljeta shakes her head and tuts. 'Never you mind how is he,' she says. 'How is Helena? It is typical, you men. How is Helena? That is important!'

Elliot shrugs unhappily, looking towards the door.

'I have no idea,' he says. 'I haven't seen her for –' he checks his watch and sighs, 'for some four hours now. The midwife sent me out and promised she'd let me know as soon as there were any ... developments. I tried to explain that I am a physician, I mean, I've never attended childbirth before, but it's not as though I were squeamish. But she was so insistent. It's so damn difficult sitting and waiting and not knowing. Do you think –'

'I'm sure she will ask for your assistance if the need arises,' Stanislav interrupts, putting his arm around Elliot's shoulder. 'Patience, my friend.'

'You have visitors?' Luljeta asks suddenly, as though she has only just become aware of the other people in the room. Her hands travel up instinctively to inspect her hair.

Henry Rickman rises.

'Miss Şagolj, Mr Dmowska, very nice to see you again,' he says with flawless pronunciation, holding his hand out to Stanislav. Stanislav steps forward and shakes Henry's hand.

'Many congratulations on your engagement to this charming lady,' Henry adds, looking in the direction of a blushing Luljeta and smiling.

'Thank you, Mr Rickman,' Stanislav answers. 'I feel indeed very grateful that she has agreed to become my wife.'

'I know precisely how that feels,' Henry says, smiling down at Julia. 'And I wish you as much happiness in your marriage as I have had in mine.'

Stanislav gives him a broad, lopsided grin.

'Oh, and congratulations also on your new position,' Henry says. 'The Borough Council, Elliot tells me.'

'Yes,' Stanislav replies. 'I have much to be grateful for.'

He and Luljeta sit down opposite the Rickmans. Elliot has never seen Luljeta so flushed before.

'Helena's parents drove up early this morning, as soon as I'd telephoned that the baby was on its way,' he says. 'I hadn't thought we would still be waiting when they arrived. It's been close to fifteen hours now.'

He rubs the side of his face, wondering how much nervous tension one man can endure. Just after midnight, he woke to a low, animal-like moan coming from Helena in the bed beside him. Helena only allowed him to summon the midwife at six in the morning ('I'd rather have a midwife at my side who's had a decent night's sleep'), and since then he has experienced alternating terror, excitement, impatience and, perversely, self-pity. He feels slightly envious of Helena – at least she is in the centre of the storm, has first-hand knowledge of what is going on inside her body. Perhaps it was wise for the midwife to send him away. But for all that, he would still rather be by his wife's side.

A heavy silence falls on the room, everyone perhaps searching for a suitable, distracting topic. It is an extremely hot and humid July day, and, although Mrs Blake drew the blinds that morning in an attempt to keep the room as cool as possible, the air feels close and doughy. Stanislav gives in to the heat and removes his heavy jacket, ignoring a disapproving look from Luljeta, which seems to say "But Mr Rickman must be hot and still he remains properly dressed." Elliot wouldn't mind, or perhaps notice, if they all stripped down to their undergarments. He is making an effort to suppress all the knowledge he has of statistics relating to childbirth – including the probability of the infant being stillborn, or worse, the mother haemorrhaging – and he feels as close to a migraine as he has for over a year, when these agonising assaults finally, mysteriously but permanently disappeared. He wipes his moist hands on his trousers and concentrates on trying to imagine how it will feel to hold his son or daughter for the first time.

Henry finally breaks the silence.

'I heard from Charles last week,' he says, addressing, it seems, no one in particular.

'Charles Beaumont?' Elliot asks. He last saw Beaumont some eight months ago at a conference in Edinburgh. They spoke briefly, politely; Beaumont didn't make any comment regarding Elliot's then recent wedding to Helena. This was perhaps too personal, too private to speak about. Of course, there was also no mention of the events surrounding Elliot's resignation from the Chapel, which was a relief to Elliot. After his return to London from Russia almost eighteen months ago and the subsequent reunion with Helena, he has no longing to look back, only to what lies ahead. Yet the understanding that Raphael was not real, but instead a projection of his broken self, still occasionally troubles him. He will never be entirely free from the unease that accompanies the knowledge of his own fragility. But for now, and with every day that passes, he feels the fracture inside him continue to heal. It will leave a permanent scar, of that he has no doubt, but one that in time, he hopes, will fade into insignificance.

And his decision to set up a private practice certainly pleased Helena's parents. In fact, many of his first patients came on recommendation from one of the Rickmans. The Chapel now seems, indeed it is, a world away. Henry's mention of Beaumont suddenly brings it back clearly.

'Yes, Charles Beaumont,' Henry continues. 'He told me that Chapelford Lane will be closing its doors at the end of the month.'

'Closing? The Chapel? But why?'

Henry shrugs. 'Very unfortunate business. This will not be the official reason given, I'm sure, but rumour has it that one of the doctors was arrested for soliciting. A certain Benjamin Eastleigh. You may remember him, Elliot.'

Elliot is astonished. Of all the male staff at the Chapel, Eastleigh, that young, bright-eyed Cambridge graduate, was the most unlikely candidate he would have imagined visiting prostitutes.

'And the trustees withdrew their funding before anyone could do anything about it,' Henry continues. 'Not that surprising really – there's word that the Church has been looking for a way out for a while now. I reckon they overestimated the influence they might have in shaping the direction psycho-analysis would take. Well, they clearly lost that one.' He pulls his pipe out of his left jacket pocket and gazes at it for a moment, as if considering whether to light it. 'Charles put up a good fight, I'm sure. It's a shame. Charles deserved better than that. But I suppose it was his time. He'll be retiring to the country to live with his daughter.'

'And the other members of staff?' Elliot asks. He will have to write to Beaumont, ask if he can be of help, perhaps take on some of the patients.

Henry shakes his head. 'I don't know. They'll all find suitable positions, Charles seems to think. Well, you know him, Elliot. He only took on the best. Oh, but come to think of it, he did mention that one of the senior nurses, Mrs Robins or something, will be joining him as his housekeeper. His final act of charity, I presume.'

For the first time that day, Elliot's mind is jolted free of his thoughts surrounding Helena upstairs. So they finally found a way to be together, Evelyn and Beaumont, and this gives him true, unadulterated pleasure. Lost in thought, and gradually becoming overwhelmed by the heat and lack of sleep, he only becomes aware of Cassandra's voice when she taps him on the shoulder, repeating more loudly what she has obviously said several times already:

'It's over, Elliot. Wake up. It's over!'

He jumps up quickly, almost losing his breath, feeling the ground swaying beneath his feet. The midwife is standing at the drawing room door, her plump skin moist with sweat and her face red and blotchy. She nods at Elliot without smiling.

'How is she?' Elliot asks.

'Which one?' the midwife replies.

Elliot feels momentarily irritated by this riddle. 'Helena. Is she all right?'

The midwife rolls her eyes. 'Yes, Dr. Taverley, she's fine. And the little girl is fine, too. They are both exhausted, but as well as any newborn and her mother.'

Elliot is vaguely aware of the excited cries and congratulations from the others as he makes his way across the room and through the door, but doesn't stop. A girl. He and Helena have a little girl. It is glorious. He somehow manages to negotiate the stairs, walking as if in a dream yet fuelled by a newly discovered energy, and reaches the bedroom door. It is wide open. The curtains have been drawn back and the windows opened, letting in streamers of bright sunshine, on which innumerable motes of dust are performing a joyous dance.

And there is Helena; her hair, transformed by the sunlight into a composition of auburn, bronze and gold, frames a pale pink face. It is a beautiful, perfect sight. She looks up from the baby in her arms as Elliot enters, and smiles tiredly.

'Look,' she whispers and turns their daughter ever so slightly around towards Elliot. 'This is Grace.'

It is the perfect name, Elliot thinks, as he stands almost drowning in rapture at the sight of his baby daughter, the tiny perfection of her shape, the rosiness of her skin. Superstitious until the end, Helena refused to discuss possible names until after the birth, and now she has chosen the one that so perfectly suits. Elliot cannot imagine her possessing any other. The baby's eyes and fists are tightly closed and her ruby lips form a pout he at once recognises as Helena's.

'Come and hold her,' Helena says tenderly, but Elliot shakes his head, afraid that this, the most fragile of all things, might shatter in his arms. Instead, he gently eases himself onto the bed next to Helena and places his arm around her. Helena lets her head drop onto his chest, and as she drifts off to sleep, Elliot stares at the sunlight reflected in the open windowpane until his eyes begin watering and he has to shut them.

*

Acknowledgements

Thanks to my family for their love, support and encouragement – Jake, Fay, David, Lilo, Amy and June.

Special thanks to my good friend Michael Walsh, who was there right from the beginning; to my agent Jenny Brown, for believing in me; to my lovely editor Gill Tasker, for her brave and insightful editing; to my übercool publisher Mark Buckland, for his enthusiasm; to my former professor Graham Richards, for introducing me to Raphael; to Chris Hannah, for the amazing cover design; to the staff at Thornaby Library; to the early readers, for their time and feedback – Carin Müller, Dorothy Allen, Al Guthrie, Julia Schooler, Harald Grosch, Henrik Olsson and Helen Sedgwick, as well as my fellow Creative Writers at Lancaster – Michelene Wandor, Sarah Roby, Kay Douglas and Mehran Waheed.

The sources I consulted for research purposes are too numerous to list in full, but special mention goes to: Ian Hacking's brilliant and eloquent *Rewriting the Soul: Multiple Personality and the Sciences of Memory*; Eugene S. Bagger's *Psycho-Graphology: A Study of Rafael Shermann*, a 1924 case study that provided the inspiration for the novel; Google; Margaret Gullan-Whur's *What Your Handwriting Reveals*; Eve Bingham's *Simply Handwriting Analysis*; Arthur Ransome's *Russia in 1919*; E.M. Halliday's *The Ignorant Armies*; and Edmund Ironside's *Archangel, 1918-1919*.

Finally, thanks to Chrissie for everything. Kisses, J.